**Praise for #1 *New York Times* bestselling author
Linda Lael Miller**

"[Linda Lael] Miller has found a perfect niche with charming western romances and cowboys who will set readers' hearts aflutter."

—*RT Book Reviews*

"[Miller's] ranch-based westerns have always entertained and stayed with me long after reading them."

—*Idaho Statesman* on *The Marriage Pact*

"Miller seems to understand her characters' thoughts and state of mind while fulfilling her reader's expectations. She doesn't disappoint."

—*Armchair Interviews* on *The Rustler*

**Praise for *New York Times* bestselling author
B.J. Daniels**

"[B.J.] Daniels is truly an expert at Western romantic suspense."

—*RT Book Reviews* on *Atonement*

"After reading *Mercy*, B.J. Daniels will absolutely move to the top of your list of must-read authors."

—*Fresh Fiction*

The daughter of a town marshal, **Linda Lael Miller** is a *New York Times* bestselling author of more than one hundred historical and contemporary novels. Linda's books have hit #1 on the *New York Times* bestseller list seven times. Raised in Northport, Washington, she now lives in Spokane, Washington.

New York Times and *USA TODAY* bestselling author **B.J. Daniels** lives in Montana with her husband, Parker, and three springer spaniels. When not writing, she quilts, boats and plays tennis. Contact her at bjdaniels.com, on Facebook or on Twitter, @bjdanielsauthor.

LINDA LAEL

MILLER

AT *Home* IN STONE CREEK

HARLEQUIN® BESTSELLING AUTHOR COLLECTION

ISBN-13: 978-0-373-01064-6

At Home in Stone Creek

Copyright © 2016 by Harlequin Books S.A.

The publisher acknowledges the copyright holders of the individual works as follows:

At Home in Stone Creek
Copyright © 2009 by Linda Lael Miller

Day of Reckoning
Copyright © 2004 by Barbara Heinlein

Recycling programs for this product may not exist in your area.

Printed in U.S.A.

HARLEQUIN®
www.Harlequin.com

CONTENTS

AT HOME IN STONE CREEK   7
Linda Lael Miller

DAY OF RECKONING   223
B.J. Daniels

AT HOME
IN STONE CREEK

Linda Lael Miller

For Karen Beaty, with love.

Chapter 1

Ashley O'Ballivan dropped the last string of Christmas lights into a plastic storage container, resisting an uncharacteristic urge to kick the thing into the corner of the attic instead of stacking it with the others. For her, the holidays had been anything *but* merry and bright; in fact, the whole year had basically sucked. But for her brother, Brad, and sister Olivia, it qualified as a personal best—both of them were happily married. Even her workaholic twin, Melissa, had had a date for New Year's Eve.

Ashley, on the other hand, had spent the night alone, sipping nonalcoholic wine in front of the portable TV set in her study, waiting for the ball to drop in Times Square.

How lame was that?

It was worse than lame—it was *pathetic*.

She wasn't even thirty yet, and she was well on her way to old age.

With a sigh, Ashley turned from the dusty hodgepodge surrounding her—she went all out, at the Mountain View Bed and Breakfast, for every red-letter day on the calendar—and headed for the attic stairs. As she reached the bottom, stepping into the corridor just off the kitchen, a familiar car horn sounded from the driveway in front of the detached garage. It could only be Olivia's ancient Suburban.

Ashley had mixed feelings as she hoisted the ladder-steep steps back up into the ceiling. She loved her older sister dearly and was delighted that Olivia had found true love with Tanner Quinn, but since their mother's funeral a few months before, there had been a strain between them.

Neither Brad nor Olivia nor Melissa had shed a single tear for Delia O'Ballivan—not during the church service or the graveside ceremony or the wake. Okay, so there wasn't a greeting card category for the kind of mother Delia had been—she'd deserted the family long ago, and gradually destroyed herself through a long series of tragically bad choices. For all that, she'd still been the woman who had given birth to them all.

Didn't that count for something?

A rap sounded at the back door, as distinctive as the car horn, and Olivia's glowing, pregnancy-rounded face filled one of the frost-trimmed panes in the window.

Oddly self-conscious in her jeans and T-shirt and an ancient flannel shirt from the back of her closet, Ashley mouthed, "It's not locked."

Beaming, Olivia opened the door and waddled across the threshold. She was due to deliver her and

Tanner's first child in a matter of days, if not hours, and from the looks of her, Ashley surmised she was carrying either quadruplets or a Sumo wrestler.

"You know you don't have to knock," Ashley said, keeping her distance.

Olivia smiled, a bit wistfully it seemed to Ashley, and opened their grandfather Big John's old barn coat to reveal a small white cat with one blue eye and one green one.

"Oh, no you don't," Ashley bristled.

Olivia, a veterinarian as well as Stone Creek, Arizona's one and only real-deal animal communicator, bent awkwardly to set the kitten on Ashley's immaculate kitchen floor, where it meowed pitifully and turned in a little circle, pursuing its fluffy tail. Every stray dog, cat or bird in the county seemed to find its way to Olivia eventually, like immigrants gravitating toward the Statue of Liberty.

Two years ago, at Christmas, she'd even been approached by a reindeer named Rodney.

"Meet Mrs. Wiggins," Olivia chimed, undaunted. Her china-blue eyes danced beneath the dark, sleek fringe of her bangs, but there was a wary look in them that bothered Ashley…even shamed her a little. The two of them had always been close. Did Olivia think Ashley was jealous of her new life with Tanner and his precocious fourteen-year-old daughter, Sophie?

"I suppose she's already told you her life story," Ashley said, nodding toward the cat, scrubbing her hands down the thighs of her jeans once and then heading for the sink to wash up before filling the electric kettle. At least *that* hadn't changed—they always had tea together, whenever Olivia dropped by—which was less and less often these days.

After all, unlike Ashley, Olivia had a life.

Olivia crooked up a corner of her mouth and began struggling out of the old plaid woolen coat, flecked, as always, with bits of straw. Some things never changed—even with Tanner's money, Olivia still dressed like what she was, a country veterinarian.

"Not much to tell," Livie answered with a slight lift of one shoulder, as nonchalantly as if telepathic exchanges with all manner of finned, feathered and furred creatures were commonplace. "She's only four-teen weeks old, so she hasn't had time to build up much of an autobiography."

"I do not want a cat," Ashley informed her sister.

Olivia hauled back a chair at the table and collapsed into it. She was wearing gum boots, as usual, and they looked none too clean. "You only *think* you don't want Mrs. Wiggins," she said. "She needs you and, whether you know it or not, you need her."

Ashley turned back to the kettle, trying to ignore the ball of cuteness chasing its tail in the middle of the kitchen floor. She was irritated, but worried, too. She looked back at Olivia over one stiff shoulder. "Should you be out and about, as pregnant as you are?"

Olivia smiled, serene as a Botticelli Madonna. "Pregnancy isn't a matter of degrees, Ash," she said. "One either is or isn't."

"You're pale," Ashley fretted. She'd lost so many loved ones—both parents, her beloved granddad, Big John. If anything happened to any of her siblings, what-ever their differences, she wouldn't be able to bear it.

"Just brew the tea," Olivia said quietly. "I'm perfectly all right."

While Ashley didn't have her sister's gift for talking to animals, she *was* intuitive, and her nerves felt all twitchy, a clear sign that something unexpected was about to happen. She plugged in the kettle and joined Olivia at the table. "Is anything wrong?"

"Funny you should ask," Olivia answered, and though the soft smile still rested on her lips, her eyes were solemn. "I came here to ask *you* the same question. Even though I already know the answer."

As much as she hated the uneasiness that had sprung up between herself and her sisters and brother, Ashley tended to bounce away from any mention of the subject like a pinball in a lively game. She sprang right up out of her chair and crossed to the antique breakfront to fetch two delicate china cups from behind the glass doors, full of strange urgency.

"Ash," Olivia said patiently.

Ashley kept her back to her sister and lowered her head. "I've just been a little blue lately, Liv," she admitted softly. "That's all."

She would never get to know her mother.

The holidays had been a downer.

Not a single guest had checked into her Victorian bed-and-breakfast since before Thanksgiving, which meant she was two payments behind on the private mortgage Brad had given her to buy the place several years before. It wasn't that her brother had been pressing her for the money—he'd offered her the deed, free and clear, the day the deal was closed, but she'd insisted on repaying him every cent.

On top of all that, she hadn't heard a word from

Jack McCall since his last visit, six months ago. He'd suddenly packed his bags and left one sultry summer night, while she was sleeping off their most recent bout of lovemaking, without so much as a goodbye.

Would it have killed him to wake her up and explain? Or just leave a damn note? Maybe pick up a phone?

"It's because of Mom," Olivia said. "You're grieving for the woman she never was, and that's okay, Ashley. But it might help if you talked to one of us about how you feel."

Weary rage surged through Ashley. She spun around to face Olivia, causing her sneakers to make a squeaking sound against the freshly waxed floor, remembered that her sister was about to have a baby, and sucked all her frustration and fury back in on one ragged breath.

"Let's not go there, Livie," she said.

The kitten scrabbled at one leg of Ashley's jeans and, without thinking, she bent to scoop the tiny creature up into her arms. Minute, silky ears twitched under her chin, and Mrs. Wiggins purred as though powered by batteries, snuggling against her neck.

Olivia smiled again, still wistful. "You're pretty angry with us, aren't you?" she asked gently. "Brad and Melissa and me, I mean."

"No," Ashley lied, wanting to put the kitten down but unable to do so. Somehow, nearly weightless as that cat was, it made her feel anchored instead of set adrift.

"Come on," Olivia challenged quietly. "If I weren't nine and a half months along, you'd be in my face right now."

Ashley bit down hard on her lower lip and said nothing.

"Things can't change if we don't talk," Olivia persisted.

Ashley swallowed painfully. Anything she said would probably come out sounding like self-pity, and Ashley was too proud to feel sorry for herself, but she also knew her sister. Olivia wasn't about to let her off the hook, squirm though she might. "It's just that nothing seems to be working," she confessed, blinking back tears. "The business. Jack. That damn computer you insisted I needed."

The kettle boiled, emitting a shrill whistle and clouds of steam.

Still cradling the kitten under her chin, Ashley unplugged the cord with a wrenching motion of her free hand.

"Sit down," Olivia said, rising laboriously from her chair. "I'll make the tea."

"No, you won't!"

"I'm pregnant, Ashley," Olivia replied, "not incapacitated."

Ashley skulked back to the table, sat down, the tea forgotten. The kitten inched down her flannel work shirt to her lap and made a graceful leap to the floor.

"Talk to me," Olivia prodded, trundling toward the counter.

Ashley's vision seemed to narrow to a pinpoint, and when it widened again, she swayed in her chair, suddenly dizzy. If her blond hair hadn't been pulled back into its customary French braid, she'd have shoved her hands through it. "It must be an awful thing," she murmured, "to die the way Mom did."

Cups rattled against saucers at the periphery of Ashley's awareness. Olivia returned to the table but stood beside Ashley instead of sitting down again. Rested a hand on her shoulder. "Delia wasn't in her right mind, Ashley. She didn't suffer."

"No one cared," Ashley reflected, in a miserable whisper. "She died and no one even *cared*."

Olivia didn't sigh, but she might as well have. "You were little when Delia left," she said, after a long time. "You don't remember how it was."

"I remember praying every night that she'd come home," Ashley said.

Olivia bent—not easy to do with her huge belly—and rested her forehead on Ashley's crown, tightened her grip on her shoulder. "We all wanted her to come home, at least at first," she recalled softly. "But the reality is, she didn't—not even when Dad got killed in that lightning storm. After a while, we stopped needing her."

"Maybe *you* did," Ashley sniffled. "Now she's gone forever. I'm never going to know what she was really like."

Olivia straightened, very slowly. "She was—"

"Don't say it," Ashley warned.

"She drank," Olivia insisted, stepping back. The invisible barrier dropped between them again, a nearly audible shift in the atmosphere. "She took drugs. Her brain was pickled. If you want to remember her differently, that's your prerogative. But don't expect me to rewrite history."

Ashley's cheeks were wet, and she swiped at them with the back of one hand, probably leaving streaks in the coating of attic dust prickling on her skin. "Fair enough," she said stiffly.

Olivia crossed the room again, jangled things around

at the counter for a few moments, and returned with a pot of steeping tea and two cups and saucers.

"This is getting to me," she told Ashley. "It's as if the earth has cracked open and we're standing on opposite sides of a deep chasm. It's bothering Brad and Melissa, too. We're *family,* Ashley. Can't we just agree to disagree as far as Mom is concerned and go on from there?"

"I'll try," Ashley said, though she had to win an inner skirmish first. A long one.

Olivia reached across the table, closed her hand around Ashley's. "Why didn't you tell me you were having trouble getting the computer up and running?" she asked. Ashley was profoundly grateful for the change of subject, even if it did nettle her a little at the same time. She hated the stupid contraption, hated anything electronic. She'd followed the instructions to the letter, and the thing *still* wouldn't work.

When she didn't say anything, Olivia went on. "Sophie and Carly are cyberwhizzes—they'd be glad to build you a website for the B&B and show you how to zip around the Internet like a pro."

Brad and his wife, the former Meg McKettrick, had adopted Carly, Meg's half sister, soon after their marriage. The teenager doted on their son, three-year-old Mac, and had befriended Sophie from the beginning.

"That would be…nice," Ashley said doubtfully. The truth was, she was an old-fashioned type, as Victorian, in some ways, as her house. She didn't carry a cell phone, and her landline had a rotary dial. "But you know me and technology."

"I also know you're not stupid," Olivia responded, pouring tea for Ashley, then for herself. Their spoons made a cheerful tinkling sound, like fairy bells, as they stirred in organic sugar from the chunky ceramic bowl in the center of the table.

The kitten jumped back into Ashley's lap then, startling her, making her laugh. How long had it been since she'd laughed?

Too long, judging by the expression on Olivia's face.

"You're really all right?" Ashley asked, watching her sister closely.

"I'm better than 'all right,'" Olivia assured her. "I'm married to the man of my dreams. I have Sophie, a barn full of horses out at Starcross Ranch, and a thriving veterinary practice." A slight frown creased her forehead. "Speaking of men…?"

"Let's not," Ashley said.

"You still haven't heard from Jack?"

"No. And that's fine with me."

"I don't think it *is* fine with you, Ashley. He's Tanner's friend. I could ask him to call Jack and—"

"No!"

Olivia sighed. "Yeah," she said. "You're right. That would be interfering, and Tanner probably wouldn't go along with it anyhow."

Ashley stroked the kitten even as she tried not to bond with it. She was zero-for-zero on that score. "Jack and I had a fling," she said. "It's obviously over. End of story."

Olivia arched one perfect eyebrow. "Maybe you need a vacation," she mused aloud. "A new man in your life. You could go on one of those singles' cruises—"

Ashley gave a scoffing chuckle—it felt good to engage in girl talk with her sister again. "Sure," she retorted. "I'd meet guys twice my age, with gold chains around their necks and bad toupees. Or worse."

"What could be worse?" Olivia joked, grinning over the gold rim of her teacup.

"Spray-on hair," Ashley said decisively.

Olivia laughed.

"Besides," Ashley went on, "I don't want to be out of town when you have the baby."

Olivia nodded, turned thoughtful again. "You should get out more, though."

"And do what?" Ashley challenged. "Play bingo in the church basement on Mondays, Wednesdays and Fridays? Join the Powder Puff bowling league? In case it's escaped your notice, O pregnant one, Stone Creek isn't exactly a social whirlwind."

Olivia sighed again, in temporary defeat, and glanced at her watch. "I'm supposed to meet Tanner at the clinic in twenty minutes—just a routine checkup, so don't panic. Meet us for lunch afterward?"

The kitten climbed Ashley's shirt, its claws catching in the fabric, nestled under her neck again. "I have some errands to run," she said, with a shake of her head. "You're going to stick me with this cat, aren't you, Olivia?"

Olivia smiled, stood, and carried her cup and saucer to the sink. "Give Mrs. Wiggins a chance," she said. "If she doesn't win your heart by this time next week, I'll try to find her another home." She took Big John's ratty coat from the row of pegs next to the back door and shoved her arms into the sleeves, reclaimed her purse from the end of the counter, where she'd set it on the way in. "Shall I ask Sophie and Carly to come by after school and have a look at your computer?"

Ashley enjoyed the girls, and it would be nice to bake a batch of cookies for someone. Besides, she was tired of being confronted by the dark monitor, tower and printer every time she went into the study. "I guess," she answered.

"Done deal," Olivia confirmed brightly, and then she was out the door, gone.

Ashley held the kitten in front of her face. "You're not staying," she said.

"Meow," Mrs. Wiggins replied.

"Oh, all right," Ashley relented. "But I'd better not find any snags in my new chintz slipcovers!"

The helicopter swung abruptly sideways in a dizzying arch, setting Jack McCall's fever-ravaged brain spinning. He hoped the pilot hadn't seen him grip the edges of his seat, bracing for a crash.

His friend's voice sounded tinny, coming through the earphones. "You belong in a hospital," he said. "Not some backwater bed-and-breakfast."

All Jack really knew about the toxin raging through his system was that it wasn't contagious—the CDC had ordered him into quarantine until that much had been determined—but there was still no diagnosis and no remedy except a lot of rest and quiet. "I don't like hospitals," he responded, hoping he sounded like his normal self. "They're full of sick people."

Vince Griffin chuckled at that, but it was a dry sound, rough at the edges. "What's in Stone Creek, Arizona?" he asked. "Besides a whole lot of nothin'?"

Ashley O'Ballivan was in Stone Creek, and she was a whole lot of somethin', but Jack had neither the strength nor the inclination to explain. Given the way he'd ducked out on her six months before, after taking an emergency call on his cell phone, he didn't expect a welcome, knew he didn't deserve one. But Ashley, being Ashley, would take him in, whatever her misgivings, same as she would a wounded dog or a bird with a broken wing.

He had to get to Ashley—he'd be all right then.

He closed his eyes, letting the fever swallow him.

There was no telling how much time had passed when he surfaced again, became aware of the chopper blades slowing overhead. The magic flying machine bobbed on its own updraft, sending the broth he'd sipped from a thermos scalding its way up into the back of his throat.

Dimly, he saw the ancient ambulance waiting on the airfield outside Stone Creek; it seemed that twilight had descended, but he couldn't be sure. Since the toxin had taken him down, he hadn't been able to trust his perceptions.

Day turned into night.

Up turned into down.

The doctors had ruled out a brain tumor, but he still felt as though something was eating his brain.

"Here we are," Vince said.

"Is it dark or am I going blind?"

Vince tossed him a worried look. "It's dark," he said.

Jack sighed with relief. His clothes—the usual black jeans and black turtleneck sweater—felt clammy against his flesh. His teeth began to chatter as two figures unloaded a gurney from the back of the ambulance and waited for the blades to stop so they could approach.

"Great," Vince remarked, unsnapping his seat belt.

"Those two look like volunteers, not real EMTs. The CDC parked you at Walter Reed, and that wasn't good enough for you because—?"

Jack didn't answer. He had nothing against the famous military hospital, but he wasn't associated with the U.S. government, not officially at least. He couldn't see taking up a bed some wounded soldier might need, and, anyhow, he'd be a sitting duck in a regular facility.

The chopper bounced sickeningly on its runners, and Vince, with a shake of his head, pushed open his door and jumped to the ground, head down.

Jack waited, wondering if he'd be able to stand on his own. After fumbling unsuccessfully with the buckle on his seat belt, he decided not.

When it was safe, the EMTs came forward, following Vince, who opened Jack's door.

Jack hauled off his headphones and tossed them aside.

His old friend Tanner Quinn stepped around Vince, his trademark grin not quite reaching his eyes.

"You look like hell warmed over," he told Jack cheerfully.

"Since when are you an EMT?" Jack retorted.

Tanner reached in, wedged a shoulder under Jack's right arm, and hauled him out of the chopper. His knees immediately buckled, and Vince stepped up, supporting him on the other side.

"In a place like Stone Creek," Tanner replied, "everybody helps out."

"Right," Jack said, stumbling between the two men keeping him on his feet. They reached the wheeled gurney—Jack had thought they never would, since it seemed to recede into the void with every awkward step—and he found himself on his back.

Tanner and the second man strapped him down, a process that brought back a few bad memories.

"Is there even a hospital in this hellhole of a place?" Vince asked irritably, from somewhere in the cold night.

"There's a pretty good clinic over in Indian Rock," Tanner answered easily, "and it isn't far to Flagstaff." He paused to help his buddy hoist Jack and the gurney into the back of the ambulance. "You're in good hands, Jack. My wife is the best veterinarian in the state."

Jack laughed raggedly at that.

Vince muttered a curse.

Tanner climbed into the back beside Jack, perched on some kind of fold-down seat. The other man shut the doors.

"I'm not contagious," Jack said to Tanner.

"So I hear," Tanner said, as his partner climbed into the driver's seat and started the engine. "You in any pain?"

"No," Jack struggled to quip, "but I might puke on those Roy Rogers boots of yours."

"You don't miss much, even strapped to a gurney." Tanner chuckled, hoisted one foot high enough for Jack to squint at it and hauled up the leg of his jeans to show off the fancy stitching on the boot shaft. "My brother-in-law gave them to me," he said. "Brad used to wear them onstage, back when he was breaking hearts out there on the concert circuit. Swigged iced tea out of a whiskey bottle all through every performance, so everybody would think he was a badass."

Jack looked up at his closest and most trusted friend

and wished he'd listened to Vince. Ever since he'd come down with the illness, a week after snatching a five-year-old girl back from her noncustodial parent—a small-time drug runner with dangerous aspirations and a lousy attitude—he hadn't been able to think about anyone or anything but Ashley. When he *could* think.

Now, in one of the first clearheaded moments he'd experienced since checking himself out of the hospital the day before, he realized he might be making a major mistake—not by facing Ashley; he owed her that much and a lot more. No, he could be putting her in danger, and putting Tanner and his daughter and his pregnant veterinarian wife in danger, as well.

"I shouldn't have come here," he said, keeping his voice low.

Tanner shook his head, his jaw clamped down hard, as though irritated by Jack's statement. Since he'd gotten married, settled down and sold off his multinational construction company to play at being an Arizona rancher, Tanner had softened around the edges a little, but Jack knew his friend was still one tough SOB.

"This is where you belong," Tanner insisted. Another grin quirked one corner of his mouth. "If you'd had sense enough to know that six months ago, old buddy, when you bailed on Ashley without so much as a fare-thee-well, you wouldn't be in this mess."

Ashley. The name had run through his mind a million times in those six months, but hearing somebody say it out loud was like having a fist close around his insides and squeeze hard.

Jack couldn't speak.

Tanner didn't press for further conversation.

The ambulance bumped over country roads, finally hit smooth blacktop.

"Here we are," Tanner said. "Ashley's place."

"I knew something was going to happen," Ashley told Mrs. Wiggins, peeling the kitten off the living room curtains as she peered out at the ambulance stopped in the street. "I *knew* it."

Not bothering to find her coat, Ashley opened the door and stepped out onto the porch. Tanner got out on the passenger side and gave her a casual wave as he went around back.

Ashley's heart pounded. She stood frozen for a long moment, not by the cold, but by a strange, eager sense of dread. Then she bolted down the steps, careful not to slip, and hurried along the walk, through the gate.

"What...?" she began, but the rest of the question died in her throat.

Tanner had opened the back of the ambulance, but then he just stood there, looking at her with an odd expression on his face.

"Brace yourself," he said.

Jeff Baxter, part of a rotating group of volunteers, like Tanner, left the driver's seat and came to stand a short but eloquent distance away. He looked like a man trying to brace himself for an imminent explosion.

Impatient, Ashley wedged herself between the two men, peered inside.

Jack McCall sat upright on the gurney, grinning stupidly. His black hair, military-short the last time she'd seen him, was longer now, and sleekly shaggy. His eyes blazed with fever.

"Whose shirt is that?" he asked, frowning.

Still taken aback, Ashley didn't register the question right away. Several awkward moments had passed by the time she glanced down to see what she was wearing.

"Yours," she answered, finally.

Jack looked relieved. "Good," he said.

Ashley, beside herself with surprise until that very instant, landed back in her own skin with a jolt. "What are you doing here?" she demanded.

Jack scooted toward her, almost pitched out of the ambulance onto his face before Tanner and Jeff moved in to grab him by the arms.

"Checking in," he said, once he'd tried—and failed—to shrug them off. "You're still in the bed-and-breakfast business, aren't you?"

You're still in the bed-and-breakfast business, aren't you?

Damn, the man had nerve.

"You belong in a hospital," she said evenly. "Not a bed-and-breakfast."

"I'm willing to pay double," Jack offered. His face, always strong, took on a vulnerable expression. "I need a place to lay low for a while, Ash. Are you game?"

She thought quickly. The last thing in the world she wanted was Jack McCall under her roof again, but she couldn't afford to turn down a paying guest. She'd have to dip into her savings soon if she did, and not just to pay Brad.

The bills were piling up.

"Triple the usual rate," she said.

Jack squinted, probably not understanding at first, then gave a raspy chuckle. "Okay," he agreed. "Triple it is. Even though it *is* the off-season."

Jeff and Tanner half dragged, half carried him toward the house.

Ashley hesitated on the snowy sidewalk.

First the cat.

Now Jack.

Evidently, it was her day to be dumped on.

Chapter 2

"What *happened* to him?" Ashley whispered to Tanner, in the hallway outside the second-best room in the house, a small suite at the opposite end of the corridor from her own quarters. Jeff and Tanner had already put the patient to bed, fully dressed except for his boots, and Jeff had gone downstairs to make a call on his cell phone.

Jack, meanwhile, had sunk into an instant and all-consuming sleep—or into a coma. It was a crapshoot, guessing which.

Tanner looked grim; didn't seem to notice that Mrs. Wiggins was busily climbing his right pant leg, her infinitesimal claws snagging the denim as she scaled his knee and started up his thigh with a deliberation that would have been funny under any other circumstances.

"All I know is," Tanner replied, "I got a call from

Jack this afternoon, just as Livie and I were leaving the clinic after her checkup. He said he was a little under the weather and wanted to know if I'd meet him at the airstrip and bring him here." He paused, cupped the kitten in one hand, raised the little creature to nose level, and peered quizzically into its mismatched eyes before lowering it gently to the floor. Straightening from a crouch, he added, "I offered to put him up at our place, but he insisted on coming to yours."

"You might have called me," Ashley fretted, still keeping her voice down. "Given me some warning, at least."

"Check your voice mail," Tanner countered, sounding mildly exasperated. "I left at least four messages."

"I was out," Ashley said, defensive, "buying kitty litter and kibble. Because *your wife* decided I needed a cat."

Tanner grinned at the mention of Olivia, and something eased in him, gentling the expression in his eyes. "If you'd carry a cell phone, like any normal human being, you'd have been up to speed, situationwise." He paused, with a mischievous twinkle. "You might even have had time to bake a welcome-back-Jack cake."

"As if," Ashley breathed, but as rattled as she was over having Jack McCall land in the middle of her life like the flaming chunks of a latter-day Hindenburg, there was something else she needed to know. "What did the doctor say? About Olivia, I mean?"

Tanner sighed. "She's a couple of weeks overdue—Dr. Pentland wants to induce labor tomorrow morning."

Worry made Ashley peevish. "And you're just telling me this now?"

"As I said," Tanner replied, "get a cell phone."

Before Ashley could come up with a reply, the front door banged open downstairs, and a youthful female voice called her name, sounding alarmed.

Ashley went to the upstairs railing, leaned a little, and saw Tanner's daughter, Sophie, standing in the living room, her face upturned and so pale that her freckles stood out, even from that distance. Sixteen-year-old Carly, blond and blue-eyed like her sister, Meg, appeared beside her.

"There's an ambulance outside," Sophie said. "What's happening?"

Tanner started down the stairs. "Everything's all right," he told the frightened girl.

Carly glanced from Tanner to Ashley, descending behind him. "We meant to get here sooner, to set up your computer," Carly said, "but Mr. Gilvine kept the whole Drama Club after school to rehearse the second act of the new play."

"How come there's an ambulance outside," Sophie persisted, gazing up at her father's face, "if nobody's sick?"

"I didn't say nobody was sick," Tanner told her quietly, setting his hands on her shoulders. "Jack's upstairs, resting."

Sophie's panic rose a notch. "Uncle Jack is sick? What's wrong with him?"

That's what I'd *like to know,* Ashley thought.

"From the symptoms, I'd guess it's some kind of toxin."

Sophie tried to go around Tanner, clearly intending to race up the stairs. "I want to see him!"

Tanner stopped her. "Not now, sweetie," he said, his tone at once gruff and gentle. "He's asleep."

"Do you still want us to set up your computer?" Carly asked Ashley.

Ashley summoned up a smile and shook her head. "Another time," she said. "You must be tired, after a whole day of school and then play practice on top of that. How about some supper?"

"Mr. Gilvine ordered pizza for the whole cast," Carly answered, touching her flat stomach and puffing out her cheeks to indicate that she was stuffed. "I already called home, and Brad said he'd come in from the ranch and get us as soon as we had your system up and running."

"It can wait," Ashley reiterated, glancing at Tanner.

"I'll drop you off on the way home," he told Carly, one hand still resting on Sophie's shoulder. "My truck's parked at the fire station. Jeff can give us a lift over there."

Having lost her mother when she was very young, Sophie had insecurities Ashley could well identify with. The girl adored Olivia, and looked forward to the birth of a brother or sister. Tanner probably wanted to break the news about Livie's induction later, with just the three of them present.

"Call me," Ashley ordered, her throat thick with concern for her sister and the child, as Tanner steered the girls toward the front door.

Tanner merely arched an eyebrow at that.

Jeff stepped out of the study, just tucking away his cell phone. "I'm in big trouble with Lucy," he said. "Forgot to let her know I'd be late. She made a soufflé and it fell."

"Uh-oh," Tanner commiserated.

"We get to ride in an ambulance?" Sophie asked, cheered.

"Awesome," Carly said.

And then they were gone.

Ashley raised her eyes to the ceiling. Recalled that Jack McCall was up there, sprawled on one of her guest beds, buried under half a dozen quilts. Just how sick was he? Would he want to eat, and if so, what?

After some internal debate, she decided on home-made chicken soup.

That was the cure for everything, wasn't it?

Everything, that is, except a broken heart.

Jack McCall awakened to find something furry standing on his face.

Fortunately, he was too weak to flail, or he'd have sent what his brain finally registered as a kitten flying before he realized he wasn't back in a South American jail, fighting off rats willing to settle for part of his hide when the rations ran low.

The animal stared directly into his face with one blue eye and one green one, purring as though it had a motor inside its hairy little chest.

He blinked, decided the thing was probably some kind of mutant.

"Another victim of renegade genetics," he said.

"Meooooow," the cat replied, perhaps indignant.

The door across the room opened, and Ashley elbowed her way in, carrying a loaded tray. Whatever was on it smelled like heaven distilled to its essence, or was that the scent of her skin and that amazing hair of hers?

"Mrs. Wiggins," she said, "get down."

"Mrs.?" Jack replied, trying to raise himself on his pillows and failing. This was a fortunate thing for the cat, who was trying to nest in his hair by then. "Isn't she a little young to be married?"

"Yuk-yuk," Ashley said, with an edge.

Jack sighed inwardly. All was not forgiven, then, he concluded.

Mrs. Wiggins climbed down over his right cheek and curled up on his chest. He could have sworn he felt some kind of warm energy flowing through the kitten, as though it were a conduit between the world around him and another, better one.

Crap. He was really losing it.

"Are you hungry?" Ashley asked, as though he were any ordinary guest.

A gnawing in the pit of Jack's stomach told him he was—for the first time since he'd come down with the mysterious plague. "Yeah," he ground out, further weakened by the sight of Ashley. Even in jeans and the flannel shirt he'd left behind, with her light hair springing from its normally tidy braid, she looked like a goddess. "I think I am."

She approached the bed—cautiously, it seemed to Jack, and little wonder, after some of the acrobatics they'd managed in the one down the hall before he left—and set the tray down on the nightstand.

"Can you feed yourself?" she asked, keeping her distance. Her tone was formal, almost prim.

Jack gave an inelegant snort at that, then realized, to his mortification, that he probably couldn't. Earlier, he'd made it to the adjoining bathroom and back, but the effort had exhausted him. "Yes," he fibbed.

She tilted her head to one side, skeptical. A smile

flittered around her mouth, but didn't come in for a landing. "Your eyes widen a little when you lie," she commented.

He sure hoped certain members of various drug and gunrunning cartels didn't know that. "Oh," he said.

Ashley dragged a fussy-looking chair over and sat down. With a little sigh, she took a spoon off the tray and plunged it into a bright-blue crockery bowl. "Open up," she told him.

Jack resisted briefly, pressing his lips together— he still had *some* pride, after all—but his stomach betrayed him with a long and perfectly audible rumble. He opened his mouth.

The fragrant substance turned out to be chicken soup, with wild rice and chopped celery and a few other things he couldn't identify. It was so good that, if he'd been able to, he'd have grabbed the bowl with both hands and downed the stuff in a few gulps.

"Slow down," Ashley said. Her eyes had softened a little, but her body remained rigid. "There's plenty more soup simmering on the stove."

Like the kitten, the soup seemed to possess some sort of quantum-level healing power. Jack felt faint tendrils of strength stirring inside him, like the tender roots of a plant splitting through a seed husk, groping tentatively toward the sun.

Once he'd finished the soup, sleep began to pull him downward again, toward oblivion. There was something different about the feeling this time; rather than an urge to struggle against it, as before, it was more an impulse to give himself up to the darkness, settle into it like a waiting embrace.

Something soft brushed his cheek. Ashley's fingertips? Or the mutant kitten?

"Jack," Ashley said.

With an effort, he opened his eyes.

Tears glimmered along Ashley's lashes. "Are you going to die?" she asked.

Jack considered his answer for a few moments; not easy, with his brain short-circuiting. According to the doctors at Walter Reed, his prognosis wasn't the best. They'd admitted that they'd never seen the toxin before, and their plan was to ship him off to some secret government research facility for further study.

Which was one of the reasons he'd bolted, conned a series of friends into springing him and then relaying him cross-country in various planes and helicopters.

He found Ashley's hand, squeezed it with his own. "Not if I can help it," he murmured, just before sleep sucked him under again.

Their brief conversation echoed in Ashley's head, over and over, as she sat there watching Jack sleep until the room was so dark she couldn't see anything but the faintest outline of him, etched against the sheets.

Are you going to die?

Not if I can help it.

Ashley overcame the need to switch on the bedside lamp, send golden light spilling over the features she knew so well—the hazel eyes, the well-defined cheekbones, the strong, obstinate jaw—but just barely. Leaving the tray behind, she rose out of the chair and made her way slowly toward the door, afraid of stepping on Mrs. Wiggins, frolicking at her feet like a little ghost.

Reaching the hallway, Ashley closed the door softly

behind her, bent to scoop the kitten up in one hand, and let the tears come. Silent sobs rocked her, making her shoulders shake, and Mrs. Wiggins snuggled in close under her chin, as if to offer comfort.

Was Jack truly in danger of dying?

She sniffled, straightened her spine. Surely Tanner wouldn't have agreed to bring him to the bed-and-breakfast—to her—if he was at death's door.

On the other hand, she reasoned, dashing at her cheek with the back of one hand, trying to rally her scattered emotions, Jack was bone-stubborn. He always got his way.

So maybe Tanner was simply honoring Jack's last wish.

Holding tightly to the banister, Ashley started down the stairs.

Jack hadn't wanted to *live* in Stone Creek. Why would he choose to *die* there?

The phone began to ring, a persistent trilling, and Ashley, thinking of Olivia, dashed to the small desk where guests registered—not that *that* had been an issue lately—and snatched up the receiver.

"Hello?" When had she gotten out of the habit of answering with a businesslike, "Mountain View Bed and Breakfast"?

"I hear you've got an unexpected boarder," Brad said, his tone measured.

Ashley was unaccountably glad to hear her big brother's voice, considering that they hadn't had much to say to each other since their mother's funeral. "Yes," she assented.

"According to Carly, he was sick enough to arrive in an ambulance."

Ashley nodded, remembered that Brad couldn't see her, and repeated, "Yes. I'm not sure he should be here—Brad, he's in a really bad way. I'm not a nurse and I'm—" She paused, swallowed. "I'm scared."

"I can be there in fifteen minutes, Ash."

Fresh tears scalded Ashley's eyes, made them feel raw. "That would be good," she said.

"Put on a pot of coffee, little sister," Brad told her. "I'm on my way."

True to his word, Brad was standing in her kitchen before the coffee finished perking. He looked more like a rancher than a famous country singer and sometime movie star, in his faded jeans, battered boots, chambray shirt and denim jacket.

Ashley couldn't remember the last time she'd hugged her brother, but now she went to him, and he wrapped her in his arms, kissed the top of her head.

"Olivia..." she began, but her voice fell away.

"I know," Brad said hoarsely. "They're inducing labor in the morning. Livie will be fine, honey, and so will the baby."

Ashley tilted her head back, looked up into Brad's face. His dark-blond hair was rumpled, and his beard was growing in, bristly. "How's the family?"

He rested his hands on her shoulders, held her at a little distance. "You wouldn't have to ask if you ever stopped by Stone Creek Ranch," he answered. "Mac misses you, and Meg and I do, too."

The minute Brad had known she needed him, he'd been in his truck, headed for town. And now that he was there, her anger over their mother's funeral didn't seem so important.

She tried to speak, but her throat had tightened again, and she couldn't get a single word past it.

One corner of Brad's famous mouth crooked up. "Where's Lover Boy?" he asked. "Lucky thing for him that he's laid up—otherwise I'd punch his lights out for what he did to you."

The phrase *Lover Boy* made Ashley flinch. "That's over," she said.

Brad let his hands fall to his sides, his eyes serious now. "Right," he replied. "Which room?"

Ashley told him, and he left the kitchen, the inside door swinging behind him long after he'd passed through it.

She kept herself busy by taking mugs down from the cupboard, filling Mrs. Wiggins's dish with kibble the size of barley grains, switching on the radio and then switching it off again.

The kitten crunched away at the kibble, then climbed onto its newly purchased bed in the corner near the fireplace, turned in circles for a few moments, kneaded the fabric, and dropped like the proverbial rock.

After several minutes had passed, Ashley heard Brad's boot heels on the staircase, and poured coffee for her brother; she was drinking herbal tea.

As if there were a hope in hell she'd sleep a wink that night by avoiding caffeine.

Brad reached for his mug, took a thoughtful sip.

"Well?" Ashley prompted.

"I'm not a doctor, Ash," he said. "All I can tell you for sure is, he's breathing."

"*That's* helpful," Ashley said.

He chuckled, and the sound, though rueful, consoled

her a little. He turned one of the chairs around backward, and straddled it, setting his mug on the table.

"Why do men like to sit like that?" Ashley wondered aloud.

He grinned. "You've been alone too long," he answered.

Ashley blushed, brought her tea to the table and sat down. "What am I going to do?" she asked.

Brad inclined his head toward the ceiling. "About McCall? That's up to you, sis. If you want him out of here, I can have him airlifted to Flagstaff within a couple hours."

This was no idle boast. Even though he'd retired from the country-music scene several years before, at least as far as concert tours went, Brad still wrote and recorded songs, and he could have stacked his royalty checks like so much cordwood. On top of that, Meg was a McKettrick, a multimillionaire in her own right. One phone call from either one of them, and a sleek jet would be landing outside of town in no time at all, fully equipped and staffed with doctors and nurses.

Ashley bit her lower lip. God knew why, but Jack wanted to stay at her place, and he'd gone through a lot to get there. As impractical as it was, given his condition, she didn't think she could turn him out.

Brad must have read her face. He reached out, took her hand. "You still love the bastard," he said. "Don't you?"

"I don't know," she answered miserably. She'd definitely loved the man she'd known before, but this was a new Jack, a different Jack. The *real* one, she supposed. It shook her to realize she'd given her heart to an illusion.

"It's okay, Ashley."

She shook her head, started to cry again. "Nothing is okay," she argued.

"We can make it that way," Brad offered quietly. "All we have to do is talk."

She dried her eyes on the sleeve of Jack's old shirt. It seemed ironic, given all the things hanging in her closet, that she'd chosen to wear that particular garment when she'd gotten dressed that morning. Had some part of her known, somehow, that Jack was coming home?

Brad was waiting for an answer, and he wouldn't break eye contact until he got one.

Ashley swallowed hard. "Our mother died," she said, cornered. "Our *mother*. And you and Olivia and Melissa all seemed—relieved."

A muscle in Brad's jaw tightened, relaxed again. He sighed and shoved a hand through his hair. "I guess I *was* relieved," he admitted. "They said she didn't suffer, but I always wondered—" He paused, cleared his throat. "I wondered if she was in there somewhere, hurting, with no way to ask for help."

Ashley's heart gave one hard beat, then settled into its normal pace again. "You didn't hate her?" she asked, stunned.

"She was my mother," Brad said. "Of course I didn't hate her."

"Things might have been so different—"

"Ashley," Brad broke in, "things *weren't* different. That's the point. Delia's gone, for good this time. You've got to let go."

"What if I can't?" Ashley whispered.

"You don't have a choice, Button."

Button. Their grandfather had called both her and

Melissa by that nickname; like most twins, they were used to sharing things. "Do you miss Big John as much as I do?" she asked.

"Yes," Brad answered, without hesitation, his voice still gruff. He looked down at his coffee mug for a second or so, then raised his gaze to meet Ashley's again. "Same thing," he said. "He's gone. And letting go is something I have to do about three times a day."

Ashley got up, suddenly unable to sit still. She brought the coffee carafe to the table and refilled Brad's cup. She spoke very quietly. "But it was a one-time thing, letting go of Mom?"

"Yeah," Brad said. "And it happened a long, long time ago. I remember it distinctly—it was the night my high school basketball team took the state championship. I was sure she'd be in the bleachers, clapping and cheering like everybody else. She wasn't, of course, and that was when I got it through my head that she wasn't coming back—ever."

Ashley's heart ached. Brad was her big brother; he'd always been strong. Why hadn't she realized that he'd been hurt, too?

"Big John *stayed,* Ashley," he went on, while she sat there gulping. "He stuck around, through good times and bad. Even after he'd buried his only son, he kept on keeping on. Mom caught the afternoon bus out of town and couldn't be bothered to call or even send a postcard. I did my mourning long before she died."

Ashley could only nod.

Brad was quiet for a while, pondering, taking the occasional sip from his coffee mug. Then he spoke again. "Here's the thing," he said. "When the chips were down, I basically did the same thing as Mom—

got on a bus and left Big John to take care of the ranch and raise the three of you all by himself—so I'm in no position to judge anybody else. Bottom line, Ash? People are what they are, and they do what they do, and you have to decide either to accept that or walk away without looking back."

Ashley managed a wobbly smile. Sniffled once. "I'm sorry I'm late on the mortgage payments," she said.

Brad rolled his eyes. "Like I'm worried," he replied, his body making the subtle shifts that meant he'd be leaving soon. With one arm, he gestured to indicate the B&B. "Why won't you just let me sign the place over to you?"

"Would you do that," Ashley challenged reasonably, "if our situations were reversed?"

He flushed slightly, got to his feet. "No," he admitted, "but—"

"But what?"

Brad grinned sheepishly, and his powerful shoulders shifted slightly under his shirt.

"But you're a man?" Ashley finished for him, when he didn't speak. "Is that what you were going to say?"

"Well, yeah," Brad said.

"You'll have the mortgage payments as soon as I get a chance to run Jack's credit card," she told her brother, rising to walk him to the back door. Color suffused her cheeks. "Thanks for coming into town," she added. "I feel like a fool for panicking."

In the midst of pulling on his jacket, Brad paused. "I'm a big brother," he said, somewhat gruffly. "It's what we do."

"Are you and Meg going to the hospital tomorrow, when Livie…?"

Brad tugged lightly at her braid, the way he'd always done. "We'll be hanging out by the telephone," he said. "Livie swears it's a normal procedure, and she doesn't want everyone fussing 'as if it were a heart transplant,' as she put it."

Ashley bit down on her lower lip and nodded. She already had a nephew—Mac—and two nieces, Carly and Sophie, although technically Carly, Meg's half sister, whom her dying father had asked her to raise, wasn't really a niece. Tomorrow, another little one would join the family. Instead of being a nervous wreck, she ought to be celebrating.

She wasn't, she decided, so different from Sophie. Having effectively lost Delia when she was so young, she'd turned to Olivia as a substitute mother, as had Melissa. Had their devotion been a burden to their sister, only a few years older than they were, and grappling with her own sense of loss?

She stood on tiptoe and kissed Brad's cheek. "Thanks," she said again. "Call if you hear anything."

Brad gave her braid another tug, turned and left the house.

Ashley felt profoundly alone.

Jack had nearly flung himself at the singing cowboy standing at the foot of his bed, before recognizing him as Ashley's famous brother, Brad. Even though the room had been dark, the other man must have seen him tense.

"I know you're awake, McCall," he'd said.

Jack had yawned. "O'Ballivan?"

"Live and in person," came the not-so-friendly reply.

"And you're sneaking around my room because...?"

O'Ballivan had chuckled at that. Hooked his thumbs through his belt loops. "Because Ashley's worried about you. And what worries my baby sister worries *me,* James Bond."

Ashley was worried about him? Something like elation flooded Jack. "Not for the same reasons, I suspect," he said.

Mr. Country Music had gripped the high, spooled rail at the foot of the bed and leaned forward a little to make his point. "Damned if I can figure out why you'd come back here, especially in the shape you're in, after what happened last summer, except to take up where you left off." He paused, gripped the rail hard enough that his knuckles showed white even in the gloom. "You hurt her again, McCall, and you have my solemn word—I'm gonna turn right around and hurt *you.* Are we clear on that?"

Jack had smiled, not because he was amused, but because he liked knowing Ashley had folks to look after her when he wasn't around—and when he was. "Oh, yeah," Jack had replied. "We're clear."

Obviously a man of few words, O'Ballivan had simply nodded, turned and walked out of the room.

Remembering, Jack raised himself as high on the pillows as he could, strained to reach the lamp switch. The efforts, simple as they were, made him break out in a cold sweat, but at the same time, he felt his strength returning.

He looked around the room, noting the flowered wallpaper, the pale rose carpeting, the intricate woodwork on the mantelpiece. Two girly chairs flanked the cold fireplace, and fat flakes of January snow drifted past the two sets of bay windows, both sporting seats beneath, covered by cheery cushions.

It was a far cry from Walter Reed, he thought.

An even further cry from the jungle hut where he'd hidden out for nearly three months, awaiting his chance to grab little Rachel Stockard, hustle her out of the country by boat and then a seaplane, and return her to her frantic mother.

He'd been well paid for the job, but it was the memory of the mother-daughter reunion, after he'd surrendered the child to a pair of FBI agents and a Customs official in Atlanta, that made his throat catch more than two weeks after the fact.

Through an observation window, he'd watched as Rachel scrambled out of the man's arms and raced toward her waiting mother. Tears pouring down her face, Ardith Stockard had dropped to her knees, arms outspread, and gathered the little girl close. The two of them had clung to each other, both trembling.

And then Ardith had raised her eyes, seen Jack through the glass, and mouthed the words, "Thank you."

He'd nodded, exhausted and already sick.

Closing his eyes, Jack went back over the journey to South America, the long game of waiting and watching, finally finding the small, isolated country estate where Rachel had been taken after she was kidnapped from her maternal grandparents' home in Phoenix, almost a year before.

Even after locating the child, he hadn't been able to make a move for more than a week—not until her father and his retinue of thugs had loaded a convoy of jeeps with drugs and firepower one day, and roared off down the jungle road, probably headed for a rendezvous with a boat moored off some hidden beach.

Jack had soon ascertained that only the middle-aged cook—and he had reason not to expect opposition from her—and one guard stood between him and Rachel. He'd waited until dark, risking the return of the jeep convoy, then climbed to the terrace outside the child's room.

"Did you come to take me home to my mommy?" Rachel had shrilled, her eyes wide with hope, when he stepped in off the terrace, a finger to his lips.

Her voice carried, and the guard burst in from the hallway, shouting in Spanish.

There had been a brief struggle—Jack had felt something prick him in the side as the goon went down—but, hearing the sound of approaching vehicles in the distance, he hadn't taken the time to wonder.

He'd grabbed Rachel up under one arm and climbed over the terrace and back down the crumbling rock wall of the house, with its many foot-and handholds, to the ground, running for the trees.

It was only after the reunion in Atlanta that Jack had suddenly collapsed, dizzy with fever.

The next thing he remembered was waking up in a hospital room, hooked up to half a dozen machines and surrounded by grim-faced Feds waiting to ask questions.

Chapter 3

Ashley did not expect to sleep at all that night; she had too many things on her mind, between the imminent birth of Olivia's baby, lingering issues with her mother and siblings, and Jack McCall landing in the middle of her formerly well-ordered days like the meteor that allegedly finished off the dinosaurs.

Therefore, sunlight glowing pink-orange through her eyelids and the loud jangle of her bedside telephone came as a surprise.

She groped for the receiver, nearly throwing a disgruntled Mrs. Wiggins to the floor, and rasped out a hoarse, "Hullo?"

Olivia's distinctive laugh sounded weary, but it bubbled into Ashley's ear and then settled, warm as summer honey, into every tuck and fold of her heart. "Did I wake you up?"

"Yes," Ashley admitted, her heart beating faster as

she raised herself onto one elbow and pushed her bangs back out of her face. "Livie? Did you—is everything all right—what—?"

"You're an aunt again," Olivia said, choking up again. "Twice over."

Ashley blinked. Swallowed hard. "Twice over? Livie, you had *twins?*"

"Both boys," Olivia answered, in a proud whisper. "And before you ask, they're fine, Ash. So am I." There was a pause, then a giggle. "I'm not too sure about Tanner, though. He's only been through this once before, and Sophie didn't bring along a sidekick when she came into the world."

Ashley's eyes burned, and her throat went thick with joy. "Oh, Livie," she murmured. "This is wonderful! Have you told Melissa and Brad?"

"I was hoping you'd do that for me," Olivia answered. "I've been working hard since five this morning, and I could use a nap before visiting hours roll around."

First instinct: Throw on whatever clothes came to hand, jump in the car and head straight for the hospital, visiting hours be damned. Ashley wanted a look at her twin nephews, wanted to see for herself that Olivia really was okay.

In the next instant, she remembered Jack.

She couldn't leave a sick guest alone, which meant she'd have to rustle up someone to keep an eye on him before she could visit Olivia and the babies.

"You're in Flagstaff, right?" she asked, sitting up now.

"Good heavens, no," Olivia replied, with another laugh. "We didn't make it that far—I went into labor at three-thirty this morning. I'm at the clinic over in Indian Rock—thanks to the McKettricks, they're equipped with incubators and just about everything else a new baby could possibly need."

"Indian Rock?" Ashley echoed, still a little groggy. Forty miles from Stone Creek, Meg's hometown was barely closer than Flagstaff, and lay in the opposite direction.

"I'll explain later, Ash," Olivia said. "Right now, I'm beat. You'll call Brad and Melissa?"

"Right away," Ashley promised. Happiness for her sister and brother-in-law welled up into her throat, a peculiar combination of pain and pleasure. "Just one more thing—have you named the babies?"

"Not yet. We'll probably call one John Mitchell, for Big John and Dad, and the other Sam. Even though Tanner and I knew we were having two babies—our secret—we need to give it some thought."

Practically every generation of the O'Ballivan family boasted at least one Sam, all the way back to the founder of Stone Creek Ranch. For all her delight over the twins' birth, Ashley felt a little pang. She'd always planned to name her own son Sam.

Not that she was in any danger of having children.

"C-Congratulations, Livie. Hug Tanner for me, too."

"Consider it done," Olivia said.

Goodbyes were said, and Ashley had to try three times before she managed to hang up the receiver.

After drawing a few deep breaths and wiping away *mostly* happy tears, Ashley regained her composure, remembered that she'd promised to pass the news along to the rest of her family.

Brad answered the telephone out at the ranch,

sounding wide-awake. The sun couldn't have been up for long, but by then, he'd probably fed all the dogs, horses and cattle on the place and started breakfast for Meg, Carly, Mac and himself. "That's great," he said, once Ashley had assured him that both Olivia and the babies were doing well. "But what are they doing in Indian Rock?"

"Olivia said she'd explain later," Ashley answered.

The next call she placed was to her own twin, Melissa, who lived on the other side of town. A lawyer and an absolute genius with money, Melissa owned the spacious two-family home, renting out one side and thereby making the mortgage payment without touching her salary.

A man answered, and the voice wasn't familiar.

A little alarmed—reruns of *City Confidential* and *Forensic Files* were Ashley's secret addiction—she sat up a little straighter and asked, "Is this 555-2293?"

"I think so," he said. "Melissa?"

Melissa came on the line, sounding breathless. "Olivia?"

"Your *other* sister," Ashley said. "Livie asked me to call you. The babies were born this morning—"

"Babies?" Melissa interrupted. "Plural?"

"Twins," Ashley answered.

"Nobody said anything about twins!" Being something of a control freak, Melissa didn't like surprises— even good ones.

Ashley smiled. "They do run in the family, you know," she reminded her sister. "And apparently Tanner and Olivia wanted to surprise us. She says all is well, and she's going to catch some sleep before visiting hours."

"Boys? Girls? One of each?" Melissa asked, rapid-fire.

"Both boys," Ashley said. "No for-sure names yet. And who is that man who just answered your phone?"

"Later," Melissa said, lowering her voice.

Ashley's imagination spiked again. "Just tell me you're all right," she said. "That some stranger isn't forcing you to pretend—"

"Oh, for Pete's sake," Melissa broke in, sounding almost snappish. She'd been worried about Olivia, too, Ashley reasoned, calming down a little, but still unsettled. "I'm not bound with duct tape and being held captive in a closet. You're watching too much crime-TV again."

"Say the code word," Ashley said, just to be absolutely sure Melissa was safe.

"You are so paranoid," Melissa griped. Ashley could just see her, pushing back her hair, which fell to her shoulders in dark, gleaming spirals, picture her eyes flashing with irritation.

"Say it, and I'll leave you alone."

Melissa sighed. "Buttercup," she said.

Ashley smiled. After a rash of child abductions when they were small, Big John had helped them choose the secret word and instructed them never to reveal it to anyone outside the family. Ashley never had, and she was sure Melissa hadn't, either.

They'd liked the idea of speaking in code—their version of the twin-language phenomenon, Ashley supposed. Between the ages of three and seven, they'd driven everyone crazy, chattering away in a dialect made up of otherwise ordinary words and phrases.

If Melissa had said, "I plan to spend the afternoon sewing," for instance, Ashley would have called out the National Guard. Ashley's signal, considerably less autobiographical, was, "I saw three crows sitting on the mailbox this morning."

"Are you satisfied?" Melissa asked.

"Are you PMS-ing?" Ashley countered.

"I wish," Melissa said.

Before Ashley could ask what she'd meant by that, Melissa hung up.

"She's PMS-ing," Ashley told Mrs. Wiggins, who was curling around her ankles and mewing, probably ready for her kitty kibble.

Hastily, Ashley took a shower, donned trim black woolen slacks and an ice-blue silk blouse, brushed and braided her hair, and went out into the hallway.

Jack's door was closed—she was sure she'd left it open a crack the night before, in case he called out— so she rapped lightly with her knuckles.

"In," he responded.

Ashley rolled her eyes and opened the door to peek inside the room. Jack was sitting on the edge of the bed, his back very straight. He needed a shave, and his eyes were clear when he turned his head to look at her.

"You're better," she said, surprised.

He gave a slanted grin. "Sorry to disappoint you."

Ashley felt her temper surge, but she wasn't about to give Jack McCall the satisfaction of getting under her skin. Not today, when she'd just learned that she had twin nephews. "Are you hungry?"

"Yeah," he said. "Bacon and eggs would be good."

Ashley raised one eyebrow. He'd barely managed chicken soup the night before, and now he wanted a trucker's breakfast? "You'll make yourself sick," she told him, hiking her chin up a notch.

"I'm already sick," he pointed out. "And I still want bacon and eggs."

"Well," Ashley said, "there aren't any. I usually have grapefruit or granola."

"You serve paying guests *health food?*"

Ashley sucked in a breath, let it out slowly. She wasn't about to admit, not to Jack McCall, at least, that she hadn't had a guest, paying or otherwise, in way too long. "Some people," she told him carefully, "care about good nutrition."

"And some people want bacon and eggs."

She sighed. "Oh, for heaven's sake."

"It's the least you can do," Jack wheedled, "since I'm paying triple for this room and the breakfast that's supposed to come with the bed."

"All right," she said. "But I'll have to go to the store, and that means *you'll* have to wait."

"Fine by me," Jack replied lightly, extending his feet and wriggling his toes, his expression curious, as though he wasn't sure they still worked. "I'll be right here." The wicked grin flashed again. "Get a move on, will you? I need to get my strength back."

Ashley shut the door hard, drew another deep breath in the hallway, and started downstairs, careful not to trip over the gamboling Mrs. Wiggins.

Reaching the kitchen, she poured kibble for the kitten, cleaned and refilled the tiny water bowl, and gathered her coat, purse and car keys.

"I'll be back in a few minutes," she told the cat.

The temperature had dropped below freezing during the night, and the roads were sheeted in ice. Ashley's trip to the supermarket took nearly forty-five minutes, the store was jammed, and by the time she got home, she was in a skillet-banging mood. She was an innkeeper, not a nurse. Why hadn't she insisted that Tanner and Jeff take Jack to one of the hospitals in Flagstaff?

She built a fire on the kitchen hearth, hoping to cheer herself up a little—and take the chill out of her bones—then started a pot of coffee brewing. Next, she laid four strips of bacon in the seasoned cast-iron frying pan that had been Big John's, tossed a couple of slices of bread into the toaster slots, and took a carton of eggs out of her canvas grocery bag.

She knew how Jack liked his eggs—over easy— just as she knew he took his coffee black and strong. It galled her plenty that she remembered those details— and a lot more.

Cooking angrily—so much for her motto that every recipe ought to be laced with love—Ashley nearly jumped out of her skin when she heard his voice behind her.

"Nice fire," he said. "Very cozy."

She whirled, openmouthed, and there he was, standing in the kitchen doorway, but leaning heavily on the jamb.

"What are you doing out of bed?" she asked, once the adrenaline rush had subsided.

Slowly, he made his way to the table, dragged back a chair and dropped into the seat. "I couldn't take that wallpaper for another second," he teased. "Too damn many roses and ribbons."

Knowing that wallpaper was a stupid thing to be sensitive about, and sensitive just the same, Ashley opened a cupboard, took down a mug and filled it, even though the coffeemaker was still chortling through the brewing process. Set the mug down in front of him with a thump.

"Surely you're not *that* touchy about your décor," Jack said.

"Shut up," Ashley told him.

His eyes twinkled. "Do you talk to all your guests that way?"

As so often happened around Jack, Ashley spoke without thinking first. "Only the ones who sneaked out of my bed in the middle of the night and disappeared for six months without a word."

Jack frowned. "Have there been a lot of those?"

Jack McCall was the first—and only—man Ashley had ever slept with, but she'd be damned if she'd tell him so. After all, she realized, he hadn't just broken her heart once—he'd done it *twice*. She'd been shy in high school, but the day she and Jack met, in her freshman year of college at the University of Arizona, her world had undergone a seismic shift.

They talked about getting married after Ashley finished school, had even looked at engagement rings. Jack had been a senior, and after graduation, he'd enlisted in the Navy. After a few letters and phone calls, he'd simply dropped out of her life.

She'd gotten her BA in liberal arts.

Melissa had gone on to law school, Ashley had returned to Stone Creek, bought the B&B with Brad's help and tried to convince herself that she was happy.

Then, just before Christmas, two years earlier, Jack had returned. She'd been a first-class fool to get involved with him a second time, to believe it would last. He came and went, called often when he was away, showed up again and made soul-wrenching love to her just when she'd made up her mind to end the affair.

"I haven't been hibernating, you know," she said stiffly, turning the bacon, pushing down the lever on the toaster and sliding his perfectly cooked eggs off the burner. "I date."

Right. Melissa had fixed her up twice, with guys she knew from law school, and she'd gone out to dinner once, with Melvin Royce, whose father owned the Stone Creek Funeral Home. Melvin had spent the whole evening telling her that death was a beautiful thing—not to mention lucrative—cremation was the way to go, and corpses weren't at all scary, once you got used to them.

She hadn't gone out with anyone since.

Oh, yes, she was a regular party girl. If she didn't watch out, she'd end up as tabloid fodder.

Not. The tabloids were Brad's territory, and he was welcome to them, as far as she was concerned.

"I'm sorry, Ashley," Jack said quietly, when they'd both been silent for a long time. She couldn't help noticing that his hand shook slightly as he took a sip of his coffee and set the mug down again.

"For what?"

"For everything." He thrust splayed fingers through his hair, and his jaw tightened briefly, under the blue-black stubble of his beard.

"Everything? That covers a lot of ground," Ashley said, sliding his breakfast onto a plate and setting it down in front of him with an annoyed flourish.

Jack sighed. "Leaving you. It was a dumb thing to do. But maybe coming back is even dumber."

The remark stung Ashley, made her cheeks burn,

and she turned away quickly, hoping Jack hadn't noticed. "You arrived in an ambulance," she said. "Feel free to leave in one."

"Will you sit down and talk to me? Please?"

Ashley faced him, lest she be thought a coward.

Mrs. Wiggins, the little traitor, started up Jack's right pant leg and settled in his lap for a snooze. He picked up his fork, broke the yolk on one of his eggs, but his eyes were fastened on Ashley.

"What happened to you?" Ashley asked, without planning to speak at all. There it was again, the Jack Phenomenon. She wasn't normally an impulsive person.

Jack didn't look away, but several long moments passed before he answered. "The theory is," he said, "that a guy I tangled with on a job injected me with something."

Ashley's heart stopped, started again. She joined Jack at the table, but only because she was afraid her knees wouldn't support her if she remained standing. "A job? What kind of job?"

"You know I'm in security," Jack hedged, avoiding her eyes now, concentrating on his breakfast. He ate slowly, deliberately.

"Security," Ashley repeated. All she really knew about Jack was that he traveled, made a lot of money and was often in danger. These were not things he'd actually told her—she'd gleaned them from telephone conversations she'd overheard, stories Sophie and Olivia had told her, comments Tanner had made.

"I've got to leave again, Ashley," Jack said. "But this time, I want you to know why."

She *wanted* Jack to leave. So why did she feel as

though a trapdoor had just opened under her chair, and she was about to fall down the rabbit hole? "Okay— why?" she asked, in somebody else's voice.

"Because I've got enemies. Most of them are in prison—or dead—but one has a red-hot grudge against me, a score to settle, and I don't want you or anybody else in Stone Creek to get hurt. I should have thought things through before I came here, but the truth is, all I could focus on was being where you are."

The words made her ache. Ashley longed to take Jack's hand, but she wouldn't let herself do it. "What kind of grudge?"

"I stole his daughter."

Ashley's mouth dropped open. She closed it again.

Jack gave a mirthless little smile. "Her name is Rachel. She's seven years old. Her mother went through a rebellious period that just happened to coincide with a semester in a university in Venezuela. She fell in with a bad crowd, got involved with a fellow exchange student—an American named Chad Lombard, who was running drugs between classes. Her parents ran a background check on Lombard, didn't like the results and flew down from Phoenix to take their daughter home. Ardith was pregnant—the folks wanted her to give the baby up and she refused. She was nineteen, sure she was in love with Lombard, waited for him to come and get her, put a wedding band on her finger. He didn't. Eventually, she finished school, married well, had two more kids. The new husband wanted to adopt Rachel, and that meant Lombard had to sign off, so the family lawyers tracked him down and presented him with the papers and the offer of a hefty check. He went ballistic, said he wanted to raise Rachel himself, and generously offered to take Ardith back, too, if she'd leave the other two kids behind and divorce the man she'd married. Naturally, she didn't want to go that route. Things were quiet for a while, and then one day Rachel disappeared from her backyard. Lombard called that night to say Phoenix P.D. was wasting its time looking for Rachel, since he had the child and they were already out of the country."

Although Ashley had never been a mother herself, it was all too easy to understand how frantic Ardith and the family must have been.

"And they hired you to find Rachel and bring her home?"

"Yes," Jack answered, after another long delay. The long speech had clearly taken a lot out of him, but the amazed admiration she felt must have been visible in her eyes, because he added, "But don't get the idea that I'm some kind of hero. I was paid a quarter of a million dollars for bringing Rachel back home safely, and I didn't hesitate to accept the money."

"I didn't see any of this in the newspapers," Ashley mused.

"You wouldn't have," Jack replied. He'd finished half of his breakfast, and although he had a little more color than before, he was still too pale. "It was vital to keep the story out of the press. Rachel's life might have depended on it, and mine definitely did."

"Weren't you scared?"

"Hell," Jack answered, "I was terrified."

"You should lie down," she said softly.

"I don't think I can make it back up those stairs," Jack said, and Ashley could see that it pained him to admit this.

"You're just trying to avoid the wallpaper," she joked, though she was dangerously close to tears. Carefully, she helped him to his feet. "There's a bed in my sewing room. You can rest there until you feel stronger."

His face contorted, but he still managed a grin. "You're strong for a woman," he said.

"I was raised on a ranch," Ashley reminded him, ducking under his right shoulder and supporting him as she steered him across the kitchen to her sewing room. "I used to help load hay bales in our field during harvest, among other things."

Jack glanced down at her face, and she thought she saw a glimmer of respect in his eyes. "*You* bucked bales?"

"Sure did." They'd reached the sewing room door, and Ashley reached out to push it open. "Did you?"

"Are you kidding?" Jack's chuckle was ragged. "My dad is a dentist. I was raised in the suburbs—not a hay bale for miles."

Like the account of little Rachel's rescue, this was news to Ashley. She knew nothing about Jack's background, wondered how she could have fallen so hard for a man who'd never mentioned his family, let alone introduced her to them. In fact, she'd assumed he didn't *have* a family.

"Exactly what *is* your job title, anyway?"

He looked at her long and hard, wavering just a few feet from the narrow bed. "Mercenary," he said.

Ashley took that in, but it didn't really register, even after the Rachel story. "Is that what it says on your tax return, under *Occupation?*"

"No," he answered.

They reached the bed, and she helped him get settled. Since he was on top of the blankets, she covered him with a faded quilt that had been passed down
through the O'Ballivan clan since the days when Mad-
die and Sam ran the ranch.

"You do file taxes, don't you?" Ashley was a very
careful and practical person.

Jack smiled without opening his eyes. "Yeah," he
said. "What I do is unconventional, but it isn't illegal."

Ashley stepped back, torn between bolting from the
room and lying down beside Jack, enfolding him in her
arms. "Is there anything I can get you?"

"My gear," he said, his eyes still closed. "Tanner
brought it in. Leather satchel, under the bed upstairs."

Ashley gave a little nod, even though he wouldn't
see it. What kind of *gear* did a mercenary carry? Guns?
Knives?

She gave a little shudder and left the door slightly
ajar.

Upstairs, she found the leather bag under Jack's bed.
The temptation to open it was nearly overwhelming,
but she resisted. Yes, she was curious—*beyond* curious—but she wasn't a snoop. She didn't go through
guests' luggage any more than she read the postcards
they gave her to send for them.

When she got back to the sewing room, Jack was
sleeping. Mrs. Wiggins curled up protectively on his
chest.

Ashley set the bag down quietly and slipped out.
Busied herself with routine housekeeping chores, too
soon finished.

She was relieved when Tanner showed up at the
kitchen door, looking worn out but blissfully happy.

"I came to babysit Jack while you go and see Olivia and the boys," he said, stepping past her and helping himself to a cup of lukewarm coffee. "How's he doing?"

Ashley watched as her brother-in-law stuck the mug into the microwave and pushed the appropriate buttons. "Not bad—for a mercenary."

Tanner paused, and his gaze swung in Ashley's direction. "He told you?"

"Yes. I need some answers, Tanner, and Jack is too sick to give them."

The new father turned away from the counter, the microwave whirring behind him, leaned back and folded his arms, watching Ashley, probably weighing the pros and cons of spilling what he knew—which was plenty, unless she missed her guess.

"He's talking about leaving," Ashley prodded, when Tanner didn't say anything right away. "I'm used to that, but I think I deserve to know what's going on."

Tanner gave a long sigh. "I'd trust Jack with my life—I trusted him with *Sophie's,* when she ran away from boarding school right after we moved here, but the truth is, I don't know a hell of a lot more about him than you do."

"He's your best friend."

"And he plays his cards close to the vest. When it comes to security, he's the best there is." Tanner paused, thrust a hand through his already mussed hair. "I can tell you this much, Ashley—if he said he loved you, he meant it, whatever happened afterward. He's never been married, doesn't have kids, his dad is a dentist, his mother is a librarian, and he has three younger brothers, all of whom are much more conventional than

Jack. He likes beer, but I've never seen him drunk. That's the whole shebang, I'm afraid."

"Someone injected him with something," Ashley said in a low voice. "That's why he's sick."

"Good God," Tanner said.

A silence fell.

"And he's leaving as soon as he's strong enough," Ashley said. "Because some drug dealer named Chad Lombard has a grudge against him, and he's afraid of putting all of us in danger."

Tanner thought long and hard. "Maybe that's for the best," he finally replied. Ashley knew Tanner wasn't afraid for himself, but he had to think about Olivia and Sophie and his infant sons. "I hate it, though. Turning my back on a friend who needs my help."

Ashley felt the same way, though Jack wasn't exactly a friend. In fact, she wasn't sure how to describe their relationship—if they had one at all. "This is Stone Creek," she heard herself say. "We have a long tradition of standing shoulder to shoulder and taking trouble as it comes."

Tanner's smile was tired, but warm. "Go," he said. "Tuckered out as she is, Olivia is dying to show off those babies. I'll look after Jack until you get home."

Ashley hesitated, then got her coat and purse and car keys again, and left for the clinic in Indian Rock.

Chapter 4

Olivia was sitting up in bed, beaming, a baby tucked in the crook of each arm, when Ashley hurried into her room. There were flowers everywhere—Brad and Meg had already been there and gone, having brought Carly and Sophie to see the boys before school.

"Come and say hello to John and Sam," Olivia said gently.

Ashley, clutching a bouquet of pink and yellow carnations, hastily purchased at a convenience store, moved closer. She felt stricken with wonder and an immediate and all-encompassing love for the tiny red-faced infants snoozing in their swaddling blankets.

"Oh, Livie," she whispered, "they're beautiful."

"I agree," Olivia said proudly. "Do you want to hold them?"

Ashley swallowed, then reached out for the bundle

on the right. She sat down slowly in the chair closest to Olivia's bed.

"That's John," Olivia explained, her voice soft with adoring exhaustion.

"How can you tell?" Ashley asked, without lifting her eyes from the baby's face. He seemed to glow with some internal light, as though he were trailing traces of heaven, the place he'd so recently left.

Livie chuckled. "The twins aren't identical, Ashley," she said. "John is a little smaller than Sam, and he has my mouth. Sam looks like Tanner."

Ashley didn't respond; she was too smitten with young John Mitchell Quinn. By the time she swapped one baby for the other, she could tell the difference between them.

A nurse came and collected the babies, put them back in their incubators. Although they were healthy, like most twins they were underweight. They'd be staying at the clinic for a few days after Olivia went home.

Olivia napped, woke up, napped again.

"I'm so glad you're here," she said once.

Ashley, who had been rising from her chair to leave, sat down again. Remembered the carnations and got up to put them in a water-glass vase.

"How did you wind up in Indian Rock instead of Flagstaff?" Ashley asked, when Olivia didn't immediately drift off.

Olivia smiled. "I was on a call," she said. "Sick horse. Tanner wanted me to call in another vet, but this was a special case, and Sophie was spending the night at Brad and Meg's, so he came with me. We planned to go on to Flagstaff for the induction when I was finished, but the babies had other ideas. I went into labor in the barn, and Tanner brought me here."

Ashley shook her head, unable to hold back a grin. Her sister, nine and a half months pregnant by her own admission, had gone out on a call in the middle of the night. It was just like her. "How's the horse?"

"Fine, of course," Olivia said, still smiling. "I'm the best vet in the county, you know."

Ashley found a place for the carnations—they looked pitiful among all the dozens and dozens of roses, yellow from Brad and Meg, white from Tanner, and more arriving at regular intervals from friends and coworkers. "I know," she agreed.

Olivia reached for her hand, squeezed. "Friends again?"

"We were never *not* friends, Livie."

Olivia shook her head. Like all O'Ballivans, she was stubborn. "We were always *sisters*," she said. "But sisters aren't necessarily friends. Let's not let the mom-thing come between us again, okay?"

Ashley blinked away tears. "Okay," she said.

Just then, Melissa streaked into the room, half-hidden behind a giant potted plant with two blue plastic storks sticking out of it. She was dressed for work, in a tailored brown leather jacket, beige turtleneck and tweed trousers.

Setting the plant down on the floor, when she couldn't find any other surface, Melissa hurried over to Olivia and kissed her noisily on the forehead.

"Hi, Twin-Unit," she said to Ashley.

"Hi." Ashley smiled, glanced toward the doorway in case the mystery man had come along for the ride. Alas, there was no sign of him.

Melissa looked around for the babies. Frowned. She did everything fast, with an economy of motion; she'd come to see her nephews and was impatient at the delay. "Where are they?"

"In the nursery," Olivia answered, smiling. "How many cups of coffee have you had this morning?"

Melissa made a comical face. "Not nearly enough," she said. "I'm due in court in an hour, and where's the nursery?"

"Down the hall, to the right," Olivia told her. A worried crease appeared in her otherwise smooth forehead. "The roads are icy. Promise me you won't speed all the way back to Stone Creek after you leave here."

"Scout's honor," Melissa said, raising one hand. But she couldn't help glancing at her watch. "Yikes. Down the hall, to the right. Gotta go."

With that, she dashed out.

Ashley followed, double-stepping to catch up.

"Who was the man who answered your phone this morning?" she asked.

Melissa didn't look at her. "Nobody important," she said.

"You spent the night with him, and he's 'nobody important'?"

They'd reached the nursery window, and since Sam and John were the only babies there, spotting them was no problem.

"Could we not discuss this now?" Melissa asked, pressing both palms to the glass separating them from their nephews. "Why are they in incubators? Is something wrong?"

"It's just a precaution," Ashley answered gently. "They're a little small."

"Aren't babies *supposed* to be small?" Melissa's eyes were tender as she studied the new additions to the family. When she turned to face Ashley, though, her expression turned bleak.

"He's my boss," she said.

Ashley took a breath before responding. "The one who divorced his latest trophy wife about fifteen minutes ago?"

Melissa stiffened. "I knew you'd react that way. Honestly, Ash, sometimes you are such a prig. The marriage was over years ago—they were just going through the motions. And if you think I had anything to do with the breakup—well, you ought to know better."

Ashley closed her eyes briefly. She *did* know better. Her twin was an honorable person; nobody knew that better than she did. "I wasn't implying that you're a home-wrecker, Melissa. It's just that you're not over Daniel yet. You need time."

Daniel Guthrie, the last man in Melissa's life, owned and operated a fashionably rustic dude ranch between Stone Creek and Flagstaff. An attractive widower with two young sons, Dan was looking for a wife, someone to settle down with, and he'd never made a secret of it. Melissa, who freely admitted that she *could* love Dan and his children if she half tried, wanted a career— after all, she'd worked hard to earn her law degree.

It was a classic lose-lose situation.

"I didn't have sex with Alex," Melissa whispered, though Ashley hadn't asked. "We were just *talking.*"

"I believe you," Ashley said, putting up both hands in a gesture of peace. "But Stone Creek is a small town. If some bozo's car was parked in your driveway all night, word is bound to get back to Dan."

"Dan has no claim on me," Melissa snapped. "*He's* the one who said we needed a time-out." She sucked in a furious breath. "And Alex Ewing is *not* a bozo. He's up for the prosecutor's job in Phoenix, and he wants me to go with him if he gets it."

Ashley blinked. "You would move to—to Phoenix?"

Melissa widened her eyes. "Phoenix isn't Mars, Ashley," she pointed out. "It's less than two hours from here. And just because you're content to quietly fade away in Stone Creek, quilting and baking cookies for visiting strangers, that doesn't mean *I* am."

"But—this is home."

Melissa looked at her watch again, shook her head. "Yeah," she said. "That's the problem."

With that, she walked off, leaving Ashley staring after her.

I am not *"content to quietly fade away in Stone Creek,"* she thought.

But wasn't that exactly what she was doing?

Making beds, cooking for guests, putting up decorations for various holidays only to take them down again? And, yes, quilting. That was her passion, her artistic outlet. Nothing wrong with that.

But Melissa's remarks *had* brought up the question Ashley usually avoided.

When was her *life* supposed to start?

Jack woke with a violent start, expecting darkness and nibbling rats.

Instead, he found himself in a small, pretty room with pale green walls. An old-fashioned sewing machine, the treadle kind usually seen only in antiques malls and elderly ladies' houses stood near the door.

The quilt covering him smelled faintly of some herb—probably lavender—and memories.

Ashley.

He was at her place.

Relief flooded him—and then he heard the sound. Distant—a heavy step—definitely *not* Ashley's.

Leaning over the side of the bed, which must have been built for a child, it was so short and so narrow, Jack found his gear, fumbled to open the bag, extracted his trusty Glock, that marvel of German engineering. Checked to make sure the clip was in—and full.

The mattress squeaked a little as he got to his feet, listening not just with his ears, but with every cell, with all the dormant senses he'd learned to tap into, if not to name.

There it was again—that thump. Closer now. Definitely masculine.

Jack glanced back over one shoulder, saw that the kitten was still on the bed, watching him with curious, mismatched eyes.

"Shhh," he told the animal.

"Meooow," it responded.

The sound came a third time, nearer now. Just on the other side of the kitchen doorway, by Jack's calculations.

Think, he told himself. He knew he was reacting out of all proportion to the situation, but he couldn't help it. He'd had a lot of practice at staying alive, and his survival instincts were in overdrive.

Chad Lombard couldn't have tracked him to Stone Creek; there hadn't been time. But Jack was living and breathing because he lived by his gut as well as his mind. The small hairs on his nape stood up like wire.

Using one foot, the Glock clasped in both hands, he eased the sewing room door open by a few more inches.

Waited.

And damn near shot the best friend he'd ever had when Tanner Quinn strolled into the kitchen.

"Christ," Jack said, lowering the gun. With his long outgoing breath, every muscle in his body seemed to go slack.

Tanner's face was hard. "That was my line," he said.

Jack sagged against the doorframe, his eyes tightly shut. He forced himself to open them again. "What the hell are you doing here?"

"Playing nursemaid to you," Tanner answered, crossing the room in a few strides and expertly removing the Glock dangling from Jack's right hand. "Guess I should have stuck with my day job."

Jack opened his eyes, sick with relief, sick with whatever that goon in South America had shot into his veins. "Which is what?" he asked, in an attempt to lighten the mood.

Tanner set the gun on top of the refrigerator and pulled Jack by the arm. Squired him to a chair at the kitchen table.

"Raising three kids and being a husband to the best woman in the world," he answered. "And if it's all the same to you, I'd like to stick around long enough to see my grandchildren."

Jack braced an elbow on the tabletop, covered his face with one hand. "I'm sorry," he said.

Tanner hauled back a chair of his own, making plenty of noise in the process, and sat down across from Jack, ignoring the apology. "What's going on,

McCall?" he demanded. "And don't give me any of your bull crap cloak-and-dagger answers, either."

"I need to get out of here," Jack said, meeting his friend's gaze. "Now. Today. Before somebody gets hurt."

Tanner flung a scathing glance toward the Glock, gleaming on top of the brushed-steel refrigerator. "Seems to me, *you're* the main threat to public safety around here. Dammit, you could have shot Ashley—or Sophie or Carly—"

"I said I was sorry."

"Oh, well, that changes everything."

Jack sighed. And then he told Tanner the same story he'd told Ashley earlier. Most of it was even true.

"You call this living, Jack?" Tanner asked, when he was finished. "When are you going to stop playing Indiana Jones and settle down?"

"Spoken like a man in love with a pregnant veterinarian," Jack said.

At last, Tanner broke down and grinned. "She's not pregnant anymore. Olivia and I are now the proud parents of twin boys."

"As of when?" Jack asked, delighted and just a shade envious. He'd never thought much about kids until he'd gotten to know Sophie, after Tanner's first wife, Katherine, was killed, and then Rachel, the bravest seven-year-old in Creation.

"As of this morning," Tanner answered.

"Wow," Jack said, with a shake of his head. "It would *really* have sucked if I'd shot you."

"Yeah," Tanner agreed, going grim again.

"All the more reason for me to hit the road."

"And go where?"

"Dammit, I don't know. Just away. I shouldn't have come here in the first place—I was out of my mind with fever—"

"You were out of your mind, all right," Tanner argued. "But I think it has more to do with Ashley than the toxin. There's a pattern here, old buddy. You always leave—and you always come back. That ought to tell you something."

"It tells me that I'm a jerk."

"You won't get any argument there," Tanner said, without hesitation.

"I can't keep doing this. Every time I've left that woman, I've meant to stay gone. But Ashley haunts me, Tanner. She's in the air I breathe and the water I drink—"

"It's called *love,* you idiot," Tanner informed him.

"Love," Jack scoffed. "This isn't the Lifetime channel, old buddy. And it's not as if I'm doing Ashley some big, fat favor by loving her. My kind of romance could get her *killed.*"

Tanner's mouth crooked up at one corner. "You watch the *Lifetime channel?*"

"Shut up," Jack bit out.

Tanner laughed. "You are so screwed," he said.

"Maybe," Jack snapped. "But you're not being much help here, in case you haven't noticed."

"It's time to stop running," Tanner said decisively. "Take a stand."

"Suppose Lombard shows up? He'd like nothing better than to take out everybody I care about."

Tanner's expression turned serious again, and both his eyebrows went up. "What about your dad, the dentist, and your mom, the librarian, and your three brothers, who probably have the misfortune to look just like you?"

Something tightened inside Jack, a wrenching grab, cold as steel. "Why do you think I haven't seen them since I got out of high school?" he shot back. "Nobody knows I *have* a family, and I want it to stay that way."

Tanner leaned forward a little. "Which means your name isn't Jack McCall," he said. "Who the hell are you, anyway?"

"Dammit, you *know* who I am. We've been through a lot together."

"Do I? Jack is probably your real first name, but I'll bet it doesn't say *McCall* on your birth certificate."

"My birth certificate conveniently disappeared into cyberspace a long time ago," Jack said. "And if you think I'm going to tell you my last name, so you can tap into a search engine and get the goods on me, you're a bigger sucker than I ever guessed."

Tanner frowned. He loved puzzles, and he was exceptionally good at figuring them out. "Wait a second. You and Ashley dated in college, and she knew you as Jack McCall. Did you change your name in high school?"

"Let this go, Tanner," Jack answered tightly. He had to give his friend something, or he'd never get off his back—that much was clear. And while they were sitting there planning his segment on *Biography,* Chad Lombard was looking for him. By that scumbag's watch, it was payback time. "I was one of those difficult types in high school—my folks, with some help from a judge, sent me to one of those military schools where they try to scare kids into behaving like human beings. One of the teachers was a former SEAL. Long story short, the Navy tapped me for their version of Special Forces and put me through college. I never went home, after that, and the name change was their idea, not mine."

Tanner let out a long, low whistle. "Hot damn," he muttered. "Your folks must be frantic, wondering what happened to you."

"They think I'm dead," Jack said, stunned at how much he was giving up. That toxin must be digesting his brain. "There's a grave and a headstone; they put flowers on it once in a while. As far as they're concerned, I was blown to unidentifiable smithereens in Iraq."

Tanner glared at him. "How could you put them through that?"

"Ask the Navy," Jack said.

Outside, snow crunched under tires as Ashley pulled into the driveway.

"End of conversation," Jack told Tanner.

"That's what *you* think," Tanner replied, pushing back his chair to stand.

"I'll be out of here as soon as I can arrange it," Jack warned quietly.

Tanner skewered him with a look that might have meant "Good riddance," though Jack couldn't be sure.

The back door opened, and Ashley blew in on a freezing wind. Hurrying to Tanner, she threw her arms around his waist and beamed up at him.

"The babies are *beautiful!*" she cried, her eyes glistening with happy tears. "Congratulations, Tanner."

Tanner hugged her, kissed the top of her head. "Thanks," he said gruffly. Then, with one more scathing glance at Jack, he put on his coat and left, though not before his gaze strayed to the Glock on top of the refrigerator.

Fortunately, Ashley was too busy taking off her own coat to notice.

Jack made a mental note to retrieve the weapon before she saw it.

"You're up," she told him cheerfully. "Feeling better?"

He'd never left her willingly, but this time, the prospect nearly doubled him over. He sat up a little straighter. "I love you, Ashley," he said.

She'd been in the process of brewing coffee; at his words, she stopped, stiffened, stared at him. "What did you say?"

"I love you. Always have, always will."

She sagged against the counter, all the joy gone from her eyes. "You have a strange way of showing it, Jack McCall," she said, after a very long time.

"I can't stay, Ash," he said hoarsely, wishing he could take her into his arms, make love to her just once more. But he'd done enough damage as it was. "And this time, I won't be back. I promise."

"Is that supposed to make me feel better?"

"It would if you knew what it might mean if I stayed."

"What would it mean, Jack? If you stayed, that is."

"I told you about Lombard. He's the vindictive type, and if he ever finds out about you—"

"Suppose he does," Ashley reasoned calmly, "and you're not here to protect me. What then?"

Jack closed his eyes. "Don't say that."

"Stone Creek isn't a bad place to raise a family," she forged on, with a dignity that broke Jack's heart into two bleeding chunks. "We could be happy here, Jack. Together."

He got to his feet. "Are you saying you love me?"

"Always have," she answered, "always will."

"It wouldn't work," Jack said, wishing he hadn't been such a hooligan back in his teens. None of this would be happening if he hadn't ended up in military school and shown a distinct talent for covert action. He'd probably be a dentist in the Midwest, with a wife and kids and a dog, and his parents and his brothers would be dropping by for Sunday afternoon barbecues instead of visiting an empty grave.

"Wouldn't it?" Ashley challenged. "Make love to me, Jack. And then tell me it wouldn't work."

The temptation burned in his veins and hardened his groin until it hurt. "Ashley, don't."

She began to unbutton her blue silk blouse.

"Ashley."

"What's the matter, Jack? Are you chicken?"

"Ashley, *stop* it." It wasn't a command, it was a plea. "I'm not who you think I am. My name isn't Jack Mc-Call, and I—"

Her blouse was open. Her lush breasts pushed against the lacy pink fabric of her bra. He could see the dark outline of her nipples.

"I don't care what your name is," she said. "I love you. You love me. Whoever you are, take me to bed, unless you want to have me on the kitchen floor."

He couldn't resist her any more than he'd been able to resist coming back every time he left. She was an addiction.

He held out his hand, and she came to him.

Somehow, they managed to get up the stairs, along the hallway, into her bedroom.

He didn't remember undressing her, or undressing himself.

It was as though their clothes had burned away in the heat.

Even a few minutes before, Jack wouldn't have believed he had the strength for sex, but the drive was deep, elemental, as much a part of him as Ashley herself.

There was no foreplay—their need for each other was too great.

The two of them fell sideways onto her bed, kissing as frantically as half-drowned swimmers trying to breathe, their arms and legs entwined.

He took her in one hard stroke, and found her ready for him.

She came instantly, shouting his name, clawing at his back with her fingernails. He drove in deep again, and she began the climb toward another pinnacle, writhing beneath him, flinging her hips up to meet his.

"Jack," she sobbed, *"Jack!"*

He fought to keep control, wondered feverishly if he'd die from the exertion. Oh, but what a way to go.

"Jack—"

"For God's sake, Ashley, lie still—"

Of course she didn't. She went wild beneath him.

Jack gave a ragged shout and spilled himself into her. He felt her clenching around him as she erupted in an orgasm of her own, with a long, continuous cry of exultant surrender.

Afterward, they lay still for a long time, spent, gasping for breath.

Jack felt himself hardening within her, thickening.

"Say it, Jack," she said. "Say you're going to leave me. I dare you."

He couldn't; he searched for the words, but they were nowhere to be found.

So he kissed her instead.

Ashley awakened alone, at dusk, naked and soft-boned in her bed.

The aftershocks of Jack's lovemaking still thrummed in her depths, even as panic surged within her. Damn, he'd done it again—he'd driven her out of her mind with pleasure and then left her.

She scrambled out of bed, pulled on her ratty chenille robe, and hurried downstairs.

"Jack?" She felt like a fool, calling his name when she knew he was already gone, but the cry was out of her mouth before she could stop it.

"In here," he called back.

Ashley's heart fluttered, and so did the pit of her stomach.

She followed the echo of his voice as far as the study doorway, found him sitting at her computer. The monitor threw blue shadows over the planes of his face.

"Hope you don't mind," he said. "My laptop came down with a case of jungle rot, so I trashed it somewhere in the mountains of Venezuela, and I haven't had a chance to get another one."

Ashley groped her way into the room, like someone who'd forgotten how to walk, and landed in the first available chair, a wingback she'd reupholstered herself, in pink, green and white chintz. "Make yourself at home," she said, and then blushed because the words could be taken so many ways.

His fingers flew over the keyboard, with no pause when he looked her way. "Thanks," he said.

"You've made a remarkable recovery, it seems to me," Ashley observed.

"The restorative powers of good sex," Jack said, "are legendary."

He was legendary. It had been hours since they'd made love, but Ashley still felt a deliciously orgasmic twinge every few moments.

"Answering email?" she asked, to keep the conversation going.

Jack shook his head. "I don't get email," he said. "After I booted this thing up and ran all the setups, I did a search. Noticed you didn't have a website. You can't run a business without some kind of presence on the Internet these days, Ashley—not unless you want to go broke."

"You're building a *Web site?*"

"I'm setting up a few prototypes. You can have a look later, see if you like any of them."

"You're a man of many talents, Jack McCall."

He grinned. He'd showered and shaved since leaving her bed, she noticed. And he was wearing fresh clothes—blue jeans and a white T-shirt. "I began to suspect you thought that while you were digging your heels into the small of my back and howling like a she-wolf calling down the moon."

Ashley laughed, but her cheeks burned. She *had* acted like a hussy, abandoning herself to Jack, body and soul, and she didn't regret a moment of it. "Pretty cocky, aren't you?" she said.

Jack swiveled the chair around. "Come here," he said gruffly.

Her heart did a little jig, and her breath caught. "Why?"

"Because I want you," he replied simply.

She stood up, crossed to him, allowed him to set her astraddle on his lap. Moaned as he opened her bathrobe, baring her breasts.

Jack nibbled at one of her nipples, then the other. "Ummm," he murmured, shifting in the chair. He continued to arouse delicious feelings in her breasts with his lips and tongue.

Her eyes widened when she realized he'd opened his jeans. He drew his knees a little farther apart, and she gave a crooning gasp when she felt him between her legs, hot and hard, prodding.

Just as he entered her, he leaned forward again, took her right nipple into his mouth, tongued it and then began to suckle.

Ashley choked out an ecstatic sob and threw back her head, her hair falling loose down her back. "Oh, God," she whimpered. "Oh, God, not yet—"

But her body seized, caught in a maelstrom of pleasure, spasmed wildly, and seized again. Taken over, possessed, she rode him relentlessly, recklessly, her very soul ablaze with a light that blinded her from the inside.

Jack waited until she'd gone still, the effort at restraint visible in his features, and when he let himself go, the motions of his body were slow and graceful. Ashley watched his face, spellbound, until he'd stopped moving.

He sighed, his eyes closed.

And then they flew open.

"You *are* on the pill, aren't you?" he asked.

She had been, before he left. After he was gone, there had been no reason to practice birth control.

Ashley shook her head.

"What?" Jack choked out.

Ashley closed her robe, moved to rise off his lap.

But he grasped her hips and held her firmly in place. "Ashley?" he rasped.

"No, Jack," she said evenly. "I'm not on the pill."

He swore under his breath.

"Don't worry," she told him, hiding her hurt. "I'm not going to trap you."

He was going hard inside her again—angry hard. His eyes smoldering, his hands still holding her by the hips, he began to raise and lower her, raise and lower her, along the growing length of his shaft.

She buckled with the first orgasm, bit back a cry of response.

Jack settled back in the chair, watching her face, already driving her toward another, stronger climax.

And then another, and still another.

When his own release came, much later, he didn't utter a sound.

Chapter 5

In some ways, that last bout of lovemaking had been the most satisfying, but it left Ashley feeling peevish, just the same. When it was over, and she'd solidified her sex-weakened knees by an act of sheer will, she tugged her bathrobe closed and cinched the belt with a decisive motion.

"Good night," she told Jack, her chin high, her face hot.

"'Night," he replied. Having already refastened his jeans, he turned casually back to the computer monitor. To look at him, nobody would have guessed they'd been having soul-bending sex only a few minutes before.

"I'll need a credit card," Ashley said.

Jack slanted a look at her. "I beg your pardon?" he drawled.

Ashley's blush deepened to crimson. "Not for the sex," she said primly. "For the room."

Jack's attention was fixed on the monitor again. "My wallet's in the bag with my other gear. Help yourself."

As she stormed out, she thought she heard him chuckle.

Fury zinged through her, like a charge.

Since she was no snoop, she snatched up the leather bag, resting on the sewing room floor, and marched right back to the study. Set it down on the desk with a hard thump, two inches from Jack's elbow.

He sighed, flipped the brass catch on the bag, and rummaged inside until he found his wallet. Extracted a credit card.

"Here you go, Madam," he said, holding it between two fingers.

Ashley snatched the card, unwilling to pursue the word *Madam*. "How long will you be staying?"

The question hung between them for several moments.

"Better put me down for two weeks," Jack finally said. "The food's good here, and the sex is even better."

Ashley glanced at the card. It was platinum, so it probably had a high limit, and the expiration date was three years in the future. The name, however, was wrong.

"'Mark Ramsey'?" she read aloud.

"Oops. Sorry." Jack took the card back.

"Is that your real name?"

"Of course not." Frowning with concentration, Jack thumbed through a stack of cards, more than most people carried, certainly.

"What *is* your name, then?" *Since I just had about fourteen orgasms straddling your lap, I think I have a right to know.*

"Jack McCall," he said sweetly, handing her a gold card. "Try this one."

"What name did you use when you rescued Rachel?"

"Not this one, believe me. But if a man calls here or, worse yet, comes to the door, asking for Neal Mercer, you've never heard of me."

Ashley's palms were sweaty. She sank disconsolately into the same chair she'd occupied earlier, before the lap dance. "Just how many aliases do you have, anyway?"

Jack was focused on the keyboard again. "Maybe a dozen. Are you going to run that card or not?"

Ashley leaned a little, peered at the screen. A picture of her house, in full summer regalia, filled it. Trees leafed out. Flowers blooming. Lawn greener than green and neatly mowed. She could almost smell sprinkler-dampened grass.

"Where did you get that?" she asked.

"The picture?" Jack didn't look at her. "Downloaded it from the Chamber of Commerce website. I'm setting you up to take credit cards next—the usual?"

She sighed. "Yes."

"Why the sigh?" He was watching her now.

"I have so much to learn about computers," Ashley said, after biting her lip. That was only part of what was bothering her, of course. She loved this man, and he claimed to love her in return, and she didn't even know who he was.

How crazy was that?

"It's not so hard," he told her, switching to another page on the screen, one filled with credit card logos. "I'll show you how."

"What's your name?"

He chuckled. "Rumpelstiltskin?"

"Hilarious. Do you even *remember* who you really are?"

He turned in the swivel chair, gazing directly into her eyes. "Jack McKenzie," he said solemnly. "As if it mattered."

"Why wouldn't it matter?" Ashley asked in a whisper.

"Because Jacob 'Jack' McKenzie is dead. Buried at Arlington, with full military honors."

She stared at him, confounded.

"Get some sleep, Ashley," Jack said, and now he sounded weary.

She was too proud to ask if he planned on sharing her bed—wasn't even sure she wanted him there. Yes, she loved him, with her whole being, there was no escaping that. But they might as well have lived in separate universes; she wasn't an international spy. She was a small-town girl, the operator of a modest B&B. Intrigue wasn't in her repertoire.

Slowly, she rose from the chair. She walked into the darkened living room, flipped on a lamp and proceeded to the check-in desk. There, she ran Jack's credit card.

It went through just fine.

She returned the card to him. "There'll be a slip to sign," she said flatly, "but that can wait until morning."

Jack merely nodded.

Ashley left the study again, scooped up a mewing Mrs. Wiggins as she passed and climbed the stairs.

Jack waited until he'd heard Ashley's bedroom door close in the distance, then set up yet another email account, and brought up the message page. Typed in his mother's email address at the library.

Hi, Mom, he typed. *Just a note to say I'm not really dead...*

Delete.

He clicked to the search engine, entered the URL of the website for his dad's dental office.

There was Dr. McKenzie, in a white coat, looking like a man you'd trust your teeth to without hesitation. The old man was broad in the shoulders, with a full head of silver hair and a confident smile—Jack supposed he'd look a lot like his dad someday, if he managed to live long enough.

The average web surfer probably wouldn't have noticed the pain in Doc's eyes, but Jack did. He looked deep.

"I'm sorry, Dad," he murmured.

His cell phone, buried in the depths of his gear bag, played the opening notes of "Folsom Prison Blues."

Startled, Jack scrabbled through T-shirts and underwear until he found the cell. He didn't answer it, but squinted at the caller ID instead. It read, "Blocked."

A chill trickled down Jack's spine as he waited to see if the caller would leave a voice mail. This particular phone, a throwaway, was registered to Neal Mercer, and only a few people had the number.

Ardith.

Rachel.

An FBI agent or two.

Chad Lombard? There was no way he could have it, unless Rachel or Ardith had told him. Under duress.

A cold sweat broke out between Jack's aching shoulder blades.

A little envelope flashed on the phone screen.

After sucking in a breath, Jack accessed his voice mail.

"Jack? It's Ardith." She sounded scared. She'd changed her name, changed Rachel's, bought a condo on a shady street in a city far from Phoenix and started a new life, hoping to stay under Lombard's radar.

Jack waited for her to go on.

"I think he knows where we are," she said, at long last. "Rachel—I mean, Charlotte—is sure she saw him drive by the playground this afternoon—oh, God, I hope you get this—" Another pause, then Ardith recited a number. "Call me."

Jack shuddered as he hit the call back button. Cell calls were notoriously easy to listen in on, if you had the right equipment and the skill, and given the clandestine nature of his life's work, Lombard surely did. If Rachel *had* seen her father drive past the playground, and not just someone who resembled him, the bastard was already closing in for the kill.

"H-hello?" Ardith answered.

"It's Jack. This has to be quick, Ardith. You need to get *Charlotte* and leave. Right now."

"And go where?" Ardith asked, her voice shaking. "For all I know, he's waiting right outside my door!"

"I'll send an escort. Just be ready, okay?"

"But where—?"

"You'll know when you get here. My people will use the password we agreed on. Don't go with them unless they do."

"Okay," Ardith said, near tears now.

They hung up without goodbyes.

Jack immediately contacted Vince Griffin, using

Ashley's landline, and gave the order, along with the password.

"Call me after you pick them up," he finished.

"Will do," Vince responded. "I take it she and the kid are right where we left them?"

"Yes," Jack said. It was beyond unlikely that Ashley's phone was bugged, but Vince's could be. He had to take the chance, hope to God nobody was listening in, that his longtime friend and employee wouldn't be followed. "Be careful."

"Always," Vince said cheerfully, and hung up.

Jack heard a sound behind him, regretted that the Glock was hidden behind a pile of quilts in the sewing room.

Ashley stood, pale-faced, in the study doorway.

"They're coming here? Rachel and her mother?"

"Yes," Jack said, letting out his breath. *You could have shot Ashley,* he heard Tanner say. A chill burned through him. "They won't be here long—just until I can find them a safe place to start over."

"They can stay as long as they need to," Ashley said, but she looked terrified. "There's no safer place than Stone Creek."

It wouldn't be a safe place for long if Lombard tracked his ex-girlfriend and his daughter to the small Arizona town, but Jack didn't point that out. There was no need to say it aloud.

Jack shut down the computer and retired to the sewing room.

Knowing she wouldn't sleep, Ashley showered, put on blue jeans and an old T-shirt, and returned to the kitchen, where she methodically assembled the ingredients for the most complicated recipe in her collec-tion—her great-grandmother's rum-pecan cake.

The fourth batch was cooling when dawn broke, and Ashley was sitting at the table, a cup of coffee un-touched in front of her.

Jack stepped out of the sewing room, a shaving kit under one arm. His smile was wan, and a little guilty. "Smells like Christmas in here," he said, very quietly. "Did you sleep?"

Ashley shook her head, vaguely aware that she was covered in cake flour, the fallout of frenzied baking. "Did you?"

"No," Jack said, and she knew by the hollow look in his eyes that he was telling the truth. "Ashley, I'm sorry—"

"Please," Ashley interrupted, "stop saying that."

She couldn't help comparing that morning to the one before, when she'd virtually seduced Jack right there in the kitchen. Was it only yesterday that she'd visited Olivia and the babies at the clinic in Indian Rock, had that disturbing conversation with Melissa outside the nursery? Dear God, it seemed as though a hundred years had passed since then.

The wall phone rang.

Jack tensed.

Ashley got up to answer. "It's only Melissa," she said.

She always knew when Melissa was calling.

"I'm picking up twin-vibes," her sister announced. "What's going on?"

"Nothing," Ashley said, glancing at the clock on the fireplace mantel. "It's only six in the morning, Melissa. What are you doing up so early?"

"I told you, I've got vibes," Melissa answered, sounding impatient.

Jack left the kitchen.

"Nothing's wrong," Ashley said, winding the telephone cord around her finger.

"You're lying," Melissa insisted flatly. "Do I have to come over there?"

Ashley smiled at the prospect. "Only if you want a home-cooked breakfast. Blueberry pancakes? Cherry crepes?"

"You," Melissa accused, "are deliberately torturing me. Your own sister. You *know* I'm on a diet."

"You're five foot three and you weigh 110 pounds. If you're on a diet, I'm having you committed." Remembering that their mother had died in the psychiatric ward of a Flagstaff hospital, Ashley instantly regretted her choice of words. This was a subject she wanted to avoid, at least until she regained her emotional equilibrium. Melissa, like Brad and Olivia, had had a no-love-lost relationship with Delia.

"Cherry crepes," Melissa mused. "Ashley O'Ballivan, you are an evil woman." A pause. "Furthermore, you have some nerve, grilling me about Alex Ewing, when Jack McCall is back."

Ashley frowned. "How did you know that?"

"Your neighbor, Mrs. Pollack, works part-time in my office, remember? She told me he arrived in an ambulance, day before yesterday. Is there a reason you didn't mention this?"

"Yes, Counselor," Ashley answered, "there is. Because I didn't want you to know."

"Why not?" Melissa sounded almost hurt.

"Because I knew I'd look like an idiot when he left again."

"Not to be too lawyerly, or anything, but why invite me to breakfast if you were trying to hide a man over there?"

Ashley laughed, but it was forced, and Melissa probably picked up on that, though mercifully, she didn't comment. "Because I'm overstocked on cherry crepes and I need the freezer space?" she offered.

"You were supposed to say something like, 'Because you're my twin sister and I love you.'"

"That, too," Ashley responded.

"I'll be over before work," Melissa said. "You're really okay?"

No, Ashley thought. *I'm in love with a stranger, someone wants to kill him, and my bed-and-breakfast is about to become a stop on a modern underground railroad.*

"I will be," she said aloud.

"Damn right you will," Melissa replied, and hung up without a goodbye. Of course, there hadn't been a "hello," either.

Classic Melissa.

The upstairs shower had been running through most of her conversation with Melissa—Ashley had heard the water rushing through the old house's many pipes. Now all was silent.

Thinking Jack would probably be downstairs soon, wanting breakfast, Ashley fed Mrs. Wiggins and then took a plastic container filled with the results of her *last* cooking binge from the freezer.

A month ago she'd made five dozen crepes, complete with cherry sauce from scratch, when one of her college friends had called to say she'd just found out her husband was having an affair.

Before that, it had been a double-fudge brownie marathon—beginning the night of her mother's funeral. She'd donated the brownies to the residents of the nursing home three blocks over, since, in her own way, she was just as calorie-conscious as Melissa.

Baking therapy was one thing. Scarfing down the results was quite another.

Half an hour passed, and Jack didn't reappear.

Ashley waited.

A full hour had passed, and still no sign of him.

Resigned, she went upstairs. Knocked softly at his bedroom door.

No answer.

Her imagination kicked in. The man had *aliases,* for heaven's sake. He'd abducted a drug dealer's seven-year-old daughter from a stronghold in some Latin American jungle.

Maybe he'd sneaked out the front door.

Maybe he was lying in there, dead.

"Jack?"

Nothing.

She opened the door, her heart in her throat, and stuck her head inside the room.

He wasn't in the bed.

She raised her voice a little. "Jack?"

She heard the buzzing sound then, identified it as an electric shaver, and was just about to back out of the room and close the door behind her, as quietly as possible, when his bathroom door opened.

His hair was damp from the shower, and he was

wearing a towel, loincloth style, and nothing else. He grinned as he shut off the shaver.

"I'm not here for sex," Ashley said, and then could have kicked herself.

Jack laughed. "Too bad," he said. "Nothing like a quickie to get the day off to a good start. So to speak."

A quickie indeed. Ashley gave him a look, meant to hide the fact that she found the idea more than appealing. "Breakfast will be ready soon," she said coolly. "And Melissa is joining us, so try to behave yourself."

He stepped out of the bathroom.

Her gaze immediately dropped to the towel. Shot back to his face.

He was grinning. "But we're alone *now,* aren't we?"

"I'm still not on birth control, remember?" Ashley's voice shook.

"*That* horse is pretty much out of the barn," Jack drawled. He was walking toward her.

She didn't move.

He took her hand, pulled her to him, pushed the door shut.

Kissed her breathless.

Unsnapped her jeans, slid a hand inside her panties.

All without breaking the kiss.

Ashley moaned into his mouth, wet where he caressed her.

He maneuvered her to the bed, laid her down.

Ashley was already trying to squirm out of her jeans. When it came to Jack McCall—McKenzie—*whoever*—she was downright easy.

Jack finally ended the kiss, proceeded to rid her of her shoes, of the binding denim, and then her practical cotton underpants.

She whimpered in anticipation when he knelt between her legs, parted her thighs, kissed her—*there*.

A shudder of violent need moved through her.

"Slow and easy," he murmured, between nibbles and flicks of his tongue.

Slow and easy? She was on fire.

She shook her head from side to side. "Hard," she pleaded. "Hard and fast, Jack. *Please*..."

He went down on her in earnest then, and after a few glorious minutes, she shattered completely, peaking and then peaking again.

Jack soothed her as she descended, stroking her thighs and murmuring to her until she sank into satisfaction.

She'd expected him to mount her, but he didn't.

Instead, he dressed her again, nipping her once through the moist crotch of her panties before tucking her legs into her jeans, sliding them up her legs, tugging them past her bottom. He even slipped her feet into her shoes and tied the laces.

"What about—the quickie?" she asked, burning again because he'd teased her with that little scrape of his teeth. Because as spectacular as her orgasm had been, it had left her wanting—*needing*—more.

"I guess that will have to wait," Jack said, sitting down beside her on the bed and easing her upright next to him. "Didn't you say your sister would be here for breakfast at any moment?"

She looked down at the towel—either it had miraculously stayed in place or he'd wrapped it around his waist again when she wasn't looking—and saw the sizable bulge of his erection. "You've got a hard-on," she said matter-of-factly.

Jack chuckled. "Ya think?"

Melissa's voice sounded from downstairs. "Ash? I'm here!"

Ashley bolted to her feet, blushing. "Coming!" she called back.

"You can say that again," Jack teased.

Smoothing her hair with both hands, tugging at her T-shirt, Ashley hurried out of the room.

"I'll be right down!" she shouted, from the top of the stairs.

Melissa's reply was inaudible.

Ashley dashed into her bathroom and splashed her face with cold water, then checked herself out in the full-length mirror on the back of the door.

She looked, she decided ruefully, like a woman who'd just had a screaming climax—and needed more.

Quickly, she applied powder to her face, but the tell-tale glow was still there.

Damn.

There was nothing to do but go downstairs, where her all-too-perceptive twin was waiting for cherry crepes. If she didn't appear soon, Melissa would come looking for her.

"You were having sex," Melissa said two minutes later, when Ashley forced herself to step into the kitchen.

"No, I wasn't," Ashley replied, with an indignant little sniff.

"Liar."

Ashley crossed the room, turned the oven on to preheat, and got very busy taking the frozen crepes out of their plastic container, transferring them to a baking dish. All the while, she was careful not to let Melissa catch her eye.

"Olivia and the twins are coming home today," Melissa said lightly, but something in her voice warned that she wasn't going to let the sex issue drop.

"I thought the babies had to stay until they were bigger," Ashley replied, still avoiding Melissa's gaze.

"Tanner hired special nurses and had two state-of-the-art incubators brought from Flagstaff," Melissa explained.

Once the crepes were in the oven, Ashley had no choice but to turn around and look at Melissa.

"You *were* having sex," Melissa repeated.

Ashley flung her hands out from her sides. "*Okay. Yes,* I was having sex!" She sighed. "Sort of."

"What do you mean, *sort of?* How do you 'sort of' have sex?"

"Never mind," Ashley snapped. "Isn't it enough that I admitted it? Do you want details?"

"Yes, actually," Melissa answered mischievously, "but I'm obviously not going to get them."

Jack pushed open the inside door and stepped into the kitchen.

"Yet," Melissa added, in a whisper.

Ashley rolled her eyes.

"Hello, Jack," Melissa said.

"Melissa," Jack replied.

Like Brad and Olivia, Melissa wasn't in the Jack McCall fan club. They'd all turned in their membership cards the last time he ditched Ashley.

"Just passing through?" Melissa asked sweetly.

"Like the wind," Jack answered. "Your brother already threatened me, so maybe we can skip that part."

Ashley raised her eyebrows. Brad had *threatened* Jack?

"As long as somebody got the point across," Melissa chimed.

"Oh, believe me, I get it."

"Will you both stop bickering, please?" Ashley asked.

Melissa sneezed. Looked around. "Is there a *cat* in this house?"

Jack grinned. "I could find the little mutant, if you'd like to pet it."

Melissa sneezed again. "I'm—*allergic!* Ashley, you *know* I'm all—all—*atchoo!*"

Ashley had completely forgotten about Mrs. Wiggins, and about her sister's famous allergies. Olivia insisted it was all in Melissa's head, since she'd been tested and the results had been negative.

"I'm sorry, I—"

Another sneeze.

"Bless you," Jack said generously.

Melissa grabbed up her coat and purse and ran for the back door. Slammed it behind her.

"Well," Jack commented, "that went well."

"Shut up," Ashley said.

Jack let out a magnanimous sigh and spread his hands.

Ashley went to the cupboard, got out two plates, set them on the table with rather more force than necessary. "You," she said, "are complicating my life."

"Are you talking to me or the cat?" Jack asked, all innocence.

"You," Ashley replied tersely. "I'm not getting rid of the cat."

"But you *are* getting rid of me? After that orgasm?"

"Shut up."

Jack chuckled, pressed his lips together, and pretended to zip them closed.

Ashley served the crepes. They both ate.

All without a single word passing between them.

After breakfast, Jack retreated to the study, and Ashley cleaned up the kitchen. Melissa called just as she was closing the dishwasher door.

"It wasn't the cat," Melissa said, first thing.

"Duh," Ashley responded.

"I mean, I thought it was, but I'm probably catching cold or something—"

"Either that, or you're allergic to Jack."

"He's bad news, Ash," Melissa said.

"I guess I could take up with Dan," Ashley said mildly. "I hear he's looking for a domestic type."

"Don't you dare!"

Ashley smiled, even though tears suddenly scalded her eyes. She was destined to love one man—Jack McCall—for the rest of her life, maybe for the rest of eternity.

And Melissa was right.

He was the worst possible news.

Chapter 6

"I'm going out to Tanner and Olivia's after work today," Melissa said. "Gotta see my nephews in their natural habitat. Want to ride along?"

By the time Melissa left her office, even if she knocked off at five o'clock—a rare thing for her—it would be dark out. Ardith and Rachel would surely arrive that night, and Ashley wanted to be on hand to welcome the pair and help them settle in.

She'd already decided to put the secret guests in the room directly across from Jack's; it had twin beds and a private bathroom. Jack would surely want to be in close proximity to them in case of trouble, and the feeling was undoubtedly mutual.

"I didn't sleep very well last night," she confessed. "By the time you leave work, I'll probably be snoring."

"Whatever you say," Melissa said gently. "Be careful, Ash. When the sex is good, it's easy to get carried away."

"Sounds like you're speaking from experience," Ashley replied. "Have you seen Dan lately?"

Melissa sighed. "We're not speaking," she said, with a sadness she usually kept hidden. "The last time we did, he told me we should both start seeing other people." A sniffle. "I heard he's going out with some waitress from the Roadhouse, over in Indian Rock."

"Is that why you're considering leaving Stone Creek? Because Dan is dating someone else?"

Melissa began to cry. There was no sob, no sniffle, no sound at all, but Ashley knew her sister was in tears. That was the twin bond, at least as they experienced it.

"Why do I have to choose?" Melissa asked plaintively. "Why can't I have Dan *and* my career? Ash, I worked so hard to get through law school—even with Brad footing the bills, it was *really* tough."

Ashley hadn't been over this ground with Melissa, not in any depth, anyway, because they'd been semi-estranged since the day of their mother's funeral. "Is that what Dan wants, Melissa? For you to give up your law practice?"

"He has two young sons, Ash. The ranch is *miles* from anywhere. In the winter, they get snowed in—Dan homeschools Michael and Ray from the first blizzard, sometimes until Easter, because the ranch road is usually impassable. Unless I wanted to travel by dogsled, I couldn't possibly commute. I'd go bonkers." Melissa pulled in a long, quivery breath. "I might even pull a 'Mom,' Ashley. If I got desperate enough. Get on a bus one fine afternoon and never come back."

"I can't see you doing that, Melissa."

"Well, *I* can. I love Dan. I love the boys—way too much to do to them what Delia did to us."

"Mel—"

"Here's how much I love them. I'd rather Dan married that waitress than someone who was always looking for an escape route—like me."

"Have you and Dan talked about this, Melissa? *Really* talked about it?"

"Sort of," Melissa admitted wearily. "His stock response was, 'Mel, we can work this out.' Which means I stay home and cook and clean and sew slipcovers, while he's out on the trail, squiring around a bunch of executive greenhorns trying to find their inner cowboys."

"How do you *know* that's what it means? Did Dan actually say so, Melissa, or is this just your take on the situation?"

"*'Just'* my 'take' on the situation?" Melissa countered, sounding offended. "I'm not some naive Martha Stewart clone like—like—"

"Like me?"

"I didn't say that!"

"You didn't have to, Counselor." *A Martha Stewart clone?* Was that how other people saw her? Because she enjoyed cooking, decorating, quilting? Because she'd never had the kind of world-conquering ambition Brad and Melissa shared?

"Ashley, I truly didn't mean—"

Ashley had always been the family peacemaker, and that hadn't changed. "I know you didn't mean to hurt my feelings, Melissa," she said gently. *Oh, but you did.* "And maybe it *is* time I had a little excitement in my life."

With Jack around, excitement was pretty much a sure thing.

Out-of-the-stratosphere sex and a drug dealer bent on revenge.

Who could ask for more?

There was a smile in Melissa's voice, along with a tremulous note of relief. "Kiss the babies for me, if you see them before I do," she said.

Ashley hadn't decided whether or not she'd make the drive out to Starcross Ranch that day. It wasn't so far, but the roads were probably slick. Although she had snow tires, her car was a subcompact, and it didn't have four-wheel drive.

"I'll do that," she answered, and the call was over.

Jack, she soon discovered, was in the study, working on potential websites for the bed-and-breakfast. He was remarkably cool, calm and collected, considering the circumstances, but Ashley couldn't help noticing that his nondescript cell phone was within easy reach.

She went upstairs, cast one yearning look toward her bed. Climbing into it wasn't an option—she might have another wakeful night if she went to sleep at that hour of the day.

Using her bedside phone, she placed a call to Olivia. Her sister answered on the second ring. "Dr. O'Ballivan," she said, all business. Olivia had taken Tanner's name when they married, but she still used her own professionally.

Olivia was managing marriage, motherhood and a career, at least so far. Why couldn't Melissa do the same thing?

"You sound very businesslike, for someone who

just went through childbirth twice in the space of ten minutes," Ashley said.

Olivia laughed. "That's modern medicine for you. Have twins one day, go home the next. Tanner hired nurses to look after the babies round the clock until I've rested up, so I'm a lady of leisure these days."

"How are they?"

"Growing like corn in August," Olivia replied.

"Good," Ashley said. "Are you up for a visitor? Please say so if you're not—I promise I'll understand."

"I'd *love* to have a visitor," Olivia said. "Tanner's out feeding the range cattle, Sophie's at school, and of course the day nurse is busy doting on the two new men in the house. Ginger isn't in the mood for chitchat, so I'm at loose ends."

Ashley couldn't help smiling. Ginger, an aging golden retriever, was Olivia's constant companion, and the two of them usually had a lot to say to each other. "I'll be out as soon as I've showered and dressed," she said. "Do you need anything from town?"

"Nope. Loaded up on groceries over the weekend," Olivia answered. "The roads have been plowed and sanded, but be careful anyway. There's another snow-storm rolling in tonight."

Ashley promised to drive carefully and said good-bye.

She tried to be philosophical about the approaching storm, but for her, once Christmas had come and gone, snow lost its charm. Unlike her siblings, she didn't ski.

The shower perked her up a little—she used her special ginseng-and-rice soap, and the scent was heavenly. After drying off with the kind of soft, thick towel one would expect a "Martha Stewart clone" to have on hand, she dressed in a long black woolen skirt, a lavender sweater with raglan sleeves, and high black boots.

She brushed her hair out and skillfully redid her braid.

Frowned at her image in the steamy mirror.

Maybe she ought to change her hair. Get one of those saucy, layered cuts, with a few shimmery highlights thrown in for good measure. Drive to one of the malls in Flagstaff and have a makeover at a department-store cosmetics counter.

Jazz herself up a little.

The trouble was, she'd never aspired to jazziness.

Her natural color, a coppery-blond, suited her just fine, and so did the style. The braid was tidy, feminine, and practical, considering the life she led.

On the other hand, she'd been wearing that same French braid since college. Spiral curls, like Melissa's, might look sexy on her.

Did she *want* to be sexier?

Look how much trouble she'd gotten herself into with the same old hairdo and minimal makeup.

Quickly, she applied lip gloss and a light coat of mascara and headed downstairs. Pausing in the study doorway, she allowed herself the pleasure of watching Jack for a few moments before saying, "I'm going out to Olivia and Tanner's. Want to come along?"

Jack turned in the swivel chair. "Maybe some other time," he said. "I think I'd better stick around, in case Vince shows up with Ardith and Rachel sooner than expected."

Ashley didn't know who Vince was, though she had caught the name when she accidentally-on-purpose overheard Jack's phone conversation with Ardith the night before.

"Did he call?" She wanted to ask Jack if he was feeling ill again, but something stopped her. "Vince, I mean?"

Jack nodded. "They're on their way."

"No trouble?"

His gaze was direct. "Depends on how you define *trouble*," he replied. "Ardith has a husband and two other children besides Rachel. She's had to leave them behind—at least for the time being."

Ashley's heart pinched. She knew what it was to await the return of a missing mother. "Aren't the police doing anything?"

"They were willing to send a patrol car by Ardith's place every once in a while. Under civil law, unless Lombard actually attacks or kills her or Rachel, there isn't much the police can do."

"That's insane!"

"It's the law."

"The husband and the other children—aren't they in danger, too?" Wouldn't the whole family be better off together, Ashley wondered, even if they had to establish new identifies? At least they'd have each other.

"The more people involved," Jack told her grimly, "the harder it is to hide. For now, they're safer apart."

"A man like Lombard—wouldn't he go after the rest of the family, if only to force Ardith out into the open?"

"He might do anything," Jack admitted. "From what I've seen, though, Lombard is fixated on getting Rachel back and not much else. Ardith is in his way, and he won't hesitate to take her out to get what he wants."

Ashley hugged herself. Even inside, wearing warm

clothes, she felt chilled. "But *why* is he so obsessed? He wasn't around when Rachel was born—he couldn't have bonded with her the way a father normally would."

"Why does he run drugs?" Jack countered. "Why does he kill people? We're not dealing with a rational person here, Ashley. If I had to hazard a guess at his motive, I'd say it's pure ego. Lombard is a sociopath, if not worse. He sees Rachel as an object, something that *belongs* to him." He paused, and she saw pain in his eyes. "Do me a favor?" he asked hoarsely.

"What?"

"Don't come back here tonight. Stay with Tanner and Olivia. Or with Brad and his wife."

Ashley swallowed. "You think Lombard's coming— Here?" She'd known Jack thought exactly that, on some level, but it seemed so incredible that she had to ask.

"Let's just say I'd rather not take a chance."

"But you *will* be taking a chance, with your own life."

"That's one hell of a lot better than taking a chance with yours. Once I figure out what to do with Ardith and Rachel, make sure they're someplace Lombard will never find them, I'm going to draw that crazy son-of-a-bitch as far from Stone Creek as I can."

"This isn't going to end, is it? Not unless—"

"Not unless," Jack said, rising from the chair, approaching her, "I kill him, or he kills me."

"My God," Ashley groaned, putting a hand to her mouth.

Jack gripped her shoulders firmly, but with a gentleness that reminded her of their lovemaking. "I'll never be able to forgive myself if you get caught in the cross fire, Ashley. If you meant it when you said you loved me, then do what I ask. Take the cat, leave this house, and don't come back until I give the all clear."

"I *did* mean it, but—"

He brushed her chin with the pad of his thumb. "I understand that you come from sturdy pioneer stock and all that, Ashley. I know the O'Ballivans have always held their own against all comers, faced down any trouble that came their way. But Chad Lombard is no ordinary bad guy. He's the devil's first cousin. You don't want to know the things he's done—you wouldn't be able to get them out of your head."

Ashley stared into Jack's eyes, so deathly afraid for him that it didn't occur to her to be afraid for herself. "When you went looking for Rachel in South America," she said, her mouth so dry that she almost couldn't get the words out, "that wasn't your first run-in with Lombard, was it?"

"No," he said, after a long, long time.

"What hap—?"

"You don't want to know. I sure as hell wish *I* didn't." He slid his hands down her upper arms, squeezed her elbows. "Go, Ashley. Do this for me, and I'll never ask you for another thing."

"That's what I'm afraid of," she told him.

He leaned in, kissed her forehead. Took a deep breath, seeming to draw in the scent of her and hold it as long as possible. "Go," he repeated.

She agonized in silence for a long moment, then nodded in reluctant agreement. She'd wanted to meet Ardith and Rachel, but maybe it would be better—for them as well as for her—if that never happened.

"You'll call when you get to your sister's place?" Jack asked.

"Yes," Ashley said.

She turned away from Jack slowly, went back upstairs, packed a small suitcase.

She didn't say goodbye to Jack; there was something too final about that. Instead, she collected Mrs. Wiggins and set out for Starcross Ranch, though when she arrived at Tanner and Olivia's large, recently renovated house, she left her suitcase and the kitten in the car.

The last thing the Quinns needed, with new babies and incubators and three shifts of nurses already in residence, was a relative looking for a place to hide out. After the visit, she would drive on to Meg and Brad's, ask to spend the night in their guesthouse.

Although she knew she'd be welcome, Brad would want to know what was going on. After all, she had a perfectly good place of her own.

Lying wouldn't do any good—her brother knew Jack was there, knew their history, at least as a couple.

She would have to tell Brad the truth—but how much of it?

Jack hadn't asked her to keep any secrets. Given the situation, though, he might have thought that went without saying.

Tanner stepped out onto the porch as she came up the walk. He smiled, but his eyes were filled with unasked questions.

Ashley dredged up a tattered smile from somewhere inside, pasted it to her mouth. "Hello, Tanner," she said.

"Jack called," he told her.

Ashley stopped in the middle of the walk. A special system of wires kept the concrete clear of ice and snow, and she could feel the heat of it, even through the soles of her boots.

"Oh," she said.

He passed her on the walk without another word. Went to her car, reached in for the suitcase and the kitten.

"I was going to spend the night over at Brad and Meg's," she said, pausing on the porch steps.

"You're staying here," Tanner said. "It's not as though we don't have room, and I promise, the dogs won't eat your cat."

"But—the babies—Olivia—the last thing you need is—"

Beside her now, Tanner tried for a smile of his own and fell short. "Brad and Meg will be over later, with the kids. Melissa's stopping by when she's through at work. Time for a family meeting, kiddo, and you're the guest of honor."

Curiously, Ashley felt both deflated and uplifted by this news. "If it's about giving up Jack, you can all forget it," she said firmly.

Tanner didn't respond to that. Somehow, even with a protesting cat in one hand and a suitcase handle in the other, he managed to open the front door. "Olivia's in the kitchen," he told her. "I'll put your things in the guestroom. Cat included."

In that house, the "guestroom" was actually a suite, with a luxurious bath, a flat-screen TV above the working fireplace, and its own kitchenette.

Ginger rose from her cushy bed, tail wagging, when Ashley stepped into the main kitchen. Ashley bent to greet the sweet old dog.

Dressed in jeans and an old flannel shirt, Olivia sat

in the antique rocking chair in front of the bay windows, a receiving blanket draped discreetly over her chest, nursing one of the babies. Seeing Ashley, she smiled, but her eyes were troubled.

Ashley went to her sister, bent to kiss the top of her head.

"Tell me what's going on, Ashley," Olivia said. "Tanner gave me a few details after he talked to Jack on the phone earlier, but he was pretty cryptic."

Ashley pulled one of the high-backed wooden chairs over from the table and sat down, facing Olivia. Their knees didn't quite touch.

Tanner came into the room, went to the coffeepot and filled a cup for Ashley. "You look like you could use a shot of whiskey," he commented. "But now that Sophie's a teenager, always having friends over, we decided to remove all temptation. This will have to do."

"Thanks," Ashley said, smiling a little and taking the cup.

Olivia was rocking the chair a little faster, her gaze fixed on Ashley. "Talk to us," she ordered.

Ashley sighed. When Brad and Meg and Melissa arrived, she'd have to repeat the whole incredible story—what little she knew of it, anyway—but it was clear that Olivia would brook no delay. So Ashley told her sister and brother-in-law what she knew about Rachel's rescue, and Chad Lombard's determination to, one, get his daughter back and, two, take revenge on Jack for stealing her away.

Tanner didn't look surprised; he probably knew more than she did, since he and Jack were close friends. Ashley didn't risk as much as a glance in Olivia's direction. She hated worrying her sister, especially now.

"Jack sent someone to bring Ardith and Rachel to Stone Creek," she finished. "And he wanted me out of the house in case Lombard managed to follow them somehow."

"It was certainly generous of Jack," Olivia said, with a bite in her tone, "to bring all this trouble straight to *your* door."

Tanner glanced at Olivia, grimaced slightly. "He was sick, Liv," he told her. "Out of his head with fever."

Olivia sighed.

"I'm in love with Jack," Ashley said bravely. "You might as well know."

Olivia and Tanner exchanged looks.

"What a surprise," Tanner said, one corner of his mouth tilting up briefly.

"You do realize," Olivia said seriously, her gaze boring into Ashley's face, "that this situation is hopeless? Even if Jack manages to get the woman and her little girl to safety, this Lombard character will always be a threat."

Tanner pulled up a chair beside Olivia and took her hand. "Liv," he said, "Jack is the best at what he does. He won't let anything happen to Ashley."

Tears filled Olivia's expressive eyes, then spilled down her cheeks. Ginger gave a little whimper and lumbered over to lay her muzzle on her mistress's knee. Rolled her brown eyes upward.

"I will *not* calm down," Olivia told the dog. "This is serious!"

This time, Tanner and Ashley looked at each other.

"I agree with Ginger," Tanner told his wife quietly. "You need to stay calm. We all do." By now, he was used to Olivia's telepathic conversations with animals.

Ashley couldn't remember a time when her big sister didn't communicate with four-legged creatures of all species.

"How can I, when my sister is in mortal danger?" Olivia snapped, watching Ashley. "All because of *your* friend."

"Jack *is* my friend," Tanner responded, his voice still even. "And that's why I'm going to do whatever I can to help him."

Olivia turned her head quickly, stared at her husband. *"What?"*

"I can't just turn my back on him, Liv," Tanner said. "Not even for you."

"What about Sophie? What about John and Sam? They need their father, and *I* need my husband!"

Tanner started to speak, then stopped himself. Ashley saw a small muscle bunch in his jaw, go slack.

Ginger whimpered again, still gazing up at Olivia in adoring sorrow, her dog eyes liquid.

"That's easy for *you* to say," Olivia told the dog.

"This is why I didn't want to stay here," Ashley told Tanner sadly. "I've been in this house for five minutes, and I'm already causing trouble."

"You didn't do anything wrong," Olivia said, her voice and expression softening, her eyes still shining with tears. "Before Big John died, when Brad was away from home, busy with his career, I promised our grandfather I'd look after you and Melissa, and I intend to keep my word, Ashley."

"I'm not a little girl anymore," Ashley reminded her sister.

Olivia didn't answer. She was intent on tucking either John or Sam against her shoulder, patting his tiny back. The receiving blanket still covered her. When the burp came, Olivia smiled proudly.

Tanner stood up, gently took his son and carried him out of the kitchen.

Olivia straightened her clothing and laid the blanket aside. Gave Ginger a few reassuring strokes on the head before sending the animal back to her bed nearby.

"You are going to be the most amazing mother," Ashley said.

"Don't try to change the subject," Olivia warned. She was smiling, but her eyes remained moist and fierce with determination to protect her little sister. "So, you really are in love with Jack McCall?"

"Afraid so," Ashley replied. "And I think it's forever."

"Is he planning to stay this time?" Olivia's tone was kind, if wary.

Ashley raised her shoulders slightly, lowered them again. "He paid for two weeks at the B&B," she said.

Olivia's eyes narrowed, then widened. "Two weeks? That's all?"

"It's something," Ashley said, feeling like a candidate for some reality show about women trying to get over the wrong man. She made a lame attempt at a joke. "If we decide to make this permanent, I won't be charging him for bed and board."

Olivia didn't laugh, or even smile. "What if he leaves?"

"I think there's a good chance that he will," Ashley admitted. Then, without thinking, she rested one hand against her lower belly.

Olivia read the gesture with unerring accuracy. "Ashley—are you *pregnant?*"

"It's too early to know, doctor," Ashley said. "Unless there's a second-day test out there that I haven't heard about."

"*Unprotected sex?* Ashley, what are you *thinking?*"

"For once, I'm not. And it's kind of a relief."

"What if there's a baby? Jack might not be around to help you raise it."

"I'd manage, Olivia, as other women do, and *have* since cave days, if not longer."

"A child needs a father," Olivia said.

"Spoken like a very lucky woman with a husband who adores her," Ashley answered, without a shred of malice.

Tanner returned before Olivia could answer, took her by both hands, and gently hoisted her to her feet. "Time for your nap, Mama Bear," he told her.

Olivia didn't resist, but she did pin Ashley with a big-sister look and say, "We're not finished with this conversation."

Ashley simply spread her hands.

Shade by shade, shadow by shadow, night finally came.

Ashley had called from Olivia's place, as promised. They hadn't exchanged more than a few words, and those had been stiff and stilted.

It was no great wonder to Jack that Ashley was projecting a chill: She'd been banished from her own house by a man who had no damn business being there at all.

He was getting antsy.

He'd heard nothing about Ardith and Rachel since his first terse conversation with Vince Griffin, right after the pickup. On the bright side, the toxin seemed to be in abeyance, though he still broke out in cold sweats at irregular intervals, and spates of weakness invariably followed in their wake.

To keep from going crazy, or maybe to make sure he did, Jack logged on to his father's website again. Clicked to the Associates page.

There were his brothers, Dean and Jim. The last time Jack had seen them, they'd been in junior high, wannabe Romeos with braces and acne. Now, they looked like infomercial hosts.

He smiled.

A blurb at the bottom of the page showed a snapshot of Bryce, the youngest. In a wild break with McKenzie tradition, he was studying to be an optometrist.

There was no mention of Jack himself, of course. But his mother wasn't on the site, either, and that bothered him.

His dad had always been a big believer in family values.

What a disappointment I must have been, Jack thought, frowning as he left the website and ran another search. There might be a recent picture of his mom on the library's site. After all, she'd been the director when he'd left for military school.

The director's face beamed from the main page, and it wasn't his mother's.

Frowning, Jack ran another search, using her name.

That was when he found the obituary, dated three years ago, a week after her fifty-third birthday.

The picture was old, a close-up taken on a long-ago family vacation.

The headshot showed her beaming smile, the bright eyes behind the lenses of her glasses. Jack's own eyes

burned so badly that he had to blink a few times before he could read beyond her name, Marlene Estes
McKenzie.

She'd died at home, according to the writer of the
obit, surrounded by family and friends. In lieu of flowers, her husband and sons requested that donations be
made to a well-known foundation dedicated to fighting breast cancer.

Breast cancer.

Jack breathed deeply until his emotions were at least
somewhat under control, then, against his better judgment, he reached for Ashley's phone, dialed the familiar number.

"Dr. McKenzie's residence," a woman's voice
chimed.

Jack couldn't speak for a moment.

"Hello?" the woman asked pleasantly. "Is anyone
there? Hello?"

He finally found his voice. "My name is—Mark
Ramsey. Is the doctor around?"

"I'm so sorry," came the answer. "My husband is out
of town at a convention, but either of his sons would be
happy to see you if this is an emergency."

"It isn't," Jack said. Then, with muttered thanks, he
quietly hung up.

He got out of the chair, walked to the window,
looked out at the street. A blue pickup truck drove
past. The house opposite Ashley's blurred.

All this time, Jack had imagined his mother visiting
his grave at Arlington. Squaring her shoulders, sniffling a little, mourning her firstborn's "heroic" death
in Iraq. Instead, she'd been lying in a grave of her own.

He rubbed his eyes with a thumb and forefinger.

How long had his dad waited, after his first wife's death, to remarry?

What kind of person was the new Mrs. McKenzie? Did Dean and Jim and Bryce like her?

Jack ached to call Ashley, needed to hear her voice.

But what would he say? *Hi, I just found out my mother died three years ago?* He wasn't sure he'd be able to get through the sentence without breaking down.

He moved away from the window. No sense making a target of himself.

The night grew darker, colder and lonelier.

And still Jack didn't turn on a light. Nor did he head for the kitchen to raid Ashley's refrigerator, even though he hadn't eaten since breakfast.

He'd done a lot of waiting in his life. He'd waited for precisely the right moment to rescue children and diplomats and wealthy businessmen held for ransom. He'd waited to be rescued himself once, with nearly every bone in his body broken.

Waiting was harder now.

In his mind, he heard the voice of a young soldier. "You'll be all right now, sir. We're United States Marines."

Jack's throat tightened further.

And then the throwaway cell phone rang.

Sweat broke out on Jack's upper lip. He'd spoken to Vince over Ashley's phone. He'd warned Ardith not to use the cell number again, in case it was being monitored.

It was unlikely that the FBI would be calling him up to chat. They had their own ways of getting in touch.

Holding his breath, he pressed the Talk button, but didn't speak.

"I'll find you," Chad Lombard said.

"Why don't I make it easy for you?" Jack answered lightly.

"Like, how?" Lombard asked, a smirk in his voice.

"We agree on a time and place to meet. One way or another, this thing will be over."

Lombard laughed. "I must be crazy. I kind of like that idea. It has a high-noon sort of appeal. But how do I know you'll come alone, and not with a swarm of FBI and DEA agents?"

"How do I know *you'll* come alone?" Jack countered.

"I guess we'll just have to trust each other."

"Yeah, right. When and where, hotshot?"

"I'll be in touch about that," Lombard said lightly. "Oh, and by the way, I've already killed you, for all intents and purposes. The poison ought to be in your bone marrow by now, eating up your red blood cells. Still, I'd like to be around to see you shut down, Robocop."

Jack's stomach clenched, but his voice came out sounding even and in charge.

"I'll be waiting to hear from you," he said, and hung up.

Chapter 7

Oh, and by the way, I've already killed you, for all intents and purposes. The poison ought to be in your bone marrow by now, eating up your red blood cells.

Lombard's words pulsed somewhere in the back of Jack's mind, like a distant drumbeat. The man was a skilled liar—and that was one of his more admirable traits, but this time, instinct said he was telling the truth.

Jack had never been afraid of death, and he still wasn't. But he was *very* afraid of leaving Ashley exposed to dangers she couldn't possibly imagine, even after all he'd told her. Tanner and her brother would *try* to protect her, and they were both men to be reckoned with, but were they in the same league with Lombard and his henchmen?

One-on-one, Lombard was no match for either of them.

The trouble was, Lombard never *went* one-on-one; he was too big a coward for that.

Coupled with the news of his mother's passing, *three years ago,* the knowledge that some concoction of jungle-plant extracts and nasty chemicals was already devouring his bone marrow left Jack reeling a little.

Suck it up, McCall, he thought. *One crisis at a time.*

It was after midnight when a local cab pulled up in front of Ashley's house.

Jack watched nervously from the study window as Vince got out of the front passenger seat, tucking his wallet into the back pocket of his chinos as he did so, and then opened the rear door, curbside.

Rachel scrambled out to the sidewalk, standing with her small hands on her hips like some miniature queen surveying her kingdom. She was soon followed by a much less confident Ardith, hunched over in a black trench coat and hooded scarf.

The cab drove away, and Vince steered Ardith and Rachel up the front walk.

Jack was quick to open the door; Rachel flashed past him, clad in jeans and a blue coat that looked like it might have been rescued from a thrift store, with Ardith slinking along behind.

"A *cab?*" Jack bit out, the minute he and Vince came face-to-face on the unlighted porch.

"Hide in plain sight," Vince said casually.

Jack let it pass for the moment, mainly because Rachel was tugging at the back of his shirt in a rapidly escalating effort to get his attention.

"My name is Charlotte now," she announced, "but you can still call me Rachel if you want to."

Jack grinned. He wanted to hoist the child into his arms, but didn't. After the conversation with Lombard, he couldn't quite shake the vision of his bones going hollow, caving in on themselves at the slightest exertion. He would need all his strength to deal with the inevitable.

Get over it, he told himself. If he lived long enough, he would check into a hospital, find out whether or not he was a candidate for a marrow transplant. In the meantime, there were other priorities, like keeping Rachel and Ashley and Ardith alive from one moment to the next.

"Are you hungry?" Jack asked, thinking of Ashley's freezer full of cherry crepes and other delicacies. God, what would it be like to live like a normal man—marry Ashley, live in this house, this Norman Rockwell town, for good?

"Just tired," Ardith said. Even trembling inside the bulky raincoat, she looked stick-thin, at least fifteen pounds lighter than the last time he'd seen her. And Ardith hadn't had all that much weight to spare in the first place.

"Yes!" Rachel blurted, the word toppling over the top of her mother's answer. "I'm *starved.*"

"I wouldn't mind something to gnaw on myself," Vince said, his gaze slightly narrowed as he studied his boss, there in the dimness of Ashley's entryway.

"We rode in a helicopter!" Rachel sang out, on the way to the kitchen.

Jack stopped at the base of the stairs, conscious of Ardith's exhaustion. She seemed to exude it through every pore. The unseen energy of despair vibrated around her, pervaded Jack's personal space.

"You two go on to the kitchen," Jack told Vince and the little girl, indicating the direction with a motion of one hand. "Help yourselves to whatever you find." Although he kept his tone even, the glance he gave the pilot said, *We'll talk about the cab later.*

Jack did not regard himself as a hard man to work for—sure, his standards were high, but he paid top wages, provided health insurance and a generous retirement plan for his few but carefully chosen employees. On the other hand, he didn't tolerate carelessness of any kind, and Vince knew that.

Vince grimaced slightly, keenly aware of Jack's meaning, and shepherded Rachel toward the kitchen.

"Don't burn too many lights," Jack added, "and stay away from the windows."

Vince stiffened at the predictability of the order, but he didn't turn around to give Jack a ration of crap, the way he might have done in less dire circumstances.

Jack shifted his gaze to Ardith, but she'd turned her face away. He put a hand to the small of her back and ushered her up the stairs.

"Are you all right?" he asked quietly.

"I'm scared to death," Ardith replied, still without looking at him.

Even through the raincoat and whatever she was wearing underneath, Jack could feel the knobbiness of her spine against the palm of his hand.

"When is this going to be over, Jack?" she blurted, when they'd reached the top. She was staring at him now, her eyes huge and black with sorrow and fear. "When can I go back to my husband and my children?"

"When it's safe," Jack said, but he was thinking, *When Chad Lombard is on a slab.*

"When it's safe!" Ardith echoed. "You know as well as I do that 'when it's safe' might be *never!*"

She was right about that; unless he took Lombard

out, once and for all, she and Rachel would probably have to keep running.

"You can't think that way," Jack pointed out. "You'll drive yourself crazy if you do." He guided her toward the room across from his, the one Ashley had set aside for Ardith and Rachel.

Although he'd been the one to send Ashley away, he wished for a brief and fervent moment that she had stayed. Being a woman, she'd know how to calm and comfort Ardith in ways that would probably never enter his testosterone-saturated brain.

And he needed to tell *somebody* that his mother had died. He couldn't confide in Vince—they didn't have that kind of relationship. Ardith had enough problems of her own, and Rachel was a little kid.

Jack opened the door of the small but still spacious suite, with its flowery bedspreads, lace curtains and bead-fringed lamps. He'd closed the shutters earlier, and laid the makings of a fire on the hearth.

Taking a match from the box on the mantel, he lit the wadded newspaper and dry kindling, watched with primitive satisfaction as the blaze caught.

Ardith looked around, finally shrugged out of the raincoat.

"I want to call Charles," she said, clearly expecting a refusal. "I haven't talked to my husband since—"

"If you want to put him and the other kids in Lombard's crosshairs, Ardith," Jack said evenly, giving her a sidelong glance as he straightened, then stood there, soaking in the warmth of the fire, "you go right ahead."

She was boney as hell, beneath a sweat suit that must have been two sizes too big for her, and her once-beautiful face looked gaunt, her cheekbones protruding, her skin gray and slack. She'd aged a decade since gathering her small daughter close in that airport.

Ardith glanced toward the open door of the suite, then turned her gaze back to Jack's face. "I have two other children besides Rachel," she said slowly.

Jack added wood to the fire, now that it was crackling, and replaced the screen. Turned to Ardith with his arms folded across his chest.

"Meaning what?" he asked, afraid he already knew what she was about to say.

She sagged, limp-kneed, onto the side of one of the twin beds, her head down. "Meaning," she replied, after biting down so hard on her lower lip that Jack half expected to see blood, "that Chad is wearing me down."

Jack went to the door, peered out into the hall, found it empty. In the distance, he could hear Vince and Rachel in the kitchen. Pans were clattering, and the small countertop TV was on.

He shut the door softly. "Don't even tell me you're thinking of turning Rachel over to Lombard," he said.

A tear slithered down one of Ardith's pale cheeks, and she didn't move to wipe it away. Maybe she wasn't even aware that she was crying. Her eyes blazed, searing into Jack. "Are you judging me, Mr. McCall? May I remind you that you work for me?"

"May I remind you," Jack retorted calmly, "that Lombard is an international drug runner? That he tortures and kills people on a regular basis—for fun?"

Ardith dragged in a breath so deep it made her entire body quiver. "I wish I'd never gotten involved with him."

"Get in line," Jack said. "I'm sure your parents

would agree, along with your present husband. The fact is, you *did* 'get involved,' in a big way, and now you've got a seven-year-old daughter who deserves all the courage and strength you can muster up."

"I'm running on empty, Jack. I can't keep this up much longer."

"Where does that leave Rachel?"

Misery throbbed in her eyes. "With you?" she asked, in a small voice. "She'd be safe, I know she would, and—"

"And you could go back home and pretend none of this ever happened? That you never met Lombard and gave birth to his child—*your* child?"

"You make me sound horrible!"

Jack thrust out a sigh. "Look, I know this is hard. It's *worse* than hard. But you can't bail on that little girl, Ardith. Deep down, you don't even want to. You've got to tough this out, for Rachel's sake and your own."

"What if I can't?" Ardith whispered.

"You can, Ardith, because you don't have a choice."

"Couldn't the FBI or the DEA help? Find her another family—?"

"Christ," Jack said. "You can't be serious."

Ardith fell onto her side on the bed, her knees drawn up to her chest in a fetal position, and sobbed, deeply and with a wretchedness that tore at the fabric of his soul. It was one of the worst sounds Jack had ever heard.

"You're exhausted," he said. "You'll feel different when you've had something to eat and a good night's sleep. We'll come up with some kind of solution, Ardith. I promise."

Footsteps sounded on the stairs, then in the hallway, and Rachel burst in. "Mommy, we found beef stew in the fridge and—" she stopped, registering the sight her mother made, lying there on the bed. Worry contorted the child's face, made her shoulders go rigid. "Why are you crying?"

Stepping behind Rachel so she couldn't see him, Jack glared a warning at Ardith.

Ardith stopped wailing, sat up, sniffled and dashed at her cheeks with the backs of both hands. "I was just missing your daddy and the other kids," she said. She straightened her spine, snatched tissues from a decorative box on the table between the beds, and blew her nose.

"I miss them, too," Rachel said. "And Grambie and Gramps, too."

Ardith nodded, set the tissue aside. "I know, sweetheart," she said. Somehow, she summoned up a smile, misty and faltering, but a smile nonetheless. "Did someone mention beef stew? I could use something like that."

Rachel's attention had shifted to the cheery fireplace. "We get our own *fireplace?*" she enthused.

Jack thought back to the five days he and Rachel had spent navigating that South American jungle after he'd nabbed her from Lombard's remote estate. They'd dealt with mosquitoes, snakes, chattering monkeys with a penchant for throwing things at them, and long, dark nights with little to cover them but the stars and the weighted, humid air.

Rachel hadn't complained once. When they were traveling, she got to ride on Jack's back or shoulders, and she enjoyed it wholeheartedly. She'd chattered incessantly, every waking moment, about all the things she'd have to tell her mommy, her stepfather, and her little brother and sister when they were together again.

"Your own fireplace," Jack confirmed, his voice husky.

He and Ardith exchanged glances, and then they all went downstairs, to the kitchen, for some of Ashley's beef stew.

Ashley waited until she was sure Olivia and Tanner were sound asleep, then crept out of the guest suite. The night nurse sat in front of the television set in the den, sound asleep.

Behind Ashley, Mrs. Wiggins mewed.

Ashley turned, a finger to her lips, hoisted the kitten up for a nuzzle, then carried the little creature back into the suite, set her down, and carefully closed the door.

Her eyes burned as the kitten meowed at being left behind.

Reaching the darkened and empty kitchen, Ashley let out her breath, going over the plan she'd spent several hours rehearsing in her head.

She would disable the alarm, then reset it before closing the door behind her. Drive slowly out to the main road, waiting until she reached the mailboxes before turning her headlights on.

Ginger, snoozing on her dog bed in the corner, lifted her golden head, gave Ashley a slow, curious once-over.

Ashley put a finger to her lips, just as she'd done earlier, with the kitten.

A voice bloomed in her mind.

Don't go, it said.

Ashley blinked. Stared at the dog. Shook her head.

No. She had *not* received a telepathic message from Olivia's dog. She was still keyed up from the family meeting, and worried about Jack, and her imagination was running away with her, that was all.

I'll tell, the silent, internal voice warned. *All I have to do is bark.*

"Hush," Ashley said, fumbling in her purse for her car keys. "I'm not hearing this. It's all in my head."

"It's snowing."

Unnerved, Ashley tried to ignore Ginger, who had now risen on all four paws, as though prepared to carry out a threat she couldn't possibly have made.

Ashley went to the nearest window, the one over the sink, and peered through it, squinting.

Snowflakes the size of golf balls swirled past the glass.

Ashley glanced back at Ginger in amazement. "Well, it *is* January," she rationalized.

"You can't drive in this blizzard."

"Stop it," Ashley said, though she couldn't have said whether she was talking to the golden retriever or to herself. Or both.

The dog simply stood there, ready to bark.

Nonsense, Ashley thought. *Olivia hears animals.* You don't.

Still, either her imagination or the dog had a point. Her small hybrid car wouldn't make it out of the driveway in weather like that. The yard was probably under a foot of snow, and visibility would be zero, if not worse.

She had to think.

As quietly as possible, she drew back a chair at the big kitchen table and sat down.

Ginger relaxed a little, but she was still watchful.

Just sitting at that table caused Ashley to flash back to the family meeting earlier that evening. Meg and Brad, Melissa, Olivia and Tanner—even Sophie and Carly and little Mac, had all been there.

As the eldest of the four O'Ballivan siblings, Brad had been the main spokesperson.

"Ashley," he'd said, "you're not going home until McCall is gone. And Tanner and I plan to make sure he is, first thing in the morning."

She'd gaped at her brother, understanding his reasoning but stung to fury just the same. Looking around, she'd seen the same grim determination in Tanner's face, Olivia's, even Melissa's.

Outraged, she'd reminded them all that she was an adult and would come and go as she pleased, thank you very much.

Only Sophie and Carly had seemed even remotely sympathetic, but neither of them had spoken up on her behalf.

"You can't hold me prisoner here," Ashley had protested, her heart thumping, adrenaline burning through her veins like acid.

"Oh, yeah," Brad had answered, his tone and expression utterly implacable. "We can."

She'd decided right then that she'd get out—yes, their intentions were good, but it was the principle of the thing—but she'd also kept her head. She'd pretended to agree.

She'd helped make supper.

She'd loaded the dishwasher afterward.

She'd even rocked one of the babies—John, she thought—to sleep after Olivia had nursed him.

The evening had seemed endless.

Finally, Meg and Brad had left, taking Mac and Carly with them. Sophie, having finished her homework, had given Ashley a hug before retiring to her room for the night.

Ashley had yawned a lot and vanished into her own lush quarters.

She'd taken a hot bath, put on her pajamas and one of Olivia's robes, watched a little television—some mindless reality show.

And she'd waited, listening to the old-new house settle around her, Mrs. Wiggins curled up on her lap, as though trying to hold her new mistress in her chair with that tiny, weightless body of hers.

Once she was sure the coast was clear, Ashley had quietly dressed, never thinking to check the weather. Such was her state of distraction.

Now, here she sat, alone in her sister's kitchen at one-thirty in the morning, engaged in a standoff with a talking dog.

"I can take the Suburban," she whispered to Ginger. "It will go anywhere."

"What's so important?" Ginger seemed to ask.

Ashley shook her head again, rubbed her temples with the fingertips of both hands. "Jack," she said, keeping her voice down because, one, she didn't want to be overheard and stopped from leaving and, two, she was talking to a *dog,* for pity's sake. "*Jack* is so important. He's sick. And something is wrong. I can feel it."

"You could ask Tanner to go into town and help him out."

Ashley blinked. Was this really happening? If the conversation *was* only in her mind, why did the other side of it just pop up without her framing the words first?

"I can't do that," she said. "Olivia and the babies might need him."

Resolved, she rose from her chair, crossed to the wooden rack where Olivia kept various keys, and helped herself to the set that would unlock and start the venerable old Suburban.

She jingled the key ring at Ginger.

"Go ahead," she said. "Bark."

Ginger gave a huge sigh. *"I'll give you a five minute head start,"* came the reply, *"then I'm raising the roof."*

"Fair enough," Ashley agreed, scrambling into Big John's old woolen coat, the one Olivia wore when she was working, hoping it would give her courage. "Thanks."

"I was in love once," Ginger said, sounding wistful.

Ashley moved to the alarm-control panel next to the back door. Racked her brain for the code, which Olivia had given to her in case of emergency, finally remembered it.

Grabbed her coat and dashed over the threshold.

The cold slammed into her like something solid and heavy, with sharp teeth.

Her car was under a mound of snow, the Suburban a larger mound beside it. Perhaps because of the emotions stirred by the family meeting, Tanner had forgotten to park the rigs in the spacious garage with his truck, the way he normally would have on a winter's night.

Hastily, she climbed onto the running board and wiped off the windshield with one arm, grateful for the heavy, straw-scented weight of her grandfather's old coat, even though it nearly swallowed her. Then she opened the door of the Suburban, got in and rammed the key into the ignition.

The engine sputtered once, then again, and finally roared to life.

Ashley threw it into Reverse, backed into the turn-around, spun her wheels for several minutes in the deep snow.

Swearing under her breath, she slammed the steering wheel with one fist, missed it, and hit the horn instead.

"Do. Not. Panic," she told herself out loud.

Just how many minutes had passed, she wondered frantically. Had Ginger already started barking? Had anyone heard the Suburban's horn when she hit it by accident?

She drew a deep breath, thrust it out in a whoosh.

No, she decided.

Lights would be coming on in the house if the dog were raising a ruckus. The howling wind had probably covered the bleat of the horn.

She shifted the Suburban into the lowest gear, tried again to get the old wreck moving. It finally tore free of the snowbank, the wheels grabbing.

As she turned the vehicle around and zoomed down the driveway, she heard the alarm system go off in the house, even over the wind and the noise of the engine.

Crap. She'd either forgotten to reset the system, or done it incorrectly.

Looking in the rearview mirror would have been useless, since the back window was coated with snow and frost, so Ashley sped up and raced toward the main road, praying she wouldn't hit a patch of ice and spin off into the ditch.

I'm sorry, she told Tanner and Olivia, the babies and Sophie and the night nurse, the alarm shrieking like a convention of angry banshees behind her. *I'm so sorry.*

Her kitchen was completely dark.

Shivering from the cold and from the harrowing ride into town, Ashley shut the door behind her, dropped her key into the pocket of Big John's coat and reached for the light switch.

"Don't move," a stranger's voice commanded. A *male* stranger's voice.

Flipping the switch was a reflex; light spilled from the fluorescent panels in the ceiling, revealing a man she'd never seen before—or had she?—seated at her table, holding a gun on her.

"Who are you?" she asked, amazed to discover that she could speak, she was so completely terrified.

The man stood, the gun still trained squarely on her central body mass. "The pertinent question here, lady, is who are *you?*"

A strange boldness surged through Ashley, fear borne high on a flood of pure, indignant rage. "I am Ashley O'Ballivan," she said evenly, "and this is my house."

"Oh," the man said.

Just then, the inside door swung open and Jack was there, brandishing a gun of his own.

What was this? Ashley wondered wildly. Tombstone?

"Lay it down, Vince," Jack said, his voice stone-cold.

Vince complied, though not with any particular

grace. The gun made an ominous thump on the table-top. "Chill, man," he said. "You told me to stand watch and that's all I was doing."

Ashley's gaze swung back to Jack. She was furious and relieved, and a host of other things, too, all at once.

"I do not allow firearms in my house," she said.

Vince chuckled.

Jack told him to get lost, shoving his own pistol into the front of his pants. The move was too expert, too deft, and the gun itself looked military.

Vince ambled out of the room, shaking his head once as he passed Jack.

"What are you doing here?" Jack asked, as though *she* were the intruder.

"Do I have to say it?" Ashley countered, flinging her purse aside, fighting her way out of Big John's coat, which suddenly felt like a straightjacket. *"I live here, Jack."*

"I thought we agreed that you wouldn't come back until I gave you a heads-up," Jack said, keeping his distance.

Considering Ashley's mood, that was a wise decision on his part, even if he *was* armed and almost certainly dangerous.

"I changed my mind," she replied, tight-lipped, her arms folded stubbornly across her chest. "And who is that—that *person,* anyway?"

"Vince works for me," Jack said.

Another car crunched into the driveway. A door slammed.

Jack swore, untucking his shirt so the fabric covered the gun in the waistband of his jeans.

Tanner slammed through the back door.

"Well," Jack observed mildly, "the gang's all here."

"Not yet," Tanner snapped. "Brad's on his way. What the *hell* is going on, Ashley? You set off the alarm, the dog is probably *still* barking her brains out, and the babies are permanently traumatized—not to mention Sophie and Olivia!"

"I'm sorry," Ashley said.

A cell phone rang, somewhere on Tanner's person.

He pulled the device from his coat pocket, after fumbling a lot, squinted at the caller ID and took the call. "She's at her place," he said, probably to Olivia. A crimson flush climbed his neck, pulsed in his jaw. And his anger was nothing compared to what Brad's would be. "No, don't worry—I think things are under control..."

Ashley closed her eyes.

Brakes squealed outside.

Tanner's voice seemed to recede, and then the call ended.

Brad nearly tore down the door in his hurry to get inside.

Jack looked around, his expression drawn but pleasant.

"Cherry crepes, anyone?" he asked mildly.

Chapter 8

"I know a place the woman and the little girl will be safe," Brad said wearily, once the excitement had died down and Ashley, her brother, Jack and Tanner were calmly seated around her kitchen table, eating the middle-of-the-night breakfast she'd prepared to keep from going out of her mind with anxiety.

Vince, the man with the gun, was conspicuously absent, while Ardith and Rachel slept on upstairs. Remarkably, the uproar hadn't awakened them, probably because they were so worn-out.

Jack shifted in his chair, pushed back his plate. For a man who believed so strongly in bacon and eggs, he hadn't eaten much. "Where?" he asked.

"Nashville," Brad replied. Then he threw out the name of one of the biggest stars in country music. "She's a friend," he added, as casually as if just *any-*

body could wake up a famous woman in the middle of the night and ask her to shelter a pair of strangers for an indefinite length of time. "And she's got more high-tech security than the president. Bodyguards, the whole works."

"She'd do that?" Jack asked, grimly impressed.

Brad raised one shoulder in a semblance of a shrug. "I'd do it for her, and she knows that," he said easily. "We go way back."

"Sounds good to me," Tanner put in, relaxing a little. Everyone, naturally, was showing the strain.

"Me, too," Jack admitted, and though he didn't sigh, Ashley sensed the depths of his relief. "How do we get them there?"

"Very carefully," Brad said. "I'll take care of it."

Jack seemed to weigh his response for a long time before giving it. "There's a woman's life at stake here," he said. "And a little girl's future."

"I get that," Brad answered. His gaze slid to Ashley, then moved back to Jack's face, hardening again. "Of course, I want something in return."

Ashley held her breath.

Jack maintained eye contact with Brad. "What?"

"You, gone," Brad said. "For good."

"Now, *wait just one minute*—" Ashley sputtered.

"He's right," Jack said. "Lombard wants me, Ashley, not you. And I intend to keep it that way."

"So when do we make the move?" Tanner asked.

"Now," Brad responded evenly, a muscle bunching in his jawline. He could surely feel Ashley's glare boring into him. "I can have a jet at the airstrip within an hour or two, and I think we need to get them out of here before sunrise."

"Can't you let Rachel and her mother rest, just for this one night?" Ashley demanded. "They must be absolutely exhausted by all this—"

"It has to be tonight," Brad insisted.

Jack nodded, sighed as he got to his feet. "Make the calls," he told Brad. "I'll get them out of bed."

Things were moving too fast. Ashley gripped the table edge, swaying with a sudden sensation of teetering on the brink of some bottomless abyss. "Wait," she said.

She might as well have been invisible, inaudible. A ghost haunting her own house, for all the attention anyone paid her.

Brad was already reaching for his cell phone. "When I get back from Nashville," he said, watching Jack, "I expect you to be history."

Jack nodded, avoiding Ashley's desperate gaze. "It's a deal," he said, and left the room.

Ashley immediately sprang out of her chair, without the faintest idea of what she would do next.

Tanner took a gentle hold on her wrist and eased her back down onto the cushioned seat.

Brad placed a call to his friend. Apologized for waking her up. Exchanged a few pleasantries—yes, Meg was fine and Mac was growing like a weed, and sure there would be other kids. Give him time.

Ashley listened in helpless sorrow as he went on to explain the Ardith-Rachel situation and ask for help.

The singer agreed immediately.

Brad called for a private jet. He might as well have been ordering a pizza, he was so casual about it. Only with a pizza, he would at least have had to give a credit card number.

When Brad said, "jump," the response was invariably, "How high?"

Because she'd always known him as her big brother, the broad scope of his power always came as a surprise to her.

Things accelerated after the phone calls.

Resigned, Ashley got to work preparing food for the trip, so Ardith and Rachel wouldn't starve, though the jet probably offered catered meals.

Her guests stumbled sleepily into the kitchen just as she was finishing, herded there by Jack, their clothes rumpled and hastily donned, their eyes glazed with confusion, weariness and fear.

The little girl favored Ashley with a wan, blinking smile. "Have you been taking care of Jack?" she asked.

Ashley's heart turned over. "I've been trying," she said truthfully, studiously ignoring Brad, Tanner and Jack himself.

Vince had wandered in behind them. "Want me to go along for the ride?" he asked, meeting no one's eyes.

"No," Jack said tersely. "You're done here."

"For good?" Vince asked.

"For now," Jack replied.

Vince turned to Brad. "Catch a ride to the airstrip with you?"

Jack gave the man a quick glance, his eyes ever so slightly narrowed. "I'll take you there myself," he said, adding a brisk, "Later."

"You stopped trusting me, boss?" Vince asked, with an odd grin.

"Maybe," Jack said.

Some of the color drained from Vince's face. "Am I fired?"

"Don't push it," Jack answered.

In the end, it was decided that Tanner would drive Vince back to his helicopter once Brad, Ardith and Rachel were aboard the jet, ready for takeoff. Later, Tanner would see that Jack boarded a commercial airliner in Flagstaff, bound for Somewhere Else.

Holding back tears, Ashley handed her brother the food she'd packed, tucked into a basket with a cheery red-and-white-checkered napkin for a cover.

Something softened in Brad's eyes as he accepted the offering, but he didn't say anything.

And neither did Ashley.

A gulf had opened between Ashley and the big brother she had always loved and admired, far wider than the one created by their mother's death. Even knowing he was doing what he thought was right— what probably *was* right—Ashley felt steamrolled, and she resented it.

Soon, Brad was gone, along with Ardith and Rachel.

Approximately an hour later, Tanner and the chastened Vince left, too.

Jack and Ashley sat on opposite sides of the kitchen table, unable to look at each other.

After a long, long time, Jack said, "My mother died three years ago. And I didn't have a clue."

Startled, Ashley sat up straighter in her chair. "I'm sorry," she said.

"Breast cancer," Jack explained gruffly, his eyes moist.

"Oh, Jack. That's terrible."

He nodded. Sighed heavily.

"I guess this is our last night together," Ashley said, at some length.

"I guess so," Jack agreed miserably.

Purpose flowed through Ashley. "Then let's make it count," she said. She locked the back door. She flipped off the lights. And then she took Jack's hand, there in the darkness, and led him upstairs to her bed.

Every moment, every gesture, was precious, and very nearly sacred.

Jack undressed Ashley the way an archeologist might uncover a fragile treasure, with a cherishing tenderness that stirred not only her body, but her soul. Head back, she surrendered her naked breasts to him, reveled in the sensations wrought by his lips and tongue.

A low, crooning sound escaped her, and she found just enough control to open his shirt, her fingers fumbling with the buttons. She needed to feel his flesh, bare and hard, yet warm against her palms and splayed fingers.

They kissed, long and deep, with a sweet urgency all the better for the smallest delay.

In time, Jack eased her onto the bed, sideways, and spread her legs to nuzzle and then suckle her until she was gasping with need and exaltation.

She whispered his name, a ragged sound, and tears burned in her eyes. How would she live without him, without this? How colorless her days would be, when he was gone, and how empty her nights. He'd taught her body to crave these singular pleasures, to need them as much as she needed air and water and the light of the sun.

But, no, she thought sorrowfully. She mustn't spoil what was probably their last night together by leaving the moment, journeying into a lonely and uncertain future. It was *now* that mattered, and only now. Jack's hands on her inner thighs, Jack's mouth on the very center of her femininity.

Dear God, it felt so good, the way he was loving her, almost too good to be borne.

The first climax came softly, seizing her, making her buckle and moan in release.

"Don't stop," she pleaded, entangling her fingers in his hair.

She hoped he would *never* cut his hair short again.

He chuckled against her moist, straining flesh, nipped at her ever so lightly with his teeth and brought her to another orgasm, this one sharp and brief, a sudden and wild flexing deep within her. "Oh, I'm a long way from finished," he assured her gruffly, before falling to her again.

Ashley could never have said afterward how many times she rose and fell on the hot tide of primitive satisfaction, flailing and writhing and crying out with each new abandoning of her ordinary self.

When he finally took her, she gloried in the heat and length and hardness of him, in the pulsing and the renewed wanting. Her body became greedier than before, demanding, reaching, shuddering. And Jack drove deep, eventually losing control, but only after a long, delicious period of restraint.

They made love time and again that night, holding each other in silence while they recovered between bouts of fevered passion.

"I'll come back if I can," Jack told her, at one point, barely able to breathe, he was so spent. "Give me a year before you fall in love with somebody else, okay?"

A year. It seemed like an eternity to Ashley, she

was so aware of every passing moment, every tick of the celestial clock. At the same time, though, she knew it was safe to promise. She'd wait a lifetime, a dozen lifetimes, because for her, there *was* no man but Jack.

She nodded, dampening his bare shoulder with her tears, and finally slept.

Jack eased himself out of Ashley's arms, and her bed, around eight o'clock the next morning. It was one of those heartrendingly beautiful winter days, with sunlight glaring on pristine snow. Everything seemed to be draped in purity.

He dressed in his own room, gathered the few belongings he'd brought with him, and tucked them into his bag.

Given his druthers, he would have sat quietly in a chair, watching Ashley sleep, memorizing every line and curve of her, so he could hold her image in his mind and his heart until he died.

But Jack was the sort of man who rarely got his druthers.

He had things to do.

First, he'd meet with Chad Lombard.

If he survived that—and it was a crapshoot, whether he or Lombard or neither of them would walk away— he'd check himself into a hospital.

Feeling more alone than he ever had—and given some of the things he'd been through that was saying a lot—Jack gravitated to the computer in Ashley's study. He called up his dad's website, clicked to the Contact Us link, wrote an email he never intended to send.

Hello, Dad. I'm alive, but not for long, probably...

He went on to explain why he'd never come home

from military school, why he'd let everyone in his family believe he was dead. He apologized for any pain they must have suffered because of his actions, and resisted the temptation to lay any of the blame on the Navy.

The mission had been a tough one, with a high price, but no one had held a gun to his head. He'd made the decision himself and, in most ways, he had never regretted it.

He went on to say that he hoped his mother hadn't had to endure too much pain, and asked for forgiveness. In sketchy terms, he described the toxin that was probably killing him.

In closing, he wrote, *You should know that I met a woman. If things were different, I'd love to settle down with her right here in this little Western town, raise a flock of kids with her. But some things aren't meant to be, and it's beginning to look as if this is one of them.*

No matter how it may seem, I love you, Dad.

I'm sorry.

Jack.

He was about to hit the Delete button—writing the piece had been a catharsis—when two things happened at once. His cell phone rang, and somebody knocked hard at the front door.

Simultaneously, Jack answered the call and admitted Tanner Quinn to the house he'd soon be leaving, probably forever.

No more cherry crepes.

No more mutant cat.

No more Ashley.

"Mercer?" Lombard asked affably, "is that you?"

Jack shifted to the Neal Mercer persona, because

Lombard knew him by that name, gestured for Tanner to come inside, but be quiet about it.

Ashley was still sleeping, and Jack didn't want to wake her. Leaving was going to be hard enough, without a face-to-face goodbye.

On the other hand, didn't he owe her that much?

"What?" he asked Lombard.

"I've decided on a place for the showdown," Lombard said. "Tombstone, Arizona. Fitting, don't you think?"

"You're a regular John Wayne," Jack told him.

Tanner raised his eyebrows in silent question. Jack shook his head, pointed to his gear bag, waiting just inside the door.

Tanner picked up the bag, carried it out to his truck. The exhaust spewed white steam into the cold, bright air.

Leavin' on a jet plane... Jack thought.

"Tomorrow," Lombard went on. "High noon."

"High *drama,* you mean," Jack scoffed.

"Be there," Lombard ordered, dead serious now, and hung up.

Jack sighed and clicked the phone shut.

Glanced up at the ceiling.

Tanner returned from the luggage run, waiting with his big rancher's hands stuffed into the pockets of his sheepskin coat.

"Give me a minute," Jack said.

Tanner nodded, his eyes full of sympathy.

Jack turned from that. Sympathy wasn't going to help him now.

He had to be strong. Stronger than he'd ever been.

Upstairs, he entered Ashley's room, sat down on the

edge of the bed, and watched her for a few luxurious moments, moments he knew he would cherish until he died, whether that was in a day, or several decades.

Ashley opened her eyes, blinked. Said his name.

For a lot of years, Jack had claimed he didn't have a heart. For all his money, love was something he simply couldn't afford.

Now he knew he'd lied—to himself and everyone else.

He had a heart, all right, and it was breaking.

"I love you," he said. "Always have, always will."

She sat up, threw her arms around his neck, clung to him for a few seconds. "I love you, too," she murmured, trembling against him. Then she drew back, looked deep into his eyes. "Thanks," she said.

"For—?" Jack ground out the word.

"The time we had. For not leaving without saying goodbye."

He nodded, not trusting himself to speak just then.

"If you can come back—"

Jack drew out of her embrace, stood. In the cold light of day, returning to Stone Creek, to Ashley, seemed unlikely, a golden dream he'd used to get through the night.

He nodded again. Swallowed hard.

And then he left.

He was boarding a plane in Flagstaff, nearly two hours later, before he remembered that he hadn't closed the email he'd drafted on Ashley's computer, spilling his guts to his father.

Ashley wasn't exactly a techno-whiz, he thought,

with a sad smile, but if she stumbled upon the message somehow, she'd know most of his secrets.

She might even send the thing, on some do-gooder impulse, though Jack doubted that. In any case, she'd know about the damage the toxin was doing to his bone marrow and be privy to his deepest regrets as far as his family was concerned.

She'd know he'd loved her, too. Wanted to spend his life with her.

That shining dream could still come true, he supposed, but a lot of chips would have to fall first, and land in just the right places. The odds, he knew, were against him.

Nothing new there.

He took his seat on the small commuter plane, fastened his seat belt, and shut off his cell phone.

Tanner had been right there when he'd bought his ticket—he'd chosen Phoenix, said he'd probably head for South America from there, and gone through all the proper steps, checking his gear bag and filling out a form declaring that there was a firearm inside, properly secured.

What he *didn't* tell his friend was that he planned to charter a flight to Tombstone as soon as he reached Phoenix and have it out with Chad Lombard, once and for all.

Takeoff was briefly delayed, due to some mechanical issue.

During the wait, Jack switched his phone on again, placed a short call that drew an alarmed stare from the woman sitting next to him and smiled as he put the cell away.

"Air marshal," he explained, in an affable undertone.

The woman didn't look reassured. In fact, she moved to an empty seat three rows forward. A word to the flight attendants about the man in 7-B and he'd be off the plane, tangled in a snarl with a pack of TSA agents until three weeks after forever.

For some reason, she didn't report him. Maybe she didn't watch the news a lot, or fly much.

Jack settled back, closed his eyes, and tried not to think about Ashley and the baby they might have conceived together, the future they might have shared.

That proved impossible, of course, like the old game of trying not to think about a pink elephant.

The plane lifted off, bucked through some turbulence and streaked toward his destiny—and Chad Lombard's.

Carly McKettrick O'Ballivan watched her aunt with concern, while Meg, who was both Carly's sister *and* her adoptive mother—how weird was that?—puttered around the big kitchen, trying to distract Ashley.

Meg was expecting a baby, and the news might have cheered Ashley up, but Carly and her mother-sister had agreed on the way into town to wait until Brad-dad was back from wherever he'd gone.

Unable to bear Ashley's pale face and sorrowful eyes any longer, Carly excused herself and wandered toward the study. She'd set up the computer, she decided. Use this strange morning constructively.

School was closed on account of megasnow, but nothing stopped members of the McKettrick clan when they wanted to get somewhere. Meg had told Carly they were going to town, fired up her new Land Rover right after breakfast, acting all mysterious and sad, buckled a squirmy Mac into his car seat, and off they'd gone.

Carly, a sucker for adventure, had enjoyed the ride into town, over roads buried under a foot of snow. Once, Meg had even taken an overland route, causing Mac to giggle and Carly to shout, "Yee-haw!"

Even the plows weren't out yet—that's how deep the stuff was.

To Carly's surprise, someone had beaten her to the computer gig. The monitor was dark, but the machine was on, whirring quietly away in the otherwise silent room.

She sat down in the swivel chair, touched the mouse.

An email message popped up on the monitor screen.

Since Brad and Meg were big on personal privacy, Carly didn't actually read the email, but she couldn't help noticing that it was signed, "Love, Jack."

She barely knew Jack McCall, but she'd liked him. Which was more than could be said for Brad and Meg.

They clearly thought the man was bad news.

Carly bit her lower lip. If Jack had gone to all the trouble of writing that long email, she reasoned, her heart thumping a little, surely he'd intended to send it.

With so much going on—Carly had no idea what any of it actually was, except that it had obviously done a real number on Ashley, so it must be pretty heavy stuff—he'd probably just forgotten.

Carly took a deep breath, moved the cursor, and hit Send.

"Carly!" Meg called, clearly approaching.

Carly closed the message panel. "What?"

Meg appeared in the doorway of the study. "School's

open after all," she said. "I just heard it on the kitchen radio."

Carly sighed. "Awesome," she said, meaning exactly the opposite.

Meg chuckled. "Get a move on, kiddo," she ordered.

"Are there snowshoes around here someplace?" Carly countered. "Maybe a dogsled and a team, so I can *mush* to school?"

"Hugely funny," Meg said, grinning. Like all the other grown-ups, she looked tired. "I'd drive you to school in the Land Rover, but I don't think I should leave Ashley just yet."

Carly agreed, with the teenage reluctance that was surely expected of her, and resigned herself to the loss of that greatest of all occasions, a snow day.

Trudging toward the high school minutes later, she wondered briefly if she should have left that email in the outbox, maybe told Meg or Ashley about it.

But her friends were converging up ahead, laughing and hurling snowballs at each other, and she hurried to join them.

Ashley both hoped for and dreaded a call from Jack, but none came.

Not while Meg was there, and not when she left.

A ranch hand from Starcross brought Mrs. Wiggins back home, and Ashley was glad and grateful, but still wrung out. She felt dazed, disjointed, as though she were truly beside herself.

She slept.

She cooked.

She slept some more, and then cooked some more.

At four o'clock that afternoon, Brad showed up.

"He's gone," she said, meaning Jack, meeting her taciturn-looking brother at the back door. "Are you happy now?"

"You know I'm not," Brad said, moving past her to enter the house when she would have blocked his way. He helped himself to coffee and, out of spite, Ashley didn't tell him it was decaf. If he expected a buzz from the stuff, something to jump-start the remainder of his day, he was in for a disappointment.

"Are Ardith and Rachel safe?" she asked.

"Yes," Brad answered, leaning back against the counter to sip his no-octane coffee and study her. "You all right?"

"Oh, I'm just fabulous, thank you."

"Ashley, give it up, will you? You know Jack couldn't stay."

"I also know the decision was mine to make, Brad—not yours."

Her brother gave a heavy sigh. She could see how drained he was, but she wouldn't allow herself to feel sorry for him. Much. "You'll get over this," he told her, after a long time.

"Gee, thanks," she said, wiping furiously at her already-clean counters, keeping as far from Brad as she could. "That makes it all better."

"Meg's going to have a baby," Brad said, out of the blue, a few uncomfortable moments later. "In the spring."

Ashley froze.

Olivia had twins.

Now Meg and Brad were adding to their family, something she should have been glad about, considering that Meg had suffered a devastating miscarriage a year after Mac was born and there had been some question as to whether or not she could have more children.

"Congratulations," Ashley said stiffly, unable to look at him.

"You'll get your chance, Ash. The right man will come along and—"

"The right man *came* along, Brad," Ashley snapped, "and now he's gone."

But at least, this time, Jack had said goodbye.

This time, he hadn't wanted to go.

Small consolations, but something.

Brad set his mug aside, crossed to Ashley, took her shoulders in his hands. "I'd have done anything," he said hoarsely, "to make this situation turn out differently."

Ashley believed him, but it didn't ease her pain.

She let herself cry, and Brad pulled her close and held her, big brother-style, his chin propped on top of her head.

"O'Ballivan tough," he reminded her. It was their version of something Meg's family, the McKettricks, said to each other when things got rocky.

"O'Ballivan tough," she agreed.

But her voice quavered when she said it.

She felt anything *but* tough.

She'd go on, just the same, because she had no other choice.

Jack arrived in Earp-country at eleven forty-five that morning and, after paying the pilot of the two-seat Cessna he'd chartered in Phoenix, climbed into a waiting taxi. Fortunately, Tombstone wasn't a big town, so he wouldn't be late for his meeting with Chad Lombard.

Anyway, he was used to cutting it close.

There were a lot of tourists around, as Jack had feared. He'd hoped the local police would be notified, find some low-key way to clear the streets before the shootout took place.

Some of them might be Lombard's men.

And some of them might be Feds.

Because of the innocent bystanders and because both the DEA and the FBI had valid business of their own with Lombard, Jack had taken a chance and tipped them off while waiting for the commuter jet to take off from Flagstaff.

He stashed his gear bag behind a toilet in a gas station restroom, tucked his Glock into his pants, covered it with his shirt and stepped out onto the windy street.

If he hadn't been in imminent danger of being picked off by Lombard or one of the creeps who worked for the bastard, he might have found the whole thing pretty funny.

He even amused himself by wishing he'd bought a round black hat and a gunslinger's coat, so he'd look the part.

Wyatt Earp, on the way to the OK Corral.

He was strolling down a wooden sidewalk, pretending to take in the famous sights, when the cell phone rang in the pocket of his jean jacket.

"Yo," he answered.

"You called in the Feds!" Lombard snarled.

"Yeah," Jack answered. "You're outnumbered, bucko."

"I'm going to take you out last," Lombard said. "Just

so you can watch all these mommies and daddies and little kiddies in cowboy hats bite the freaking dust!"

Jack's blood ran cold. He'd known this was a very real possibility, of course—that was the main reason he'd called in reinforcements—but he'd hoped, against all reason, that even Lombard wouldn't sink that low.

After all, the man had a daughter of his own.

"Where are you?" Jack asked, with a calmness he sure as hell didn't feel. Worse yet, the weakness was rising inside him again, threatening to drop him to the ground.

Lombard laughed then, an eerie, brittle sound. "Look up," he said.

Jack lifted his eyes.

Lombard stood on a balcony overlooking the main street, opposite Jack. And he was wearing an Earp hat and a long coat, holding a rifle in one hand.

"Gun!" Jack yelled. "Everybody out of the street!"

The crowd panicked and scattered every which way, bumping into each other, screaming. Scrambling to shield children and old ladies and little dogs wearing neckerchiefs.

Lombard raised the rifle as Jack drew the Glock.

But neither of them got a chance to fire.

Another shot ripped through the shining January day, struck Lombard, and sent him toppling, in what seemed like slow motion, over the balcony railing, which gave way picturesquely behind him, like a bit from an old movie.

People shrieked in rising terror, as vulnerable to any gunmen Lombard might have brought along as backup as a bunch of ducks in a pond.

Feds rushed into the street, hustling the tourists into

restaurants and hotel lobbies and souvenir shops, crowd control at its finest, if a little late.

Government firepower seemed to come out of the woodwork.

Somebody was taking pictures—Jack was aware of a series of flashes at the periphery of his vision.

He walked slowly toward the spot where Chad Lombard lay, either dead or dying, oblivious to the pandemonium he would have enjoyed so much.

Lombard stared blindly up at the blue, blue sky, a crimson patch spreading over the front of his collarless white shirt. Damned if he hadn't pinned a star-shaped badge to his coat, just to complete the outfit.

The Feds closed in, the sniper who had taken Lombard out surely among them. A hand came to rest on Jack's shoulder.

More pictures were snapped.

"Thanks, McCall," a voice said, through a buzzing haze.

He didn't look up at the agent, the longtime acquaintance he'd called from the plane in Flagstaff. Taking the cell phone out of his pocket, he turned it slowly in one hand, still studying Lombard.

Lombard didn't look like a killer, a drug runner. Jack could see traces of Rachel in the man's altar-boy features.

"We had trouble spotting him until he climbed out onto that balcony," Special Agent Fletcher said. "By our best guess, he stole the gunslinger getup from one of those old-time picture places—"

"Why didn't you clear the streets earlier?" Jack demanded.

"Because we got here about five seconds before you did," Fletcher answered. "Are you all right, McCall?"

Jack nodded, then shook his head.

Fletcher helped Jack to his feet. "Which is it?" he rasped. "Yes or no?"

Jack swayed.

His vision shrank to a pinpoint, then disappeared entirely.

"I guess it's no," he answered, just before he lost consciousness.

Chapter 9

The first sound Jack recognized was a steady *beep-beep-beep*. He was in a hospital bed, then, God knew where. Probably going about the business of dying.

"Jack?"

He struggled to open his eyes. Saw his father looming over him, a pretty woman standing wearily at the old man's side. If it hadn't been for her, Jack would have thought he was hallucinating.

Dr. William "Bill" McKenzie smiled, switched on the requisite lamp on the wall above Jack's head.

The spill of light made him wince.

"I see you've still got all your hair," Jack said, very slowly and in a dry-throated rasp. "Either that, or that's one fine rug perched on top of your head."

Bill laughed, though his eyes glistened with tears. Maybe they were goodbye tears. "You always were a smart-ass," he said. "This is my real hair. And speaking of hair, yours is too long. You look like a hippie."

People still used the word *hippie?*

Obviously, his dad's generation did. For all he knew, Bill McKenzie had been a hippie, once upon a time. There was so much they didn't know about each other.

"How did you find me?" Jack asked. The things he felt were too deep to leap right into—there had to be a transition here, a gradual shift.

"It wasn't too hard to track you down. You were all over the Internet, the TV and the newspapers after that incident in Tombstone. You were treated in Phoenix, and then some congressman's aide got in touch with me—soon as you were strong enough, I had you brought home, where you belong."

Home, Jack thought. *To die?*

Jack's gaze slid to the woman, who looked uncomfortable. *My stepmother,* he thought, and felt a fresh pang of loss because his mom should have been standing there beside his dad, not this stranger.

"Abigail," Bill explained hoarsely. "My wife."

"If you'll excuse me," Abigail said, after a nod of greeting, and headed for the nearest exit.

Bill sighed, trailed her with his eyes.

Jack glimpsed tenderness in those eyes, and peace. "How long have I been here?" he asked, after a long time.

"Just a few days," Bill answered. He cleared his throat, looking for a moment as though he might make a run for the corridor, just as Abigail had done. "You're in serious condition, Jack. Not out of the woods by any means."

"Yeah," Jack said, trying to accept what was probably inevitable. "I know. And you're here to say good-bye?"

The old man's jaw clamped down hard, the way it used to when he was about to give one of his sons hell for some infraction and then ground him for a decade. "I'm *here*," he said, almost in a growl, "because you're my son, and I thought you were dead."

"Like Mom."

Bill's eyes, hazel like Jack's own, flashed. "We'll talk about your mother another time," he said. "Right now, boy, you're in one hell of a fix, and that's going to be enough to handle without going into all the *other* issues."

"It's a bone marrow thing," Jack recalled, but he was thinking about Ashley. She wasn't much for media, but even she had probably seen him on the news. "Something to do with a toxin manufactured especially for me."

"You need a marrow donor," Bill told him bluntly. "It's your only chance, and, frankly, it will be touch and go. I've already been tested, and so have your brothers. Bryce is the only match."

A chance, however small, was more than Jack had expected to get. He must have been mulling a lot of things over on an unconscious level while he was submerged in oblivion, though, because there was a sense of clarity behind the fog enveloping his brain.

"Bryce," he said. "The baby."

"He wouldn't appreciate being called that," Bill replied, with a moist smile. His big hand rested on Jack's, squeezed his fingers together. "Your brother will be ready when you are."

Jack imagined Ashley, the way she'd looked and smelled and felt, warm and naked beneath him. He saw her baking things, playing with the kitten, parking herself in front of the computer, her brow furrowed slightly with confusion and that singular determination of hers.

If he got through this thing, he could go back to her.

Swap his old life for a new one, straight across, and never look back.

But suppose some buddy of Lombard's decided to step up and take care of unfinished business?

No, he decided, discouraged to the core of his being. There were too many unknown factors; he couldn't start things up with Ashley again, even if he got lucky and survived the ordeal he was facing, until he was sure she'd be in no danger.

"So when is this transplant supposed to go down?" he asked his dad.

"Yesterday wouldn't have been too soon," Bill replied. "They were only waiting for you to stabilize a little."

"I'd like to see my brothers," Jack said, but even as he spoke, the darkness was already sucking him back under, into the dreamless place churning like an ocean beneath the surface of his everyday mind. "If they're speaking to me, that is."

Bill dashed at his wet eyes with the back of one large hand. "They're speaking to you, all right," he replied. "But if you pull through, you can expect all three of them to read you the riot act for disappearing the way you did."

If you pull through.

Jack sighed. "Fair enough," he said.

Reaching deep into her mind and heart in the days after Jack's leaving, Ashley had found a new strength.

She'd absorbed the media blitz, with Jack and Chad Lombard playing their starring roles, with a stoicism that surprised even her. After the first wave, she'd stopped watching, stopped reading.

Enough was enough.

Every sound bite, every news clip, every article brought an overwhelming sense of sorrow and relief, in equal measures.

Two days after the Tombstone Showdown, as the reporters had dubbed it, a pair of FBI agents had turned up at Ashley's door.

They'd been long on questions and short on answers.

All they'd really been willing to divulge was that she was in no danger from Chad Lombard's organization; some of its members had been taken into federal custody in Arizona. The rest had scattered to the four winds.

And Jack was alive.

That gave her at least a measure of relief.

It was the questions that fed her sorrow, innocuous and routine though they were. Something about the tone of them, a certain sad resignation—there were no details forthcoming, either in the media or from the visiting agents, but she sensed that Jack was still in trouble.

Had Jack McCall told her anything about his association with any particular government agencies and if so, what? the agents wanted to know.

Had he left anything behind when he went away?

If Mr. McCall agreed, would she wish to visit him in a location that would be disclosed at a later time?

No, Jack hadn't told her anything, beyond the things the FBI already knew, and no, he hadn't left anything behind. Yes, she wanted to see him and she'd appreciate it if they'd disclose the mysterious location.

They refused, though politely, and left, promising to contact her later.

After that, she'd heard nothing more.

Since then, Ashley had been seized by a strange and fierce desperation, a need to do *something,* but she had no idea where Jack was, or what kind of condition he was in. She only knew that he'd collapsed in Tombstone—there had been pictures in the newspapers and on the web.

Both Brad and Tanner had "their people" beating the bushes for any scrap of information, but either they'd really come up with nothing, as they claimed, or they simply didn't want Jack McCall found. Ever.

Melissa was searching, too; even though she wasn't any fonder of Jack than Brad and Olivia were, she and Ashley had the twin link. Melissa knew, better than any of the others, exactly what her sister was going through.

The results of that investigation? So far, zip.

After a week, Jack disappeared from the news, displaced by accounts of piracy at sea, the president's latest budget proposal, and the like.

By the first of February, Ashley was very good at pretending she didn't care where Jack McCall was, what he was doing, whether or not he would—or could—come back.

She'd decided to Get on with Her Life.

Carly and Sophie had spent hours with her, after school, when they weren't rehearsing their parts in the drama club's upcoming play, fleshing out one of the websites Jack had created, showing her how to surf the Net, how to run searches, how to access and reply to email.

In fact, they'd both managed to earn special credit at school for undertaking the task.

Slowly, Ashley had begun to understand the mysteries of navigating cyberspace.

She quickly became proficient at web surfing, and especially at monitoring her modest but attractive website, already bringing in more business than she knew what to do with.

The B&B was booked solid for Valentine's Day weekend, and the profit margin on her "Hearts, Champagne and Roses" campaign looked healthy indeed.

With two weeks to go before the holiday arrived, she was already baking and freezing tarts, some for her guests to enjoy, and some for the annual dance at the Moose Lodge. This year, the herd was raising money to resurface the community swimming pool.

She'd agreed to serve punch and help provide refreshments, not out of magnanimity, but because she baked for the dance every year. And, okay, partly because she knew everybody in town was talking about her latest romantic disaster—this one had gone national, with CNN coverage and an article in *People,* not that she'd been specifically mentioned—and she wanted to show them all that she wasn't moping. No, sir, not her.

She was O'Ballivan tough.

If she still cried herself to sleep once in a while, well, nobody needed to know that. Nobody except Mrs. Wiggins, her small, furry companion, always ready to comfort her with a cuddle.

As outlined in the piece in *People,* Ardith and Rachel were back home, in a suburb of Phoenix, happily reunited with the rest of the family.

Yes, Ashley thought, sitting there at her computer long after she should have taken a bubble bath and gone to bed, day by day, moment by moment, she was getting over Jack.

Really and truly.

Or not.

Glancing out the window, she saw Melissa's car, a red glow under the streetlight, swinging into her driveway.

"Good," Ashley said to Mrs. Wiggins, who was perched on her right shoulder like a parrot. "I could use a little distraction."

Melissa was just coming through the back door when Ashley reached the kitchen. Her hair was flecked with snow and her grin was wide. Looking askance at Mrs. Wiggins, now nestling into her basket in front of the fireplace, Ashley's twin gave a single nose twitch and carefully kept her distance.

"It happened!" she crowed, hauling off her red tailored coat. "Alex got the prosecutor's job, and I'm going to be one of his assistants! I start the first of March and I've already got a line on a condo in Scottsdale—"

"Wonderful," Ashley said.

Melissa narrowed her beautiful eyes in mock suspicion. "Well, *that* was an enthusiastic response," she replied, draping the coat over the back of one of the chairs at the table.

Ashley's smile felt wobbly on her mouth, and a touch too determined. "If this is what you want, then I'm happy for you. I'm going to miss you a lot, that's all. Except for when you were in law school, we've never really been apart."

Melissa approached, laid a winter-chilled hand on each of Ashley's shoulders. "I'll only be two hours away," she said. "You'll visit me a lot, and of course I'll come back to Stone Creek as often as I can."

"No, you won't," Ashley said, turning away to start some tea brewing, so she wouldn't have to struggle to keep that stupid, slippery smile in place any longer. "You'll be too busy with your caseload, and you know it."

"I need to get away," Melissa said, so sadly that Ashley immediately turned to face her again, no longer concerned about hiding her own misgivings.

"Because?" Ashley prompted.

Melissa rarely looked vulnerable—a good lawyer appeared confident at all times, she often said—but she did then. That sheen in her eyes—was she crying?

"Because," Melissa said, after pushing back her spirally mane of hair with one hand, "things are heating up between Dan and the waitress. Her name is Holly and according to one of the receptionists at the office, they've been in Kruller's Jewelry Store three times in the last week, looking at rings."

Ashley sighed, wiped her hands on her patchwork apron, her own creation, made up of quilt scraps. "Sit down, Melissa," she said.

To her amazement, Melissa sat.

Of the two of them, Melissa had always been the leader, the one who decided things and gave impromptu motivational speeches.

Forgetting the tea preparations, Ashley took the chair closest to her sister's. "That's why you're leaving Stone Creek?" she asked quietly. "Because Dan and this Holly person might get married?"

"'Might,' nothing," Melissa huffed, but her usually straight shoulders sagged a little beneath her very professional white blouse. "As hot and heavy as things were between Dan and me, he never said a *word* about looking at engagement rings. If he's shopping for diamonds, he's *serious* about this woman."

"And?"

Melissa flushed a vibrant pink, with touches of crimson. "And I *might* still be *just a little* in love with him," she admitted.

"You can't have it all, Melissa," Ashley reminded her sister gently. "No one does. You made a choice and now you either have to change it or accept things as they are and move on."

Melissa blinked. "That's easy for *you* to say!"

"Is it?" Ashley asked.

"What am I saying?" Melissa immediately blurted out. "Ash, I'm sorry—I know the whole Jack thing has been—"

"We're not talking about Jack," Ashley said, a mite stiffly. "We're talking about Dan—and you. He's probably marrying this woman on the rebound—if the rumors about the rings are even true in the first place—because he really cared about you. And he might be making the mistake of a lifetime."

"That's *his* problem," Melissa snapped.

"Don't be a bitch," Ashley replied. "You didn't want him, or the life he offered, remember? What did you expect, Melissa? That Dan would wait around until you retire from your seat on the Supreme Court someday, and write your memoirs?"

"Whose side are you on, anyway?" Melissa asked peevishly.

"Yours," Ashley said, and she meant it. "Just talk to Dan before you take the job in Phoenix, Melissa. Please?"

"*He's* the one who broke it off!"

"Don't you want to be sure things can't be patched up?"

"Have you been paying attention? It's *too late,* Ashley."

"Maybe it is, maybe it isn't," Ashley said, getting up to resume the tea making. "You'll never know if you don't talk things over with Dan while there's still time."

"What am I supposed to do?" Melissa demanded, losing a little steam now. "Drive out there to the back of beyond, knock on his door, and ask him if he'd like to live in a city and be Mr. Melissa O'Ballivan? I can tell you right now what the answer would be—and besides, what if I interrupted—well—*something*—?"

"Like what? Chandelier-swinging sex? Dan has kids, Melissa—he and Holly Hot-Biscuits probably don't go at it in the living room on a regular basis."

Melissa sputtered out a laugh, wholly against her will. *"Holly Hot-Biscuits?"* she crowed. "Ashley O'Ballivan, could it be that you actually have a *racy* side?"

"You'd be surprised," Ashley said, recalling, with a well-hidden pang, some of the sex she and Jack had had. A chandelier would have been superfluous.

"Maybe I wouldn't," Melissa teased. At least she'd cheered up a little. Perhaps that could be counted as progress. "You miss Jack a lot, don't you?"

"When I let myself," Ashley admitted, though

guardedly, concentrating on scooping tea leaves into a china pot. "The other night, I dreamed he was—he was standing at the foot of my bed. I could see through him, because he was—dead."

Melissa softened, in that quicksilver way she had. Tough one minute, tender the next—that was Melissa O'Ballivan. "Jack can't be dead," she reasoned, looking as though she wanted to get up from her chair, cross the room, and wrap Ashley in a sisterly embrace, but wisely refraining.

Ashley wasn't accepting hugs these days—from anybody.

She felt too bruised, inside and out.

"Why not?" she asked reasonably, over the sound of the water she ran to fill the kettle.

"Because someone would have told Tanner," Melissa said, very gently. "Come to Scottsdale with me, Ash. Right now, this weekend. Help me decide on the right condo. It would be good for you to get away, change your perspective, soak up some of that delicious sunshine—"

The idea had a certain appeal—she was sick of snow, for one thing—but there was the B&B to think about. She had guests coming for Valentine's Day, after all, and lots of preparations to make. She'd even rented out her private quarters, planning to sleep on the couch in her study.

"Maybe after the holiday," she said. Except that she'd have skiers then, with any luck at all—she'd been pitching that on her new blog, on the website. And after that, it would be time to think about Easter.

"Can you handle Valentine's Day, Ash?" Melissa asked, with genuine concern. "You're still pretty raw."

"And you're not?" Ashley challenged, but gently. "Yes, I can 'handle' it, because I have to." She brought two cups to the table, along with milk and sugar cubes. "What is it with us, Melissa? Brad got it right with Meg, and Olivia with Tanner. Why can't we?"

"I think we're romantically challenged," Melissa decided.

"Or stubborn and proud," Ashley pointed out archly. Her meaning was clear: *Melissa* was stubborn and proud. *She* would have crawled over broken glass for Jack McCall, if it meant they could be together.

Not that she particularly wanted anyone else to know that.

All of which probably made her a candidate for an episode of *Dr. Phil,* during Unhealthy Emotional Dependency week. She would serve as the bad example. *This could happen to you.*

"Don't knock pride," Melissa said cheerfully. "And some people call stubbornness 'persistence.'"

"*Some* people can put a spin on anything," Ashley countered. "Are you going to clear things up with Dan before you leave, or not?"

"Not," Melissa said brightly.

"Chicken."

"You got it. If that man looks me in the eye and says he's in love with Holly Hot-Biscuits, I'll die of mortification on the spot."

"No, you won't. You're too strong. And at least you'd know where you stand." *I'd give anything for another chance with Jack.*

"I *know* where I stand," Melissa answered, pouring tea for Ashley and then for herself, and then warming her hands around the cup instead of drinking the brew. "Up the creek without a paddle."

"That's a mixed metaphor," Ashley couldn't help pointing out.

"Whatever," Melissa said.

And that, for the time being, was the end of the discussion.

A week after the transplant, the jury was still out on whether the procedure had been successful or not, but by pulling certain strings Jack had been reluctantly released from the hospital, partly on the strength of his well-respected father's promise to make sure he was looked after and did not overexert himself. He went home to Oak Park, Illinois, his old hometown, and let Abigail and the old man install him in his boyhood bedroom in the big brick Federal on Shady Lane.

Not that there were any leaves on the trees to provide shade.

Abigail, though shy around him, had taken pains to get his room ready for occupancy—she'd put fresh sheets on the bed, dusted, aired the place out.

The obnoxious rock-star posters, a reminder of his checkered youth, were still on the walls. The antiquated computer, which he'd built himself from scavenged components, remained on his desk, in front of the windows. Hockey sticks and baseball bats occupied every corner.

The sight of it all swamped Jack, made him miss his mother more acutely than ever.

And that was nothing compared to the way he missed Ashley.

Bryce, soon to be an optometrist, appeared in the

doorway. He was in his mid-twenties, but he looked younger to Jack.

"You're going to make it, Jack," Bryce said, and he spoke in a man's voice, not a boy's.

So many things had changed.

So many hadn't.

"Thanks to you, maybe I will."

"No maybe about it," Bryce argued.

There was a brief, awkward pause. "What do you think of Abigail?" Jack asked, pulling back the chair at his desk and sitting down. He still tired too easily.

Bryce closed the door, took a seat on the edge of Jack's bed. Loosely interlaced his fingers and let his hands dangle between his blue-jeaned knees. "She's been good for Dad. He was a real wreck after Mom died."

"I guess that must have been a hard time," Jack ventured, turning his head to look out over the street lined with skeleton trees, waiting for spring.

"It was pretty bad," Bryce admitted. "Did Dad tell you the government is having your headstone removed from the cemetery at Arlington, and the empty box dug up?"

"Guess they need the space," Jack said, as an infinite sadness washed over him. Once, he'd been a hotshot. Now he was sick of guns and violence and war.

"Yeah," Bryce agreed quietly. "Who's the woman?"

Jack tensed. "What woman?"

"The one you mentioned in the email you sent to Dad's office."

Jack closed his eyes briefly, longing for Ashley. Wondering if she'd finally mastered the fine art of computing well enough to check out the Sent Messages folder.

"I'm getting engaged on Valentine's Day," Bryce said, to fill the gap left by Jack's studied silence. "Her name is Kathy. We went to college together."

"Congratulations," Jack managed.

"I wanted to be like you, you know," Bryce went on. "Raise hell. Get sent away to military school. Maybe even bite the sand in Iraq."

Jack managed a tilt at one corner of his mouth, enough to pass for a grin—he hoped. "Thank God you changed your mind," he said. "Mom and Dad— after I disappeared—how were they?"

"Devastated," Bryce answered.

Jack shoved a hand through his hair. Sighed. What had he expected? That they'd go merrily on, as if nothing had happened? *Oh, well, Jack's gone, but we still have three sons left, don't we, and they're all going to graduate school.*

"I need to see Mom's grave," he said.

"I'll take you there," Bryce responded immediately. "After my last class, of course."

Jack smiled. "Of course."

Bryce rose, made that leaving sound by huffing out his breath. "Be nice to Abigail, okay?" he said. "Dad loves her a lot, and she's really trying to fit in without usurping Mom's place."

"I haven't been nice?"

"You've been…reserved."

"Staying alive has been taking up all my time," Jack answered. "Again, thanks to you, I've got a fighting chance. I'll never forget what you did, Bryce. No two ways about it, donating marrow hurts."

Bryce cleared his throat, reached for the doorknob, but didn't quite turn it. "It could take time," he said, letting Jack's comment pass. "All of us being a family again, I mean. But don't give up on us, okay? Don't just take off or something, because I can't even tell you how hard that would be for Dad. He's already lost so much."

"I'm not going anywhere," Jack promised. "I might need that grave at Arlington after all, you know. Maybe they shouldn't be too quick to lay the new resident to rest."

Bryce flushed. "Who's the woman?" he asked again.

Jack met his brother's gaze. "Her name is Ashley O'Ballivan. She runs a bed-and-breakfast in Stone Creek, Arizona. Do me a favor, little brother. Don't get any ideas about calling her up and telling her where I am."

"Why don't *you* call her?"

"Because I still don't know if I'm going to live or die."

Bryce finally turned the knob, opened the door to go. "Maybe she'd like to hear from you, either way. Spend whatever time you have left—"

"And maybe she'd like to get on with her life," Jack broke in brusquely.

After Bryce was gone, Jack booted up the ancient computer—or tried to, anyhow. The cheapest pay-as-you-go cell phone on the market probably had more power.

Giving up on surfing the web, catching up on all he'd missed since Tombstone, he tried to interest himself in the pile of high school yearbooks stacked on a shelf in his closet.

What a hotheaded little jerk he'd been, he thought. A throwback, especially in comparison to his brothers.

He revisited his junior year, flipping pages until he found Molly Henshaw, the love of his adolescent life. Although he hadn't been a praying man, Jack had begged God to let him marry Molly someday.

Looking at her class picture, he remembered that she'd had acne, which she tried to cover with stuff closer to orange than flesh tone. Big hair, too. And a come-hither look in her raccoonlike eyes. Even in the photograph, he could see the clumps of mascara coating her lashes.

Must have been the come hither, he decided.

And thank God for unanswered prayers.

Having come to that conclusion, Jack decided to go downstairs, where Abigail was undoubtedly flitting around the kitchen. Time to make a start at getting to know his father's new wife, though their acquaintance might be a short one if his body rejected Bryce's marrow.

For his dad's sake, because there were so many things he couldn't make up for, he had to give it a shot. Ironically, he knew it was what his mother would have wanted.

Later, he'd log on to his dad's computer, in the den. See if Ashley's website was up and running.

With luck, there would be a picture of her, smiling like the welcoming hostess she was, dressed in something flowered, with her hair pulled back into that prim French braid he always wanted to undo.

For now, that would have to be enough.

Abigail was in the kitchen, the room where Jack had had so many conversations with his mother. Feminine and modestly pretty, Abigail wore a flowered apron, her hair was pinned up in a loose chignon at her nape, and her hands were white with flour.

She smiled shyly at Jack. "Your father likes peach pie above all things," she confided.

"I'm pretty fond of it myself," Jack answered, grinning. "You're a baker, Abigail?"

His stepmother shrugged. She couldn't have been more different, physically anyway, from his mom. She'd been tall and full-figured, always lamenting humorously that she should have lived in the 1890s, when women with bosoms and hips were appreciated. Abigail was petite and trim; she probably gardened, maybe knitted and crocheted.

His mother had loved to play golf and sail, and to Jack's recollection, she'd never baked a pie or worn an apron in her life.

"A baker and a few other things, too," Abigail said, with a quirky little smile playing briefly on her mouth. "I retired from real estate a year before Bill and I met. Sold my company for a chunk of cash and decided to spend the rest of my life doing what I love…baking, planting flowers, sewing. Oh, and fussing over my husband."

Jack swiped a slice of peach from the bowl waiting to be poured into the pie pan, and she didn't slap his hand. "Married before?" he asked casually. "Any kids?"

Abigail shook her head, and a few tendrils of her graying auburn hair escaped the chignon. "I was too busy with my career," she said, without a hint of regret. "Besides, I always promised myself I'd wait for

the right man, no matter how long it took. Turned out
to be Bill McKenzie."

He'd underestimated Abigail, that much was clear.
She was an independent woman, living the life she
chose to live, not someone looking for an easy life
married to a prosperous dentist. In fact, Abigail probably had a lot more money than his dad did, and that
was saying something.

"He's happy, Abigail. Thank you for that." Jack
reached for a second slice, and this time, she did swat
his hand, smiling and shaking her head.

She took a cereal bowl from the cupboard, scooped
in a generous portion of fruit with a soup spoon, and
handed him the works.

Jack decided he knew all he needed to know about
Abigail—she loved his father, and that was as good as
it got. Leaning in a little, he kissed her cheek.

"Welcome aboard, Abigail," he said hoarsely.

She smiled. "Thanks," she replied, and went back
to building the pie.

Chapter 10

"Ms. O'Ballivan? My name is Bryce McKenzie and I—"

Ashley shifted the telephone receiver from her left ear to her right, hunching one shoulder to hold it in place, busy rolling out pie dough on the butcher's block next to the counter. "I'm sorry, Mr. McKenzie," she said, distracted, "but we're all booked up for Valentine's Day—"

The man replied with an oddly familiar chuckle. Something about the timbre of it struck a chord somewhere deep in Ashley's core. "Excuse me?" he said.

"The bed-and-breakfast—I guess I just assumed you were calling because of the publicity my website's been getting—"

Again, that sense of familiarity flittered, in the pit of Ashley's stomach now.

"I'm Jack McKenzie's brother," Bryce explained.

McKenzie. The name finally registered in Ashley's befuddled memory, the one Jack had admitted leaving behind so long ago. "Oh," she said, stretching the phone cord taut so she could collapse into a kitchen chair. *"Oh."*

"I probably shouldn't be calling you like this, but— well—"

"Is Jack all right?"

Bryce McKenzie sighed. "Yes and no," he said carefully.

Ashley put a floury hand to her heart, smearing her T-shirt with white finger marks. "Tell me about the 'no' part, Mr. McKenzie," she said.

"Bryce," he corrected. And then, after clearing his throat, he explained that Jack had needed a bone marrow transplant. The patient was up and around, and he was taking antirejection drugs, but he didn't seem to be recovering—or regressing—and his family was worried.

They'd had a family meeting, Bryce concluded, one Jack hadn't been privy to, and decided as a unit that seeing Ashley again might be the boost he needed to get better.

Ashley listened with her eyes closed and her heart hammering.

"Where is he now?" she asked, very quietly, when Bryce had finished.

"We live in Chicago, so he's here," he answered. "There's plenty of room at my dad's place, if you wanted to stay there. I mean, if you even want to come in the first place, that is."

Ashley's heart thrummed. Valentine's Day was a

week away and she had to be there to greet her guests, make them comfortable—didn't she? This was her chance to take the business to a whole new level, make some progress, stay caught up on her payments to Brad and fortify her faltering savings.

And none of that was as important as seeing Jack again.

"I think," she said shakily, "that if Jack wanted to see me, he would have called himself."

"He wants to make sure he's going to live through this first," Bryce answered candidly. Then, after sucking in an audible breath, he added, "Will you come? It could make all the difference in his recovery—or, at least, that's what we're hoping."

Ashley looked around her kitchen, cluttered now with the accoutrements of serious cooking. The freezer was full, the house was ready for the onslaught of lovers planning a romantic getaway.

How could she leave now?

How could she *stay?*

"I'll be there as soon as I can book a flight," she heard herself say.

"One of us will pick you up at O'Hare," Bryce said, his voice light with relief. "Just call back with your flight number and arrival time."

Ashley wrote down the cell numbers he gave her and promised to get in touch with him as soon as she had the necessary information.

"This is crazy," she told Mrs. Wiggins, as soon as she'd hung up.

"Meooow," Mrs. Wiggins replied, curling against Ashley's ankle.

Having made the decision, Ashley was full of sudden energy. She made airline reservations for the next day, flying out of Flagstaff, connecting in Phoenix, and then going on to Chicago. When that was done, she called Bryce back.

"You're sure Jack wants to see me?" she asked, having second thoughts.

"I'm sure," Bryce said, with a smile in his voice.

The next call was to Melissa, at her office, and Ashley was almost panicking by then. The moment Melissa greeted her with a curious "Hello"—Ashley never called her at work—the whole thing spilled out.

Ashley held her breath, after the spate of words, awaiting Melissa's response.

"I see," Melissa said cautiously.

"I might be back before Valentine's Day," Ashley blurted, anxious to assuage her sister's misgivings about Jack, "but I can't be absolutely sure, and I need you to cover for me if necessary."

"I don't know beans about running a bed-and-breakfast," Melissa said gamely, "much less *cooking*. But I'll be there, Ash. Get your bags packed."

Tears burned Ashley's eyes. She could always count on Melissa, on any member of her family, to come through in a pinch. Why had she doubted that, even for a moment? "Thanks, Melissa."

"You'll have to send the cat to Olivia's place," Melissa warned, though her tone was good-natured. "You know how my allergies flare up when I'm around anything with fur."

"I know," Ashley said sweetly, "that you're a hypochondriac. But I love you anyway."

"Gee, thanks," Melissa replied. "No cat," she clarified firmly. "The deal's off if Olivia won't take him."

"Her," Ashley said, smiling. "How many male cats do you know with the name 'Mrs. Wiggins'?"

"I don't know *any* cats, whatever the gender," Melissa answered, "and I don't want to, either."

Ashley grinned to herself. "I'm sure Olivia will cat-sit," she conceded. "One more thing. Could you serve punch at the Valentine's Day dance? I promised and I did all this baking and I'm not sure I'll be back in time—"

"Oh, for Pete's sake," Melissa said. *"Yes,* if it comes to that, but you'd better do your darnedest to be home before the first guests arrive. I mean well, but we're taking a risk here. I'm not the least bit domestic, remember, and I could put you out of business without half trying."

Ashley laughed, sniffled once. "I promise I'll do my O'Ballivan best," she said. "Have you seen Dan yet?"

"No," Melissa said, "and don't mention his name again, if you don't mind."

After the call ended, Ashley wrestled her one and only suitcase down from the attic—she rarely traveled—and set it on her bed, open.

Mrs. Wiggins immediately climbed into it, as though determined to make the journey with her mistress.

"Not this time," Ashley said, gently removing the furball.

The next dilemma was, what did a person pack for a trip to Chicago in the middle of winter?

She decided on her trademark broomstick skirts, lightweight tunic sweaters, and some jeans, for good measure.

When she called Starcross Ranch, hoping to speak

to Olivia, Tanner answered instead. Ashley asked if Mrs. Wiggins could bunk in for a few days.

"Sure," Tanner said, as Ashley had known he would. But he also wanted an explanation. "Where are you off to, in such a hurry?"

Tanner was Jack's friend, and he'd surely been as worried about him as Ashley had. Although it was possible that the two men had been in touch, her instincts told her they hadn't.

Ashley drew a deep breath, let it out slowly, and hoped she was doing the right thing by telling Tanner. And by jetting off to Chicago when Jack hadn't asked her to come.

"Jack's in Chicago," she said. "He's had a bone marrow transplant—something to do with the toxin—and his family is worried about him. He's not getting worse, but he's not getting better, either."

Tanner murmured an exclamation. "I see," he said. "Jack didn't call you himself?"

"No," Ashley admitted, her shoulders sagging a little.

Tanner considered that, must have decided against giving an opinion, one way or the other. "You'll keep me in the loop?" he asked presently.

"Yes," Ashley said.

"I'll be there to get the cat sometime this afternoon. Do you want a ride to the airport?"

"I've got that covered," Ashley replied. "Thanks, Tanner. I really appreciate this."

"We're family," Tanner pointed out. "Brad could probably charter a jet—"

"I don't need a jet," Ashley interrupted, though

gently. "And I'm not really ready to discuss any of this with Brad. Not just yet, anyhow."

"Is there a plan?" Tanner asked. "And if so, what is it?"

Ashley smiled, even though her eyes were burning again. "No plan," she said. "I'm not even sure Jack wants me there. But I have to see him, Tanner."

"Of course you do," Tanner agreed, sounding both relieved and resigned. "Brad is going to wonder where you've gone, though. He keeps pretty close tabs on his three little sisters, you know. But don't worry about that—I'll handle him."

She heard Olivia's voice in the background, asking what was going on.

"Let me talk to her," Ashley said, and told the whole story all over again.

"I don't like it that you're going alone," Olivia told her, a minute or so later. "I've got the babies to look after, and I think Sophie is coming down with a cold, but maybe Melissa could go along—"

"Melissa is going to house-sit," Ashley said. "And she'll have her hands full holding down the fort, especially if I'm not back before Valentine's Day. I'll be *fine,* Livie."

"You're sure? What if Jack—?"

"What if he doesn't want to see me? I'll handle it, Liv. I'm a big girl now, remember?"

Olivia's laugh was warm, and a little teary. "Godspeed, little sister," she said. "And call us when you get there."

"I will," Ashley said, thinking how lucky she was.

The next few hours passed in a haze of activity—

there were project lists to make for Melissa, and dozens of other details, too.

As promised, Tanner showed up late that afternoon to collect a mewing Mrs. Wiggins in the small pet carrier Olivia had sent along.

"Tell Jack I said hello," Tanner said, as he was leaving.

Ashley nodded, and her brother-in-law planted a light kiss on the top of her head.

"Take care," he told her. And then he was gone.

Melissa showed up when she got off work, and she and Ashley went over the lists—which guests to put where, how to reheat the food she'd prepared ahead of time, frozen and carefully labeled, how to take reservations and run credit cards, and a myriad of other things.

Melissa looked overwhelmed, but in true O'Ballivan spirit, she vowed to do her best.

Knowing she wouldn't sleep if she stayed in Stone Creek that night, Ashley loaded her suitcase into the car and set out for Flagstaff, intending to check into a hotel near the airport and have a room-service supper.

Her flight was leaving at six-thirty the next morning.

Along the way, though, she pulled off onto the snowy road leading to the cemetery where her mother was buried, parked near Delia's grave, and waded toward the headstone.

There were no heartfelt words, no tears.

Ashley simply felt a need to be there, in that quiet place. Somehow, a sense of closure had stolen into her heart when she wasn't looking. She could let go now, move on.

The weather was bitterly cold, though, and she soon

got back in her car and made her steady, careful way toward Flagstaff.

She would always love the mother she'd longed to have, she reflected, but it was time to go forward, appreciate the *living* people she loved, those who loved her in return: Brad and Meg, Olivia and Tanner, Melissa and little Mac and Carly and sweet Sophie and the babies.

And Jack.

She didn't obsess over what might happen when she arrived in Chicago. For once in her life, she was taking a risk, going for what she wanted.

And she wanted Jack McCall—McKenzie—whoever he was.

Once she'd arrived in Flagstaff, she chose a hotel and checked in, ordered a bowl of cream of broccoli soup, ate it, and soaked in a warm bath until the chill seeped out of her bones. Most of it, anyway.

A part of her would remain frozen until she'd seen Jack for herself.

"You did *what?*" Jack demanded, after supper that night, when he and Bryce wound up the evening sitting in chairs in front of the fireplace. It had been a hectic thing, supper, with brothers and their wives, nieces and nephews, and even a few neighbors there to share in the meal celebrating Jack's return from the dead.

"I called Ashley O'Ballivan," Bryce repeated, with no more regret than he'd shown the first time. "She'll be here late tomorrow afternoon. I'm picking her up at O'Hare."

Jack sat back, absorbing the news. A part of him soared, anticipating Ashley's arrival. Another part wanted to find a place to hide out until she was gone again.

"You've got a lot of nerve, little brother," he finally said, with no inflection in his voice at all. "Especially considering that I told you I'm not ready to see her."

"Until you're sure you won't die," Bryce confirmed confidently. "Jack, *all* of us are terminal. Maybe you won't be around long. Maybe you'll live to be a hundred. But in the meantime, you need to see *this woman,* even if it's only to say goodbye."

Saying goodbye to Ashley the last time had been one of the hardest things Jack had ever had to do. Saying goodbye to her again, especially for eternity, might be more than he could bear.

His conscience niggled at him. What about what *Ashley* had to bear?

Jack closed his eyes. "I'll get you for this," he told his brother.

Bryce chuckled. "You'll have to get well first," he replied.

"You think you can take me?" Jack challenged, grinning now, both infuriated and relieved.

"I'm not a little kid anymore," Bryce pointed out. "I might be able to take you—even with all your paramilitary skills."

Jack opened his eyes, looked at his younger brother with new respect. "Maybe you could," he said.

Bryce stood, stretched and yawned mightily. "Better get back to my apartment," he said. "Busy day tomorrow."

Ashley, Jack thought, full of conflicting emotions he couldn't begin to identify. What was he so afraid of?

Not commitment, certainly—at least as far as Ashley was concerned.

"After this," he told his departing brother, "mind your own business."

"Not a chance," Bryce said lightly.

And then he was gone.

The first signs of an approaching blizzard hit Chicago five minutes after Ashley's plane landed at O'Hare, and the landing had been so bumpy that her knuckles were white from gripping the armrests—letting go of them was a slow and deliberate process.

She was such a homebody, completely unsuited to an adventurer like Jack. If she'd had a brain in her head, she decided, gnawing at her lower lip, she would have turned right around and flown back to Arizona where she belonged, blizzard or no blizzard.

She waited impatiently while all the passengers in the rows ahead of hers gathered their coats and carry-ons and meandered up the aisle at the pace of spilled peanut butter.

They had all the time in the world, probably.

Ashley knew she might not.

She hurried up the Jetway when her turn finally came, having returned the flight attendant's farewell smile with a fleeting one of her own.

Finding her way along a maze of moving walkways took more time, and she was almost breathless when she finally stepped out of the secure area, scanning the waiting sea of strange faces. Bryce had promised to hold up a sign with her name on it, so they could recognize each other, but even standing on tiptoe, she didn't see one.

"Ashley?"

She froze, turned to see Jack standing at her elbow. A strangled cry, part sob and part something else entirely, escaped her.

He looked so thin, so pale. His eyes were, as Big John used to say, like two burned holes in a blanket.

"Hey," he said huskily.

Ashley swallowed, still unable to move. "Hey," she responded.

He grinned, resembling his old self a little more, and crooked his arm, and she took it.

"You're glad to see me?" she asked, afraid of the answer. His grin, after all, could have been a reflex.

"If I'd been given a choice," he replied, "I would have asked you not to come. But, yeah, I'm glad to see you."

"Good," Ashley said uncertainly, aware of the strangeness between them. And the ever-present electrical charge.

"My interfering brother is waiting over in baggage claim," he said. "Let's go find him, before this storm gets any worse and we get stuck in rush-hour traffic. It's a long drive out to Oak Park."

Ashley nodded, overjoyed to be there and, at the same time, wishing she'd stayed home.

Once she'd met Bryce McKenzie—he was taller than his brother, though not so broad in the shoulders—and collected her solitary, out-of-style suitcase, the three of them headed for the parking garage, Bryce carrying the bag.

Fortunately, Bryce drove a big SUV with four-wheel drive, and he didn't seem a bit worried about the weather. Ashley sat in the front passenger seat, while Jack climbed painfully into the back.

The snow was coming down so hard and so fast by then, and the traffic was so intense, that Ashley wondered if they would reach Oak Park alive.

They did, eventually, and all the McKenzies were waiting in the entryway of the large brick house when they pulled into the circular driveway out front.

Introductions were made—Jack's father and step-mother, his brothers and their wives, Bryce's fiancée, Kathy—and most of their names went out of Ashley's head as soon as she'd heard them.

She could think of nothing—and no one—but Jack.

Jack, who'd sat silent in the backseat of his brother's SUV all the way from the airport. Bryce, bless his heart, had tried hard to keep the conversation going, asking Ashley if her flight had been okay, inquiring about Stone Creek and what it was like there.

Ashley, as uncomfortable in her own way as Jack was in his, had given sparse answers.

She shouldn't have come.

Just as she'd feared, Jack didn't want her there.

The McKenzies welcomed her heartily, though, and Mrs. McKenzie—Abigail—served a meat-loaf supper so delicious that Ashley made a mental note to ask for the recipe.

Jack, seated next to her, though probably not by his own choosing, ate sparingly, as she did, and said almost nothing.

"You must be tired," Jack's father said to her, when the meal was over and Ashley automatically got up to help clear the table. The older man's gaze shifted to his eldest son. "Jack, why don't you show Ashley to her room so she can rest?"

Jack nodded, gestured for Ashley to precede him, and followed her out of the dining room.

The base of the broad, curving staircase was just ahead.

Ashley couldn't help noticing how slowly Jack moved. He was probably exhausted. "You don't have to—"

"Ashley," he interrupted blandly, "I can still climb stairs."

She lowered her gaze, then forced herself to look at him again. "I'm sorry, Jack—I—I shouldn't have come, but—"

He drew the knuckles of his right hand lightly down the side of her cheek. "Don't be sorry," he said. "I guess—well—it's hard on my pride, your seeing me like this."

Ashley was honestly puzzled. Sure, he'd lost weight, and his color wasn't great, but he was still *Jack*. "Like what?"

Jack spread his arms, looked down at himself, met her eyes again. She saw misery and sorrow in his expression. "I might be dying, Ashley," he said. "I wanted you to remember me the way I was before."

Ashley stiffened. "You are *not* going to die, Jack McCall. I won't tolerate it."

He gave a slanted grin. "Is that so?" he replied. "What do you intend to do to prevent it, O'Ballivan?"

"Take a pregnancy test," Ashley said, without planning to at all.

Jack's eyes widened. "You think you're—?"

"Pregnant?" Ashley finished for him, lowering her

voice lest the conversation carry into the nearby dining room.

"Yeah," Jack said, somewhat pointedly.

"I might be," Ashley said. This was yet another thing she hadn't allowed herself to think about—until now. "I'm late. *Very* late."

He took her elbow, squired her up the stairs with more energy than he'd shown since she'd come face-to-face with him at O'Hare. "Is that unusual?"

"Yes," Ashley whispered, *"it's unusual."*

He smiled, and a light spread into his eyes that hadn't been there before. "You're not just saying this, are you? Trying to give me a reason to live or something like that?"

"If you can't come up with a reason to live, Jack Mc-Call," Ashley said, waving one arm toward the distant dining room, where his family had gathered, "you're in even sorrier shape than I thought."

He frowned. "Jack *McKenzie,*" he said, clearly thinking of something else. "I'm going by my real name now."

"Well, bully for you," Ashley said.

"'Bully for me'?" He laughed. "God, Ashley, you should have been born during the Roosevelt administration—the *Teddy* Roosevelt administration. Nobody says 'Bully for you' anymore."

Ashley folded her arms. *"I* do," she said.

His eyes danced—it was nice to know she was so entertaining—then went serious again. "Why are you here?"

She bristled. "You *know* why."

"No," Jack said, sounding honestly mystified. "I

thought we agreed that I'd come back to Stone Creek after this was all over, and we'd stay apart until then."

Ashley's throat constricted as she considered the magnitude of what Jack was facing. "And *I* thought we agreed that we love each other. Whether you live or die, I want to be here."

Pain contorted his face. "Ashley—"

"I'm not going anywhere until I know what's going to happen to you," Ashley broke in. "When will you know whether the transplant worked or not?"

The change in him was downright mercurial; Jack's eyes twinkled again, and his features relaxed. He made a show of checking his watch. "I'm expecting an email from God at any minute," he teased.

"That isn't funny!"

"Not much is, these days." He took her upper arms in his hands. "Ashley, as soon as this blizzard lets up, I want you to get on an airplane and go back to Stone Creek."

"Well, here's a news flash for you: just because you *want* something doesn't mean you're going to get it."

He grinned, shook his head. "Strange that I never noticed how stubborn you can be."

"Get used to it."

He crossed the hall, opened a door.

She peeked inside, saw a comfortable-looking room with an antique four-poster bed, a matching dresser and chest of drawers, and several overstuffed chairs.

"I won't sleep," she warned.

"Neither will I," Jack responded.

Ashley turned, faced him squarely. Spoke from her heart. "Don't die, Jack," she said. "Please—whatever happens between us—don't just give up and die."

He leaned in, kissed her lightly on the mouth. "I'll do my best not to," he said. Then he turned and started back toward the stairs.

"Aren't you going to bed?" Ashley asked, feeling lonely and very far from home.

"Later," he said, winking at her. "Right now, I'm going to call drugstores until I find one that delivers during snowstorms."

Ashley's heart caught; alarm reverberated through her like the echo of a giant brass gong. "Are you running low on one of your medications?"

"No," Jack answered. "I'm going to ask them to send over one of those sticks."

"Sticks?" Ashley frowned, confused.

"The kind a woman pees on," he explained. "Plus sign if she's pregnant, minus if she's not."

"That can wait," Ashley protested. "Have you looked out a window lately?"

"I've got to know," Jack said.

"You're insane."

"Maybe. Good night, Ashley."

She swallowed. "Good night," she said. Stepping inside the guestroom, she closed the door, leaned her forehead against it, and breathed deeply and slowly until she was sure she wouldn't cry.

Her handbag and suitcase had already been brought upstairs. Sinking down onto the side of the bed, Ashley rummaged through her purse until she found the cell phone she'd bought on a wave of technological confidence, after she'd finally mastered her computer.

She dialed her own number at the bed-and-breakfast, and Melissa answered on the first ring.

"Ashley?" The twin-vibe strikes again.

"Hi, Melissa. I'm here—in Chicago, I mean—and I'm—I'm fine."

"You don't *sound* fine," Melissa argued. "How's Jack?"

"He looks terrible, and I don't think he's very happy that I'm here."

"Oh, Ash—I'm sorry. Was the bastard rude to you?"

Ashley smiled, in spite of everything. "He's not a bastard, Melissa," she said, "and no, he hasn't been rude."

"Then—?"

"I think he's given up," Ashley admitted miserably. "It's as if he's decided to die and get it over with. And he doesn't want me around to see it happen."

"Look, maybe you should just come home—"

"I can't. We're socked in by the perfect storm. I've never seen so much snow—even in Stone Creek." She paused. "And I wouldn't leave anyway. How's everything there?"

"It's fine. I've had to turn away at least five people who wanted to book rooms for Valentine's Day weekend." Melissa still sounded worried. "You do realize that you might be there a while? Do you have enough money, Ash?"

"No," Ashley said, embarrassed. "Not for a long haul."

"I can help you out if you need some," Melissa offered. "Brad, too."

Ashley gulped down her O'Ballivan pride, and it wasn't easy to swallow. "I'll let you know," she said, with what dignity she had left. "Do me a favor, will you? Call Tanner and Olivia and let them know I got here okay?"

"Sure," Melissa said.

They said their goodbyes soon after that, and hung up.

As tired as she was, Ashley knew she wouldn't sleep.

She took a bath, brushed her teeth and put on her pajamas.

She watched a newscast on the guestroom TV, waited until the very end for the weather report.

More snow on the way. O'Hare was shut down, and the police were asking everyone to stay off the roads except in the most dire emergencies.

At quarter after ten, a knock sounded on Ashley's door.

"It's me," Jack called, in a loud whisper. "Can I come in?"

Before Ashley could answer, one way or the other, the door opened and he stepped inside, carrying a white bag in one hand.

"Nothing stops the post office or pharmacy delivery drivers," he said, holding out the bag.

The pregnancy test, of course.

Ashley's hand trembled as she reached out to accept it. "Come back later," she said, moving toward her bathroom door.

Jack sat down on the side of her bed. "I'll wait," he said.

Chapter 11

Huddled in the McKenzies' guest bathroom, Ashley stared down at the plastic stick in mingled horror and delight.

A plus sign.

She was pregnant.

Ashley made some rapid calculations in her head; normally, if she hadn't been under stress, it would have been a no-brainer to figure out that the baby was due sometime in September. Because she was frazzled, it took longer.

"Well?" Jack called from the other side of the door. As a precaution, Ashley had turned the lock; otherwise, he might have stormed in on her, he was so anxious to learn the results.

Ashley swallowed painfully. She was bursting with the news, but if she told Jack now, she would, in effect, be trapping him. He'd feel honor-bound to marry her, whether he really wanted to or not.

And suppose he died?

That, of course, would be awful either way.

But maybe knowing about the baby would somehow heal Jack, inspire him to try harder to recover. To believe he could.

The knob jiggled. "Ashley?"

"I'm all right."

"Okay," Jack replied, "but are you *pregnant?*"

"It's inconclusive," Ashley said, too earnestly and too cheerfully.

"I read the package. You get either a plus or a minus," Jack retorted, not at all cheerful, but very earnest. "Which is it, Ashley?"

Ashley closed her eyes for a moment, offered up a silent prayer for wisdom, for strength, for courage. She simply wasn't a very good liar; Jack would see through her if she tried to deceive him. And, anyway, deception seemed wrong, however good her intentions might be. The child was as much Jack's as her own, and he had a right to know he was going to be a father.

"It's—it's a plus."

"Open the door," Jack said. Was that jubilation she heard in his voice, or irritation? Joy—or dread?

Ashley pushed the lock button in the center of the knob, and stepped back quickly to avoid being run down by a man on a mission. She was still holding the white plastic stick in one hand.

Jack took it from her, examined the little panel at one end, giving nothing away by his expression. His shoulders were tense, though, and his breathing was fast and shallow.

"My God," he said finally. "Ashley, *we made a baby.*"

"You and me," Ashley agreed, sniffling a little.

Jack raised his eyes to hers. She thought she saw a quickening there, something akin to delight, but he looked worried, too. "You weren't going to tell me?" he asked. "I wouldn't exactly describe a plus sign as 'inconclusive.'"

"I didn't know how you'd react," Ashley said. She *still* couldn't read him—was he glad or sad?

"How I'd react?" he echoed. "Ashley, this is the best thing that's ever happened to me, besides you."

Ashley stared at him, stricken to silence, stricken by joy and surprise and a wild, nearly uncontainable hope.

"You do *want* this baby, don't you?" Jack asked.

"Of course I do," Ashley blurted. "I wasn't sure *you* did, that's all."

Jack looked down at the stick again, shaking his head and grinning.

"I peed on that, you know," Ashley pointed out, reaching for the test stick, intending to throw it away.

Jack held it out of her reach. "We're keeping this. You can glue it into the kid's baby book or something."

"Jack, it's not sanitary," Ashley pointed out. Why was she talking about trivial things, when so much hung in the balance?

"Neither are wet diapers," Jack reasoned calmly. "Sanitation is all well and good, but a kid needs good old-fashioned germs, too, so he—or she—can build up all the necessary antibodies."

"You don't have to marry me if you don't want to," Ashley said, too quickly, and then wished she could bite off her tongue.

"Sure, I do," Jack said. "Call me old-fashioned, but I think a kid ought to have two legal parents."

"Sure, you *have* to marry me, or sure, you *want* to?" Ashley asked.

"Oh, I want to, all right," Jack told her, his voice hoarse, his eyes glistening. "The question is, do you want to spend the rest of your life with me? You could be a widow in six months, or even sooner. A widow with a baby to raise."

"Not if you fight to live, Jack," Ashley said.

He looked away, evidently staring into some grim scenario only he could see. "There's plenty of money," he said, as though speaking to someone else. "If nothing else, I made a good living doing what I did. You would never want for anything, and neither would our baby."

"I don't care about money," Ashley countered honestly, and a little angrily, too. *I care about you, and this baby, and our life together. Our long, long life together.* "I love you, remember?"

He set the test stick carefully aside, on the counter by the sink, and pulled Ashley out into the main part of the small suite. "I can't propose to you in a bathroom," he said.

Ashley laughed and cried.

Awkwardly, Jack dropped to one knee, still holding her hand. "I love you, Ashley O'Ballivan. Will you marry me?"

"Yes," she said.

He gave an exuberant shout, got to his feet again and pulled her into his arms, practically drowning her in a deep, hungry kiss.

The guestroom door popped open.

"Oops," Dr. McKenzie the elder said, blushing.

Jack and Ashley broke apart, Jack laughing, Ashley embarrassed and happy and not a little dazed.

Bill looked even more chagrined than before. "I heard a yell and I thought—"

"Everything's okay, Dad," Jack said, with gruff affection. "It's better than okay. I just asked Ashley to marry me, and she said yes."

"I see," Bill said, smiling, and quietly closed the door.

A jubilant "Yes!" sounded from the hallway. Ashley pictured her future father-in-law punching the air with one fist, a heartening thought.

"I still might die," Jack reminded her.

"Welcome to the human race," Ashley replied. "From the moment any of us arrive here, we're on our way out again."

"I'd like to make love to you right now," Jack said.

"Not here," Ashley answered. "I couldn't—not in your dad's house."

Jack nodded slowly. "You're as old-fashioned as I am," he said. "As soon as this storm lets up, though, we're out of here."

They sat down, side by side, on the bed where both of them wanted to make love, and neither intended to give in to desire.

Not just yet, anyway.

"How soon can we get married?" Jack asked, taking her hand, stroking the backs of her knuckles with the pad of his thumb.

Ashley's heart, full to bursting, shoved its way up into her throat and lodged there. "Wait a second," she protested, when she finally gathered the breath to speak. The aftershocks of Jack's kiss were still banging around inside her. "There are things we have to decide first."

"Like?"

"Like where we're going to live," Ashley said, nervous now. She liked Chicago, what little she'd seen of the place, that is, but Stone Creek would always be home.

"Wherever you want," Jack told her quietly. "And I know that's the old hometown. Just remember that your family isn't exactly wild about me."

"They'll get over it," Ashley told him, with confidence. "Once they know you're going to stick around this time."

"Just *try* shaking me off your trail, lady," Jack teased. He leaned toward her, kissed her again, this time lightly, and in a way that shook her soul.

"Does that mean you won't go back to whatever it is you do for a living?" Ashley ventured.

"It means I'm going to shovel snow and carry out the trash and love you, Ashley. For as long as we both shall live."

Tears of joy stung her eyes. "That probably won't be enough to keep you busy," she fretted. "You're used to action—"

"I'm sick of action. At least, the kind that involves covert security operations. Vince can run the company, along with a few other people I trust. I can manage it from the computer in your study."

"I thought you didn't trust Vince anymore," Ashley said.

"I got a little peeved with him," Jack admitted, "but he's sound. He'd have been long gone if he wasn't."

"You wouldn't be taking off all of the sudden— on some important job that required your expertise?"

"I'm good at what I do, Ashley," Jack said. "But I'm not so good that I can't delegate. Maybe I'll hang out with Tanner sometimes, though, riding the range and all that cowboy-type stuff."

"Do you know how to ride a horse?"

Jack chuckled. "It can't be that much different from riding a camel." He grinned. "And I'd be a whole lot closer to the ground."

That last statement sobered both of them.

Jack might not be just closer to the ground, he might wind up *under* it.

"I'm going to make it, Ashley," he assured her.

She dropped her forehead against his shoulder, wrapped her arms around him, let herself cling for a few moments. "You'd better," she said. "You'd just better."

Three days later, the storm had finally moved on, leaving a crystalline world behind, trees etched with ice, blankets of white covering every roof.

A private jet, courtesy of Brad, skimmed down onto the tarmac at a private airfield on the fringes of the Windy City, and Jack and Ashley turned to say temporary farewells to Jack's entire family, gathered there to see them off.

The whole clan would be traveling to Stone Creek for the wedding, which would take place in two weeks. Valentine's Day would have been perfect, but with so many guests already booked to stay at the bed-and-breakfast, it was impossible, and neither Jack nor Ashley wanted to wait until the next one rolled around.

Bill McKenzie pumped his eldest son's hand, the hem of his expensive black overcoat flapping in a brisk breeze, then drew him into a bear hug.

"Better get yourselves onto that plane and out of this wind," Bill said, at last, his voice choked. He bent to kiss Ashley's cheek. "I always wanted a daughter," he added, in a whisper.

Jack nodded, then shook hands with each of his brothers. Every handshake turned into a hug. Lastly, he embraced Abigail, his stepmother.

Ashley looked away, grappling with emotions of her own, watched as the metal stairs swung down out of the side of the jet with an electronic hum. The pilot stood in the doorway, grinning, and she recognized Vince Griffin—the man who'd held a gun on her in her own kitchen, the night Ardith and Rachel arrived.

"Better roll, boss," he called to Jack. "There's more weather headed this way, and I'd like to stay ahead of it."

Jack took Ashley's arm, steered her gently up the steps, into the sumptuous cabin of the jet. There were eight seats, each set of two facing the other across a narrow fold-down table.

"Aren't you going to ask what I'm doing here?" Vince asked Jack, blustering with manly bravado and boyishly earnest at the same time.

"No," Jack answered. "It's obvious that you wangled the job so you could be the one to take us home to Stone Creek."

Home to Stone Creek. That sounded so good to Ashley, especially coming from Jack.

Vince laughed. "I'm trying to get back in your good graces, boss," he said, flipping a switch to retract the stairs, then shutting and securing the cabin door. "Is it working?"

"Maybe," Jack said.

"I hate it when you say 'maybe,'" Vince replied.

"Just fly this thing," Jack told him mildly, with mischief in his eyes. "I want to stay ahead of the weather as much as you do."

Vince nodded, retreated into the cockpit, and shut the door behind him.

Solicitously, Jack helped Ashley out of her coat, sat her down in one of the sumptuous leather seats and swiveled it to buckle her seat belt for her.

A thrill of anticipation went through her.

Not yet, she told herself.

Jack must have been reading her mind. "As soon as we get home," he vowed, leaning over her, bracing himself on the armrests of her seat, "we're going to do it like we've never done it before."

That remark inspired another hot shiver. "Are we, now?" she said, her voice deliberately sultry.

Jack thrust himself away from her, since the plane was already taxiing down the runway, took his own seat across from hers and fastened his belt for takeoff.

Four and a half hours later, they landed outside Stone Creek.

Brad and Meg were waiting to greet them, along with Olivia and Tanner, Carly and Sophie, and Melissa.

"*Thank God* you're back," Melissa said, close to Ashley's ear, after hugging her. "I thought I was going to have to *cook.*"

Brad stood squarely in front of Jack, Ashley noticed, out of the corner of her eye, his arms folded and his face stern.

Jack did the same thing, gazing straight into Brad's eyes.

"Uh-oh," Melissa breathed. "Testosterone overload."

Neither man moved. Or spoke.

Olivia finally nudged Brad hard in the ribs. "Behave yourself, big brother," she said. "Jack will be part of the family soon, and that means the two of you have to get along."

It didn't mean any such thing, of course, but to Ashley's profound relief, Brad softened visibly at Olivia's words. Then, after some hesitation, he put out a hand.

Jack took it.

After the shake, Brad said, "That doesn't mean you can mistreat my kid sister, hotshot."

"Wouldn't think of it," Jack said. "I love her." He curved an arm around Ashley, pulled her close against his side, looked down into her upturned face. "Always have, always will."

Two weeks later
Stone Creek Presbyterian Church

"It's tacky," Olivia protested to Melissa, zipping herself into her bridesmaid's dress with some difficulty, since she was still a little on the pudgy side from having the twins. "Coming to a wedding with a U-Haul hitched to the back of your car!"

Melissa rolled her eyes. "I have to be in Phoenix bright and early Monday morning to start my new job," she said, yet again. The three sisters had been over the topic many times. Most of Melissa's belongings had already been moved to the fancy condo in Scottsdale; the rented trailer contained the last of them.

Initially, flushed with the success of helping Ashley steer the bed-and-breakfast through the Valentine's Day rush, Melissa had seemed to be wavering a little on the subject of moving away. After all, she liked her job at the small, local firm where she'd worked since graduating from law school, but then Dan Guthrie had suddenly eloped with Holly the Waitress. Now nothing would move Melissa to stay.

She was determined to shake the dust of Stone Creek off her feet and start a whole new life—elsewhere.

Ashley turned her back to her sisters and her mind to her wedding, smoothing the beaded skirt of her ivory-silk gown in front of the grainy full-length mirror affixed to the back of the pastor's office door. She and Melissa had scoured every bridal shop within a two-hundred-mile radius to find it, while Olivia searched the Internet, and the dress was perfect.

Not so the bridesmaids' outfits, Ashley reflected, happily rueful. They were bright yellow taffeta, with square necklines, puffy sleeves, big bows at the back, and way too many ruffles.

What was I thinking? Ashley asked herself, stifling a giggle.

The answer, of course, was that she *hadn't* been thinking. She'd fallen wholly, completely and irrevocably in love with Jack McKenzie, dazed in the daytime, *crazed* at night, when they made love until they were both sweaty and breathless and gasping for air.

The yellow dresses must have seemed like a good idea at the time, she supposed. Olivia and Melissa had surely argued against that particular choice—but Ashley honestly had no memory of it.

"We're going to look like giant parakeets in the pictures," Olivia complained now, but her eyes were warm and moist as she came to stand behind Ashley in front of the mirror. "You look so beautiful."

Ashley turned, and she and Olivia embraced. "I'll

make it up to you," Ashley said. "Having to wear those awful dresses, I mean."

Melissa looked down at her billowing skirts and shuddered. "I don't see how," she said doubtfully.

A little silence fell.

Olivia straightened Ashley's veil.

"I wish Mom and Dad and Big John could be here," Ashley admitted softly.

"I know," Olivia replied, kissing her cheek.

The church organist launched into a prelude to "Here Comes the Bride."

"Showtime," Melissa said, giving Ashley a quick squeeze. "Be happy."

Ashley nodded, blinking. She couldn't cry now. It would make her mascara run.

A rap sounded at the office door, and Brad entered at Olivia's "Come in," looking beyond handsome in his tuxedo. "Ready to be given away?" he asked solemnly, his gaze resting on Ashley in surprised bemusement, as though she'd just changed from a little girl to a woman before his very eyes. A grin crooked up a corner of his mouth. "We can always duck out the back door and make a run for it if you've changed your mind."

Ashley smiled, shook her head. Walked over to her brother.

Brad kissed her forehead, then lowered the front of the veil. "Jack McKenzie is one lucky man," he said gravely, but a genuine smile danced in his eyes. "Gonna be okay?"

Ashley took his arm. "Gonna be okay," she confirmed.

"We're supposed to go down the aisle first," Melissa said, grabbing Olivia's hand and dragging her past Brad and Ashley, through the open doorway, and into the corridor that opened at both ends of the small church.

"Is he out there?" Ashley whispered to Brad, suddenly nervous, as he escorted her over the threshold between one life and another.

"Jack?" Brad pretended not to remember. "I'm pretty sure I spotted him up front, with Tanner beside him. Guess it could have been the pastor, though." He paused for dramatic effect. "Oh, yeah. The pastor's wearing robes. The man I saw was in a tuxedo, tugging at his collar every couple of seconds."

"Stop it," Ashley said, but she was smiling. "I'm nervous enough without you giving me a hard time, big brother."

They joined Melissa and Olivia at the back of the church.

Over their heads, and through a shifting haze of veil, extreme anticipation, and almost overwhelming joy, Ashley saw Jack standing up front, his back straight, his head high with pride.

In just two weeks, he'd come a long way toward a full recovery, filling out, his color returning. He claimed it was the restorative power of good sex.

Ashley blushed, remembering some of that sex, and looking forward to a lot more of it.

The organist struck the keys with renewed vigor.

"There's our cue," Brad whispered to Ashley, bending his head slightly so she could hear.

"Go!" Melissa said to Olivia, giving her a little push.

Olivia moved slowly up the aisle, between pews jammed with McKenzies, O'Ballivans, McKettricks, and assorted friends.

Just before starting up the aisle herself, Melissa

turned, found Ashley's hand under the bouquet of snow-white peonies Brad had had flown in from God-knew-where and squeezed it hard.

"Go," Brad told Melissa, with a chuckle.

She made a face at him and started resolutely up the aisle.

Once she and Olivia were both in front of the altar, opposite Jack and Tanner, the organist pounded the keys with even more vigor than before. Ashley *floated* toward the altar, gripping Brad's strong arm, her gaze fixed on Jack.

The guests rose to their feet, beaming at Ashley.

Jack smiled, encouraged her with a wink.

And then she was at his side.

She heard the minister ask, "Who giveth this woman in marriage?"

Heard Brad answer, "Her family and I."

Ashley's eyes began to smart again, and she wondered if anyone had ever died of an overdose of happiness.

Brad retreated, and after that, Ashley was only peripherally aware of her surroundings. Her entire focus was on Jack.

Somehow, she got through the vows.

She and Jack exchanged rings.

And then the minister pronounced them man and wife.

Jack raised the front of Ashley's veil to kiss her, and his eyes widened a little, in obvious appreciation, when he saw that she'd forsworn her usual French braid for a shoulder-length style that stood out around her face.

She'd spent the morning at Cora's Curl and Twirl

over in Indian Rock, Cora herself doing the honors, snipping and blow-drying and phoofing endlessly.

The wedding kiss was chaste, at least in appearance.

Up close and personal, it was nearly orgasmic.

"Ladies and gentlemen," the minister said triumphantly, raising his voice to be heard at the back of the church, "may I present Mr. and Mrs. Jack McKenzie!"

Cheers erupted.

The organ thundered.

Jack and Ashley hurried down the aisle, emerging into the sunlight, and were showered with birdseed and good wishes.

The reception, held at the bed-and-breakfast, was everything a bride could hope for. Even the weather cooperated; the snow had melted, the sun was out, the sky cloudless and heartbreakingly blue.

"I ordered a sunny day just for you," Jack whispered to her, as he helped her out of the limo in front of the house.

For the next two hours, the place was crammed to the walls with wedding guests. Pictures were taken, punch and cake were served. So many congratulatory hugs, kisses and handshakes came their way that Ashley began to wish the thing would *end* already.

She and Jack would spend their wedding night right there at home, although they were leaving on their honeymoon the next day.

The sky was beginning to darken toward twilight when the guests began to leave, one by one, couple by couple, and then in groups.

Bill and Abigail McKenzie and their large extended family would occupy all the guestrooms at the bed-and-breakfast, so they lingered, somewhat at loose ends until Brad diplomatically invited them out to Stone Creek Ranch, where the party would continue.

Goodbyes were said.

Except for the caterers, already cleaning up, Melissa was the last to leave.

"I may never forgive you for this wretched dress," she told Ashley, tearing up.

"Maybe you'll get back at me one of these days," Ashley answered softly, as Jack moved away to give the twins room to say their farewells. Melissa planned to drive to Scottsdale that same night. "You'll be the bride, and I'll be the one who has to look like a giant parakeet."

Melissa huffed out a breath, shook her head. "I think you're safe from that horrid fate," she said wistfully. "I plan to throw myself into my career. Before you know it, I'll be a Supreme Court Justice, just as you said." She gave a wobbly little smile that didn't quite stick. "At least my memoirs will probably be interesting."

Ashley kissed her sister's cheek. "Take care," she said.

Melissa chuckled. "As soon as I swap this dress for a pair of jeans and a sweatshirt, and the heels for sneakers, I'll be golden."

With that, Melissa headed for the downstairs powder room, where she'd stashed her getaway clothes.

When she emerged, she was dressed for the road, and the ruffly yellow gown was wadded into a bundle under her right arm.

"Will you still love me if I toss this thing into the first Dumpster I see?" she quipped, as she and Ashley stood at the front door.

"I'll still love you," Ashley said, "no matter what."

Melissa gave a brave sniffle. "See you around, Mrs. McKenzie," she said.

And then she opened the front door, dashed across the porch and down the front steps, and along the walk. She got into her little red sports car, which looked too small to pull a trailer, tossed the offending bridesmaid's dress onto the passenger seat and waved.

Jack was standing right behind Ashley when she turned from closing the door, and he kissed her briefly on the mouth. "She's an O'Ballivan," he said. "She'll be all right."

Ashley nodded. Swallowed.

"The caterers will be out of here in a few minutes," Jack told her, with a twinkle. "I promised to overtip if they'd just kick it up a notch. Wouldn't you like to get out of that dress, beautiful as it is?"

She stood on tiptoe, kissed the cleft in her husband's chin. "I might need some help," she told him sweetly. "It has about a million buttons down the back."

Jack chuckled. "I'm just the man for the job," he said.

Mrs. Wiggins came, twitchy-tailed, out of the study, where she'd probably been hiding from the hubbub of the reception, batted playfully at the lace trim on the hem of Ashley's wedding gown.

"No you don't," she told the kitten, hoisting the little creature up so they were nose to nose, she and Mrs. Wiggins. "This dress is going to be an heirloom. Someday, another bride will wear it."

"Our daughter," Jack said, musing. "If she's as beautiful as her mother, every little boy under the age of five ought to be warned."

Ashley smiled, still holding Mrs. Wiggins. "Get rid of the caterers," she said, and headed for the stairs.

Barely a minute later, she was inside the room that had been hers alone, until today—not that she and Jack hadn't shared it every night since they got back from Chicago.

The last wintry light glowed at the windows, turning the antique lace curtains to gold. White rose petals covered the bed, and someone had laid a fire on the hearth, too.

Their suitcases stood just outside the closet door, packed and ready to go. Tomorrow at this time, she and Jack would be in Hawaii, soaking up a month of sunshine.

Ashley's heart quickened. She put a hand to her throat briefly, feeling strangely like a virgin, untouched, eager to be deflowered, and a little nervous at the prospect.

The room looked the same, and yet different, now that she and Jack were married.

Married. Not so long ago, she'd pretty much given up on marriage—and then Jack "McCall" had arrived by ambulance, looking for a place to heal.

So much had happened since then, some of it terrifying, most of it better than good.

Mrs. Wiggins leaped up onto a slipper chair near the fireplace and curled up for a long winter's snooze.

Carefully, Ashley removed the tiara that held her veil in place and set the mound of gossamer netting aside. She stood in front of the bureau mirror and fluffed out her hair with the fingers of both hands.

Her cheeks glowed, and so did her eyes.

The door opened softly, and Jack came into the room, no tuxedo jacket in evidence, unfastening his cuff links as he walked toward Ashley. Setting the cuff links aside on the dresser top, he took her into his arms, buried his hands in her hair, and kissed her thoroughly.

Ashley's knees melted, just as they always did.

Eventually, Jack tore his mouth from hers, turned her around, and began unfastening the buttons at the back of her dress. In the process, he bent to nibble at her skin as he bared it, leaving tiny trails of fire along her shoulder blades, her spine and finally the small of her back.

The dress fell in a pool at her feet, leaving her in her petticoat, bra, panty hose and high heels.

She shivered, not with fear or cold, but with eagerness. She wanted to give herself to Jack—as his wife.

But he left her, untucking his white dress shirt as he went. Crouched in front of the fireplace to light a blaze on the hearth.

Another blaze already burned inside Ashley.

Jack straightened, unfastened his cummerbund with a grin of relief, and tossed it aside. Started removing his shirt.

His eyes smoldered as he took Ashley in, slowly, his gaze traveling from her head to her feet and then back up again.

As if hypnotized, she unhooked her bra, let her breasts spill into Jack's full view. His eyes went wide as her nipples hardened, eager for his lips and tongue.

It seemed to take forever, this shedding of clothes, garment by garment, but finally they were both naked, and the fire snapped merrily in the grate, and Jack eased Ashley down onto the bed.

Because of her pregnancy—news they had yet to share with the rest of the family, because it was too new and too precious—his lovemaking was poignantly gentle.

He parted her legs, bent her knees, ran his hands from there to her ankles.

Ashley murmured, knowing what he was going to do, needing it, needing him.

He nuzzled her, parted the curls at the juncture of her thighs, and his sigh of contented anticipation reverberated through her entire system.

She tangled her fingers in his hair, held him close.

He chuckled against her flesh, and she moaned.

And then he took her full in his mouth, now nibbling, now suckling, and Ashley arched her back and cried out in surrender.

"Not so fast," Jack murmured, between teasing flicks of his tongue. "Let it happen slowly, Mrs. McKenzie."

"I—I don't think I—can wait—"

Jack turned his head, dragged his lips along the length of her inner thigh, nipped at her lightly as he crossed to the other side. "You can wait," he told her.

"*Please,* Jack," she half sobbed.

He slid his hands under her bare bottom, lifted her high, and partook of her with lusty appreciation.

She exploded almost instantaneously, her body flexing powerfully, once, twice, a third time.

And then she fell, sighing, back to the bed.

He was kissing her lower belly, where their baby was growing, warm and safe and sheltered.

"I love you, Jack," Ashley said, weak with the force of her releases.

He turned her to lie full length on the bed, poised himself over her, took her in a slow, even stroke.

"Always have," she added, trying to catch her breath and failing. "Always will."

FREE Merchandise is 'in the Cards' for you!

Dear Reader,

We're giving away FREE MERCHANDISE!

Seriously, we'd like to reward you for reading this novel by giving you **FREE MERCHANDISE** worth over **$20** retail. And no purchase is necessary!

You see the Jack of Hearts sticker above? Paste that sticker in the box on the Free Merchandise Voucher inside. Return the Voucher promptly...and we'll send you valuable Free Merchandise!

Thanks again for reading one of our novels—and enjoy your Free Merchandise with our compliments!

Pam Powers

Pam Powers

P.S. Look inside to see what Free Merchandise is **"in the cards"** for you!

W

e'd like to send you two free books like the one you are enjoying now. Your two books have a combined price of over $10 retail, but they are yours to keep absolutely FREE! We'll even send you 2 wonderful surprise gifts. You can't lose!

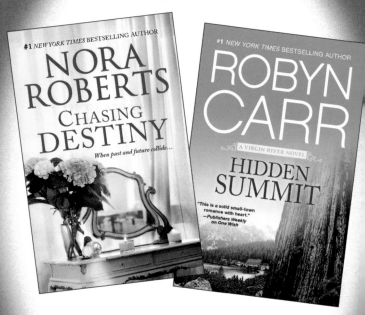

#1 *NEW YORK TIMES* BESTSELLING AUTHOR

NORA ROBERTS
CHASING DESTINY

When past and future collide...

#1 *NEW YORK TIMES* BESTSELLING AUTHOR

ROBYN CARR

A VIRGIN RIVER NOVEL

HIDDEN SUMMIT

"This is a solid small-town romance with heart."
—*Publishers Weekly*
on *One Wish*

REMEMBER: Your Free Merchandise, consisting of **2 Free Books** and **2 Free Gifts**, is worth over $20 retail! No purchase is necessary, so please send for your Free Merchandise today.

Get TWO FREE GIFTS!
We'll also send you 2 wonderful FREE GIFTS (worth about $10 retail), in addition to your 2 Free books!

Visit us at:
www.ReaderService.com

Books received may not be as shown.

YOUR FREE MERCHANDISE INCLUDES...

2 FREE Books **AND** 2 FREE Mystery Gifts

FREE MERCHANDISE VOUCHER

Please send my Free Merchandise, consisting of
2 Free Books and **2 Free Mystery Gifts**.
I understand that I am under no obligation to buy
anything, as explained on the back of this card.

194/394 HDL GKCK

Please Print

FIRST NAME

LAST NAME

ADDRESS

APT.#   CITY

STATE/PROV.   ZIP/POSTAL CODE

Offer limited to one per household and not applicable to series that subscriber is currently receiving.
Your Privacy—The Reader Service is committed to protecting your privacy. Our Privacy Policy is available online at www.ReaderService.com or upon request from the Reader Service. We make a portion of our mailing list available to reputable third parties that offer products we believe may interest you. If you prefer that we not exchange your name with third parties, or if you wish to clarify or modify your communication preferences, please visit us at www.ReaderService.com/consumerschoice or write to us at Reader Service Preference Service, P.O. Box 9062, Buffalo, NY 14240-9062. Include your complete name and address.

NO PURCHASE NECESSARY!

ROM-516-FMH16

▲ Detach card and mail today. No stamp needed. ▲

© 2015 HARLEQUIN ENTERPRISES LIMITED. ® and ™ are trademarks owned and used by the trademark owner and/or its licensee. Printed in the U.S.A.

READER SERVICE—Here's how it works:

Epilogue

December 24
Stone Creek, Arizona

Jack McKenzie stood next to his daughter's crib, gazing down at her in wonder. Katie—named for his grandmother—was nearly three months old now, and she looked more like Ashley every day. Although the baby was too young to understand Christmas, they'd hung up a stocking for her, just the same.

The door of his and Ashley's bedroom opened quietly behind him.

"The doctor is on the phone," she said quietly.

Jack turned, took her in, marveled anew, the way he did every time he saw his wife, that it was possible to go to sleep at night loving a woman so much, and wake up loving her even more.

"Okay," he said.

She approached, held out the cell phone he'd left downstairs when he brought Katie up to bed. They'd been putting the finishing touches on the Christmas tree by the front windows, he and Ashley, and the place was decorated to the hilt, though there would be no paying guests over the holidays.

Busy with a new baby, not to mention a husband, Ashley had decided to take at least a year off from running the bed-and-breakfast. She still cooked like a French chef, which was probably why he'd gained ten pounds since they'd gotten married, and she was practically an expert on the computer.

So far, she didn't seem to miss running a business.

She'd been baking all day, since half the family would be there for a special Christmas Eve supper, after the early services at the church.

They'd stayed home, waiting for the call.

He took the cell phone, cleared his throat, said hello.

Ashley moved close to him, leaned against his side, somehow supporting him at the same time. Her head rested, fragrant, against his shoulder.

He kissed her crown, drew in the scent of her hair.

"This is Dr. Schaefer," a man said, as if Jack needed to be told. He and Ashley had been bracing themselves for this call ever since Jack's last visit to the clinic up in Flagstaff, a few days before, where they'd run the latest series of tests.

"Yes," Jack said, his voice raspy. Wrapping one arm around Ashley's waist. He felt fine, but that didn't mean he was out of danger.

And there was so very much at stake.

"All the results are normal, Mr. McKenzie," he

heard Dr. Schaefer say, as though chanting the words through an underwater tunnel. "I think we can safely assume the marrow transplant was a complete success, and so were the antirejection medications."

Jack closed his eyes. "Normal," he repeated, for Ashley's benefit as well as his own.

She squeezed him hard.

"Thanks, Doctor," he said.

A smile warmed the other man's voice. "Have a Merry Christmas," the doctor said. "Not that you need to be told."

"You, too," Jack said. "And thanks again."

He closed the phone, tucked it into the pocket of his shirt, turned to take Ashley into his arms.

"Guess what, Mrs. McKenzie," he said. "We have a future together. You and me and Katie. A long one, I expect."

She beamed up at him, her eyes wet.

Downstairs, the doorbell chimed.

Ashley squeezed Jack's hand once, crossed to the crib, and tucked Katie's blanket in around her.

"I suppose they'll let themselves in," Jack said, watching her with the same grateful amazement he always felt.

Ashley smiled, and came back to his side, and they went down the stairs together, hand in hand.

Brad and Meg, with Carly and Mac and the new baby, Eva, stood in the entryway, smiling, snow dusting the shoulders of their coats and gleaming in their hair.

Olivia and Tanner arrived only moments later, with the twins, who were walking now, and Sophie.

"Where's Melissa?" Olivia asked, looking around.

"She'll be here soon," Ashley said. "She called about

an hour ago—there was a lot of traffic leaving Scotts-dale."

Ashley looked up at Jack, and they silently agreed to wait until everyone had arrived before sharing the good news about his test results.

The men spent the next few minutes carrying brightly wrapped packages in from the trucks parked out front, while the women and smaller children headed for the kitchen, where a savory supper was warming in the ovens.

Ashley and Meg and Olivia carried plates and silverware into the dining room, while Carly and Sophie kept the smaller children entertained.

A horn tooted outside, in the snowy driveway, and then Melissa hurried through the back door.

"It's cold out there!" she cried, spreading her arms for the rush of small children, wanting hugs. "And I think I saw Santa Claus just as I was pulling into town."

Soon, they were all gathered in the dining room, the grand tree in the parlor in full view through the double doors.

"I have news," Melissa said, just as Jack was about to offer a toast.

Everyone waited.

"I'm coming back to Stone Creek," Melissa told them all. "I'm about to become the new county prosecutor!"

The family cheered, and when some of the noise subsided, Ashley and Jack rose from their chairs, each with an arm around the other.

"The test results?" Olivia asked, in a whisper. Then,

reading Jack's and Ashley's expressions, a joyous smile broke over her face. "They were good?"

"Better than good," Ashley answered.

Supper was almost cold by the time the cheering was over, but nobody noticed.

It was Christmas Eve, after all.

And they were together, at home in Stone Creek.

* * * * *

**Also available from
B.J. Daniels
and HQN Books**

The Montana Hamiltons

Wild Horses
Lone Rider
Lucky Shot
Hard Rain

Beartooth, Montana

Unforgiven
Redemption
Forsaken
Atonement
Mercy

Look for *Into Dust,* the next book
in the Montana Hamiltons series!

DAY OF RECKONING

B.J. Daniels

This one is for Uncle Norb and Aunt Ginny.
I love being part of your family.
Thanks for all the support and encouragement,
and my best to you both always.

Prologue

The blur of red taillights on the highway ahead suddenly disappeared in the pouring rain and blackness.

Rozalyn Sawyer hit her brakes, shocked to realize she didn't know where she was. The road didn't look familiar. But it was hard to tell in this part of Oregon with an impenetrable jungle of green just off the pavement.

She'd been following the vehicle ahead of her for the past twenty miles. She'd picked it up outside of Oakridge, happy to see another car on this lonely stretch of highway tonight, especially at this time of year.

In her headlights she'd seen the solitary driver silhouetted behind the wheel of the pickup and felt an odd kinship. Between the rain, the darkness and the isolation, she'd been a little uneasy. But then she'd been feeling that way ever since she'd heard her father hadn't returned from his recent camping trip.

She vaguely remembered seeing a detour sign in the middle of the highway just before the pickup had turned. She'd followed the truck in front of her as the driver turned on to the narrower road to the left, and didn't remember any other roads off of this one.

But now she saw that the pavement ended. With a shock she realized where she was. Lost Creek Falls. She felt shaken, confused. How had she ended up on the dead-end road to the waterfall?

She'd been following the red taillights in front of her and not paying attention, that's how. The driver must have taken a wrong turn back at the detour sign and she'd blindly followed him. She'd been distracted, worrying about her father. As far as she could tell, no one had seen or heard from him in more than two weeks— and that included Emily, his bride of six months.

"I told you. He took his truck and camper and his camera, just like he always does," Emily had said when Roz called her yesterday. "He said he'd be back when he came back and not to concern myself. He was very clear about that."

Yes, for a few days. Not for two weeks. Liam Sawyer was in great shape for his age. He would be sixty on Thanksgiving Day, but Roz worried he might be trying to act even younger after marrying a woman fifteen years his junior.

Since no one had heard from him, Roz was sick with worry that something had happened. And now this "detour" would only make her arrival in Timber Falls all that much later.

The other driver had turned around in the gravel

parking lot and stopped, his headlights blinding her as she pulled past and started to turn around.

The moonless rainy darkness and the dense forest closed in around her car as she began her turn. Remote areas like this had always unnerved her, especially since from the time she was a child she'd known what was really out there.

Suddenly someone ran through her headlights. All she caught was a flash of yellow raincoat. She hit her brakes and stared ahead of her as the person wearing the bright yellow hooded raincoat climbed over the safety barrier at the top of the falls and disappeared in the trees that grew out over the water.

The driver of the pickup? Why would he venture out to the falls on a night like this, she wondered, watching to see if he reappeared.

Suddenly, she spotted the yellow raincoat through the trees at the edge of the falls. The figure seemed to be teetering on the precipice above the roaring water as if—

"Oh, God, no." Roz threw open her door and ran coatless through the icy cold rain toward the waterfall, fear crushing her chest making it nearly impossible to breathe. Not again. Dear God, not again.

"Don't!" she cried, still a dozen yards away.

The person didn't look her way, didn't even acknowledge hearing her. Through the rain and darkness, Roz ran, watching in horror as the bright yellow raincoat seemed to waver before it fell forward, dropping over the edge, and being instantly swallowed up in the spray of the falls.

Roz raced to the railing but couldn't see anything past the trees. Panicked, she ran around the barrier and pushed her way through the tree limbs, praying she'd find the person clinging to the edge.

The roar of the waterfall was deafening. She could feel the spray, warmer than the rain falling around her as she worked her way out onto the moss-slick boulders. She'd had a horrible fear of heights for the past ten years.

But her fear for the jumper was stronger than for herself as she grasped the slim branch of a pine tree leaning out over the waterfall.

Holding on fiercely, she stepped to the edge, her heart dropping as she glimpsed something bright yellow churning in the dark waters below.

She let out a cry and tried to step back. The limb in her hand broke and suddenly she was trying to find purchase on the wet, slick moss at her feet.

With the roar of the waterfall in her ears, she didn't hear him. Nor did she realize he'd come out onto the rocks above the dizzying dark water until he grabbed her from behind.

Chapter 1

November 14

It was late when Charity Jenkins heard someone come in to the *Timber Falls Courier* newspaper office, and realized she'd forgotten to lock the front door.

Her hand dropped to the desk drawer and the Derringer she now kept there. She'd put it in the desk after almost being killed a few weeks before. Unfortunately, as the days had gone by, she'd become lax again about security. Probably because for almost thirty years, she'd been safe in Timber Falls.

"Dammit, Charity, if you're going to work late, you've got to lock the door," Sheriff Mitch Tanner barked as he came through the dark doorway.

She let out the breath she'd been holding and gently lowered the gun back into the drawer. "Forgot." She smiled up at him as he moved in to the pool of light at her desk. Her heart did a little dippy-do-da dance, as it always did at the sight of him.

He was tall and dark with two perfect deep-set dimples, a Tanner trait. Gorgeous and impossible and the only man for her.

She watched him glance around the small newspaper office. As owner, publisher, editor and reporter, she often worked late. Her only help was a high school student who came in some evenings. This wasn't one of those evenings.

So it was just the two of them. Which was nice since it had been a few days since she'd seen the good sheriff.

For years she'd been trying to get him to realize he couldn't live without her. True, there'd been moments when he'd weakened and kissed her. But he'd always taken off like a shot, holding fast to his conviction that he wasn't good marriage material and that the two of them together would be murder.

That is, until recently. A few weeks ago, after she'd almost been killed, Mitch had asked her out. On a real date. It had been nothing short of miraculous. Same with the date. And there'd been more kissing. He'd even given her a silver bracelet she'd once admired. The entire episode had bowled her over completely. Maybe there was hope after all.

Unfortunately, she could tell that he was still fighting the inevitable as if he thought there was some doubt that they'd be getting married. Obviously, he didn't believe, like Charity did, that love conquered all.

"You're working late," he said, coming around to pull up a chair next to her desk. His gaze went to the open drawer and her gun. With a groan, he reached over to close the drawer. "Tell me it isn't loaded."

"What would be the point of an unloaded gun?" she asked, wondering why he'd stopped by.

"Try not to shoot yourself, okay?"

She grinned at him. Just the sight of him made her day. Maybe he was here to ask her to that dance at the community center this coming weekend. Or maybe he'd just come by for a kiss. Her lips tingled expectantly at the thought.

But that hope was quickly dashed when he pushed back his sheriff's hat and put on his official business face.

He cleared his throat and said, "You're going to hear about this anyway so I thought the best thing to do—"

"What is it?" she asked, sitting up a little straighter. He'd come to tell her something he didn't want to tell her. This ought to be good. Almost as good as a kiss. Almost.

"You were right," he said, the words clearly difficult for him.

She sat back. Oh yeah, this day just couldn't get any better. "I'm sorry. I don't think I heard you correctly?"

"You heard me. You were right. The shot that killed Bud Farnsworth didn't come from Daisy Dennison's gun. It came from Wade's."

Charity jerked back in her chair, the ramifications of his words nearly flooring her. "I knew it. I told you Wade Dennison was in on the kidnapping!"

Wade Dennison was the owner of Dennison Ducks, the local decoy factory outside of town and the largest employer in Timber Falls. Wade had shocked the town by bringing home a much younger wife thirty years ago.

They had a daughter right away, Desiree. Then two years later another one, Angela. Several weeks after Angela's birth the baby disappeared from her crib never to be seen again. There'd been rumors that the baby wasn't Wade's.

No ransom demand was ever made. No body ever found. Daisy Dennison, who'd been the talk of the town, became a recluse after her youngest daughter's disappearance. That is until Halloween, when she'd showed up with a gun at the Dennison Ducks factory and helped save Charity's life when the decoy foreman had tried to kill them both.

Bud Farnsworth had abducted Charity to retrieve a letter that implicated him in Angela Dennison's disappearance. A Dennison Ducks employee named Nina Monroe had mailed the letter to the *Timber Falls Courier,* Charity's newspaper, right before she was killed. Nina had more than a few secrets, it turned out, and a flair for blackmail.

Bud destroyed the letter before anyone could read it—including Charity much to her regret—but there was no doubt now that he was somehow involved in kidnapping the baby.

The only question that had remained was: Did he act alone?

Charity was sure he didn't. In fact, she was damned sure that Wade Dennison had hired Bud to get rid of the baby because he believed Angela wasn't his. Just before Bud died, he'd tried to talk and he'd been looking right at Wade at the time.

Charity was convinced that Wade had shot Bud to

shut him up, and now that she knew Wade had fired the fatal shot that killed Bud—and not his wife, Daisy— Charity was even more convinced of Wade's guilt.

"Wade *was* behind the kidnapping," Charity said.

"This is exactly why I wanted to tell you about this myself."

She rolled her eyes. "You told me because you knew I was going to find out." And here she'd been hoping he'd come by just to see her.

"Maybe I thought I could keep you from doing a story that might get you killed."

"You romantic, you."

"I'm serious, Charity. I'm worried about you and what you're going to do next."

"Mitch, I saw Bud try to say something to Wade right before he died," Charity said, feeling a chill at the memory. "He was going to incriminate Wade. That's why Wade shot him, so the truth would never come out."

"We don't know that for a fact and speculating only leads to trouble. Especially in print. I would have thought you'd have learned that by now."

She smiled. This was an old argument between them. "I'm a newspaper woman. It's my job to get to the truth, and sometimes I have to rattle a few cages to do that and you wouldn't be worried unless you thought I was right about Wade Dennison being a dangerous man."

Mitch took off his hat and raked his fingers through his hair. "Is there any way I can talk you out of this?"

She cocked her head at him. "What did you have in mind?" And to think not long ago she'd thought, if she could just write a Pulitzer Prize-winning story, Mitch would finally realize he couldn't live without her and ask her to marry him.

Instead, she'd realized that Mitch would have been happier if she wasn't a journalist at all. For some reason, he worried about her safety. Maybe because a lot of her stories got her into trouble.

He put his hat back on—and his official face.

She could play that game, too. "Have you talked to Wade?" she asked, knowing there was no way Wade was going to speak to her on the record or off.

"He admits he could have fired the fatal shot but says all he could think about was saving his wife, Daisy. That's the official statement." Mitch reached in to his coat and brought out a folded sheet of paper. He handed it to her.

"I figured that would be his story," she said, unfolding the paper to see that it was an official statement from the sheriff's office. She tossed it aside. "I'll be careful what I print, but Mitch, what if I'm right?"

His dark eyes settled on her. "If you're right, then Wade Dennison is a killer. You might want to keep that in mind."

"But how do we prove it?" she cried. "We can't let him get away with murder."

"*We* aren't going to prove it," he said getting to his feet. "I am. I have no intention of letting him get away with murder—if he's guilty. But Charity, as hard as this is for you, you might be wrong this time."

She smirked at that. "You know I'm right ninety-nine percent of the time."

He shook his head but seemed unable not to smile down at her. "You *are* something."

A person could take that a number of ways.

"Try to accept the fact that we may never know what happened to Angela Dennison," he said after a moment.

She couldn't stand the thought. "There has to be a way."

Mitch was shaking his head. "Charity, getting involved last time almost cost you your life."

True. But it had also made Mitch realize that he cared for her. She wisely didn't point this out to him though.

He stood looking down at her as if there was more he wanted to say. She waited for him to ask her to the dance. Or maybe to a late dinner. It had been almost a week since he'd kissed her.

"Just be careful, okay?" he said quietly.

She smiled up at him. "You know me."

"Yeah, that's what worries me." He turned to leave. "See you later." She hoped so as she watched him go, her lips feeling neglected.

She got up and locked the front door as he drove away. Then she turned back to her computer. She had a story to write.

The phone rang. She picked it up, already knowing who it would be.

"I got that ballistics report you wanted," said her source on the other end of the line. "Are you sitting down?"

She sat, even though she already knew the results.

"Wade Dennison's gun killed Bud Farnsworth."

"You're the best, Tommy." A thought had been percolating ever since Mitch left. If she was right and Wade Dennison had hired Bud Farnsworth to do his dirty work, then there would be a money trail. "Tommy, I have another little favor."

"Little?" he cried when he heard what she wanted. "Do you realize how many years in prison I could get for hacking in to bank records?"

"More years than hacking in to the state investigation's office for a ballistics report?" she asked innocently.

He laughed. "What's the name on the account?"

"Two accounts. Wade Dennison and Bud Farnsworth. And I'm interested in old records—say twenty-seven years ago? Let me give you the dates."

Tommy let out a low whistle when she'd finished. "I hope you know what you're doing."

"Are you kidding?" She hung up and typed Wade Dennison Fired Fatal Bullet To Silence Kidnapper or Save Wife? Angela Dennison Kidnapping Still A Mystery and stopped, reminding herself that Wade had threatened her life not that long ago. True, he did it in front of the sheriff—and she hadn't taken it all that seriously. But now...now she wasn't so sure she didn't have something to fear.

Not that it would stop her from doing the story. Or doing a little checking into both Dennison's and Farnsworth's bank accounts. After all, she was a journalist whether Mitch liked it or not and she came from a family of the best gossips in four counties. She hated not knowing what was really going on. There had to be a way to get to the truth.

The problem was Wade might be the only one left alive who knew the truth about Angela Dennison's kidnapping. Maybe it was possible to make Wade angry enough to do something that would get him caught.

She began to type again, telling herself that Mitch wasn't going to be happy about this. Nothing new about that. Too bad, though, that he hadn't kissed her. She feared that by tomorrow morning when the paper came out, kissing her would be the furthest thing from his mind.

The roar of the waterfall drowned out Roz's scream as she tried to fight off the strong arms that grabbed her from behind.

Frantic, she struggled to regain her balance, to free herself of his hold. As she lost her footing on the wet moss-slick boulder, she felt the earth tilt and all she could see was the dizzying darkness of the water below as she slipped and started to fall toward the gorge.

The arms around her loosened as if he realized he was going to pitch over the waterfall with her if he didn't let go with one arm and try to grab something to save himself.

She drove her elbow into his ribs and heard him let out an oath, but he held on and suddenly she was jerked backward. He took her down with him, both of them hitting hard as they fell under the wide base of a pine tree a few feet from the edge of the falls.

"Stay away from me," she cried, scooting back from him as her hands searched for something to defend herself with. Her fingers closed around a chunk of wet wood. She held it up, brandishing the wood like a club, as she struggled to get her feet under her.

It was dark under the tree. Not even the light from her SUV's headlamps could reach it. But she could see that he was large as he also rose to his feet. His face was in a shadow, his features a blur, but his eyes— The irises were so pale they seemed almost iridescent in the dim light.

He advanced on her, his hands out as if in surrender, but she knew he was just looking for another opening to lunge for her again.

"You come near me and I'll hit you," she yelled over the roar of the waterfall as she backed up as far as she could. "I'm warning you."

"Fine," he said and stopped. "Go ahead, jump. I don't care. My mistake for trying to save you from yourself."

She blinked at him through the mist and rain. "Save me from myself? I wasn't going to *jump*."

"Right. Whatever. Go ahead. Have at it. Believe me, I won't try to stop you again." He crossed his arms over his chest. She noticed for the first time that, like her, he wasn't wearing a coat. His shirt and slacks were soaked. Just as hers were.

"You weren't trying to push me off the waterfall?"

He glared at her. "Are you crazy? What am I saying? Of course you're crazy or you wouldn't be up here in the middle of a damned rainstorm trying to commit suicide. And this is the thanks I get for attempting to save your life."

"Thanks? You almost killed us both," she snapped. "And I told you, I wasn't trying to kill myself." She shuddered at the thought.

"Uh-huh. You just wanted to get a good look at the waterfall." He started to turn away. "Well, have a good look. I won't bother you anymore."

"I saw someone jump."

He stopped and turned slowly. "What?"

"I saw someone in a yellow raincoat jump." She glanced off to the side toward the waterfall, sick with the memory. "That's why I rushed over here."

"You saw someone?"

Could his tone be any more mocking?

"I think it was a woman." Had she caught a glimpse of long blond hair just before the figure disappeared over the top of the falls? "I saw her—" her voice broke "—lean forward and drop over the edge. When I got to the top of the falls, the yellow raincoat she was wearing was in the water below."

"Uh-huh," he said and looked around. "And this woman who jumped, where is her car?"

"Right over—"

"That's my truck. But you ought to know that. You've been following me for the past twenty miles."

She looked past her own car, the engine still running, the interior light on since she'd left her door open in her haste. The headlights sliced a narrow swath of pale gold through the pouring rain and darkness. There were no other vehicles. Just hers. And his. Nor had she seen any other cars on the highway tonight.

"How did this mysterious jumper get out here?" he asked.

She shook her head, confused. The waterfall was too far from anything for anyone to have walked. Especially this time of year in a rainstorm.

"You and I are the only ones out here," he said.

She opened her mouth, then closed it. She'd seen someone in a bright yellow raincoat, seen the person jump, seen the coat in the water below the falls.

Even back here under the shelter of the large old pine, she could still feel that falling sensation, the roaring in her ears, the warm spray on her face, feel the watery grave far, far below as her feet slipped on the mossy rock.

"You had to have seen her," Roz said, trembling hard now but not from the cold.

"All I saw was you in my side mirror as I started to leave. I saw you throw on your brakes, bolt from your car and run to the edge of the waterfall."

He'd been watching *her*? That's why he hadn't seen the person in the yellow raincoat. So he'd just been trying to save her? "If I was wrong about your intentions—"

He waved off her apology. "Forget it."

"We have to call the sheriff." Even as she said it, she knew no one could have survived that fall into the rocks and water below. It would just be a matter of recovering the body.

"You have a cell phone that works up here?" he asked. "I tried mine when I stopped. No service."

She shook her head. Of course there wouldn't be any service up here. "I'll call the sheriff when I get closer to Timber Falls."

"You sure you want to do that?"

She rubbed a hand over her wet face, still holding the chunk of wood in the other. She was exhausted, emotionally drained. She leveled her gaze at him. "I *did* see someone jump." She didn't know where the person had come from but she knew what she'd seen.

He shrugged. "Whatever you say."

She hated his scornful tone. Had he really been trying to save her? Or kill her? If he'd just left her alone, she would have been perfectly fine. She was pretty sure that was true. He was making her doubt everything.

"I have family in Timber Falls," she said, and hated herself for trying to reassure him that she was the sane one here. "I'm on my way there."

"If your family lives in Timber Falls, I'd think you would know the road."

"I wasn't paying attention. I was following *you*. And I haven't been up here in years." She wouldn't be here at all if she wasn't worried about her father. When she'd left ten years before, she'd thought nothing could ever get her back to Timber Falls. And nothing had, not even when her father had remarried, moved back and reopened her childhood home. Until now. "I came up here tonight because—"

"Thanks, but I'd prefer not to know any more about you," he said.

"Are you always this disagreeable?" she snapped.

"Actually, I'm trying to be on my best behavior right now."

"Really?"

"Really," he said, wringing the water from his shirt-tail. "You should see me when I'm not."

"No, thanks."

"Did I mention that I'm late for a dinner engagement?"

"Then please don't let me keep you," she said.

He started backing away from her. "And please don't thank me for saving your life. Really."

"No problem. I hadn't wanted to jump but now that I've met you I might change my mind."

His laugh held little humor as he turned his back on her and stalked through the rain toward the parking lot and his pickup.

She headed for her car, still gripping the chunk of wood just in case he was a psycho killer and planned to double back. He didn't. He went straight to his pickup, climbed in and a moment later the engine turned over and the headlights came on. He drove away without looking back as far as she could tell.

Her driver's-side seat was soaked and so was she. Not that she wasn't already chilled to the bone from everything that had happened.

She locked her car door, feeling scared and not sure why as she kicked up the heat. There was no other vehicle. Maybe the person who'd jumped from the waterfall had hidden her car somewhere. But why do that?

As Roz pulled out of the parking lot, tears stung her eyes. She hadn't imagined the person in the yellow raincoat. And history was not repeating itself.

Chapter 2

Rain pounded the windshield, the wipers making a steady *whap-whap* as Roz drove the narrow road back out to the main highway. She didn't see the pickup's taillights. He obviously didn't want her following him anymore and had sped off to avoid any further contact. Fine with her.

Stopping at the intersection, she looked through the rain for the detour sign she vaguely remembered seeing earlier.

It was gone.

Had he picked it up? He hadn't seen the person in the yellow raincoat. Was it possible he hadn't seen the detour sign, either? She shook off the thought. Why had he turned down the road to the waterfall then?

She hit the gas, even more anxious to get to Timber Falls. The night seemed too dark, too rainy, too isolated. She couldn't wait to see the lights of town, to get to the house, to see that her father had returned so that all her worry had been for nothing.

The rainforest grew in a dark, wet canopy over the top of the narrow, winding highway. Rain splattered down through the vegetation, striking the windshield like pebbles as mist rose ghostlike up from the pavement.

A few miles down the highway, the trees opened a little, and she dug out her cell phone, saw that she had service and called 9-1-1. She related briefly what she'd seen at Lost Creek Falls to the dispatcher and left her cell phone number for the sheriff to call her back.

When the lights of Timber Falls appeared out of the rain and mist, Roz felt such a surge of relief she almost wept. Home—the feeling surprised her given why she'd left here. This hadn't been home for ten years. Nor would it ever be again. But right now, she was overjoyed to finally be here, the one place she'd once felt safe and happy.

She drove down Main Street past the city offices, the Duck Inn bar, the *Timber Falls Courier* and the Busy Bee. The No Vacancy sign glowed red at the Ho Hum Motel and Betty's Café was packed, a half dozen cars parked out front. That was odd. She frowned, wondering why everything was so busy given the time of year—and the weather. Something must be going on.

As she turned down the once familiar tree-lined lane, she felt as if time had stood still here as well. Anxiously she awaited her first glimpse of the large old house where she'd been raised.

She'd never understood why her father had hung on to the house given the painful memories. He alone had come here over the years, paying to see that the empty house didn't fall into disrepair.

But as the structure came into view in her headlights, she was overwhelmed with emotion and thankful that he hadn't been able to part with it. The house stood fighting back the rainforest, the towering roofline etched black against the night sky. She caught her breath at the sight of it. As a child she thought it a castle. Even now it seemed larger than life.

This had been home for her first seventeen years. It had been a fun, rambling place with lots of space to play and great hiding places. Her mother always had flowers growing in large pots on the porch and brightly colored curtains at the windows.

But Roz saw that the pots of flowers were gone— just as the brightly colored curtains were, just as her mother was.

Roz looked away, fighting the same sorrow she had for the past ten years, and hoped to see her father's truck and camper parked next to the other cars in the open carport beside the house.

There were three cars. The new Cadillac her father had bought Emily as a wedding present and two new sports cars, a bright yellow one and a shiny black one. The yellow one belonged to Emily's twenty-four-year-old daughter, Suzanne, the black one to her twenty-six-year-old son, Drew.

Roz felt a sliver of apprehension to see that the whole family was here. Her father obviously hadn't returned. Was that what had brought Suzanne and Drew all the way in from Portland? Had something happened since Roz had talked to Emily?

Even more worried, Roz parked in front of the house

and made a run through the rain to the porch. She stood
waiting for her father's new family to answer the bell.
It felt so strange not to be able to just open the door
and walk in. But the people who lived here now were
virtual strangers. She'd only been around the new family on a few awkward occasions. Even her father had
become a stranger the last six months since his quickie
marriage in Las Vegas.

"Give Emily a chance," her dad had asked after
the wedding. "I know this happened pretty fast." She
should say so! "But please try. For me."

And she was trying. Really.

She rang the bell and managed a smile, relieved to
see the door opened by her newly acquired stepbrother
Drew, the least objectionable member of her father's
new family.

"Hey, you made it. I was starting to worry about
you," he said, flashing her a big smile. Drew was blond,
blue-eyed and drop-dead handsome if you went for that
type. Roz didn't. She found his classically featured face
devoid of character with no sign that he'd experienced
life, although he was only two years her junior.

Drew's saving grace was the fact that he was the
only member of his family who seemed to care one
way or another about her. His interest in her definitely
wasn't romantic. Roz suspected he paid attention to her
because it annoyed his mother.

He hugged Roz, then stepped back in surprise.
"You're freezing." He ushered her inside out of the
cold and dampness. "What happened?"

She knew she must look like a drowned cocker span-
iel, her strawberry-blond hair a tousle of damp curls.

"I had a…flat." She really didn't want to get into her "detour" or what she'd seen at the waterfall.

"Has anyone heard from my father?" she asked as she stepped in.

Drew shook his head. "Sorry."

She glanced past him, trying hard not to cry. She hadn't realized how scared she was, how worried that something had happened to him. If only she hadn't missed his call the other day.

What little of the house she could see had changed more than she could have imagined. When Roz's mother, Anna, had been alive, the house had smelled of baked bread and brownies. This house smelled of cleaner, new carpet and fresh paint.

Her father had warned her a few months ago that Emily was doing a little redecorating, but it still came as a shock to see everything of her mother gone. Through the French doors, she could see the living room. All of the beautiful old things her mother had collected had been replaced with new, modern furniture.

That wasn't the only shock. While Roz's mother, Anna, had loved vibrant colors, it seemed Emily was partial to indistinguishable shades of off-white. The furnishings didn't fit the house any more than Emily did, she thought uncharitably.

"Don't worry, all of your mother's things have been moved up to the attic," Drew said, following her gaze. "Your father insisted everything be saved."

The attic. How appropriate.

Emily came breezing out of the dining room looking harried. "Rozalyn," the woman gushed, rushing over to give her a quick air kiss.

Emily Lane Sawyer was blond with blue eyes like her two grown children. She was a tall, statuesque woman, far different from Roz's mother, who'd been petite with soft brown eyes and strawberry-blond hair that curled in the humidity just like her daughter's. Everyone had always said Roz was the spitting image of her mother, something that Emily had remarked on more than one occasion.

In her late forties, Emily was a good fifteen years younger than her new husband. Intellectually, Roz could understand what her father had seen in the woman. She had a great body for her age and she was quite attractive.

What worried Roz was what Emily had seen in Liam Sawyer.

"You made it in time for dinner," Emily said.

Roz heard the "just barely" in her tone. Dinner was the last thing Roz wanted but it would be rude to try to get out of dining with the family. "Drew says you haven't heard from my father." She couldn't bring herself to call him dad with these people.

"No, but like I told you on the phone, Liam said he didn't know when he'd be back and not to worry about him. I hope that isn't the only reason you drove all the way up here."

What other reason than to see her father? "It isn't like him to be gone this long without any word," Roz said, not mentioning the other reason she was so concerned. The strange message on her answering machine. He'd sounded upset, said little, asking her to call as soon as possible.

That had been two days ago. Emily said she hadn't heard from Liam for more than two weeks.

Also he'd left his cell phone number. Not the number at the house. And when Roz had tried to reach him she'd gotten the message that the phone was either out of the calling area or turned off.

He'd said it was important but it had been his tone that scared her. Something had happened, and it had to be something big for her father, the most laid-back man alive, to sound that upset.

And yet no one in this family seemed even concerned about him. Why was that? Because they didn't want her to know that something had happened before he'd left on his latest camping trip. And Roz was certain it had something to do with Emily.

"He's always checked in after a few days," Roz said now. "It's hard to believe you haven't heard from him."

"Well, you know him better than I do," Emily said distractedly. "I have to admit, I don't understand his need to go off into the mountains like he does at his age."

"He loves the Cascades. I'm sure that's one reason he moved back here with you." Actually, it was a mystery why her dad had done something that ridiculous, bringing this woman to Timber Falls. Roz figured there was a lot about Liam that a woman like Emily wouldn't be able to understand. Could her father have picked a woman any more different from him?

"Drew, would you see what is keeping your sister?" Emily said, glancing past Roz. "Our dinner guest will be arriving soon."

Dinner guest? Roz knew her shock must have shown. Emily wasn't letting any concern over Liam keep her from entertaining, it seemed.

Drew buzzed his sister on the intercom near the front door. "No answer," he said to his mother.

"Has anyone looked for my father?" Roz asked.

Emily seemed surprised by the question. "We wouldn't even know where to look. It would be like searching for a needle in a haystack." She glanced at her watch, obviously more worried about her dinner than her husband, then up at Roz again. "You said yourself he's always done this, gone off alone, no matter the weather, taking his camera and camper back into the mountains, out searching for Bigfoot like everyone else in this town right now. I can't see this time is any different except this time there was an actual sighting."

"There's been a sighting?" That explained the large number of people in town this time of year.

"Two weeks ago. I thought you would have heard," Emily said. "Some fool bread man claimed he saw Bigfoot just outside of town and your father took off like a shot."

Was it possible her father was on the trail of Bigfoot and that's why he hadn't come back? Why he'd sounded the way he had on the phone message? Except he hadn't sounded excited. He'd sounded…upset, almost scared. And he'd been gone way too long.

"I'm afraid he's hurt, trapped somewhere, unable to get out for help," Roz said. "I think we should contact the sheriff."

Emily touched her temple and winced as if she suddenly had a headache. "He's *your* father. Whatever you think is best. I just feel it's a little premature to be calling in the sheriff."

"I don't," Roz said.

Emily sighed. "Drew, darling, would you get my

medicine. It's in my purse." She looked past Roz and groaned. "Oh, where is he off to now? He's never around when I need him." She rubbed her temples. "I must see to dinner. By the way, a friend of your father's is joining us. I thought you'd like that."

Roz felt a stab of guilt for her earlier uncharitable thoughts about Emily. "That was very kind of you. Maybe he'll have some idea where my father has gone."

Emily checked her watch again.

"Emily, why do I feel as if there is something you aren't telling me?"

The older woman blinked blank blue eyes at her.

"Did you and Dad have a fight before he left?"

"Of course not." Emily brought herself up to her full height. "I really need to see to my dinner."

Roz sighed. She could hear at least two of her staff in the kitchen doing the actual cooking. It was obvious Emily just wanted to get away. But Roz was sorry she'd brought up the subject now. "So who is this friend of my father's who's coming to dinner?"

"It's a surprise. You really should get into some dry clothing before you catch your death. You can have a drink before dinner with Suzanne."

Roz would rather catch her death than have a drink with Drew's sister who was probably half-sloshed by now.

As Emily headed toward the kitchen, Roz heard the front door open behind her and turned to find Drew standing in the foyer. He had her suitcase in one hand, her camera bag in the other. She hadn't heard him leave.

"It finally stopped raining but I've heard there's an-other storm on the way. I brought your things in," he said, studying her openly as if concerned about her conversation with his mother.

"Thank you." She appreciated his thoughtfulness more than he could know.

"Where's Mother?" he asked.

"She's seeing to dinner. She said she invited a friend of my father's to join us." Drew seemed surprised. "I'm hoping he might know where my father went. I know your mother isn't concerned—"

"Mother hides her feelings," he said as he started for the stairs. "She was just telling me earlier that she wished Liam had shown up before your visit. She's much more worried than she's letting on."

Sure she was.

When Roz didn't comment, he said in an obvious attempt to change the subject, "Planning to do some shooting while you're here?"

"I never go anywhere without my camera."

"You must have gotten that from your dad," Drew said. "Except he says for him it's just a hobby and he could never be as good as you. Your photographs really are amazing. I saw your latest book. It's your best yet."

"Thank you." She was surprised he even knew she had a new photography book out but if he was trying to flatter her, he was succeeding quite well.

"Mother had the maid get your old room ready," he said over his shoulder.

She barely heard him. "Were you here when my father left?" she asked, still convinced Emily wasn't telling her something. Something important.

"I guess I was."

Was it just her imagination that his back stiffened at her question? Her dad had told her that Drew had moved in after getting a new job so he could work from Timber Falls via computer and help his mother with the house remodeling.

"Did my father seem…upset? Or act differently?"

"Not that I noticed." He reached the second floor landing and continued on up to the third floor without turning to look back at her.

Roz stared after him, more convinced than ever that something had happened before her father's departure. Something Drew and his mother were keeping from her.

As Roz passed the second floor, she heard a voice she recognized. Drew's sister, Suzanne, had a distinct whine that was easily recognizable even from a distance. She must be on the phone. Roz wondered why Suzanne hadn't answered the intercom when Drew had buzzed her.

As Roz hurried up the stairs after Drew, she couldn't help but remember the happy times in this house. She and her best friend, Charity, used to pretend that each room was a separate house in town where they lived happily ever after with their husbands and children and neighbors. She smiled ruefully at the memory of this house ringing with their laughter. She and Charity had both thought that one day their own children would race along these worn wooden floors as they had done.

She pushed the thought away as she and Drew reached the third floor.

"Mother hasn't gotten this far yet in her remodel," Drew said.

Roz swallowed hard as she looked down the hallway. This floor looked exactly as it had ten years ago. Her room had always been on the third floor just down from her mother's sewing room and her father's studio and darkroom. When she was young, they would put her to bed, then her mother would sew, her father would work in his darkroom. They had wanted her close by.

Her parents' bedroom had been on the second floor along with several guest rooms. Her mother had installed an intercom so she could always be within earshot of her daughter.

It was crazy, but for a moment, Roz thought she heard her mother's favorite song playing on the old phonograph in the sewing room. If she listened hard, she thought she would hear her father whistling a little off key in his darkroom down the hall. But hadn't he told her that Emily was doing away with the darkroom because she'd purchased him a digital camera?

Drew stopped in front of Roz's former bedroom door and waited for her. "Don't look so worried. Your room is exactly as you left it. Liam insisted."

Her feet felt like leaded weights as she walked down the hall to slowly turn the knob.

As the door swung open, Roz caught a glimpse of the whimsical quilt her mother had spent months stitching in secret for her thirteenth birthday. It was still on the bed, just where she'd left it. Albert, the stuffed teddy bear she'd loved threadbare, sat in the corner still wearing the tuxedo her mother had made for the tea parties she and Charity always had at the brightly painted table and chairs. On the table was the little tin tray her mother served the tiny chocolate chip cookies she'd made for them.

Roz swallowed, fighting the stinging tears that burned her eyes and choked off her throat. Drew was right. Her room was exactly as she'd left it ten years ago after her mother's death. Everywhere she looked in this room she saw her mother.

"Roz, are you all right?"

The room magnified her loss. Forcing her back to those horrible days after her mother's death. She couldn't face the loss any more now than she could at seventeen.

"Roz?"

"I'm fine," she said, realizing it wasn't near the truth. She could feel Drew's gaze on her. She glanced over at him, ready to reassure him. What she saw in his expression stopped her.

"Hey, maybe you'd better sit down," he said, putting down her suitcase and camera bag to take her arm and lead her over to the wicker chair by the window.

Had she only imagined that he'd seemed to be enjoying her discomfort at seeing this room? He looked and sounded concerned *now.* She told herself she was tired. Imagining things. Like she'd imagined someone in a yellow raincoat leaping into Lost Creek Falls?

"I'm fine. Really," she said to Drew, watching him for some sign of the expression she'd thought she'd seen only moments before. "I just need to get out of these damp clothes."

He backed toward the door, still studying her openly. "I know how hard this must be for you. Come on down soon for a drink before dinner. You look like you could use one."

She nodded and tried to smile.

"Mother went all out on dinner tonight."

"Do you know who the guest is?" she asked, getting to her feet to see Drew out. She needed some time alone. Pretending she was all right was exhausting.

"It's a surprise." He shrugged as if to say, "You know Mother."

Except she didn't know Emily. She suspected though that the woman was big on surprises. She'd certainly surprised Roz by somehow getting Liam to marry her.

"Buzz me on the intercom if you need *anything*. Two buzzes, okay?"

She nodded. "Thanks." Closing the door behind him, she turned to look at the room again, fighting tears of grief and worry and anger. How could her father bring his new wife back to this house? This house so filled with memories of Roz's mother? The room seemed to echo all the unanswered questions Roz had been asking herself for the past ten years.

First her mother and now there was the chance that her father—

She brushed at her tears, refusing to let herself even think that she might lose him, too. Cold, her clothing still damp, she went to the large antique bureau. In the third drawer she found what she'd been looking for. The thick rust-colored sweater her mother had knitted for her. It was the last thing her mother had made her. The sweater still fit.

She pulled on a pair of jeans from her suitcase and hiking boots, needing to get out of the house for a few minutes. She took the back stairs, exiting through a door that opened into her mother's garden.

The night felt cold and damp but for the moment the rain had stopped. Only the faint tingle of electricity in the air foretold of an approaching storm. She took a deep breath and let it out slowly as she started down the stone path to the rear of the property.

Like the house, her father had seen that the garden

had been maintained. But in this part of the country, it was a constant battle to hold back the rainforest and no one had a way with plants like Anna Sawyer had. Roz could see where there had been recent digging. Emily must have hired someone to redo the garden as well as the house.

Roz walked down the winding overgrown path as far as the rock arch where a tangle of vines and tree limbs had left only a narrow opening. Quiet settled over her as she stood in the shadowed darkness. From here she could barely see the house through the trees and vines.

She no longer felt like crying, which was good. She needed to be strong now—for her father. She felt like she was the only person here who was worried about him.

"What does that tell you?" she asked the night as she looked back at the house. "I can't understand how you could have gotten involved with someone like her." A younger, good-looking woman? "Okay, maybe I can understand the attraction—at first. You were lonely." The thought broke her heart. "Of course you were lonely. But something happened, didn't it?" She knew her father. He wouldn't just stay away like this. He'd called her the night before last and hadn't tried to get back to her. "What happened? What was it you needed to talk to me about?"

A breeze stirred the tops of the trees in a low moan. She took another deep breath and looked up at the night sky as if it held all the answers. Clouds skimmed over the faint glitter of distant stars. No moon. She tried to fight back her growing panic. Her every instinct told her that her father needed her, and it was imperative that she find him. Was it too much to hope that this mystery dinner guest and friend of her father's might know something?

Mist rose from the wet ground around her. She hugged herself against the dampness, not ready to go back inside. Not yet. She took another deep breath, the air scented with cedar and rainwater and damp fertile earth, and so wonderfully familiar except for—

She took another sniff. A chill skittered across her bare arms. Her heart began to knock as she picked up a scent that didn't belong on the night breeze—and, eyes adjusting to the darkness, she saw a large, still shape that didn't belong in the garden.

Someone was hiding just inches from her on the other side of the rock arch.

Chapter 3

"Wait!" Ford reached for her, hoping to stop her before she panicked and did something crazy. Like scream bloody murder. Too late. She got out one startled cry as she stumbled back from him, then she let out a bloodcurdling shriek that he knew could be heard in three counties.

He cursed himself for not warning her he was out here. At first he hadn't wanted to scare her. Once he recognized her voice, he wasn't about to open his mouth. What the hell was she doing here, anyway?

He caught her arm and spun her around, figuring once she recognized him she'd at least quit screaming. But her eyes were squeezed tightly shut, her mouth open, a shriek coming out.

Behind them, twenty yards away through the trees, the back porch light blinked on. Any moment the lady of the house would be calling the sheriff and—

He did the first thing that came to mind short of throttling the woman. When she took a breath, he kissed her, covering any future screams as his mouth dropped to hers. She gasped in surprise, eyes fluttering open for an instant, then shuttering closed again.

She had a great mouth, and for a few seconds, he got lost in her lush lips, in the warmth of her breath mingling with his, in the taste of her.

For those few seconds, he forgot whom he was kissing. He loosened his hold on her as the kiss deepened.

The right hook came out of nowhere. He managed to duck that one. But he hadn't been expecting the kick. Her boot connected with his shin.

"Damn." *He* should have been the one screaming.

She turned to run, mouth open, ready to let out another shriek. He grabbed her around the waist, dragged her back to his chest and clamped a hand over her mouth.

They were both breathing hard now, hidden in the dark shadows of the trees out of sight of whoever was now on the porch calling, "Rozalyn?"

"Listen," he whispered next to her ear. "I didn't mean to scare you."

She tried to slug him again in answer.

"I'm just trying to get to dinner, dammit," he whispered in exasperation.

The instant his words registered, Roz stopped struggling and groaned. She could hear Emily calling her name, and saw through the tree limbs the dim glow of the porch light in the distance. This man in the dark was no crazed killer hiding in the backyard. Just the dinner guest. She kicked herself mentally and wished the ground would open up and swallow her whole.

He slowly removed his hand from her mouth, obviously afraid she'd scream again. Behind her, she heard him clear his throat and step back almost as if he were afraid she'd kick him again.

She turned, an apology on the tip of her tongue. It never made it to her lips as she got her first good look at him.

"You?!" she whispered in horror. His face was bathed in the mottled pattern of light coming through the trees from the porch lamp. Her first impression earlier at the waterfall had been true. He was tall, broad-shouldered and dark except for his eyes, which were an eerie, pale blue-green.

He wasn't even handsome. His expression was too severe, brows pinched together, full mouth a grim line between the rough stubble of his designer beard. But he was definitely the man who'd almost killed her at Lost Creek Falls. "You *can't* be the dinner guest."

"Emily *invited* me," he said, obviously also trying to keep his voice down. "Anyway, why can't I?"

"Because you were sneaking in the back way!" she hissed.

"I'm *staying* in the guesthouse. What other way should I be coming from for dinner?" he whispered back.

"You're staying in the guesthouse?"

"Emily was kind enough to offer it."

"Emily is *so* thoughtful." Roz couldn't believe her stepmother would let a perfect stranger stay in the guesthouse. But this man wasn't a perfect stranger—not to her father and maybe not to Emily.

She could not believe her father would befriend such an obnoxious man. "So when was the last time you saw Liam?" she asked.

"It's been a while. Any chance we could discuss this after dinner? I'm hungry."

"Rozalyn!" Emily called again. "Is that you out there?" She sounded as if she were straining to see into the trees and darkness.

"Answer her," he whispered. "I would, but then she'd think I was the one who was screaming."

"Rozalyn?" Emily's tone had an almost hysterical edge to it.

He gave Roz a pleading look.

She groaned. "Yes, it's me," she called back through the trees and the distance between her and the house.

"Well, why in heaven's name were you screaming?" Emily yelled.

Roz sighed. "There was a big disgusting rat by the stone arch."

"Cute," he whispered.

"Ohhhhhhhh," Emily cried. "Rats? Oh! Please come in. Our guest will be arriving any moment now for dinner. I don't want you scaring him out of his wits."

"Too late for that," he muttered under his breath and narrowed his gaze at her. "You're having dinner, too, I take it?" He didn't sound any happier about that than she was. "So, this must be the family you said you had here."

"This is *not* my family," she snapped.

"Whatever." He glanced toward the house. "But don't you think we should go in to dinner? Emily is going to wonder what's keeping me if not you."

Let her wonder, Roz thought. "Why didn't you say

something to let me know you were by the arch?" What had he overheard? She hated to think.

"I didn't want to interrupt the conversation you were having with yourself. I thought you might lose your train of thought."

Funny.

"Rozalyn, who are you talking to out there?" Emily called.

"And the kiss?" Roz whispered, ignoring Emily. "What was *that* about?"

"*Nothing.* Absolutely nothing. I just wanted to shut you up before you got the whole household out here."

Flatterer. She fought the urge to kick him again.

"Are you finished interrogating me?" he asked quietly. "I'm going in even if you aren't." He stepped past her.

She let him lead the way to the house, not trusting him behind her anyway. While she could think of nothing she wanted to do less than to have dinner with this man, she didn't feel like hiding in the garden all night. And now she was curious as to how Emily knew this man well enough to invite him to stay in the guesthouse. Especially with her husband gone. Especially since this man was closer to Emily's age than Liam was. Especially since Emily would find him attractive, Roz would just bet on that.

If he was telling the truth and he really was a friend of her father's, she was dying to know how they'd met and what they could possibly have in common.

As she followed him along the winding path through the thick vegetation, she realized she didn't even know his name. Not that she really cared. She'd already found out one important thing about the man: he lied. The kiss was hardly *nothing*.

If he'd lie about a kiss… Who knew what else he'd lied about? And how much of a coincidence was it that the two of them had met at Lost Creek Falls earlier tonight under very strange circumstances only to have him turn up here?

Ford couldn't believe his bad luck. Running into the woman not once tonight but twice. Worse, it seemed Emily had invited her to dinner. He swore under his breath as he neared the house. Why hadn't this Rozalyn gone to her own family for dinner? Whoever she was, she was obviously nuts even if she really hadn't been trying to leap off the waterfall earlier.

She was a looker, too. That wild head of strawberry-blond curls, those big brown eyes and that obviously nicely put together body. Why were the great-looking ones the most cuckoo? And this one was unpredictable to boot.

A deadly combination.

He shook his head at his misfortune. But he could get through one dinner with this bunch. After all, he didn't have much choice if he hoped to accomplish what he'd come here for.

"Rozalyn?" Emily called again.

"We were just coming in," she answered behind him, adding an irritated sigh.

"We?" Emily inquired as he and Rozalyn came into view. "Oh. I see you've met."

"We were just getting acquainted," he said.

"You look like you've been wrestling in the weeds," Emily said, eyeing them both.

Rozalyn plucked a leaf from his hair and smiled at him with a devilish gleam in her eyes. She was actually enjoying ticking off her host.

"Let's go right on into the dining room. The rest are already seated," Emily said, clearly annoyed.

"I hope I didn't hold up dinner," he said. Rozalyn, he noticed, hung back as he mounted the steps of the back porch to Emily.

"Oh, no, you're right on time," Emily said, gracing him with a smile as she took his arm and led him toward the back door. "We're just delighted that you could join us."

"As am I," he said, the tension between the two women like sloughing through neck-deep mud, as Rozalyn followed them inside.

Emily still had hold of his arm as they stepped through a set of French doors into a large dining room.

He thought for a moment that Rozalyn had changed her mind about joining them for dinner, but when he glanced over his shoulder, he saw that she'd stopped in the wide French doorway and was now watching him with obvious suspicion.

"I just realized—"

"I hope you're hungry," Emily said as if Rozalyn hadn't spoken.

"—that I didn't catch your—"

"Starved," he said.

"—name," Rozalyn finished.

"I'd like you to meet my daughter," Emily said. A woman in her late twenties was seated at the round dining room table. She and a young man who resembled her had had their heads together when he and Emily had come in. Now the two looked up in surprise, cutting off an obviously intimate conversation in midsentence and appearing almost…guilty.

"This is my daughter Suzanne and my son Drew," Emily said. "Mr. Lancaster has graciously accepted my invitation to dine with us tonight."

"Lancaster?" Rozalyn said behind him in the doorway.

He turned to look at her and felt himself tense at the frown on her face. Clearly, she was trying to place the name.

Drew, who appeared to be a few years older than his sister, had gotten to his feet and was holding out his hand. Ford took it but noticed the young man's attention was more on Rozalyn.

"Mr. Lancaster is staying in our guesthouse for a while," Emily was saying.

"Really?" Suzanne was a younger version of her mother. Slim, blond and blue-eyed. Her eyes seemed a little glazed, and he noticed that not only was her dirty wineglass empty, but also the bottle in front of her was almost spent.

"Lancaster?" Rozalyn repeated from the doorway.

"Why don't you sit by my daughter," Emily said to him.

He went around the table, aware that Rozalyn still hadn't joined them. Emily had left a chair between Suzanne and Drew for her other guest.

"Rozalyn, if you'd care to join us," Emily said, her tone as sharp as a glass shard. "Let's not have a scene in front of Liam's friend and our dinner guest."

Rozalyn didn't seem to hear her. Nor was she looking at the older woman. Instead, her gaze was locked on Ford. "I missed your first name, *Mr. Lancaster.*"

He met Rozalyn's brown-eyed gaze, almost afraid to tell her but not sure why. Emily hadn't even raised an eyebrow when he'd told her. "Ford. Ford Lancaster."

"Ford Lancaster?!" Roz spat and stepped toward him as if she planned to leap the table and go for his throat. She definitely looked like she wanted to. "You lying bastard. You're no friend of my father's. What the hell are you doing here?"

Sheriff Mitch Tanner sat in his patrol car outside the *Timber Falls Courier* trying to decide what to do about Charity. A few weeks ago he'd almost lost her to a killer. Bud Farnsworth was dead, but Mitch feared that the man who killed him was even more dangerous.

Whatever Charity wrote in her newspaper would set Wade Dennison off. The owner of Dennison Ducks was a powerful man in this town and he used that power and money to get his way. Men like that often thought they were above the law.

One thing was for certain, Bud would never have come up with the idea of kidnapping the Dennison baby by himself. Mitch suspected he'd been paid. That's why Mitch had subpoenaed Wade Dennison's and Bud Farnsworth's financial records. Wade's attorney had held up the process for two weeks, arguing the case was closed. The kidnapper was dead.

But Mitch wasn't giving up because he knew in his heart that the true kidnapper, the person who'd planned the whole thing and paid Bud Farnsworth to snatch Angela Dennison, was still out there. Still walking around thinking he'd gotten away with it.

A tap on the glass made Mitch jump. "Jesse," he

said, rolling down his window. "I wish you'd quit sneaking around in the dark."

Jesse's smile was all Tanner dimples. He was just a little shorter than Mitch, stockier though, with long black hair pulled back in a ponytail, a gold earring in his right ear and handsome to a fault. "Hey, little bro. Spying on your woman?"

Mitch shook his head, not wanting to talk about Charity, especially with his brother. It was no secret that Jesse wished Charity had fallen for him. Mitch was just getting used to having his brother back in town. There'd been a time when he believed his wild, older brother was headed straight for a life of crime.

But Jesse had come back to Timber Falls a few weeks ago and really seemed to be trying to make up for his past mistakes. Mitch couldn't help but respect his brother for that. Jesse had also brought Mitch and their father closer.

"I thought you'd like to know," Jesse said now. "I just saw Wade Dennison move lock, stock and barrel into one of the units out at Florie's."

Mitch stared at him. "Nina's old unit? Aries?" Florie, a self-proclaimed psychic, had turned her motel into bungalow rentals years ago and named each of the twelve for the signs of the Zodiac. "What's up with that?" Mitch asked.

"Looks like Daisy threw him out."

What were the chances of that? Nil. Unless Daisy had something on Wade that she was holding over his head. Like she knew he was behind the kidnapping of their daughter, Angela. Or Daisy and her lover's daughter.

Mitch looked at Jesse, both of them no doubt thinking the same thing. If Angela had been a love child, then the father of that baby might very well be their own father, Lee Tanner. Lee and Daisy had had an affair in the year before Angela was born.

"How'd Wade seem?" Mitch asked, even more worried about Charity now.

Jesse shook his head. "He didn't look good. I'd say the man was about at the end of his rope. Can you imagine what will happen when this gets around town?"

And it wouldn't take long for that to happen given that Charity's Aunt Florie was one of the biggest gossips in town. And then there was Charity.

Mitch groaned at the thought of Charity's newspaper hitting the streets in the morning. There would be fireworks, sure as hell. He just hoped no one got killed.

"Damn," he swore, wondering if he should pay Wade a visit tonight. By the next day, Mitch was pretty sure he'd have the financial reports on Wade Dennison and Bud Farnsworth. And he figured he'd be paying Wade a visit once he had proof in hand anyway. No reason to court trouble tonight.

The patrol car radio squawked. Mitch took the call. A man had been found unconscious at the bottom of a cliff, not far from the recent Bigfoot sighting spot, and dropped off at the hospital. No ID.

Mitch turned to his brother. "Sounds like one of those damned Bigfoot hunters fell off a cliff and is over at the hospital."

"You need any help? I was headed home but I could tag along."

Mitch shook his head. In remote areas of Oregon, sheriffs worked alone—unless they needed to call in state investigators for help—or they could deputize someone locally for the short term.

"Later, then," Jesse said and headed toward his motorcycle parked in the alley.

Chapter 4

"Rozalyn! Have you lost your mind?" Emily cried.

Roz stood glaring at Ford Lancaster, so angry she couldn't speak.

This man sitting in the house that had once been her home was *Ford Lancaster,* the man who had ruined her father's reputation. The man who had almost killed her at the waterfall. The man who had lied about being Liam's friend. The man who had finagled his way into the guesthouse.

And if that wasn't bad enough, he'd...*kissed* her!

"Do you have any idea who this man is you're letting stay in the guesthouse?" she demanded, turning her hard-eyed gaze on Emily.

"Of course I do. Ford Lancaster. He's a scientist up here doing some research and a friend of *your* father's."

Emily never ceased to amaze her. "This man is no friend of his. Quite the opposite."

"Wait a minute," Ford interrupted loudly. "Who the hell is your father?"

"Liam Sawyer," Rozalyn snapped. "But if you really were his friend, wouldn't you know that?"

"You'd think so, wouldn't you?" Ford stared at her. And just when he thought his luck couldn't get any worse. Liam Sawyer's daughter. *I'll be damned.*

His gaze went to her lips. Her mouth was a wide, full mouth, sensual. He wished he'd taken more time with that kiss in the garden. All that kiss had done was whet his appetite. But if he got another chance—

Then his gaze drifted up to her eyes. He couldn't help but chuckle. If looks could kill, he'd be pushing up daisies right now. He didn't even want to think about his chances of ever getting to kiss this woman again.

"You think this is funny?" she demanded.

"Not really." Ironic? Tragic? Just his luck that this crazy doe-eyed strawberry blonde was Liam Sawyer's daughter.

He couldn't help but think about earlier when he'd had her in his arms. Unconsciously, he rubbed his shin and saw the hint of a smile curve her lips. No question about it, she was a menace and now she was his.

Why hadn't someone told him Liam had a daughter? Didn't he remember Rozalyn saying something about it having been years since she'd been up here? Yeah. So maybe that was the reason he was taken completely unaware.

He knew the old man had remarried and had a couple of adult stepchildren—but a *daughter* who looked like this? Worse, a daughter who was obviously going to make things harder for him? Oh, hell. This changed things considerably.

"I can't believe you'd be so rude to our guest," Emily said, sounding close to tears.

"This man is not *our* guest," Rozalyn said, narrowing those eyes at him with obvious venom.

He figured her bite was probably worse than her bark—or her kick. Clearly, Rozalyn was a woman to be reckoned with.

"Why don't you tell us, *Mr. Lancaster,* what you're *really* doing here?" She glared at him as if she hadn't missed him giving her the once-over. Those big brown eyes were hot with anger and a clear warning.

This wasn't going to be easy. But there were ways. Even with a woman like her. A woman who thought she didn't need a man.

"I guess the cat has his tongue. Mr. Lancaster here is the man who wrote the article about my father, calling him a liar and a fraud," Rozalyn said, still glaring at him.

"What article?" Emily asked.

"The article that accused him of faking photographs of Bigfoot and perpetuating a hoax," Rozalyn said. "It was my father's word against Ford Lancaster and his so-called experts."

Not exactly, Ford thought. There'd been another man with Liam Sawyer, another witness, who had also been discredited. And that article had been years ago. "I need to talk to you," he said to Rozalyn as he got to his feet.

She shot him a when-hell-freezes-over look.

"Maybe it was another Ford Lancaster," Emily suggested.

"How many Ford Lancasters do you think there are?" Rozalyn demanded.

A maid appeared in the doorway behind Rozalyn. "Excuse me. There's someone here to see you."

No one seemed to hear her.

"Wasn't that article years ago?" Drew asked.

"Yes," Emily chimed in. "Who would even remember, let alone care—"

"I remember and I care," Rozalyn shot back. "So does my father. Do you know the man you married at all? Or what matters to him? Do you have any idea what that article did to him?"

"I'm sure Mother didn't know Mr. Lancaster wrote the article when she offered him the guesthouse," Drew said.

"Of course not," Emily said. "I would never do anything to hurt Liam. Or you, Rozalyn, dear. He told me he was a friend of Liam's, and since there was no place in town to stay…"

"Excuse me. There is someone here to see you," the maid repeated.

"Ilsa, can't you see we're about to have dinner?" Emily snapped. "Tell whoever it is to come back some other time and close the doors behind you." She shot Rozalyn a look as if to say now everyone in town will be talking about your behavior.

"It's the sheriff. He wants to speak to Rozalyn," Ilse persisted.

"Rozalyn? Why would the sheriff want to talk to her?" Emily said as if it was the prince at the door with a glass slipper. "Oh Rozalyn, you didn't already involve the sheriff in our affairs, did you?"

"What do you want me to tell the sheriff?" the maid asked nervously. "Should I tell him to come back?"

"No, Rozalyn and I will both see him," Ford said.

The maid turned tail and disappeared down the hall. "If you will excuse me," he said to Emily and the others. "I apologize, Emily, but Rozalyn and I really do need to talk to the sheriff."

Ford took Roz's arm and practically dragged her out into the hallway, closing the French doors firmly behind them.

"We have to talk," he whispered. "I had no idea Liam had a daughter. But now that I do… I'm here because I think your father is in trouble." He held up a hand to ward off her questions. "I will explain later. Right now we need to see the sheriff. I assume you called him about earlier and that's why he's here?"

She jerked free, but he could see her anger deflating at his words. "My father's in trouble?"

"Possibly. Look, you called the sheriff about what you thought you saw at the falls, right? Let's get this over with, then you can tell me what you think of me at length," he said reasonably. "And I'll tell you everything I know about your father."

She obviously didn't feel like being reasonable. "I want to know why my father is in trouble and what that has to do with you and I want to know now," she said, keeping her voice down.

He groaned. "There isn't time now." He looked past her to where the sheriff was standing and watching them, then lowered his head and said quietly, "If you say anything to the sheriff, I'll deny it and you will never know why I'm here."

Her eyes flared with anger.

"Let's tell the sheriff what you saw," he added, loud enough that the officer of the law could hear.

Her body trembled with obvious rage as he took her arm and drew her toward the front door and the sheriff.

"Mitch," she said when she saw the uniformed man at the door. She broke free of Ford's grasp and rushed toward the sheriff.

Mitch? She knew him? Of course she might. She must have lived here until her mother had died. Sure. The conversation he'd overheard in the garden was starting to make sense. So was her relationship with the people in the dining room.

Ford met the sheriff's interested gaze, and felt his insides tighten. The sheriff had come for more than just a statement from Rozalyn about a possible suicide at Lost Creek Falls. Ford stood back, watching the sheriff's face and Rozalyn's body language. She hugged the cop and they exchanged a few pleasantries, then Ford heard the words he'd been dreading.

"A fall? Is Dad all right?"

The sheriff had taken off his hat. "He's in a coma, Roz."

"We have to get him flown out to Eugene, to the hospital there—"

The sheriff was shaking his head. "His condition is such that the doc says he can't be moved right now."

"I'm going to the hospital to see him," she said, pushing past Ford as he joined them. She ran up the stairs, no doubt to get her purse and car keys.

Ford found himself under the sheriff's intense scrutiny.

"I don't believe we've met," the lawman said.

"No, I'm Ford Lancaster." From the sheriff's negative reaction it was obvious Ford's reputation had preceded him.

The sheriff started to ask him something, but behind them, the dining room doors burst open. Ford was surprised it had taken Emily this long.

"What's going on?" she demanded.

As the sheriff filled her in, she burst into tears and called for Drew. Suzanne finally came out seeming more irritated than anything else. "Liam's been hurt," Emily cried. "Drew, will you drive me to the hospital?"

"Of course, Mother," he said.

"I just need to change," she said looking down at her shoes. Ford would guess she didn't want to get them wet.

"I'll stay here, Mother," Suzanne said. "In case anyone calls."

Why would anyone call? Ford wondered. Suzanne still held her wineglass. She drained it and turned back to the dining room. A look passed between Suzanne and Emily before a tearful Emily ascended the stairs with Drew following after her.

Ford noticed that Emily hadn't asked about Liam's accident. "Where was he found?" he asked as the others left him and the sheriff alone.

"Up Maple Creek. When did you get to town?"

"Rozalyn followed me in from Oakridge."

"Then you saw the jumper at Lost Creek Falls?" The sheriff sounded surprised.

Ford shook his head. "I'm not sure there was a jumper. I think she might have…imagined it. She's been pretty upset about her father—and with good reason it seems. Who found him?"

"Some Bigfoot hunters. They dropped him at the hospital." The sheriff glanced up the stairs as Rozalyn hurried down.

Ford reached for the keys dangling from her fingers. "I'm driving you."

"I'd like to have a few words with you at the hospital," the sheriff was saying to Ford.

"No problem." He took the keys from Rozalyn before she could protest. The sheriff raised a brow, probably expecting Rozalyn to put up a fight. "We'll see you at the hospital, Sheriff," Ford said.

Roz let Ford open the passenger side door of her SUV for her, then watched him hurry around to slide behind the wheel.

She leaned back against the seat, fighting panic, as she gave him the four-block directions to the Timber Falls hospital. Her father was in a coma. Mitch said he'd fallen from a cliff up Maple Creek Road and had been found by some Bigfoot hunters. Hadn't she known something had happened to him? If only she'd come sooner. If only—

Her gaze swung to Ford, suddenly remembering what he had said. "What did you mean when you told me my father was in trouble?" she asked as they neared the hospital.

He shot her a look, then turned back to his driving. "Let's just go to the hospital and find out what we can for now, all right?"

"No," she said, sitting up a little straighter. "You said it was the reason you were here. Did you mean Timber Falls? Or the house?"

"There isn't time to get into this right now. I'll tell you everything," he said, meeting her gaze. "After you see your father."

Ford swung the SUV into the hospital emergency entrance. Roz closed her eyes tightly for a moment, trying to hold it together. She had to be strong—for her father. She'd deal with Ford later.

Before he had the car parked, she was out and running toward the emergency room door. He caught up with her in time to open the door for her.

She rushed into the small hospital entry with him right behind her. The nurse's station was empty.

Her heart dropped. What if her father had gotten worse? What if—

She could make out a steady beep coming from down the dim hallway. She rushed toward the sound, the hurried footfalls of her and Ford echoing on the linoleum floor, as she prayed her father was alive even if still in a coma.

At the open doorway, Roz had a passing impression of a nurse and a doctor, both dressed in white beside a hospital bed. The nurse was round and rosy-cheeked with a halo of white hair. The doctor was blond, late forties, nice-looking.

Roz looked past both to the bandaged man lying in the bed, monitors making soft bleating noises, a respirator breathing in and out, in and out.

Her throat constricted at the sight of her father. He looked as white as the sheets and so incredibly frail but he was still alive! Thank God.

"How is he?" Roz asked, rushing into the room.

"No change, but he's holding his own," the nurse said. She smiled when she saw Roz as if she knew her. "I'm so glad you're here and I know your father is, too." Her eyes twinkled. "He knows you've come to see him, don't worry about that."

"Thank you," Roz said. "I'm—"

"Rozalyn," she said and smiled more broadly. "You

look just like your mother. I'm Kate Clark. I know you don't remember me, but I was at your birth. Don't worry about your father. He's in good hands. I'll be here all night."

"I won't, knowing you're taking care of him," Roz said.

"This is Dr. Harris," the nurse said.

The doctor had been looking at her father's chart. He looked up and frowned. "Who are you?" He sounded irritated.

"I'm his daughter, Rozalyn," she said looking down at her dad. She fought back tears as she whispered, "I'm here, Dad," and squeezed his hand. No response. She glanced up, expecting to see Ford in the doorway. But he was gone. "He's in a coma?"

The doctor nodded. "That's typical with this kind of head injury."

"The sheriff said he fell?" Roz asked.

"Probably slipped. Didn't fall far, I would guess, but struck his head on something," the doctor said.

"Who brought him in?" Roz looked at the nurse, who shook her head, then the doctor.

"They didn't leave names," he said. "Just out-of-towners up here looking for Bigfoot. Your father really needs his rest—" Dr. Harris broke off when he saw Ford reappear in the doorway again. The doctor put down the clipboard and started to leave the room. "Please keep your visit short."

He had reached the doorway when Emily and Drew rushed past Ford and into the room.

"Oh, no!" Emily cried, stopping in the center of the room to cover her face. "How bad is it, Dr. Harris?"

"I'm optimistic and you should be, too, Mrs. Sawyer.

He's a strong, stubborn man. He won't give up easily," the doctor said. "I was going to call you with the news but the sheriff insisted on doing it."

"Yes," Emily said and glanced at Roz. "I guess he wanted to tell Liam's daughter first."

Rozalyn hardly noticed the bitterness in the woman's tone. She was too surprised that Emily seemed to know the doctor. But the new Mrs. Sawyer had been in town for over a month. Emily probably knew everyone in Timber Falls by now.

"Oh, Drew," Emily said as he moved to put his arm around her shoulders.

Roz looked up at Ford who was still in the doorway. He motioned for her. "I'll give you a moment alone with Liam," she said as she squeezed her dad's hand, then laid it gently back on the bed beside him and left the room, surprised to find both Mitch and Ford waiting for her out in the hall. She could feel the tension between them, and could only guess what had been going on.

Ford closed the hospital room door but watched through the window as Mitch said, "Lancaster here feels your father needs protection."

Her gaze leaped to Ford. He didn't seem to notice. He was watching the group in the hospital room, looking worried, his jaw tight. He'd said her father was in trouble *before* Mitch told her Liam was in the hospital. It was almost as if Ford had been expecting this to happen. Why was that? She remembered his promise to tell her everything as soon as they left here.

She stared at Ford, reminding herself of all the reasons she shouldn't trust the man. And yet something in his worried expression—

"I think that's a good idea, Mitch," she said, making the decision not only to keep quiet about what Ford had told her—but to trust that he had his reasons for wanting her father protected.

Mitch was staring at her in obvious surprise. "Why?"

"Is there someone I can hire to stay with him, not let him out of sight even for a moment?" Ford asked, finally looking at the sheriff. "Is there someone in town who would be reliable and willing to take the job? Someone you trust?"

But Mitch was still looking at Roz. "You think your father is in danger?" he asked.

She nodded. "I can't explain it, but I do, Mitch."

He let out a long sigh and looked at Ford. "I know someone. My brother, Jesse Tanner. No one will get past Jesse to Liam. But I need to know why you feel Liam needs that kind of protection."

"Let's just say I have a bad feeling that his fall wasn't an accident," Ford said.

Roz must have looked as shocked as Mitch.

"You have any proof of that?" the sheriff asked.

"Not yet," Ford said. "But if you want to keep him alive, then I suggest you call your brother and get him up here. If you're sure he can be trusted."

"I'd trust him with my life and Liam's," Mitch said.

Ford looked to Roz, then nodded. "Call him." He glanced back through the hospital room window as if he wasn't moving an inch until Jesse Tanner arrived to take over.

"Can I have a word with you?" Mitch asked Roz as he stepped down the hall, pulled out his cell and punched in a series of numbers. When the line answered, he said, "It's me," and briefly explained the situation. A few seconds later, he disconnected. "Jesse's on his way. I've deputized him so there won't be any question as to his authority for being here."

"Thanks, Mitch."

"Look, Roz, I don't know what the deal is with you and Lancaster—"

"There's nothing between us. I just don't want to take any chances with my dad, that's all," she said.

He nodded, but she could tell he wasn't buying it for a minute.

"It just isn't like him to fall off a cliff," she said and shuddered at the thought of how long he'd lain there before he'd been found. She couldn't bear the thought that he'd been in pain, worse that he may have been pushed, may have even seen his assailant.

"No, it's not like Liam, but accidents do happen," Mitch said. "What's odd is that I was up Maple Creek Road earlier tonight and I didn't see his pickup and camper. Is it possible someone dropped him off at the trailhead?"

That *was* odd. "I don't know. His truck isn't at the house. Emily said he took it when he left two weeks ago."

"I'm sure it will turn up," Mitch assured her. "And don't worry. Your dad's going to pull through. You know how tough he is. Then he'll tell us just what happened."

She nodded and smiled through her tears. She was counting on it, she thought as she looked down the hall at Ford standing outside her father's hospital room. In the meantime, any answers were going to have to come from Ford Lancaster.

She balked at the idea but still couldn't wait until

Jesse Tanner arrived so she could find out why the man who'd tried to destroy Liam in print years ago was now trying to save him.

"How long have you been sheriff?" she asked Mitch, not wanting to go back down to her father's room until Emily and Drew were finished.

"Pretty much since Sheriff Hudson retired."

She knew the sheriff had retired shortly after her mother's death. She tried not to think about that right now and looked into Mitch's handsome face instead, then at his ring finger.

He laughed. "No, Charity hasn't lassoed me yet—but not for lack of trying."

When she and Charity used to play house, Charity was always married to Mitch Tanner while Roz's pretend husband was not only nameless but also faceless.

"Have you seen Charity?" he asked.

She shook her head. "Not for a while."

"I know she'd love to see you. She has breakfast every morning at Betty's."

Roz nodded. "I'd love to see her, too."

Mitch pulled out a small notebook and pen. "Why don't we go over what you saw at Lost Creek Falls while we're waiting."

Roz hugged herself against the memory as she told him.

"What made you think it was a woman?" he asked, taking notes.

She shook her head. "All I really saw was the bright yellow raincoat but at one point I thought I saw long blond hair. It was too dark to make out much." She hesitated. "And it happened so fast."

"Lancaster says he didn't see anything."

She shook her head ruefully. "He thought I was going to jump and tried to save me. He almost killed me instead."

Mitch didn't look pleased to hear this. "Where is he staying?"

"Our guesthouse. Emily invited him. Says she didn't know who he was, thought he was a friend of Liam's." Obviously Ford had led her to believe that.

Mitch raised a brow. "What is Lancaster doing in town?"

She shook her head, watching Ford. She wished she knew.

The sheriff put his notebook away. "I'll drive up to the falls and take a look tonight but doubt there is anything I can do until morning." They both knew that at this point he would just be retrieving the body. She shuddered at the thought. If there really was a body to retrieve. And shuddered again.

"Lancaster say how long he's staying?" Mitch asked following her gaze down the hall to Ford.

"No." He hadn't told her anything. Yet.

Mitch pulled off his hat and raked a hand through his dark hair. "Come on, Roz, you drove all the way up here from Seattle because you were worried about your father. Why?"

She told him about the message her dad had left on her answering machine. "He sounded upset. I tried to call him back but couldn't reach him. No one had heard from him at the house. Of course I was worried."

Mitch put his hat back on. "Emily have any idea why Liam might have been upset?"

"I didn't tell her about the call." She could feel the sheriff's gaze on her. "But I asked her if they'd had an argument. She denied it. I think she's lying. I think something happened between the two of them before he left."

Mitch was looking down the hall again. Emily came out of Liam's room with Drew at her side. Dr. Harris came out of another room and led Emily and Drew down the hallway in the opposite direction. They disappeared into one of the offices.

"Be careful, okay?" Mitch said quietly, watching after them.

Roz looked over at him in surprise. "You think I'm right?"

"I don't know what to think," Mitch said. "But I'd watch Lancaster." He smiled over at her. "You're too smart to fall for any line he might try to give you, right?"

Right. She turned as the front door of the hospital opened and a dark broad-shouldered man with a ponytail and a black biker jacket came through the door. It had been years since she'd seen Jesse Tanner. Mitch's older brother had been in reform school most of the time. This was the man Mitch had guarding her father?

"Hey, Rozie," Jesse said coming toward her. He had the Tanner black hair and eyes and those deep dimples. Only Jesse was handsome in a dangerous way. He also appeared very capable of keeping her father safe.

"Sorry about your papa. But don't worry. I'll see that no one does him any harm as long as I'm around."

She trusted Mitch's judgment. "I believe you," she said. "Thank you, Jesse."

"My pleasure." He gave her a grin. There was a rakishness about Jesse, a raw sexuality. This man was a danger to women. Just like another man she'd recently met, she thought, looking down the hall to where Ford lounged against the wall, eyes hooded, his body looking deceptively relaxed.

She had the feeling that he could spring like a big cat at a moment's notice. He was watching her father's room. But she knew he was also aware of her. Just as she was him.

"I want some answers," Rozalyn demanded the moment they walked out of the hospital.

Ford was surprised she'd been able to hold her tongue that long. He opened the passenger side door of her SUV for her. She got in without seeming to notice he intended to drive. Without a word, he slid behind the wheel, started the car and headed down the street.

"You really think someone purposely tried to kill my father?"

"I just feel better with a guard in his room, all right? Just until we find out what happened," Ford said. "Like I said—"

"You have a bad feeling. I heard. Why didn't you tell the sheriff what you told me?"

He pulled up in front of Betty's Café. It was early enough the place was still open but late enough there were only a few people inside still eating.

"What are you doing?" she asked as he shut off the engine and started to get out.

"Getting something to eat. I'm still hungry. You might remember I didn't get any dinner." As he got out, he heard her open her door and follow him.

"How can you even think about food at a time like this?" she demanded, catching up with him before he opened the café door for her.

"I'm sorry about your dad but we both need to eat if we're going to keep up our strength so we can find out what happened to him." He held open the door. "After you."

She mumbled something under her breath but entered, going to a booth at the back out of earshot from the other diners. He followed her, glad to see her angry. Earlier when she'd been with her father, she'd looked broken. He needed her to be strong and if being angry was what it took, he could oblige.

He also needed her to trust him. That, he realized as he slid in the booth across from her, was going to take some doing.

A young waitress Roz didn't recognize brought them menus. Roz didn't even bother to open hers, knowing she wouldn't be able to eat a bite. She was worried about her father, although knowing that Jesse Tanner was in the hospital room watching over him helped. Now if her father would just come out of his coma—

"Give us two western omelettes, extra cheese, and two cups of black coffee," Ford said without opening his menu, either. He didn't even bother to ask Roz if she would have liked cream.

"Well?" she demanded the moment the waitress was out of earshot. "You got me here, now talk."

"Are you always this impatient?" he asked.

"No, I'm actually on my best behavior. You wouldn't want to see me when I'm not," she snapped.

He smiled, obviously recognizing his own words from earlier.

He wasn't bad-looking when he smiled. Under the bright fluorescent lights of Betty's Café, she could see featherings of gray at his temples and tiny laugh lines around his sea-green eyes. He had a rugged look about him as if he'd spent a lot of time outdoors.

It surprised her. He was nothing like she had pictured him in her mind all these years. He must have been very young when he'd written the article about her father, she realized.

The waitress returned with the coffees.

Roz cradled the mug of hot coffee in her hands, needing the warmth as she sat waiting, glaring across the table at a man she had hated since the age of sixteen without ever knowing anything more about him than his name. Ford Lancaster. Her idea of the devil incarnate.

She was sixteen when the article had come out about her father. She felt cold inside as she remembered how it had devastated him.

Liam Sawyer had been on a camping trip with a friend when the two had stumbled across a large creature in the woods. Her father, who always had his camera, had hit the motordrive. But his hands had been shaking from shock and surprise, and the photographs of the creature were out of focus, the image blurred.

But still the photographs had been big news when they'd hit print. Liam had believed that his discovery would change the world's attitude about Bigfoot's existence.

That seemed the case, until Ford Lancaster called in some so-called experts to denounce the photographs as an elaborate hoax instigated by her father.

No one had believed Liam or his friend after Ford Lancaster's article came out and the news hit the papers. No one except people who knew him. But Liam

Sawyer had never gotten over the humiliation. Whenever there was a Bigfoot sighting in the years since, his photographs and the incident were always mentioned.

Her father had sworn that he'd get irrefutable proof of Bigfoot's existence or die trying. But as many times as he had returned to the Cascades, he'd never seen the creature again.

Some years later another photographer had admitted that his Bigfoot photos had been faked, casting even more suspicion on her father's photos.

Roz had spent over a decade hating Ford Lancaster and now he was sitting across the table from her.

Ford didn't seem to notice her glaring in his direction. He was without a doubt the most arrogant, rude, obnoxious man—

"I'm sorry about the way I acted earlier," he said, lifting that pale gaze to meet hers. "At the waterfall."

She shrugged and looked down at her coffee, a little thrown by the fact that he'd apologized. Not so thrown that she didn't have a comeback. "Now that I know who you are, I wouldn't expect anything less than your behavior at the waterfall."

He pretended to be wounded. "Seriously, I'm trying to change."

"Not having much luck, huh?"

He smiled. He had a nice mouth, but then she already knew that from earlier in the garden.

"Stop stalling. Don't make me sorry I covered for you with the sheriff."

He shook his head, still smiling as if he found her amusing. "Why did you?"

"Why did you lie to Emily about being a friend of my father's?"

"What makes you so sure it's a lie?"

She reached into her purse and pulled out her cell phone and started to dial the sheriff. He reached across the table and gently touched her hand holding the phone. She met his gaze.

"Can you sit still long enough for me to tell you my way?" He shook his head, answering for her. "Then I'll try to make it quick. I was twenty-four when I wrote the article about your father's photographs." She did the math. That made him thirty-six now, eight years older than she was. "It wasn't just about your father. There was someone else with him when he took those photos."

"John Wells." Her father's friend.

Ford nodded. "His name is John *Ford* Wells. He's my father."

Her jaw dropped. "How could that be since his name is Wells and yours—"

"My parents divorced when I was four. My mother remarried. I hardly ever saw my biological father—just enough to…resent the hell out of him."

She felt her eyes widen with understanding.

He nodded. "It wasn't your father I was going after in that article. It was mine."

She was dumbstruck. "You did that to your own father."

"Yeah, well, I'm a jerk, but you already know that about me." He met her gaze, his eyes the color of a warm Caribbean lagoon she'd once photographed for one of her books.

"That makes it easy for you, doesn't it."

"No, actually, nothing has been easy." He seemed to turn serious and she felt her breath catch at his next words. "John Wells hadn't been well. I was with him the day Liam called." He nodded. "I took the call. Liam sounded...scared. He wasn't making a lot of sense, almost as if he'd been drinking."

She was shaking her head. "My father never has more than a glass of wine with dinner."

"You want to hear this or not?"

She made a face at him and he continued, "He sounded as if he'd been drinking. He said he couldn't get through to the sheriff, that he was in trouble, that he'd found something. I thought he said bones."

"Bones?"

Ford nodded. "Then he said what I thought was, 'John, they're trying to kill me' and we were cut off."

She felt a shiver but couldn't help being skeptical given who was telling the story. "Why would my father call *you?*"

"I answered the phone. I guess I sounded enough like John Wells, and that Liam just assumed—"

"Why didn't you give the phone to your father?"

Ford chewed at his cheek for a moment, glancing out the window before settling that blue-green gaze on her again. "Because John Ford Wells had died just minutes before Liam's call."

Chapter 5

Ford watched her eyes fill with tears. "I'm so sorry about your father," she said and reached across the table to cover his hand.

"It's all right," he said taking back his hand. He didn't want her sympathy. It made him feel guilty and he felt guilty enough already. "We were never close."

"That's too bad." She looked down, her brown eyes swimming in tears, as she cupped her coffee mug.

He could see that she was thinking about her father, worrying that she might lose him. They were obviously very close. Or had been before his recent marriage, Ford guessed.

Her gaze lifted to his. "Why didn't you call the sheriff right away?"

"I thought your father was drunk. But the more I thought about it… So I came up here determined to get to the bottom of it."

She was eyeing him suspiciously, obviously realizing there was a lot more to it.

"Look, I called your father's house. I talked to Emily. She told me everything was fine, that she expected to hear from Liam at any time and not to concern myself."

"Emily," Rozalyn said under her breath like a curse.

"My old man said Liam Sawyer was one of the toughest men he ever knew and one of the best."

Hope shimmered along with her tears now. "He is something for his age, isn't he?"

Ford nodded.

She shook her head as if she found it all too unbelievable. "Why would anyone hurt him?"

"If he really did find bones—"

"What kind of bones would be worth trying to kill a man over?"

Ford hesitated, then lowered his voice. "Given what Liam had been doing up in the mountains, I'd say Bigfoot bones."

Roz stared at him as if too shocked to speak. "Excuse me? You scientists have discredited the thousands of Bigfoot-like creature sightings around the world saying that if such a beast existed, then why hadn't a skeleton ever been found. Are you telling me now that *you* think it's possible he could have found a Bigfoot skeleton?"

"Possible. Not probable." Hadn't he been waiting most of his life for this? He didn't believe and yet, God knew, he wanted to.

Roz eyed him, trying to put her finger on her misgivings about Ford Lancaster. Misgivings, hell. She didn't trust him. He was the enemy. Wasn't he?

"Why would anyone try to kill my father over Bigfoot bones?" she asked, still wondering why he hadn't gone to the sheriff.

"You aren't really that naive, are you? A Bigfoot skeleton would be an incredible find. It would set the scientific world on its ear." Excitement crept into his voice and his sea-green eyes shone in the café lights. "The bones could prove to be hominid, a subspecies of us, human."

"You make it sound as if you believe they exist," she said, surprised by the enthusiasm she heard in his voice.

"It's possible," he said slowly. "After all the Ishii, the last of a Stone Age Indian tribe, had remained hidden in a canyon only eight miles from Oroville, California, in the early 1900s until they voluntarily came out and made themselves known. The mountain gorilla wasn't proven to exist until 1902. It would make the person who found the bones famous. Not to mention rich."

"Rich?"

"Those bones are worth a fortune," he said. "Not just in the rewards being offered for definitive proof that such a creature exists, but to private collectors."

She'd never thought of a find like that in monetary terms because she knew her father wouldn't have, either. "My father would never have sold them. He would have donated them to a museum."

"But that doesn't mean that someone else out there doesn't realize their value and intends to cash in on the find."

"You're saying that someone found out about the bones and—" A sob choked off her words.

"Liam sounded like he was running scared when he called."

Running scared. That's how she felt right now. "And you think he's still in danger?" she said, brushing at her tears.

"If the bones are Bigfoot bones, then your father is in danger as long as someone thinks he is going to tell about the discovery."

He reached over and touched her hand, sending a jolt through her. He jerked his hand back, looking embarrassed as he picked up his cup, his gaze set on the coffee.

She stared at him, her heart beating too fast, and all he'd done was touch her. Who was this man who could be so kind one moment and so awful the next? And why did her body have to react this way with Ford Lancaster of all people?

He must feel the same way, she thought as she watched him stare into his coffee. Touching her had been a mistake. No kidding.

She took a drink of her own coffee and realized her hands were shaking.

He didn't look up as he said, "Until the bones are found—"

"But by now, wouldn't the person have gotten the bones out of the woods?"

"I don't think so or we would have heard about it. The bones could be too large to move. Or embedded in the rock. I don't know. Maybe your father found something portable like a skeleton and hid it. But if someone had the bones in their possession, they would have made the announcement by now."

"You think my father might have hidden what he

found?" Roz realized her dad had been making some really bad decisions lately. Marrying Emily. Bringing her to the house here at Timber Falls. Maybe he had hidden the bones, knowing someone was following him. She just hoped it wouldn't cost him his life.

"Until Liam regains consciousness we have no way of knowing," Ford was saying. "Or until I find the bones. The sheriff told me where Liam was found. At least I have a place to start looking in the morning."

"I'm going with you."

His gaze locked with hers. "It's too dangerous. If I'm right and your father's fall wasn't an accident, then whoever did it won't hesitate to do the same thing to you if given a chance."

"You don't know this area like I do," she argued. "My dad has taken me up in those mountains since I was old enough to ride in a backpack. I probably know more about Bigfoot hunting than you do and I know my father. You need me."

She wanted to find those bones before whoever had hurt her father profited from them. She also wanted to find the person who'd done this to her father. If his fall really hadn't been an accident. If Ford Lancaster was telling her the truth. "I am going with you," she told him. "So don't even try to stop me."

She caught something in his gaze just an instant before he said, "I should have known I couldn't talk you out of it." What was it that she'd seen in his eyes? Relief? Or triumph?

She took a sip of her coffee, watching him over the rim of her cup as he ate. "What I don't understand is why you would risk your life to help my father."

He smiled as if he'd been expecting the question. "Let's just say I owe him for the article I wrote on him."

"You could just write a retraction," she said. "Instead of risking your life."

He shook his head. "The photographs your father took were too blurry to prove anything one way or the other. The experts I had look at them were as convinced as I was that they'd been faked." He held up a hand quickly to keep her from biting his head off. "Look, I didn't know your father. Or mine, for that matter. And yes, I did have an ax to grind. I'm not proud of it. But like I said, that's the past. There's no going back and changing that."

That seemed a bit too simple, but she let it ride. After all, Ford's father had been Liam's best friend— and had been hurt by the article as well. Maybe Ford also wanted to make up some things to his own father.

"I think we should keep this just between the two of us," Ford said, looking up at her. "It sounds like there are enough people out there searching for Bigfoot as it is without word of this getting out. If we stand any hope of finding the bones—"

"And the person who injured my father," she said.

"Yes. If we announce what we're looking for, we'll scare him off. Or force him to move quicker to get the bones out before we can find them."

Their food arrived. To her surprise, Roz realized she was hungry after all. She'd felt so helpless at the hospital but now there seemed to be something she could do besides pray and wait beside her father's hospital bed for him to recover.

They ate in silence, wolfing down their meals as if

neither had eaten in weeks. By the time they finished, it was getting late.

"I want to stop by the hospital and see my father again."

"I thought you might. Mind if I go with you?"

She didn't mind in the least. In fact, she was glad for the company. Ever since he'd told her about the danger he thought her father was in, she'd found herself looking over her shoulder. She wanted to make sure Liam was safe—and hoped he'd be conscious by the time they got there.

Jesse Tanner was sprawled in a chair in the hospital room when she walked in. He nodded at her as she entered the room. Ford stayed in the doorway.

Roz pulled up a chair beside her father's bed. "I'm here, Dad," she whispered and squeezed his hand. No response. She began to talk softly to him, talking about the past, reliving memories she'd buried ten years ago when her mother died. He never moved, never gave any indication he heard her.

She was crying softly by the time she finally stood and let go of his hand. "I'll be back." She needed to find out what had happened to him. Ford was right about that, she thought, glancing toward the door.

But even as she thought it, she wondered again at Ford's motivations. What was it about the man that made her so suspicious of him? Was it just the article he'd written so many years ago or something else? Something she couldn't quite put her finger on.

Roz hadn't realized how tired she was until she and Ford walked out of the hospital. The night was dark, the clouds damp and low. In the distance lightning flashed above the tree line.

"I'm going to walk back," Ford said and handed her the keys as thunder rumbled softly to the west. "Will you be all right?"

"It's only a few blocks," Roz said, surprised she was a little disappointed he wasn't coming with her.

"I'll see you in the morning. Good night."

When she drove away, he was still standing in front of the hospital. She wondered if he was worried about security for her father or if he just wanted some time alone. She could understand that.

Roz thought of her father and felt a chill. Who was it he had to fear? It could be anyone...

Even Ford Lancaster?

As a car came around the dark corner at the end of the street from the hospital, Ford stepped back into the shadows. A sports car pulled up next to the emergency room entrance. Drew Lane got out and looked around before walking to the passenger side and opening the car door. His mother emerged, also glancing around before rushing inside.

Drew held the car door open as Suzanne Lane stumbled out from the small space in the back. She shoved away his offered hand for help, obviously intoxicated, and wound her way toward the hospital entrance. "I don't know why I had to be here," she said to her mother.

Emily said something under her breath that Ford couldn't make out but whatever it was, it wasn't nice.

Drew followed the two women inside. Neither noticed Ford in the shadows watching them. Or heard him enter the hospital a few minutes later behind them.

"Who are you?" he heard Emily exclaim from Liam's room.

Ford smiled to himself as he quietly stepped into the room after the trio. Jesse was still sprawled in the chair in the corner of Liam Sawyer's room but Ford didn't doubt from watching the man move that he could spring from that chair in a heartbeat if he needed to.

"Haven't you met Jesse Tanner yet?" Ford asked behind them. "He's the sheriff's brother."

Emily spun around, breathing heavily with obvious surprise and displeasure. "What is he doing here?" she demanded, then lowered her voice to add, "Liam needs his rest."

Ford nodded. "The deputy is here to make sure he gets it."

"Deputy?" Emily was visibly trying to calm herself. "I'd like a moment alone with my husband."

"Jesse doesn't leave the room," Ford said. "But don't worry. He won't disturb you."

"On whose orders?"

"Rozalyn's," Ford said, knowing that he carried no weight at all in this matter. But Rozalyn did. She was the man's daughter, his blood, although legally Emily could put up a fight. But it would take time and a lawyer. "She just wants to make sure her father is safe."

"Safe?! He's in a hospital! What is wrong with that girl?" Emily snapped with disgust. "The sheriff told me that she thought she saw someone jump from Lost Creek Falls?" She was shaking her head as if the idea was ludicrous. "You know her mother committed suicide. Jumped from the widow's walk in the attic."

He tried not to show his shock. No wonder Rozalyn had freaked out at the falls like she had.

Emily nodded, obviously pleased that she'd shocked him. "I have to live in that house knowing what that poor deranged woman did just upstairs...."

"You can't get me *near* that attic," Suzanne said, slurring her words.

"The worst part is that this sort of thing runs in Rozalyn's family," Emily said with a shudder. "I'm sure she just imagined seeing someone jump from the falls. It wouldn't be the first time. Her father told me she heard voices and music all the time after her mother's death."

Ford wished now that he'd seen the jumper. He didn't want to agree with this woman that Rozalyn had just imagined the whole thing. "Losing a parent like that has to be a shock," he said, thinking of his own father's quiet death and how it had affected him.

He couldn't imagine what Rozalyn must have gone through after her mother's suicide.

"Rozalyn is unstable. Why else would she think she saw a jumper at the river? Or that Liam was in danger?" Emily demanded.

"I'll leave you alone to visit with your husband," Ford said. He glanced in Jesse's direction, their eyes meeting in silent understanding. Nothing could get Jesse Tanner out of that room short of a stretcher.

"I just wanted to tell Liam good night," Emily said and went around to the side of the bed to pat her husband's pale hand. Drew and Suzanne hadn't moved from their spots near the door.

As Ford headed down the hall, he passed Dr. Harris and heard Emily greet the doctor with, "Oh Mark, I'm so worried about Liam." Ford heard the doctor reassuring her in a soft caring tone. "Is there any way you can get that awful man out of Liam's room?"

"I guess the sheriff insisted at the request of the daughter. My hands are tied, Em."

As Ford left the hospital, the sky to the west glittered with lightning. He could practically feel the low rumble of thunder echo in his chest. It wouldn't be long now before all hell broke loose, he thought, thinking of the coming storm—and the one inside him.

Roz parked in front of the house noticing that, while a couple of lights burned inside, Drew's car was gone. Were they still at the hospital?

Roz had hoped everyone had gone to bed. She could feel the approaching storm in the air as she walked quickly up the steps and across the porch. She was relieved that the porch light was on and the front door wasn't locked. She felt a little chilled and couldn't wait to have a hot bath as lightning flickered in the distance, thunder echoing behind it, the night suddenly feeling colder.

She hurried inside, trying to be as quiet as possible in hopes of avoiding running into any of the family again tonight—just in case any were home.

She didn't see anyone as she closed the front door behind her and started up the stairs. From the kitchen came the clatter of pots and pans, but no other sound.

Roz hurried up the stairs, trying not to think about Ford Lancaster. Impossible. If even half of what he'd told her was the truth—

As she passed the second floor, she heard nothing but silence. Was it possible even Suzanne had gone to the hospital? Could she be wrong about the level of their concern for her father?

She *was* tired. Exhausted with worry and from being around these people. Biting her tongue took so much energy. Not that she'd done much tongue biting tonight.

She opened the door to her room, thankful now that it hadn't been changed. It felt like a sanctuary in this house and she needed that right now. She closed the door and caught the scent of chocolate—her one weakness.

In a dish next to her bed were two perfect pieces of her favorite Swiss chocolates—and a note. "I thought you might enjoy these after the day you've had, Drew."

How thoughtful. Roz popped one of the chocolates into her mouth and closed her eyes, letting the rich, smooth delicacy melt on her tongue. "Ahhhhh."

She'd save the other one for after a hot bath.

As she turned, she caught a movement out of the corner of her eye. Her pulse jumped and she had to stifle a scream.

It was only the curtain billowing in on a gust of wind. Her relief was short-lived. She hadn't left the window open. Maybe Drew had opened it to let in some fresh air. Odd, though, she couldn't imagine anyone doing that with a thunderstorm on the way.

A cold draft of damp air curled around her neck as she went to the window, frowning as she looked down. Past the narrow window ledge was a drop of three stories to the garden below. She glanced up through the limbs of the large tree directly outside her room and caught sight of a dark figure moving along the garden path toward the guesthouse. Ford?

She started to close the window but stopped as she noticed how close the branches of the tree were to her room. It would be easy for someone to climb the tree and right into her room.

She shook off the thought as she closed the window and locked it. Why would anyone go to the effort, let alone the danger of falling from a rain-slick tree limb to climb in her window? Especially when the window had been closed and locked when she'd left earlier. Hadn't it? It had definitely been closed. She couldn't swear it had been locked though.

She turned to survey the room, her gaze settling on her open suitcase.

Earlier when she'd left, her suitcase hadn't been open on the trunk at the end of her bed.

But it was now.

She stepped to it, seeing at once that the contents had been gone through—and not very neatly—as if the person had been in a hurry. Drew? It seemed unlikely that it had been him. He wouldn't leave her chocolates and a note, and then rummage through her suitcase in such a way that she'd notice. Someone else had been in her room!

Her mouth went dry as she looked around. What had someone been searching for? Had he climbed the tree?

Or just left the window open to make her think the intruder had come from outside the house—rather than from within?

Ford Lancaster looked more than capable of scaling that tree and coming in through her bedroom window. That image tantalized her imagination a little too much and she quickly moved on to other suspects.

Emily was nosey enough that Roz could easily see

her going through the suitcase. But she was also cheap enough that she wouldn't leave the window open. Too much heat loss.

Roz sighed. As far as in-house suspects, that left Suzanne. Suzanne didn't seem motivated or sober enough to go through her suitcase let alone open the window to make her think someone had just left moments before Roz arrived.

Roz looked out, thinking of Ford.

That pretty much left Ford. She'd just seen him from the window. He could have scaled down the tree only moments before. That *had* been him she'd seen heading for the guesthouse, hadn't it? He'd certainly made good time walking back, even though Timber Falls was small and the hospital was only a few blocks away.

But what would Ford have been looking for in her suitcase? What would anyone have been looking for?

She locked the window and froze as she heard a familiar song playing in the room next door, her mother's sewing room. The song was her mother's favorite—and the same song Roz heard in her nightmares.

Heart pounding, she moved across her bedroom and opened the door to peer out. The hallway was empty. She was only imagining the music—just as she had earlier tonight. Just as she had right after her mother's death. Just as she did when she dreamed about her mother's death.

But this time it sounded so real. And this time there was no mistaking where the music was coming from.

She tiptoed down the hallway, stopping at the sewing room door. The knob felt cold to the touch. It turned in her hand and the door swung open.

The room, like her own, was exactly the same as it

had been ten years ago. Some of her mother's fabric was still spread out on the cutting table, the scissors lying next to it, as if any moment her mother would pick them up.

The song stopped, and in the silence that followed, she thought she really had imagined it. But then the record began to play again, startling her and she saw why.

Her mother's old automatic phonograph. The single 45 spinning on the turntable. The record scratchy, the speakers tinny sounding.

She stepped into the chilly room, lifted the needle off the 45 and turned the record player to off. Silence filled the room.

She wasn't going to cry. Wasn't that exactly what someone wanted her to do? Why else had they turned on the phonograph? But how? Wasn't everyone at the hospital?

As she started to turn toward the open doorway to leave, she heard a soft click behind her and froze.

An instant later the phonograph needle began to scratch across the record again.

Chapter 6

As Ford walked to the guesthouse from the hospital, the town of Timber Falls was quiet and dark as if holding its breath before the next rainstorm hit.

He stopped on the porch, took out his keys and started to unlock the guesthouse door. He froze, the hair rising on the back of his neck. The door was already open and he had the feeling that whoever had broken in either hadn't been gone long—or was still inside.

He reached into his pocket for his penlight but didn't turn it on as he slowly pushed open the door. It was black inside the guesthouse except for a sliver of light under his bedroom door. He could hear a faint rustling on the other side.

Cautiously, he moved closer. A floorboard creaked under his shoe. The light under the door went out. He snapped on the penlight and threw open the door just in time to see a dark figure rush out through the patio doors and out into the night.

He gave chase but the intruder was quickly swallowed up by the rainforest. Ford swore under his breath. He couldn't even be sure if it had been a man or a woman. Nor could he make out a footprint in the mossy ground outside.

Closing the patio doors, he found marks where a tool had been used to break the lock. So why had the front door been open? Had someone just wanted him to believe they'd broken in when in truth, the intruder had used a key and not closed the door properly?

He closed the drapes and pulled a chair up under the doorknob of the patio door for the night. He would do the same to the front door when the time came.

As he turned back to the room, he saw that his things had been gone through. His papers were scattered on the floor where they'd been dropped.

Adrenaline shot through him. Where was his laptop computer?

He hurried around the bed, relieved to see it lying next to the bed on the floor. Even before he reached for it, he knew that the disk would be gone.

It was.

He swore again. Whoever had stolen the disk now knew as much about Liam Sawyer's find as Ford did. But then again, whoever had broken in here had already known something or he wouldn't have come here tonight.

Ford mentally kicked himself. He'd provided the thief with the perfect opportunity by staying away so long. But that was the least of his worries. That disk had more than Liam's find on it. If any of that information should get to Rozalyn—

He rubbed his sore shin where she'd kicked him earlier in the garden and thought about, of all things, the kiss.

He'd lied. It hadn't been *nothing*. In fact those few delightful moments in the garden made him curious enough to want to kiss her again. He swore at the thought, reminding himself of the kind of woman Rozalyn Sawyer was. The kind who would risk her life for a phantom stranger at a waterfall.

Just his luck that the one person who actually might be able to help him would be the least predictable and the most honest.

Roz stood, her back to the sewing room as the heartbreakingly familiar record began to play on the phonograph again. A chill skittered across her skin, the tiny hairs on the back of her neck rising. That same song had been playing the day her mother jumped from the fourth floor widow's walk to fall to her death. No one had believed Roz that the song had been playing any more than they believed that she'd heard voices in the attic before her mother was found.

Nor would anyone believe that Roz had turned off the record player.

And that *someone* had turned it back on.

Out of the corner of her eye, she spied her mother's scissors on the cutting table. Holding her breath, she grabbed for the scissors. The instant her hand closed over them, she whirled around, brandishing the sharp weapon.

There wasn't another soul in the room. Just as she

knew there wouldn't be. The record whirled on the phonograph. The music filled the room. She was completely alone.

Tears of terror blurred her eyes as she rushed back in, grabbed the cord and jerked the plug from the wall. A final note hung in the air as the needle scratched across the vinyl, the arm dropping away from the record.

She stood over the phonograph, the silence louder and more eerie than the music had been. She stared down at the 45 as if she half expected the record to begin spinning again and the needle to rise and drop to the scratchy vinyl surface.

The scissors clattered to the floor. She grabbed the record from the turntable and began to break it into tiny pieces that fell to the floor like dark confetti until her trembling hands were empty and she ran from the room, slamming the door behind her.

She wanted to keep going, out of this house, out of this town, away from all the painful memories. But she couldn't leave her father. She ran to her bedroom and hurriedly locked the door behind her.

Nor would she be frightened away.

Checking under the bed, in the closet and even behind the shower curtain in the bathroom, she tried to still her panic.

Lightning splintered the sky beyond her window, followed moments later by a deafening boom of thunder. She cried out, backing up against the wall as she watched the sky outside flash with light.

She had to calm down. Someone was trying to scare her and damn but it was working. Exhaustion made her brain foggy. She tried to think, tried to get her composure back. Her mother's spirit hadn't started that phonograph playing. Nor was it the electrical storm or some quirk of nature. Someone had to have rigged the phonograph to keep playing even when she'd turned it off.

Emily! The woman had resented her from the beginning. She definitely didn't want her here. Drew was the only one who seemed to care anything about her.

Roz saw the second piece of chocolate on the plate by her bed and almost dove for it. Once in her mouth, the rich chocolate began to melt, and Roz felt her heart rate drop a little. She would never be able to sleep unless she got a hot bath even as late as it was. She was too worried about her father. Too keyed up over everything.

But she'd also seen too many movies where the heroine foolishly climbed into the tub not realizing the killer was in her bedroom. She double-checked the closet, under the bed and made sure the window was locked, then she barricaded herself in the bathroom after first looking behind the shower curtain again.

The chocolate was starting to take effect. She felt a mellowness wash over her as she turned on the faucet and the large claw-foot tub began to fill.

She could hardly hear the thunder rumbling outside. Without a window, she couldn't see the flashes of lightning. Maybe by the time she was through bathing, the storm would have died down to just rain.

She tried not to worry about her father, praying he would have regained consciousness by morning. She also tried not to think about the phonograph. Or the open window she'd found earlier in her bedroom. Or the fact that someone had gone through her suitcase.

As the tub filled, she opened the bottle of jasmine bubble bath that had been set out for her and poured a large dollop into the water. Drew again?

She yawned, stripped off her clothing and stepped into the tub, groggily sinking neck-deep into the warm water and jasmine-scented bubbles. The water felt like silk as it caressed her skin, warming her to her core. She closed her eyes.

Heaven. She was surprised how drowsy she felt suddenly, and behind her lids, saw a figure in a yellow raincoat running through the golden beams of her headlights and the pouring rain, heading for the brink of a waterfall.

Her eyes flew open. She shoved the image away. She didn't want to think what the sheriff would find at Lost Creek Falls.

As she lay back in the tub, she let herself drift to the soft lap and warm feel of the water, pretending she was supine on a raft under the summer sun, the ocean beneath her the color of Ford's eyes.

Her eyes closed, her lids too heavy to keep open. Ford's image appeared as if conjured up. Those insolent sea-green eyes met hers. His gaze caressed her face, her neck, her—

Her eyes flew open and she sat up, sloshing water in the tub. She looked around the room. His image had been so real that she expected to see Ford standing over her. The room was empty. Of course it was. The door was locked. She must have dozed off. She could have drowned.

"That's enough of that." It seemed to take all her energy to pull herself from the tub, rub herself dry with the towel, don the long white cotton nightgown she'd brought and unlock the bathroom door, let alone climb into bed.

As exhausted as she was, she found herself fighting sleep, afraid to close her eyes for fear of what she might see. Worse, what she might hear—the unbroken favorite 45 playing again on her mother's phonograph in the next room.

She stared hard at the ceiling, willing her lids open. It took all her effort. The old house creaked and groaned. Lightning flashed beyond the window curtains, thunder rattled the glass, echoing like a heartbeat inside her. Roz didn't even remember closing her eyes.

Ford couldn't sleep. After tossing and turning for a while, he finally gave up. He pulled on only a pair of jeans and padded barefoot into the kitchen to make himself a drink. He could feel the electricity in the air and smell the scent of the approaching rain as he took his glass out to the covered porch.

The wind groaned in the swaying tops of the trees, as lightning cut huge zigzagged seams in the darkness and thunder cracked like a shot overhead. He waited out the storm, restless and edgy.

The first sip of Scotch burned all the way down. Just what he needed. He knew he wouldn't be able to sleep until the storm moved on, until the rain fell in a monotonous downpour.

He looked toward the house, wondering if Rozalyn was asleep. She'd looked exhausted at the hospital. Why wouldn't she be asleep after the night she'd had. He tried not to feel sorry for her. A weird stepfamily. Her father in the hospital in a coma. And maybe even worse, Ford Lancaster dropping into her life. Talk about bad karma.

And there was her past. Her family's history of instability. He knew how that could haunt a person. It certainly could explain her reaction at Lost Creek Falls tonight. Of course, he hadn't seen a thing. Another sore point between them. Another reason she wouldn't want to trust him. As if she needed any more reasons.

He took another sip of his drink and smiled ruefully. He'd pretty much blown it with her. Except maybe for the kiss. For that moment he'd thought he had her right where he wanted her. She had been responding quite nicely. Until she kicked him.

He shook his head, amazed she'd come back here after her mother had committed suicide in that house. The woman had grit, that was for damned sure. Look at how she'd stood up to Emily and the rest of them. He smiled to himself. *Look how she stood up to you.*

He walked to the edge of the porch railing. This was the last place in the world he wanted to be. Worse, he hated what he was going to have to do. One thing was for certain, he couldn't let Rozalyn find out the truth from whoever had taken the disk. Not before she helped him find whatever it was Liam Sawyer had discovered in the woods before his injury.

Ford glanced toward the main house again. He couldn't see most of the structure because of the trees. But he could see the attic windows clearly. At first he thought he'd just imagined the flicker of light behind one of the windows.

He waited for the light to come on again.

It didn't.

Lightning ripped through the darkness in a blinding flash. A heartbeat later, thunder boomed.

Still no light flickered in the attic. Odd. Maybe he had just imagined it. Or the glow had been the reflection of lightning on the windowpane.

He looked down at his glass, surprised it was empty, and went back in to make another drink, trying to convince himself that whatever happened to Rozalyn Sawyer, she wasn't his responsibility. He would just get what he wanted and get out. Like he always had.

Inside the guesthouse, he sloshed a little more Scotch into his glass. The screen door banged against the door frame as the storm picked up. The first few drops of rain splattered loudly on the porch roof.

Ford could feel the power of the storm in the cold air blowing in through the screen door. He was already wired but now the night held an odd expectation that made the hair rise on his forearms.

He slipped on athletic shoes and a T-shirt, picked up his drink and went back out on the porch again to watch the storm. Between the crashes of thunder, he could hear the rain pelting the leaves out in the darkness as the storm centered itself over the town as if hunkering down for the duration.

He breathed a sigh of relief. Finally. Rain. Wonderful monotonous rain that would let him sleep. He realized he didn't need the Scotch and dumped the contents of his glass over the railing, anxious now for the oblivion of sleep, the one place he might find peace.

But as he turned to go back inside, he made the mistake of glancing toward the house again. This time there was no mistaking the flicker of a flashlight beam behind one of the attic windows. He watched the light bob across the attic and wondered what someone was doing up there. He imagined most of the family agreed with Suzanne; they wouldn't be caught dead up there.

The flashlight went out as a lamp flared in the right-hand corner of the attic. Odd. The person who had turned it on was behind a pillar. He waited for the person to step out.

Instead, the movement came from off to the right. A figure in a long white nightgown appeared as if an apparition. Even from this distance he recognized the hair. Long and strawberry-blond, it floated around her shoulders, shimmering in the lamplight.

She moved to one of the windows at the center of the attic. For the first time he noticed the widow's walk.

His glass slipped from his fingers. He was already running toward the house as Rozalyn Sawyer opened the windows wide and climbed out onto the widow's walk four stories above the ground, the wind whipping the cloth of the white nightgown around her slim body, her strawberry-blond hair now aglow in the light of the storm, as rain fell in large, hard and angry drops from the darkness.

Chapter 7

Ford let out an oath as he barreled through the dense vegetation of the garden to the back of the house. Above him, Rozalyn balanced on the edge of the widow's walk—just as she had at the falls. The hem of her nightgown snapped in the wind through a curtain of rain.

He didn't dare call to her. Didn't dare draw her attention downward. Running to the back door, he tried the knob, not surprised to find it locked. *Bang on the door. Get someone up there. Quick.*

He rejected the idea as quickly as it had come. The noise alone might cause her to jump. Looking upward, he realized there was only one way to reach her. He'd have to climb the tree next to the house.

The cold soaking rain beat down on him as he quickly began to climb. Lightning fractured the darkness. Thunder detonated overhead.

Climbing a tree in a thunderstorm. *Great, Lancaster.* And all to save a woman who was bound and determined to kill herself. If he lucked out and didn't slip and fall from the wet tree limbs, he'd probably get struck by lightning.

And as if his luck couldn't get any worse, the tree wasn't high enough to take him all the way to the attic. He crawled out on a limb near one of the windows on the third floor. He started to break the window but saw that someone had already broken the lock. A screwdriver lay on the edge of the windowsill out of view from inside.

He took the screwdriver, inserted it between the window and frame in the same grooves made earlier and lifted. The window rose with a groan.

A flash of lightning illuminated a girl's room. Rozalyn's former bedroom?

Still hanging on to the limb, he swung over to the windowsill, then ducking down, dropped into the room with a thud. A cat burglar he wasn't.

On top of the open suitcase on a trunk at the end of the bed was the rust-colored sweater Rozalyn had been wearing earlier. It was her bedroom all right. Except she should have been sacked out, sound asleep. But the bed was empty, the covers thrown back.

He rushed out into the hallway wondering how to get to the attic as he glanced toward the staircase. Not that way. He swung his gaze back down the hallway and felt a chill. There was a dark space between the paneling and wall at the end the hall. A secret door of some kind.

He ran down the hall. Definitely a secret door. A faint light glowed at the top of a set of steep narrow steps that rose upward. On the closest step he saw one small barefoot print in the dust. Rozalyn.

With only a moment's hesitation at the thought of the door closing behind him and being trapped inside, he scrambled up the steps, hoping he could get out at the top as easily as he'd gotten in.

He hadn't gone far when he heard something that made him miss a step. A shudder tore through him. Cripes, what the hell was that?

But he knew even before he reached the top of the stairs, grateful to see another hidden door—also open, and beyond it the source of the light and the bloodcurdling sound.

A small lamp glowed in a corner of the huge attic. Most of the room was filled with antiques that had been piled along one side, leaving the side along the windows open.

His breath caught when he recognized the source of the high-pitched keening. Rozalyn. He followed the horrific sound and her dusty barefooted prints across the attic, drawing up short just behind the widow's walk.

The hair rose on the back of his neck. Rozalyn stood framed against the darkness, her feet balancing on the six-inch wide railing, nothing else but air between her and the ground four stories below. Her head was thrown back, the hideous pain-filled cry emanating from her throat.

"Rozalyn?" he said softly, afraid that he might startle her. He thought of when he'd grabbed her earlier tonight at the waterfall. Unfortunately, he wasn't as close this time.

He took a couple of steps toward her. The old wooden floorboards under him groaned. He froze.

She hadn't moved, hadn't seemed to have heard him over her cries. Her arms stretched out as if she planned to do a swan dive off a high board. Her soaking wet nightgown clung to her body, the hem snapping in the wind.

He took another couple of steps toward her, afraid to say anything this close to her for fear she might fall. Or jump. Another step or two and he would be close enough to make a grab for her. But her flesh would be wet and slick. She'd be damned hard to hang on to.

The keening sound stopped with a suddenness that rattled him. The deathly silence that followed was almost more frightening. Suddenly her head jerked to one side as if she heard something on the wind.

His breath caught in his throat as she turned her head slowly toward him. He feared seeing him would frighten her.

Her eyes. Oh God, her eyes.

He swore under his breath and grabbed for her.

The moment his fingers clamped over her wrist, she blinked, the glazed eyes fighting to focus on him. She let out a cry of alarm, swaying on the railing. Her wrist was slick from the rain. He got his arm around her waist as she tried to pull away, seeming confused, frightened, disoriented.

She looked down then at the ground far below her and let out a startled cry, staggering backward. He caught her in his arms and carried her away from the widow's walk and the four-story drop back into the attic.

"Where is she?" Rozalyn cried the moment he set

her down a safe distance from the windows. She sunk to the floor as if her legs wouldn't hold her. She was trembling and her eyes were still glassy. "Where is she?"

His heart quickened.

She looked past him as if she thought there was someone else in the attic with them. "Didn't you hear her?"

"Who?" he asked on a breath.

"My mother. She was calling me." Her voice broke with emotion as she glanced toward the widow's walk and shuddered, tears welling in her eyes. "Tell me you heard her," she said in a whisper, looking up at him as if she was depending on him.

You're looking at the wrong guy, he thought. "Sorry."

"I don't understand—" A sob broke from her.

"You were walking in your sleep. I have a little sister who does the same thing." He couldn't get the frightening image of her eyes from his mind. She'd looked blind, lost in another world miles away.

"Sleepwalking?" She was trembling so hard he could practically hear her teeth chatter. He dragged a worn quilt from a pile on one of the ornate antique tables and draped it around her.

"Lisa usually walked during a bad dream." He hoped that was all it was in Rozalyn's case.

"I heard something."

Just like she'd seen something earlier at the waterfall? "Old houses make strange noises sometimes—"

"It wasn't the house." She shuddered. "My mother. She was calling me, *to help her*." Eyes swimming in tears, she glanced toward the widow's walk where her mother had committed suicide. Her face crumpled. "What was I doing out there?"

He wished he knew. "I'm sure it was just a bad dream," he said, not sure of that at all. If anything, it was more like a nightmare since something had gotten her to climb out onto the railing of that widow's walk.

She looked around again, clearly not so sure now, still seeming disoriented. "It was so real," she whispered.

"Dreams can be like that," he said softly and brushed a lock of wet hair back from her cheek. Just before her brown eyes boiled over with tears again, he got a good look at them. "What are you on?"

"What?" She wiped at her tears, staring up at him.

"Drugs, what did you take?"

"Nothing. I don't take drugs."

"Not even something to sleep?"

She shook her head, quickly stopping the motion, eyes closing tightly as if the movement had made her sick.

"You're coming with me." He pulled her to her feet. She swayed, obviously woozy. He expected her to put up a fight but without a word she let him carry her to the paneled opening and the hidden staircase.

She was trembling, from the cold, fear and whatever drug dulled her eyes as he helped her descend the narrow steps. Then he carried her to her bedroom.

"We have to get you into something dry," he said quietly as he closed the door behind them. When he turned back to her, she had slumped on the edge of the bed clutching the quilt as if lost.

He went into the bathroom, came back with a couple of large towels and toweled the rainwater from her hair. He was tempted to get her into the bathtub but it would take too long to fill. He had a shower in the guesthouse. All he had to do was get her there.

He found clothing, hiking boots, her toothbrush and stuffed everything into a pillowcase from the bed. He handed it to her, swept her up again and quietly carried her down the stairs, out the back door and through the rain and garden to the guesthouse.

Once inside, he took her into the bathroom. She sat on the toilet seat still wrapped in the quilt as he turned on the shower. Steam filled the room quickly and, when he was sure it was warm enough, he gently pulled her to her feet and slipped the quilt off her shoulders.

The nightgown clung to her like a second skin. He sucked in a breath at the sight of her body flushed under the thin white fabric.

"Damn," he breathed. She was beautiful, her skin lightly freckled and pale, her breasts full and round, her nipples dark and hard against the wet cotton. She had a slim waist, a flat stomach and a small mound of strawberry-blond hair at the vee between her legs.

She took his breath away.

"Rozalyn," he said softly as he looked into her dark eyes. She trembled, still looking dazed, and he couldn't be sure if it was because of the drug she'd ingested or hypothermia setting in. He had to get her warmed up and straightened out. "I'm going to take off your wet nightgown."

She didn't resist, didn't speak or even blink as he pulled the nightgown up over her head and drew her toward the shower. She stumbled and leaned into him as if her legs still would not hold her.

Kicking off his shoes, still in his jeans and T-shirt,

he stepped into the shower with her, holding her as the warm water cascaded over her naked body. She wrapped her arms around his neck, her face against his chest, and he held her to him and thought about baseball rather than the naked woman in his arms.

After a few minutes, her trembling slowed. Warm steam filled the small bathroom like thick warm fog. He stood with her until they'd emptied the hot water tank, until her skin was bright pink.

She seemed stronger, more steady once they were out of the shower as if shedding the effects of the drug—if not the horror of what could have happened up there on the widow's walk.

Mentally reciting major league statistics, he quickly toweled her dry and pulled one of his dry T-shirts over her head. It was large enough that it dropped to below her knees, covering her glorious body.

Wrapping her in a dry quilt from the bed, he carried her to the living room couch where he deposited her while he went into the bedroom to change into dry clothes himself. He needed a drink. Desperately.

When he came back out, she looked up. She hadn't said a word in the shower or out. She looked a hundred percent better. "I know what you're thinking."

"I doubt that," he said softly.

"You think I went up there to jump," she said in a whisper.

He shook his head. "I think someone drugged you and somehow tricked you into going up to the attic and getting on that widow's walk."

"How is that possible?"

"I don't know. You appeared to be in a hypnotic

state. At first I thought you were walking in your sleep. Until I got a good look at your pupils."

"My mother jumped to her death from that same widow's walk," she said shakily.

He nodded.

"Don't you think it's a little strange that I would go up there like I did and—" Her voice broke.

"You weren't up there trying to kill yourself or you would have jumped before I got to you," he said.

She didn't look so sure about that. "How *did* you happen to see me in the attic? I don't remember anything except being really drowsy and going to bed."

He sighed. "I was out on the guesthouse porch waiting for the storm when I saw a light in one of the attic windows. Then I saw you. I climbed the tree beside the house, went through your bedroom and up those stairs hidden in the wall."

"The door was open?" she asked surprised.

He nodded. "Your bare footprints were in the dust so I knew that was the way you'd gone up." Now that he thought about it, there were no other footprints.

"You climbed the tree outside my bedroom?" Her cheeks flushed.

He wondered why she was blushing. "The lock was already broken. There was a screwdriver on the ledge where someone had pried open the window before I came along."

"Well, whatever made me go up there, thank you for—" she waved a hand through the air, her gaze shifting toward the bathroom, her cheeks in high color "—for saving me."

He met her gaze and didn't like what he saw. She thought he was some kind of hero. Far from it. "You would have awakened and climbed down if I hadn't shown up."

She gave him a look that said they both knew better than that.

"After you came back from the hospital, what did you have to drink?" he asked.

She frowned. "Nothing. I had a couple of Swiss chocolates—"

"Ones you brought with you?"

She shook her head slowly. "No, they were in a dish beside the bed with a note from Drew."

He swore under his breath. "I didn't see a note when I was looking for a change of clothing for you. Are you sure Drew left the chocolates?"

"No. His name was on the note but I wouldn't know his handwriting." She stared at him as if just starting to comprehend what he was saying. "You think there was something in the chocolates? You can't think that someone in the house put drugs in—"

"Any member of *that* family is capable, Emily included. They all had access to your room and someone had either gone in your bedroom window or wanted you to believe they had."

She bit her lower lip. "That's what I thought when I returned from the hospital to find the window open. Someone had gone through my suitcase." She looked at him. "You don't think I'm crazy?"

"I'm not saying that." He smiled. "You want some coffee?"

She shook her head. "I want to sleep for a week."

Her brown eyes were clearer, the effects of the drug wearing off. He went to the bar and sloshed some

Scotch into a glass. He pressed it into her hand. "Just a sip."

She stared down at it, lifted the glass to her lips, drank a little and made a face.

He smiled at her. "It's an acquired taste."

"Not one I care to acquire," she said and handed him back the glass.

He drained what little was left and looked down at her. She looked as if she'd been dragged through the wringer. Right now she was giving him one of her narrowed-eye looks. He could almost hear the wheels turning in her head. She was trying to figure him out, no doubt finally realizing that he might have an ulterior motive for everything he'd been doing. He smiled to himself, liking the fact that the woman was sharp.

"Why are you being so nice to me?" she asked.

"What makes you think I'm not always nice?"

"I'm serious."

"I can see that."

She studied him. He tried not to flinch.

"I don't mean to sound unappreciative but… I just feel like there might be some reason you keep saving me."

"Just my bad luck at being in the wrong place at the wrong time," he said.

"Or my good luck?"

He wanted to tell her that his coming into her life would be considered anything but good luck. But hell, that would be counterproductive to getting what he wanted now, wouldn't it?

"You can have the bed," he said and turned his back to walk down the short hall to the linen closet where he took out bedding. "I'll take the couch."

* * *

Roz couldn't believe it. Damn, if she wasn't careful she was going to start trusting him. She stared after the man, reminding herself who he was. Ford Lancaster. But how could everything that had happened tonight *not* change her original opinion of him?

He'd written that article years ago and he'd had his reason for wanting to hurt his father. Now he was trying to make up for what he'd done by helping her and her father.

So why was something still niggling at her, something that warned her not to be taken in by him no matter how kind or caring he appeared to be?

She looked into those pale green eyes as he returned to the room and felt a slight tremor. "You aren't just trying to get me to lower my defenses by being nice to me, are you?"

His smile was disarming. "You're too smart for that."

She gave him a wary look as he put the bedding on the couch next to her and felt a moment's alarm.

He chuckled. "Rozalyn, sex is the last thing on my mind right now."

Really? She wished *she* could say that. She didn't like the feeling just looking into his eyes gave her. She thought about his arms around her in the shower, her naked body pressed against—

"You should try to get some sleep," he said. "We can talk about my plans to get you to lower your defenses in the morning."

He was trying to make light of it but was it possible he was feeling what she was? Obviously not. She got to her feet. "Thank you. For everything tonight."

He smiled at that. "You make it sound like I took you on a date."

Why did he have to make it so hard to thank him?

"Before our date ends, there's something I need you to do." He went into the kitchen and came back with a paper cup. He handed it to her. "Give me a sample."

"You aren't serious."

"Humor me, okay? It's not like I asked you to get naked again." His gaze met hers. "Or have sex with me."

She felt herself flush in spite of the fact that he was baiting her. "You don't take compliments well."

He raised a brow obviously finding humor in that. "I've had so few I'm at a loss as to how to take them."

"Are you ever serious?"

"I'm serious right now," he said, his pale aqua gaze boring into hers. He pushed the paper cup at her. "Just leave it beside the sink."

She thought of him in the shower with her, how strong and solid and comforting he'd been. A different man than the one standing in front of her now. Or was that just what he wanted her to believe? Her defenses had definitely been down when they'd been in the shower together. If he had wanted to take advantage of her, he could have and she sensed he'd known it. So why hadn't he?

Was it possible he really was in Timber Falls to make amends for what he did to her father—and his own?

She pushed aside her misgivings. The man had saved her life and she was here with him now, planning to spend the rest of the night under the same roof, just feet from him.

"I didn't bring you out here to jump your bones, if that's what you're worried about," he said, looking amused.

"It never crossed my mind."

"Right." The look in his eyes curled her toes as he smiled lazily at her. "Just get some rest, okay?"

"You're an impossible man, you know that?" she said.

"It's been pointed out to me on numerous occasions."

"I'm sure it has." She started toward the bedroom.

"I need to do a couple of things early in the morning. I'm sure you'll want to go see your father before we head out into the woods. Why don't I meet you back here at, say, nine o'clock?"

She turned to look at him, wondering what he had to do in the morning. "Okay."

His back was to her as he started to make a bed on the couch for himself.

"See you in the morning," she said to his broad back, then turned, noticing that a chair had been wedged under the knob of the patio door in the bedroom. "What's with the chair under the doorknob?"

Ford had forgotten for a moment about the break-in. He turned to find her standing in the doorway and realized that wasn't all he'd forgotten. "I had an uninvited visitor earlier. Don't worry, he won't be back. The chair is just a precaution."

"Did he take anything?"

For just a moment, he actually thought about telling her the truth. "No. I guess he must have been looking for something valuable."

"Or something about my father's find," she said quietly. "You think it was the person who attacked my father?" If she hadn't been scared before, she was now. But he couldn't tell if it was for herself or her father. He suspected it was the latter. "We have to find whatever this person is after," she said with brave determination. "My father won't be safe until we do."

We. Ford nodded, torn between his relief and his guilt. Wasn't this exactly what he'd hoped for? She knew her father—and the area—better than he did. If he could just keep her alive, she might prove invaluable.

Yep, he had her right where he wanted her.

Now if he just didn't screw things up—

He stepped to her, thinking about nothing but the fear in her dark eyes and the slight tremble of her lips as her words died off. He hadn't planned to take her in his arms, let alone kiss her.

But she felt so right as his arms closed around her and the soft curves of her body pressed into him. When she looked up and met his gaze, all he could think about was her lush mouth, the feel of her lips, the taste of her.

He lowered his mouth, brushed his lips over hers, a quiver of desire quaking through him. She pushed herself up on tiptoes and kissed him tenderly, a sigh escaping her lips.

All his restraint from earlier in the shower evaporated in an instant as she drew back to look into his eyes. He dropped his mouth to hers, dragging her closer, crushing her to him as he kissed her with a passion that he hadn't known he possessed.

How he wanted her, needed her. The thought left him feeling like he'd been dunked in a bucket of ice water.

He pushed himself back from her. Damn, but he *was* going to screw this up, maybe already had. He could hear his pulse thundering in his ears as he tried to catch his breath and get his equilibrium again. "I'm sorry, I didn't mean to—I..."

She looked as shaken and stunned as he felt as she stumbled back, away from him. She touched her tongue to her upper lip and took a ragged breath. "Good night," she said, looking a little sheepish as she closed the bedroom door.

"Good night." He smiled to himself as he heard her lock the door. Did she think he would force himself on her? If he had wanted her, he could have taken her earlier in the shower. And without even trying. Or taken her a few moments ago with only a little effort.

No, if they ever made love, it would be with a lot more than just her consent. She'd have to want him as badly as he did her, which was saying a lot.

He chuckled ruefully at the odds of that happening. Sure she'd kissed him back. And it wouldn't be a kiss he'd soon forget. But he knew it had been a kiss born of gratitude. He didn't kid himself about that. He hadn't begun to chip away at her reserve let alone get her to lower her defenses.

But the idea held great appeal. Much more than it should have. He wanted her. Worse, he wanted her to want him with the same fervor. What the hell was wrong with him? He didn't need this, didn't want this.

Lie to everyone else, but don't start lying to yourself, Lancaster. You kissed her because you're starting to feel something for her.

He scoffed at the idea as he walked into the kitchen.

He was too smart to fall for Liam Sawyer's daughter. Cripes, how foolish would that be?

No, it was just physical. Nothing more.

He started to pour himself a drink but changed his mind. Now, more than ever he needed his senses about him.

The rain was falling, a hypnotic shower that drummed softly on the roof. He went back into the living room and sprawled on the couch but he knew he wasn't going to be able to sleep.

He closed his eyes, listening to the downpour, thinking about the kiss, angry with himself not only for initiating it but for enjoying it so much.

What kind of fool was he? When she found out the truth about him, she would have nothing to do with him. Worse, if he wasn't careful, he would lose his focus, forget why he was here, forget what really mattered.

But even as he thought it, he remembered the way she'd felt in his arms. Soft. Lush. Amazing…

His eyes flew open and he sat up with a start. The light in the attic. The first one he'd seen had been a flashlight beam. But later when he'd spotted Roz—

He scrubbed his hands over his face and looked toward the closed bedroom door. Rozalyn hadn't had a flashlight. The light had been coming from a lamp as she moved across to the balcony. That meant— The person with the flashlight had turned on the lamp and then…

Rozalyn had been right about one thing, she hadn't been alone in the attic. Someone had been up there. Waiting for her.

He fell back on the couch, but sleep was now out of

the question. Someone had drugged Rozalyn tonight, sure as hell. The urine sample would give him an idea of what drug was used once he had it tested. But how did that person get her up to the attic and trick her into climbing out onto the widow's walk where her mother had committed suicide?

And was it just to mess with her mind?

Or to kill her?

One disturbing thought kept him awake long into the rainy night. Rozalyn Sawyer wasn't safe. Not in that house. Not in Timber Falls. Maybe not anywhere.

And he feared he knew the reason.

Bones.

Chapter 8

Roz woke to the sun. Outside the patio doors was one of Oregon's famous sunshowers complete with a double rainbow. The storm had passed, leaving the sky clear, sunshine spilling down through the trees like a sign from heaven.

Her father was going to come out of his coma.

She and Ford would find whatever her father had discovered and who had tried to kill him…if someone really had tried. She shuddered at the thought. But Ford believed it so strongly, how could she not?

She got up and showered, reminded of Ford and the night before, the two of them in this shower together. Her cheeks flamed at the memory—including the kiss! Was he still in the next room sleeping or had he already gone out on those errands he had to run?

She promised herself she would keep him at arm's

length. No more mistakes like the one last night. If he hadn't stopped the kiss when he had—

She shoved away the thought. The two of them would find out the truth about her father's fall, but there was no way she was lowering her defenses around Ford Lancaster again. He might be attractive to look at but he was dangerous. That was probably what attracted her. She had always picked boring men, safe men. Men she could never get serious about.

She glanced at the closed door, imagining the man behind it. Ford Lancaster was nothing like those men and that's what scared her. With Ford, it would be all or nothing. Total surrender.

As she dumped out the clothes he'd put in the pillowcase for her last night, she was touched again by his kindness. It made her feel a little guilty for still having misgivings about his motivations.

He'd saved her life last night on the widow's walk. Had she just been sleepwalking or was he right? Was it possible someone had put drugs in the chocolates? Drugged or asleep, why would she follow her mother's voice to the attic?

She remembered her mother's favorite record playing on the old phonograph. She would rather believe it was just a short in the wiring. Or a peculiarity of the electrical storm. What she didn't want to believe was that someone in this house actually wanted to hurt her. Even kill her.

And not necessarily someone in the house, she thought, remembering what Ford had said about finding a screwdriver on the ledge outside her window.

She shook her head, as confused as she'd been when she'd awakened to find herself standing on the widow's walk railing about to— About to what? Not jump. No, she would never have done that. Would she have?

Didn't she once read that people often walked in their sleep when they were under a great deal of stress?

Except Ford is convinced you were drugged.

If she had been, she didn't feel any aftereffects. In fact, she was surprised how good she felt. It was as if this was the first good night's sleep she'd had in years. She could only hope her father had also had a good night's rest and was better this morning.

As she finished dressing, the only things she couldn't find were her shoes. She was sure she'd seen her hiking boots here last night. Hadn't she seen Ford dump them out of the pillowcase?

She looked around the room. When she was a teenager, she and Charity had sleepovers in the small guesthouse. They had stayed up half the night giggling and talking about boys. Of course Charity only talked about Mitch, but Roz would imagine a stranger, some white knight she had yet to meet, who would ride in and carry her away on his trusty steed.

She thought of the man sleeping on the couch in the room beyond the door. No Sir Lancelot that one. Oh, he'd sweep her off her feet, carry her away on his trusty steed, then drop her off without ceremony while she watched him ride into the sunset.

The problem was, he was starting to look like a knight to her. One more heroic act and she'd be a goner.

She thought of how he'd behaved in the shower. She'd been stark naked with the man and he'd been the perfect gentleman.

But that kiss just before she'd gone to bed had been anything but gentlemanly. She felt her face flame. He'd aroused more than just sexual feelings. His tenderness in the shower coupled with saving her life had drawn her in like a lasso.

She reminded herself that he'd been the one who'd stopped the kiss. Put a halt to what was bound to have happened after the kiss.

Was it possible he had no interest in her other than to keep her alive so she could help him find whatever her father had discovered in the woods?

Well, he'd missed his chance last night.

So why did she feel like she'd missed hers, too?

Because no man had ever stirred these kinds of feelings in her.

It's just gratitude, she told herself as she made the bed and remembered where she'd last seen her hiking boots. Ford had taken them out of the pillowcase and put them down beside the couch.

She moved to the bedroom door and opened it a crack. If he was still here, she didn't want to wake him. And if he was already gone—

He was still here. He lay on the couch, head back, lips parted, snoring lightly. She couldn't help smiling. Something about him snoring made him more human.

And there in front of the couch were the toes of her boots peeking out from under the quilt spread over him.

She tiptoed closer, leaning down to inch toward her boots, enjoying watching him sleep. He looked vulnerable asleep, and the sight touched something deep inside her.

She dropped to her hands and knees and had just reached out for her boots when he let out a sigh and rolled over onto his side, his face just inches from hers.

She snagged hold of her boots and slowly slid them toward her.

She was close enough she could see his lashes, black against his skin. His stubborn jawline was dark with stubble and looked rough to the touch. She fought the urge to cup his cheek in her hand, remembering the rough feel of his beard last night when he'd kissed her.

He sighed again, his lashes fluttered, then his lips turned up at the corners in a slow, sexy smile. She felt her heart kick up a beat. She drew her boots to her and slipped back from him. Terrified by the feelings he evoked in her.

Even if everything he'd told her was the truth, he was a disagreeable man, egotistical and self-righteous and impossible. And yet for a startling moment, she had the strongest urge to cup his face in her palms, to press her lips against his, to be a part of that smile. This time it would end in more than a kiss.

Crazy. She was crazy. Maybe she *had* gone up to the attic last night to jump. Maybe she'd been stone-cold sober and awake.

She took one last look at him before retreating out the door into the sunshine. Her heart was pounding and she felt light-headed as she cut through the garden and around the side of the house to her SUV. Then impulsively, as it was such a nice day, she decided to walk to the hospital.

Ford cracked one eyelid open as he heard the door close and smiled to himself. For a moment there, he'd thought she was going to kiss him. He'd held his breath, willing himself not to move, not to think about closing her in his arms. He could still smell her scent in the air as he rolled over onto his back and stared up at the ceiling. Damn, he was going to have to take a cold shower. An ice-cold one.

You're enjoying this way too much.

He smiled at that thought. Hell, yes.

It struck him that he wanted her to like him.

He groaned at the thought. "Let's not lose sight of what's at stake here, all right?" he said to himself as he threw back the quilt. "Eventually she's going to find out the truth and you're going to be a bastard again."

So true. He headed for the shower, unable not to remember the night before and the naked woman he'd held in his arms as the warm water cascaded over her skin. He turned the water on cold and threw himself under the icy spray.

He'd just gotten out and dressed when he heard a knock at the door. He thought about ignoring it but whoever it was knew he was in. His pickup was parked right outside.

He opened the door, disappointed to find Drew Lane standing there. He'd rather hoped that Rozalyn had come back to wake him with that kiss.

"Mother thought you might like to join us for breakfast," Drew said as he tried to see past Ford into the room. "Unless you have other plans. Then we're all going to the hospital to see how Liam is doing."

Obviously Drew had discovered Rozalyn wasn't in her bedroom and thought she might be here. "Please give my apologies to your mother but I do have other plans."

Drew glanced at Ford's still damp dark hair. "Mother will be disappointed," he said, sounding angry.

"Tell her thanks for the invite. Maybe some other

time." Ford closed the door and watched with too much satisfaction as Drew scowled and turned to head back through the garden to the house.

Ford reminded himself that if he was right, someone had drugged Rozalyn last night and got her up on that widow's walk railing. That someone could have been Drew Lane. But now wasn't the time to confront him about the chocolates. First Ford had to be sure they'd been drugged.

He hoped Drew would think that Rozalyn was under his watchful eye—if not in his bed. Both were a lie. But then, Drew didn't know that, did he?

As Ford left the house, he thought about what else? Rozalyn Sawyer. What if she really had been at the top of that waterfall last night to jump? What if she hadn't been sleepwalking or drugged? What if she was more damaged by her mother's death than even he was by his father's?

Then the urine sample he had sealed in a container on the seat beside him wouldn't show any drugs, he thought as he drove to the lab and dropped it off. The lab tech put a rush on it for the hundred-dollar incentive Ford offered. He left his cell phone number and the tech promised to get back to him as soon as possible.

Ford picked up three egg-muffin specials at Betty's Café and washed down one on his way to the hospital with one of the two coffees he'd purchased.

A different nurse was at the desk.

"Any change in Liam Sawyer's condition?" he asked.

"The same," she said as he headed down the hall to Liam's room. As far as he could tell, Liam was the hospital's only patient.

From the doorway he saw Rozalyn beside her father's bed, holding his hand, her head bent toward him, talking quietly. Ford motioned to Jesse to come out.

"Hey, breakfast," the deputy said. "Thanks, man." He snarfed down the egg and ham muffins and gulped the coffee Ford had brought him.

"I thought you might need a break," Ford said.

"A short one," Jesse agreed and grinned before sprinting down the hall to the men's lavatory.

Ford stood outside the hospital room door, watching Rozalyn with her father, touched by her tenderness, worried what it would do to her to lose another parent now. He cursed himself as he realized he liked her more all the time and didn't want to see her hurt.

But she would be hurt, he reminded himself.

Jesse returned, his face washed shiny, his long hair wet and tied back again in a ponytail.

"I'm not sure how long I'll be gone today," Ford said.

"No problem. Everything's cool here. Mitch said he'd stop by to relieve me later. Thanks for breakfast." He slipped back into the hospital room. Rozalyn didn't seem to notice.

Ford left, reminding himself that it was just a matter of time before Rozalyn learned the truth about him— even if the thief who took the computer disk didn't rat him out.

And then there would be no convincing her that he wasn't everything she thought he was.

He just hoped to hell he knew what he was doing. A lot was riding on this. He slid behind the wheel of his pickup and started the engine. He'd better quit thinking about Rozalyn Sawyer and go to work.

But first he had to find out if what he feared about her just might be true.

* * *

Charity had just taken a bite of her banana cream pie when she heard the bell tinkle over the front door of Betty's Café. She closed her eyes. For months now, whenever she ate something rich and wonderful and closed her eyes, she had visions of Sheriff Mitch Tanner. Lately, he was always dressed in a tuxedo and—be still her racing heart—he was standing in front of an altar at the church and he was looking at her, smiling, as if he loved her more than even he could imagine.

"Morning, Charity," Mitch said, taking his usual stool next to her.

She opened her eyes and turned to smile at him. "Good morning, Sheriff." Mitch seemed to think he still had a chance of remaining a bachelor. Men could be such fools.

"I saw the paper this morning," he said after Betty slid a cup of coffee and a slice of banana cream pie in front of him without a word and took off as if she knew all hell was going to break loose any moment. Betty knew the two of them well—and had seen today's *Timber Falls Courier.*

Plus Mitch had a copy of the newspaper gripped in his right hand. "Charity," he said under his breath. "I thought I warned you about printing anything that could get you killed."

She looked over at him in surprise. "You think it's that good?"

He groaned. "Do you have a death wish, woman?"

"You said yourself we might never know the truth about the kidnapping unless we rattle a few cages," she whispered back.

"I believe you just misquoted me," he said through

gritted teeth. "I said we might never know the truth. Period. The cage rattling was all yours."

"I stand corrected." She smiled at him. "The banana cream pie is amazing this morning." She took another bite and licked her lips.

His dark eyes softened as he watched her, desire sparking in them. Finally, he shook his head as if at something he just couldn't believe. "What am I going to do with you?"

"Oh, I have some great ideas."

"I'm sure you do." He picked up his fork and took a bite of his pie. "I think you'd better get your Aunt Florie to come stay with you until this blows over."

Oh no, they'd been here before. "Not Florie. Look what happened last time."

Last time Mitch had not only had her Aunt Florie staying with her, but also a deputy, and she'd still been abducted and almost killed.

"You're right," he said. "Protecting you from yourself is impossible."

"There is only one man who can protect me," she said and took a forkful of pie, closing her eyes, waiting to see that image of Mitch in the tux. She opened her eyes and winked at him.

"Don't start," Mitch said but there was no humor in his tone.

She took another bite of pie, closed her eyes and saw Mitch at the altar again. She did love him in a tux.

When she opened her eyes he was studying her as if he wondered where she'd gone and what she'd seen behind those closed eyelids. *If he only knew.*

"I know what you're thinking," she said.

"Do you?" he asked, sounding as if he hoped that wasn't the case.

"I'm a journalist. It's like a degree in human nature."

He rolled his eyes. "You have a degree in nosy is all."

She shrugged and smiled. "You might be surprised." She picked up her fork and took a bite of her pie, closing her eyes, waiting for that image of Mitch in the tux.

"I think you should move in with me."

Her eyes flew open. "You're that worried about Wade?"

"I wasn't thinking about Wade."

She cocked her head at him, her heart hammering in her chest. "What exactly are you proposing, Mitch Tanner?"

His dark gaze held hers. He looked nervous as hell. "I think... I think we should be together right now."

Easy, heart. Okay, it was progress. Just not the progress she'd hoped for. A date and he thought they should move in together?

"You're saying you want to take this to the next step or that you're just trying to protect me?" she asked carefully, trying not to start cheering wildly.

He looked around the café. No one was sitting close by but still he seemed to have trouble saying the words. "All I think about is kissing you," he whispered. "It's driving me crazy. I want to make love to you. In a bed. And I don't want to leave afterward and go home. I want you there when I wake up in the morning and when I go to bed at night."

She couldn't catch her breath. How many years had she wished he'd say those words, dreamed he would, waited for him to?

There was just one problem. She wanted to do this right. She came from a family of alternative thinkers, a hippie mom, a fortune-telling aunt, two sisters who spent more time moving in and out of apartments with different boyfriends than Mayflower movers.

But just the thought of going to bed and waking up in Mitch's arms was almost more than she could take. Tears stung her eyes. "Could you be a little more specific?"

He looked past her. "Here comes Roz," he said, sounding relieved. "I have to go anyway. We'll talk later."

She wanted to scream no! "Aren't you even going to finish your pie?" she asked, afraid she'd only dreamed this conversation.

"No, but I'm sure you won't let it go to waste." Then he did something so out of character it left her speechless—a natural occurrence in its own right. He bent close and kissed her. A quick kiss but right on the lips and then he was gone, saying hello to Roz on his way out.

Charity stared after him, in surprise and delight. She really was making progress with that man. Who would have guessed after all these years?

Her gaze shifted to her old friend. "Roz," she cried, jumping up from the stool and rushing to give her a hug. She would see Mitch later and with a lot of luck, he would finally get up the guts to say the "M" word: marriage.

Ford Lancaster worked his way down the embankment at Lost Creek Falls, telling himself he was crazier than Rozalyn Sawyer—which was saying a lot.

The slope was treacherous, steep and slippery with moss and spray from the waterfall. He clung to rocks and tree limbs and did his best to keep his feet under him. To make matters worse, he was quickly soaked to the skin from the spray.

He slid down the last few feet to the creek bottom and stood for a moment looking back up at the waterfall—and the huge rock at the top where he'd first met Rozalyn the night before. Just seeing how far up it was made him dizzy and sick to his stomach. If she had fallen or been pushed—

He didn't even want to think about that. Maybe he hadn't rescued her, hadn't saved her life. Maybe she would have kept her footing and not fallen from the top of the waterfall—let alone jumped. Maybe she wouldn't have done a swan dive off the widow's walk railing last night, either.

But that was why he was here, wasn't it? He told himself he just didn't know and if there was one thing he hated, it was not being one hundred percent certain. It's why he'd become a scientist.

Next to him the water churned and splashed over the rocks, roaring on down the narrow canyon. He stared into the deep green holes as he walked from the base of the waterfall downstream. He was looking for a yellow raincoat, one he didn't expect to find. How crazy was that?

He shook his head, disgusted with himself. He had better things to do and little time. But he wanted desperately to believe her. That was the bottom line, wasn't it? He wanted to believe a woman who didn't believe a word that came out of his mouth—and shouldn't. If he wasn't crazy, he damned sure was some kind of fool.

He moved along the slick moss-covered wet rocks, following the creek as it cut down through the gorge. He told himself he wouldn't be here if it hadn't been for that detour sign. This morning he'd checked. There was only one road off the highway and that came to a dead end here at the falls. He'd called the road department as well.

No mistake. Whoever had put that detour sign there hadn't been authorized to do so.

No, he thought, the person who'd put it there had wanted to get someone to turn off to the falls last night.

Him? Or Rozalyn? There hadn't been anyone else on the highway and with the pouring rain and the lack of traffic this time of year, Ford didn't think it was just an idle prank. Someone had known they would be driving up this way last night and had been waiting for them.

Except he didn't think the detour sign had been put there for him. That meant someone had wanted Rozalyn to see a suicide from the top of the waterfall. And it was too much of a coincidence that Rozalyn's mother had also jumped to her death.

It was a wild theory given he had no proof. Especially for a scientist who operated on fact. Ford prided himself on only believing in things he could see and prove.

But dammit, he'd seen a detour sign in the middle of that highway last night. That's why he'd turned off onto the dead-end road. And that's why Rozalyn had followed him. Unfortunately, she'd been the only one to see someone jump from the falls. Because he'd already turned around and was leaving the waterfall parking lot last night. He shouldn't have seen anything. If he hadn't just happened to look in his side mirror—

Around several bends in the creek, the falls became only a dull roar in the distance. The water slowed, pooling and circling in the rocks. He was no longer looking for just a yellow raincoat anymore. He was looking for a body. If there had been a detour sign, then there'd been a jumper and that meant there was a body down here somewhere.

And that meant that Rozalyn hadn't imagined it.

He turned another bend, not sure how far he'd gone when he caught a glimpse of something that stopped his heart dead. He swore, slipping and almost falling as he stumbled forward. No yellow raincoat. No, not even close.

In a narrow space between two large rocks were wedged the fingers of a slim hand, the nails painted bright red.

Chapter 9

Roz hugged Charity and they started chattering as if they'd seen each other only yesterday rather than several months before.

"Let's go sit in a booth," Charity suggested, grabbing a piece of half-eaten banana cream pie and her diet cola. She didn't look any different than she had the last time Roz had seen her in Seattle a few years ago. Except she seemed to glow with happiness.

Roz hadn't missed that kiss the sheriff had given Charity. "I see some things haven't changed," she said as they slid into a booth.

Charity grinned. "Can you believe it? I might convince Mitch that I'm the only woman for him yet." She sobered and reached across the table to clutch her hand. "Oh, Roz, I was so sorry to hear about your dad."

Roz had forgotten how fast news traveled in Timber Falls. "He's going to come out of the coma and be all right."

"Of course he is," Charity agreed. "I'm sure he is just so glad you're here. Just as I am. The last time I saw your dad was a few weeks ago when I accosted him on the street. This black pickup had been following me and your dad was driving a black pickup—"

"Someone was following you?"

Charity waved that off. "Long story. Anyway, it wasn't the same black pickup obviously. Rather embarrassing since your dad's new wife was with him."

"So you met Emily." She didn't have to ask Charity what she thought; she knew her friend too well.

Betty came over to say hello and take Roz's order and then they were finally alone again.

"What's this I hear about Ford Lancaster staying at your guesthouse?" Charity whispered.

"It's a long story." She felt her cheeks flush.

"A long story I'm going to have to hear some time. He really is good-looking, isn't he? I saw him when he was in town a couple of weeks ago. Didn't Emily know who he was?"

"She says she didn't." Roz frowned. "Ford was in town two weeks ago?"

"Ford, is it?" Charity grinned. "Two weeks ago almost to the day. He was sitting right over there at that table by the window. I couldn't believe it when I saw him and Betty told me who he was."

Roz couldn't believe her ears. He hadn't mentioned being in Timber Falls before. "You're sure it was Ford Lancaster?"

"Tall, dark and intense?" Charity said.

"That's him. But you left out conceited, rude and

generally nasty." Except in the shower. "Charity, he thinks my father's fall wasn't an accident. He thinks someone might have pushed him. We're going up into the mountains this morning to see if we can find any evidence." She didn't mention the "bones" her father had supposedly found right before his "accident."

"We?" Charity echoed.

"Don't get any ideas. I wouldn't trust Ford as far as I could throw him." Ford had left out the part about him being here two weeks ago. Before her father had gone into the woods? Or right after?

"It seems odd he would be worried about your father."

"Doesn't it though. It turns out that Ford is the son of John Wells, Dad's good friend who used to hike with him. Ford's parents divorced when he was young and his mother remarried, thus the Lancaster."

"Aha," Charity said. "So he wrote that article about your father's photos—and *his* father. Oooo, small world, huh?"

Roz nodded. "Tell me about it. Not only that, strange things have been happening ever since I hit town. Even before I arrived." She told Charity about what she'd seen at Lost Creek Falls.

"Roz, that's horrible."

"And last night…" She sighed. "I walked in my sleep." She didn't want to get into all the details, especially the part about Ford Lancaster saving her—again—if he was to be believed. Or about the possibility that she'd been drugged—if she actually had been.

"I'm not sure of anything or anyone at this point,"

Roz admitted. "Especially Ford Lancaster. He seems to always turn up whenever I need him."

Charity quirked a brow. "Not a bad thing to have in a man."

Roz had to laugh. "You are such a romantic. Ford Lancaster is the most arrogant, infuriating, obstinate man I've ever met."

"So you say," Charity said with a half smile.

Wishing she hadn't let the friendship lapse, Roz reached across the table for Charity's hand. "It really is good to see you. I missed you so much, but after my mother...died, I just couldn't face Timber Falls."

"I know. I should have made an effort to get up to Seattle more often," Charity said. "Just tell me what I can do to help your dad."

"There is nothing at this point except mention him in your prayers."

"You got it. So you and Ford are looking for some sort of evidence that it wasn't an accident."

Ford had warned Roz not to mention to anyone that her father might have found something in the woods that might be Bigfoot bones. If word got out, everyone and his brother would be up there looking, trying to solve the mystery and making it even harder for her and Ford. There were enough people in town looking for Bigfoot as it was.

"We just want to take a look," Roz said. "I'm not convinced but it gives me something positive to do while I'm waiting for Dad to regain consciousness. I'm sure once he does, he'll be able to tell us what happened."

Charity nodded. "Hopefully, he just fell and that's

all there is to it. I'd hate to think anyone would hurt Liam."

"Me, too." Roz had left her cell phone number with the hospital. Now she gave the number to Charity.

Betty slid the breakfast special in front of Roz, and refilled her coffee cup and Charity's diet cola. The café was filling up fast so Betty only visited for a minute and was gone.

"It must be hard for you to come back here, especially to stay in the house," Charity said.

Roz nodded, tears stinging her eyes. "I miss Mom so much. Being in that house just makes me wonder why she did it, you know?"

"Yeah. That is one of the hardest things about a suicide when there is no note. You always wonder why."

Roz wiped her tears and looked toward the street as a bright red sports car swung into a parking space out front and a young dark-haired woman emerged. She stalked toward the café, flinging open the door, and charged toward their booth, the bell tinkling wildly behind her.

Roz watched in shock as the woman stormed over to them, gaze locked on Charity, a newspaper rolled up in her hand.

"Stop printing lies about my father!" the woman screamed, throwing the rolled-up paper at Charity. "I've warned you. If you say another word about my father I'll… I'll burn that stupid newspaper of yours to the ground with you in it!"

The woman turned and stormed back out. Roz watched in amazement as the brunette climbed into the red sports car and sped off, tires squealing. "Who was that?"

Charity was busy ironing the wrinkles out of the newspaper on the café table—and smiling. "You didn't recognize her? No, I guess you wouldn't since she went to private school and was seldom home during her formative years. That was Wade Dennison's daughter, Desiree."

Roz stared at her friend. "Dennison Ducks?" She looked after the red sports car, then down at the headline in today's paper.

Turning the newspaper so she could read the first part of the story, Roz learned that Wade Dennison's gun had been used to kill his foreman Bud Farnsworth, and that Farnsworth had allegedly been involved in the kidnapping of Angela Dennison and responsible for the murder of Nina Monroe, one of the decoy painters at the plant.

"Charity? You were almost killed?"

She nodded, then said conspiratorially, "There are some people in this town who believe Wade shut Bud up before he could implicate him in the kidnapping."

Roz was shaking her head in disbelief. "You think Wade was involved in his own daughter's kidnapping?"

"I said 'some' people."

"Right." Roz wished she didn't know her friend so well. "Charity, Desiree just threatened to burn down your newspaper with you in it. I think you should call Mitch and tell him."

Charity's eyes twinkled. "Maybe you're right about calling Mitch." She smiled and toyed with the bracelet on her wrist.

"A gift from Mitch?" Roz asked, admiring the bracelet.

Charity nodded shyly.

Roz felt a stab of envy. Charity had never wavered when it came to her love for Mitch. Roz had never known any man who could make *her* look like that, and her fear was that she never would. Hearing the café door open again, she turned and realized she was hoping to see Ford Lancaster fill that doorway.

Mitch spotted the dark blue pickup parked in the lot at Lost Creek Falls as he pulled in. He parked his cruiser and walked to the top of the falls in time to see Ford Lancaster clambering up the steep side of the creek gorge.

Lancaster didn't seem in the least surprised to see him. But he did look guilty—something Mitch had come to recognize after ten years as a sheriff in a remote part of Oregon.

"Morning, Sheriff," Lancaster said casually enough. He was younger than Mitch had expected, and reminded Mitch a little of his older brother Jesse. There was a wildness about him that Ford Lancaster seemed to keep well hidden behind his no-nonsense scientist veneer.

What worried Mitch was that Ford seemed to have already conned Roz. And now Ford Lancaster was at the site of an alleged suicide. What was he doing here? More to the point, what was he doing back in Timber Falls? And just how involved was he with Roz—and Liam Sawyer? Enough that he thought Liam needed protection. Now why was that?

They were all answers Mitch planned to get. "Looking for something?"

"Same thing you are." Ford's pale aquamarine eyes gave nothing away.

Mitch would have distrusted him just based on what he knew of him. He definitely didn't like him hanging around Roz.

"Did you find the body?" Mitch asked. Which begged the question, why Ford Lancaster would risk his neck to climb down into the gorge to look for a body to begin with when he'd already said he didn't see anyone jump and thought Rozalyn Sawyer had just imagined it.

"There is no body."

"Is that right?" Mitch marveled at the man's arrogance. "What makes you so sure of that?" Bodies often got caught in the rocks or in tree limbs and didn't come up for weeks, even months.

"I found this." Ford stuck his hand in his pocket.

Mitch was startled to see what he withdrew. A mannequin's hand, the painted bright red nails chipped.

"There are broken parts all down the creek about a quarter mile."

Mitch took the piece of plastic and turned it in his fingers. "You think this is what Roz saw last night? A mannequin falling off the top of the falls?" He frowned down at the slightly curved fingers.

"Someone hid in the trees at the top of the falls and pushed it off, yes, that's exactly what I think."

Mitch glanced toward the large old pine that grew out over the rocks at the top of the waterfall. "It was pouring last night. Odd time for a prank."

Ford nodded as Mitch shifted his gaze back to him. "There was a detour sign in the middle of the highway at the falls turnoff. Whoever planned this knew about what time Rozalyn would be coming up that road."

"Someone staged this explicitly for her?" Mitch asked in surprise. "Why?"

Ford shook his head. "All I know is that I found some footprints where I think he waited for her to drive up. He already had the mannequin hidden in the trees at the top of the falls. When she started to turn around, he rushed through her headlights wearing a bright yellow raincoat so she couldn't miss him."

"Roz said she thought the jumper was a *woman,*" Mitch pointed out.

Ford nodded. "If you ask Rozalyn, I'm willing to bet she'd tell you the person had the hood up on the raincoat the first time she saw him or her. Anyway, as I was saying, the person rushed to the top of the falls, made the switch behind that tree, putting the raincoat on the mannequin and pushed it off, staying hidden in the trees and darkness. I think he or she stayed hidden long enough to witness Rozalyn's reaction—or lay in wait."

Mitch shook his head. "Don't tell me. He planned to push Roz off the falls." This man seemed to have all the answers.

Ford shrugged. "I don't think the person who did this expected me to be on the road last night—let alone that I would race back to save her. I was starting to drive off. If I hadn't glanced in my side mirror and seen her go tearing over to the falls, who knows what would have happened."

"That makes you a hero," Mitch said. Not likely.

Ford made a face as if he couldn't see himself a hero any more than Mitch could. "It's just my theory of what happened."

Mitch nodded. "And a damned interesting one, too.

You seem to have it all worked out. Lucky for Roz that you were here." Or was it?

Ford could hear the accusation in the sheriff's tone. He'd known what he was up against. He was an outsider in this close-knit community. Worse, his name seemed to be legend.

"As a scientist, I've uncovered my share of hoaxes," he said.

"Yes, I recall that about you. Handy that when we find your prints on this hand you have an explanation for that, too."

Ford gritted his teeth, curbing his impatience. "You have a better theory than mine?"

"Not yet. Where was this person's vehicle?"

"I would imagine it was hidden in the trees. I found an old logging road up that way." He pointed to the south. "It's practically grown in. The driver would have had to know it was there."

"Someone local then?"

Ford shrugged. "Or someone who had a map of the old logging roads around here." That definitely opened up the possibilities.

"How many people knew what time Roz was supposed to arrive?"

"I wouldn't know, Sheriff." But he knew someone had laid in wait for Rozalyn Sawyer up here last night. He didn't have an ounce of solid proof. The mannequin, the footprints, all circumstantial. But he knew in his heart that this whole show had been for her.

What he didn't know was why. Or if it had only been to scare her—or kill her. He'd know that when he got the results from the urinalysis. If the chocolate she ingested last night was drugged…

"You've certainly taken an interest in Roz's well-being as well as her father's."

Ford smiled. "Don't beat around the bush, Sheriff. You want to know why I just happen to be there every time Rozalyn needs me?" He shrugged. "I wish I knew. Just lucky, I guess."

"Let's try a question you can answer. What are you doing in Timber Falls?"

Ford hesitated. He wished now that he'd let the sheriff find the mannequin downstream on his own and come up with his own conclusions as well. "Isn't it possible I just came to town to investigate the Bigfoot sightings and got caught up in the Sawyers' lives?"

"No," Mitch said. "You're holding out on me, Lancaster. I'm thinking I should run you in for further questioning."

Ford looked toward the falls. He needed his freedom, whatever price it took. "You'll hear about this sooner or later anyway. Liam's best friend was my father."

"John Wells?" Mitch asked, in obvious surprise.

Ford explained how his parents had divorced when he was young, how his mother had remarried, his stepfather had adopted him and he hadn't seen much of his biological father—until two days ago when he'd been with him when he died.

"I guess that explains the article you did on Liam," the sheriff said.

"I guess."

"Great job you have, making fools of people in print."

"It pays the bills," Ford said with a shrug.

The sheriff didn't even try to hide his contempt. "It still doesn't answer my question."

"My father just passed away. Before he did, I promised him I'd try to make amends with Liam for what I did." Lying was becoming almost too easy.

The sheriff studied him for a long moment, then nodded. "I'll keep this if you don't mind," he said, pocketing the mannequin hand.

As if Ford had a choice. "There's more of the body downstream about a half mile." He hesitated, then jumped in with both feet. "Do me a favor. Take a look at Rozalyn's mother's suicide."

The sheriff frowned. "Why?"

Ford shook his head. "Just a feeling."

"You have a lot of those, don't you?" His gaze seemed to soften. "This is about Rozalyn, isn't it?"

Ford looked toward the falls again but said nothing. He hated being so transparent. He wanted to give Rozalyn some peace of mind. Had Anna Sawyer gone up those stairs, climbed out on that widow's walk and taken a dive all on her own? Worse, was it possible Rozalyn might have done the same thing last night—if he hadn't stopped her? He wished the lab would call back. He found himself praying there were drugs in that chocolate. He didn't want to even think about the alternative.

"I'm just curious about the case, all right?" he said at last, kicking himself mentally for getting involved with the woman. But involved he was. And in ways he didn't even want to think about.

"What specifically am I looking for?" Mitch asked.

"Inconsistencies. You remember the case?"

Mitch nodded. "I was undersheriff then, getting ready to take over for our sheriff who was retiring. But all of that information is confidential."

Ford nodded, knowing the sheriff would pull out the old file and, if there was something there, would use it to help Rozalyn. Mission accomplished.

Without another word, Ford turned and started toward his pickup wondering if the sheriff was really going to let him walk that easily. He had a piece of the mannequin's face in his pocket that he'd saved to show Rozalyn and that he didn't want the sheriff to know about.

"You're not planning to leave town for a while, are you?" the sheriff called after him.

Ford wanted nothing more than to get in his pickup and drive away from all of this—especially the lies. But as he opened his truck door, he looked back at the sheriff and the falls. It was too easy to imagine someone hiding in that warped old pine at the top. He couldn't leave now. He was in too deep.

"Don't worry, Sheriff. I'll be here."

Chapter 10

Mitch hadn't thought about the Anna Sawyer case in years. Sheriff Tim "Hud" Hudson had done all the real investigating on the case but he'd talked to Mitch about it. Several things had been troubling about it.

Anna hadn't left a note, which wasn't all that rare in a suicide. What had bothered Hud was a visit by the interim local doctor just minutes before Anna had committed suicide. Liam had passed a car driving going too fast on the road out, and had been forced to drive into the shallow ditch to miss it.

Liam hadn't been able to see the person driving because of the sun glare on the windshield but he'd recognized the car. It was Dr. Morrow's car, Anna's physician.

Hud's first thought was that the doc had come out to give Anna bad news, but that theory hadn't panned out. According to Anna's medical records, she'd been fine.

Liam had tried unsuccessfully to reach Dr. Morrow later only to discover the man had left town. Left two weeks earlier than he'd planned. Hud didn't have any luck reaching the doc, either. He was told by the doctor's nurse that Dr. Morrow had decided to take a trip and couldn't be reached. Then Hud had retired and Mitch had taken over and that part of the investigation had fallen through the cracks.

Another thing that had troubled Hud was the fact that Rozalyn had been in the house the day her mother committed suicide. The then-teenager had been in her room with her stereo on. But later she recalled hearing voices in the attic and something heavy hitting the floor.

When Hud reached the house though, he found no sign that anyone else had been there other than the doctor—nor any sign of a struggle.

Hud had wondered if there'd been something going on between Anna Sawyer and the doc since Dr. Morrow closed up his practice and left town so suddenly. A love affair gone wrong? Hud hadn't bought that since he'd known Anna and believed her happy in her marriage. But without talking to the doctor to see what he'd been doing there that day...

Now ten years had passed. Even if there was something in the old file, it wouldn't bring Anna Sawyer back. Nor would it necessarily give Roz any peace.

But Mitch knew he was going to have to take a look anyway.

Roz was only momentarily disappointed when the person coming in through the door at Betty's Café wasn't Ford Lancaster. She'd hoped he'd finished his errands early and had come to pick her up.

Instead it was Charity's aunt Florie who came in a gust of wind.

"Brace yourself," Charity said.

Florie was dressed just as Roz remembered: a flowing colorful caftan, dyed bright red hair wound turban-style around her small head, and blue eyes glittering beneath a smear of turquoise eye shadow. It felt so good to see that some things never changed.

Roz slid from the booth to hug the elderly woman.

"I couldn't believe it when I looked into my coffee grounds and saw that you were coming back to town," Florie said, holding her at arm's length studying her a moment before sliding into the booth across from Roz, next to her niece. "Are you all right? I was worried about you. I'm sorry your homecoming hasn't been a happy one."

"Thank you," Roz said, sitting back down across from them.

Betty called to Florie across the room. "Just coffee," Florie called back and turned to Charity. "I have some news for you."

Charity looked skeptical. "Tell me this news didn't come via the stars."

Florie made a face at her. "One of these days you're going to take my sight seriously. One of these days soon," she said ominously, "you'll be begging me for a reading."

"Uh-huh," Charity said. "What news?"

"Daisy Dennison," Florie said as if announcing the topic.

Clearly, she had her niece's full attention now. "The

last time I saw Daisy she was in a hospital in Eugene recovering from a gunshot wound," Charity said.

Florie nodded. "Well she's home and *cleaning* house." Roz could almost hear the drumroll. "Daisy threw Wade out."

Charity lifted a brow. "That house is his pride and joy. He'd never leave it."

"He's living in one of my units," Florie said. "Moved in late last night and let me tell you his aura looked bad."

"I don't believe it," Charity said. "For him to move out of the house—" She looked from her aunt to Roz. "Do you know what this means?"

Roz shook her head. "Not a clue."

"Daisy *knows* he was in on the kidnapping. And he knows she knows. She's got him over a barrel and is calling the shots now."

"Why doesn't she tell Mitch?" Roz asked, noticing the clouds outside.

"Probably for the same reason Mitch hasn't arrested Wade," Charity said, clearly excited about this news. "A distinct lack of evidence. The evidence seems to have died with Bud Farnsworth. We may never know what happened to Angela Dennison now."

"How horrible," Roz said. As kids, they'd believed that Angela was buried in the woods behind the Dennison house. Once on Halloween, when they'd gone to the Dennison house to trick-or-treat, Charity swore she heard a baby crying and turned to see what she believed to be Angela's ghost behind her.

"Wade must have found out that the baby wasn't his and got rid of it," Charity whispered. "A man with an ego like his, he probably couldn't live with the thought that he might be raising another man's child."

"Worse, falling in love with that child," Roz said.

"You're right," Charity said. "That must be why he had Angela kidnapped so quickly after she was born. He couldn't risk bonding with the baby only to find out it was another man's—and a constant reminder of his wife's infidelity."

"I think there are few men who could handle that kind of knowledge," Roz said. "But what if he was wrong? What if he got rid of his *own* daughter?"

Charity shook her head, obviously unable to imagine. "Unless that baby's body turns up, we will never know who the father really was. Maybe Daisy doesn't even know herself."

Florie hadn't said anything for several minutes but Roz saw her shiver as she reached for her coffee cup and knocked it over. "Clumsy," Florie muttered under her breath as coffee spilled across the table.

"What's wrong?" Roz asked, seeing Florie's expression.

Florie was shaking her head, staring at the spilled coffee as if it were spilled blood. "Liam. Have you heard from him since he went into the woods after the most recent Bigfoot sighting?"

Roz and Charity exchanged a surprised look.

"Auntie, I thought you knew," Charity said. "Liam was found last night."

"Something happened to him! I knew it." All the color drained from Florie's face. She grabbed the edge of the table. "I saw his misery in the cards but I thought it was his marriage...." She looked up at Roz.

"He's in the hospital. Mitch thinks he fell from a cliff. He's in a coma," Roz told her.

Tears welled in Florie's wizened eyes.

Charity put an arm around her aunt's shoulder as Roz reached across the table to take one of the woman's bejeweled hands.

"I thought you had heard," Charity said.

"I was on the Internet working most of the night and morning," Florie whispered. Roz knew that Florie had her own website and did psychic readings via email.

"Are you all right?" Roz asked, surprised the woman was so upset.

"I have to go splash my face with cold water." She rose unsteadily.

"I'll go with you," Roz said.

Florie waved her off. "I'll be fine. I just need a moment alone."

"Should we let her go by herself?" Roz asked in concern as Florie traipsed off to the ladies' room.

"She'll be fine. She hates being fussed over. She's been in a tizzy ever since Liam remarried—and she wasn't the bride," Charity said. "Ah, unrequited love."

Roz blinked. "Your aunt is in love with my father?" she asked in disbelief.

"Has been for years. I thought you knew. She says she saw it in the stars. She and your father. Every time Liam came up to check the house or make repairs, Florie just happened to stop by with some fresh-baked goods for him. Tofu or carob chips. No wonder he married someone else."

"Emily can't boil water," Roz said, still shocked by the news about Florie and Liam. Did Liam have any idea of her feelings? Men could be so dense sometimes.

"Florie's coming back," Charity whispered. "Don't mention Emily. You'll just get her started. She thinks Emily is only after your father's money and somehow tricked him into marrying her."

"That's exactly what I think," Roz said.

"Florie's never even seen the woman—except in her coffee grounds," Charity confided.

Florie returned, full of questions about Liam. Roz did her best to answer them.

"Uh-oh," Charity said under her breath as she looked out the café window.

Roz followed her gaze. Emily was coming up the street, her blond head peering out from under a dark umbrella. Roz looked over at Florie as Emily swept past the window.

"Don't do it, Aunt Florie," Charity said.

"Do what?" the older woman asked innocently as she crossed herself even though she wasn't Catholic.

"Just don't." Charity shook her head at Roz. "Don't believe anything she tells you."

"All I'm going to say is that someone should warn the woman," Florie said. "Emily is about to come to a bad end."

"It's just jealousy talking," Charity said.

"I'm not jealous," Florie argued. "Liam deserves better, that's for sure, but my feelings toward his…wife have nothing to do with what I see for her future. She isn't long for this world."

"Only if she meets you in a dark alley," Charity said, obviously trying to laugh off her aunt's prediction.

"She doesn't believe I have the sight," Florie said, unperturbed to Roz.

"She did when we were *kids*," Roz said.

Charity groaned. "We were kids. It was fun. Now, it's…different."

Emily came out of the drug store next door and stopped just feet from them at the curb. As she closed her umbrella and reached for the door handle of Drew's sports car as he pulled up for her, Florie let out a gasp.

"I've seen that woman somewhere before, a long time ago," Florie said.

Charity rolled her eyes so only Roz could see.

"Except her hair used to be a different color," Florie was saying. "It's been years but I never forget an aura and that woman's is dark as sin."

"Auntie, you're either confusing her with someone else or—"

"I know where I saw her," Florie said, eyes wide. "It was here in Timber Falls only…only it was years ago."

Charity looked even more skeptical. "She's from Portland and I'm positive I heard she'd never been to Timber Falls before Liam brought her here after the wedding." She looked at Roz for confirmation.

Roz nodded. "This is the first time you've seen her since she married Dad and moved here?"

"She's kept to herself since she hit town," Charity said. "Few people have seen her except in passing."

Emily didn't fit in here and must have realized it. "She was married to some hotshot lawyer in Portland and part of the social whirl, I guess," Roz said. "He died about a year ago and left her well off."

Florie let out a "humph."

"If that were true, she wouldn't have had to snag Liam six months later."

Charity did another eye roll, but Roz thought Florie had a good point. Was it possible Emily had exaggerated about her rich, famous lawyer husband? Or even outright lied? Liam wouldn't have checked up on Emily. He took everyone at his or her word. But Roz had no problem with doing some checking. And she could see that Charity was thinking the same thing.

"It's how she's dressed that's throwing me off," Florie mumbled. "She was wearing something…different." Her face lit up. "A uniform! A nurse's uniform. That's it! She worked for that young doctor who filled in for a while when Doc Purdy broke his leg. Morrow that was his name. James Morrow. A real looker he was, and married."

Charity was staring at her aunt. "I remember that woman. She was brunette and much chubbier."

Florie nodded enthusiastically. "You think that blond doesn't come out of a bottle? *Please.* And she was heavier because I think she was pregnant with the young doctor's baby."

"Are you sure you didn't see this on some soap opera?" Charity teased. "Auntie, you have Emily Sawyer mixed up with some other woman."

Florie was shaking her head. "I can almost remember her name."

"Don't look at me. Hope, Faith and I went into Eugene to that woman doctor down there," Charity said of her and her sisters.

"I remember Doc Purdy breaking his leg," Roz said. "But Dr. Morrow…"

"You should remember him," Florie said. "Didn't your mother see him professionally during the time right before—" She broke off realizing what she was about to say. Right before Anna Sawyer killed herself.

"Dr. Morrow," Roz said slowly.

"Roz, you must have seen her," Florie said, not letting it drop.

She shook her head. "The doctor came to the house alone or Mom went to his office." But why had her mother been going to the doctor? She remembered her dad trying to find out, but couldn't remember what he'd found out other than her mother hadn't been diagnosed with cancer or anything that would make her want to commit suicide.

Dr. Morrow hadn't stayed long after her mother's death, the memory coming back now. She could recall little about him except that he was nice. And he had made at least one house call, the day her mother died. She couldn't remember any scandal involving the man's nurse but then she didn't remember ever seeing her.

Roz looked up to see that Charity and Florie were looking at her with sympathy in their eyes.

Charity took a bite of her pie, then pushed the plate away. "Did I tell you about that guy we used to go to school with, Arnie—"

"Lynette. That was her name," Florie exclaimed. "I knew it would come to me. Lynette…"

"You see where I get it," Charity joked and tried again to change the subject. "I was raised on gossip. What other career path could I have taken but journalism?"

"Why can't I think of her last name?" Florie muttered to herself. "Charity, wasn't she the woman who took care of you when you sprained your ankle wrestling with that boy that time at the hospital?"

"It wasn't just some boy. It was Mitch," Charity said and grinned. "And Kate Clark was the emergency room nurse. Dr. Morrow was already gone by then and his nurse, as well."

"Kate's taking care of Dad," Roz said. "And a doctor named… Harris?"

"Mark Harris," Charity said, nodding. "He took the job here about a month ago. It's so hard to get doctors to stay in Timber Falls. Too isolated and the money's not that great."

"Hargrove," Florie said and snapped her fingers. "Her name was Lynette Hargrove."

Charity shook her head. "Auntie, it's not the same woman, okay? Give it a rest."

Florie wasn't paying attention. She had reached into her purse and now took out a small velvet bag. From the bag she withdrew a set of worn tarot cards.

"Auntie, don't do this, okay?"

Florie didn't pay her niece any mind.

Betty came over to refill the coffee cups and Charity's diet cola. She stood for a moment and watched Florie adeptly deal out three cards, then close her eyes tightly before placing a card facedown on top of each of them.

One of the patrons called to Betty. It was obvious she hated to leave but had to.

Roz watched, mesmerized as Florie slowly turned over the first card and then pressed her hand to her mouth, tears swimming in her eyes. "Liam is going to regain consciousness," she whispered and smiled over at Roz.

Charity said nothing as Florie turned over the next card and frowned. Her gaze came up to meet Roz. "But he will only be in more danger." She turned over the third card and let out a gasp as her gaze flew up to Roz.

"What is it?" Roz cried.

Florie had gone deathly pale again. With shaking hands she hurriedly scooped up the cards. "It's nothing." She dropped the pack of cards back into the velvet bag and thrust them deep into her purse.

"See why I hate it when she does this?" Charity said to Roz. "You scare people, Auntie."

But Roz could see that Florie had scared herself, as well. Tears welled in the older woman's eyes and she was still visibly shaking.

"Florie, you have to tell me what you saw," Roz pleaded, clutching at the woman's arm. "I know Dad is in danger. I need to know what you saw. Please."

Florie's voice broke as she whispered, "I saw an open dirt grave with...the *bones* still in it."

Roz felt all the air rush from her. *"Bones?"*

"Old bones." The woman shuddered and stumbled to her feet. "I have to go to the hospital and see Liam." Without another word, she hurried off, her brightly colored caftan blowing in the breeze behind her, leaving Roz to stare after her in shock and growing fear.

Charity gave Roz a ride back to the house since it was raining again, a light drizzle that made the once sunny day as dreary and dark as her mood. Roz avoided the main house, walking around to the guesthouse through the garden.

The chill she suddenly felt had nothing to do with the light rain. Someone was watching her. She stopped to look toward the main house but, in the dull light, couldn't see if anyone was looking out of the attic windows.

She felt spooked and afraid and couldn't wait to see Ford. She had never thought she'd admit it, but she was glad he was here. Glad they would be looking for the bones together.

Florie's revelations still had her reeling. Bones. And her conviction that Emily wasn't really Emily Lane but some woman named Lynette Hargrove, a former nurse in Timber Falls. A nurse who'd worked for the doctor who'd been taking care of Roz's mother.

Florie had to be wrong. Liam would have mentioned if Emily had ever been a nurse. Especially in Timber Falls. Unless he hadn't known. And what about the name change? Lynette Hargrove. It couldn't be the same woman.

Roz was disappointed to find Ford hadn't returned. She checked her watch. He was late. Because he was a scientist, she'd somehow expected him to be more exacting than this. Maybe he'd been held up.

A sliver of worry began to fester inside her at the thought that something might have happened to him. If he'd gone off asking questions about Liam...

She stepped up onto the porch out of the rain and tried the door. He'd left it unlocked for her. That was considerate.

As she stepped in, she heard something and realized she wasn't alone. The rustle of papers came from the bedroom. She didn't close the door, instead stepped into the guesthouse quietly to peer around the corner into the bedroom.

He had his back to her and appeared to be going through something on a desk by the bed.

"Drew?"

He swung around, obviously surprised to see her. "I didn't hear you come in."

No, she'd gathered that by his surprise. She looked to the papers in his hands. "What are you doing?"

"I had to see what Ford Lancaster was up to." He put the papers back on the desk and moved toward her. "I'm worried about you. I can see that you're starting to trust him."

Right now she trusted Ford more than she did Drew, she realized. She took a step back, glad she'd left the door open.

Drew stopped advancing toward her, looking hurt. "I'm sorry if I scared you. Roz, I was upstairs earlier looking for you and I noticed the door open to your mom's old sewing room and the broken record on the floor."

She held her breath.

"You're going to think I'm crazy but a few weeks ago I heard that record playing," he said. "I went up and turned off the phonograph but it came right back on. Blew me away. I unplugged it but the next night I heard it again. Totally freaked me out."

She found herself nodding. "It did that last night."

He laughed. "I was afraid of that." The smile died on his lips. "I *am* worried about you."

"I appreciate that," she said, feeling a little more at ease with him. "Drew, phonographs don't plug themselves back in."

"I know. I caught my mother in that room several nights later."

His admission surprised her.

"I know she's jealous of you," he said. "She resents the fact that Liam insisted on returning to Timber Falls because of you."

"Because of *me?* But I live in Seattle."

Drew nodded. "Your dad has this idea that one day you will come back here with your own family and settle in Timber Falls in the house where you were raised."

Roz couldn't believe her ears. Her father had never said anything to her about it.

"He keeps talking about your kids racing through the old house, putting laughter back in it and how Anna would have wanted that desperately. You can imagine how that makes my mother feel."

"So you think she rigged the phonograph to…scare me away?"

"I think it's possible. If you don't come back to Timber Falls, then your father will eventually move her somewhere so they can have a fresh start. She really hates it here."

Roz could see how hard the admission was for him. He was protective of his mother. But he was obviously worried about Roz and maybe what lengths his mother might go to.

"Do you know who left me the chocolates by my bed last night?"

Drew seemed surprised by the question. "I did. Didn't you get my note? They were all right, weren't they?"

She nodded, even though she wasn't sure about that. "You didn't happen to hear me walking in my sleep last night, did you?"

His eyes widened. "No. I hope you avoided the stairs."

"I didn't walk far," she said and looked toward the desk where she'd found Drew going through a stack of papers.

"You're wrong to trust Ford," Drew said, following her gaze. "Roz, look what he did to your father. I wish my mother had never told him he could stay in the guesthouse. I'll tell her to kick him out."

"No," Roz said.

He looked at her with obvious concern. "You don't really think he's in town to help your dad, do you? Men like him don't change."

Her greatest fear. It was obvious from Drew's expression that he could see that he'd struck a chord.

"He wants something, Roz, and you have to ask yourself what," Drew continued. "He acts as if he's protecting Liam, but what if it's just the opposite? What if he doesn't want any of us in the hospital room when Liam wakes up because Ford Lancaster has something to hide?"

Her cell phone rang, startling her.

"Just think about it," Drew said and headed for the door. "In the meantime, be careful."

She wondered if he meant because of Ford. Or his mother. Roz was still chilled by what Florie had seen in the cards. Now she wondered if Emily really might not be the person she was pretending to be.

The phone rang again. Roz checked the number. Charity.

"I didn't want to say anything in front of my aunt but I did some quick checking on Emily," Charity said without preamble.

Roz had known she would. She held her breath.

"There was a hotshot attorney named Andrew Lane who died about a year ago. According to his obit, he is survived by his wife, Emily, and two grown children, Andrew Junior and Suzanne of Portland, Oregon."

Roz let out the breath she'd been holding.

"As for Lynette Hargrove, she died in a car wreck about a year after she left Timber Falls," Charity said. "You see why I warned you not to listen to Aunt Florie? So just ignore that thing about bones, okay?"

She wished she could. "Thank you so much."

"No problem. Better to set your mind at ease."

Roz couldn't agree more as she snapped off her phone. She just wished Charity could ease her mind about Ford. Why wasn't he back yet? She was starting to worry about him.

It was quiet inside the guesthouse. Roz checked the bathroom, remembering the urine sample she'd left on the back of the bathroom sink. It was gone. He must have taken it to the lab.

Was that the only errand he had to run this morning? She hoped she'd just been sleepwalking, and that there was no plot against her or her father.

She turned and looked toward the desk where she'd caught Drew. Ford's laptop sat on top of what appeared to be a stack of papers that had been hurriedly shoved under it. Drew's doing? Or Ford's?

Stepping toward it, she saw the corner of a magazine article sticking out from the pile of papers. She recognized the photograph. It was one her father had taken of a large hairy creature he and John Wells had seen deep in the Cascades and believed was Bigfoot.

She lifted the laptop and pulled the jumble of papers from beneath it. On the top was the piece Ford Lancaster had written about her father for a scientific journal along with various newspaper articles quoting Lancaster and his experts speculating on how Liam Sawyer had manufactured the fraudulent Bigfoot photographs.

She stared down at the photograph of her father for a moment, then ruffled through the other papers. They were all articles about Bigfoot. One headline caught her attention: One Million Dollar Reward Offered For Bigfoot Evidence. The article said the man would pay for definitive proof that a Bigfoot existed. At the bottom, how to contact the man to collect had been circled.

Heart in her throat, she sifted through the papers and found what appeared to be the beginning of a new article typed double-space on plain white paper. It was entitled Bigfoot Hysteria In Timber Falls: Home Of The Infamous Photographer by Ford Lancaster.

"Oh God," she breathed, tears burning her eyes as she saw her father's name in the first paragraph of the story.

She stumbled back, all the papers slipping from her fingers and fluttering to the floor except for the old article about her father. She balled it up in her hands. She should have listened to that nagging feeling she'd had about Ford. But she'd thought she didn't trust him because he made her feel things she had never felt with any other man. Like hatred, she told herself angrily. Not desire. Dammit, not desire ever again.

She couldn't believe how naive she'd been, she thought as she threw the article about her father across the room. Ford had lied about everything. And she'd just wanted to believe he'd lied about a stupid kiss.

He didn't feel guilty about what he'd done to her father—or to his own. He was only in this for the money. Or the notoriety. Or both.

Hadn't she known deep down inside he wasn't telling her the real reason he was here risking his life? Why he insisted her father be protected? Just to get closer to her. All he wanted was to find the bones—or whatever had put her father in danger.

Oh Roz, you fool, you. She thought about how Ford had been in the shower with her last night, how he'd kissed her. Not once but twice. Tears sprang to her eyes. *He was just trying to gain your trust, you silly goose. He planned to use you to help him. Don't you remember that look you caught in his eyes at the café? He thinks he has you right where he wants you.*

He *did,* she thought. But not anymore.

She was so angry her first instinct was to wait for him to return and confront him. While that might make her feel better, it wouldn't help her father. No, she had to find the bones, bones her father had mistakenly told Ford about—and she had to do it before Ford did.

Unlike Ford, her father wouldn't have sold the bones to the highest bidder. Nor would she.

As Roz left the guesthouse and got into her car, she still couldn't shake the feeling that someone was watching her. Where was Ford? And what did he have planned next for her? She hated to think as she drove out to the highway and headed toward Maple Creek Bridge Road.

She couldn't help glancing in her rearview mirror. How much of what Ford had told her was a lie? Was her father really in danger? Was *she?* Or had everything that had happened been Ford's doing?

She thought about the person who'd climbed in her window and went through her suitcase, leaving the window open—and the suitcase a mess—so she'd know he'd been there.

Her heart somersaulted in her chest. Ford hadn't left the chocolates. Drew had. Ford couldn't have known her favorites. And anyway, he'd acted as if he hadn't known that Liam had a daughter. That could have been a lie though, too.

But he could have drugged the chocolates when he climbed in through her window. And he could have pretended to rescue her from the widow's walk. For all she knew, he took her up there.

But why go to so much trouble? Because he needed her to trust him. By making her think she was in danger, she had turned to him. She had played right into his hands.

Oh God, how far would he go to get what he wanted?

As far as was needed, she thought, remembering the kisses. And the reward for the Bigfoot bones.

At least now she knew. The only person she had to fear was Ford Lancaster.

Chapter 11

When Ford got to the guesthouse, he couldn't believe Rozalyn hadn't returned given how late he was. After what he'd found in the creek, he had raced back to town, anxious to see her and make sure she was safe.

But how much trouble could she get into since all she had planned was a trip to the hospital and breakfast with her friend?

He opened the guesthouse door. Had someone come in again? Hadn't the intruder gotten what he'd broken in for the first time?

"Rozalyn?" Ford called.

No answer.

But *someone* had been here. He'd locked the door when he'd left.

The moment he opened the bedroom door he saw the papers on the floor and stopped dead. He'd forgotten all about them after he'd discovered the computer disk gone. Then after he'd brought Roz to the guesthouse he couldn't very well retrieve them without making her suspicious. He'd planned to take care of them this morning and, in his haste to find out what had happened last night at the falls, he'd forgotten.

That mistake would cost him, he realized, as he picked up the papers and spotted a balled up magazine article he'd started about Liam Sawyer. He swore. Rozalyn had been here. She had come back and found the papers he'd stuffed under the laptop computer after the break-in.

Wait a minute. He didn't make a copy of this article, did he? But here was the article he'd started…

He shoved it away. Nothing mattered now but finding Rozalyn.

Ford swore again as he straightened. He had to find her and try to explain. *Good luck.* She knew the truth. Knew what he considered his father's legacy to him. In the end, John Ford Wells had left him more than his name. He'd left him the chance to be not only wealthy—but also famous. That was one hell of an inheritance.

But he only got it if he found the Bigfoot bones his father's partner had discovered. Funny the way life was. The only fly in the ointment now was Rozalyn Sawyer.

At least he knew where she'd go. Maple Creek Bridge Road. As crazy as she was she'd try to find out the truth on her own. And as crazy as he was, he'd try to save her again.

He grabbed his backpack, threw what he thought he'd need into it and headed for his pickup. He had to find her and quickly. The fool woman was going to get herself killed.

What about the bones?

Screw the bones. For the time being, Rozalyn mattered more.

That realization made him laugh out loud. The woman had put a spell on him. Like he said, life was funny. How else could he explain falling for Liam Sawyer's daughter?

Obviously his life was cursed.

Still upset with her aunt, Charity stopped by the hospital to find Florie sitting by Liam's bedside. She cringed at the thought of what might happen should Emily drop by to see how her husband was doing. That was a confrontation Charity hoped to avoid. After Charity had talked to Roz, she couldn't get Emily and Lynette Hargrove off her mind so she'd put in a couple more calls and was waiting to hear. Florie had to be wrong. And yet, Charity didn't want to take any chances.

And what was that business about bones? What bothered Charity was her friend's reaction. Roz had turned three shades of white over some old bones in a dirt grave. Odd.

Charity watched her aunt through the hospital room window and decided not to interrupt Florie's visit. She left the flowers she'd brought for Liam with the nurse on duty and headed for the newspaper office in the relentless drizzle, windshield wipers flapping. Emily—or whatever her name was—was on her own if she came by the hospital while Florie was there.

A block away, a large figure in a dark raincoat

stepped off the curb directly in front of her car. She hit her brakes as Wade Dennison slammed down his palms on the front of her VW Bug, his glaring eyes huge with malice.

Charity scrambled to lock her door, but Wade—for his age—moved too damned fast. He jerked open her car door, his face flushed with anger.

"You meddling bitch!" he bellowed.

Behind her, Charity fumbled for the cell phone in her purse, keeping her hand hidden from Wade's view as she hit the On button, then speed-dialed Mitch's number.

"Listen, Wade—"

"No, you listen to me." Suddenly all the heat went out of him. He seemed to slump against her car, head down, the rain pattering on his raincoat to the sound of…crying?

The unexpected, heart-wrenching sound chased away her fear. She stared at the broken man, suddenly wondering if she could be wrong about him.

"I would never have hurt Angela. Never. I loved her." He looked up, his face wet from the rain, from his tears. "I don't care if she was my daughter by blood. Don't you get it? I love Daisy. She was Daisy's daughter. That's all that ever mattered."

Charity realized now probably wasn't the time to remind him of his words the night Angela disappeared from her crib. But hey, she was a journalist. "You were overheard telling Daisy that you would put her back on the street and take Desiree from her."

His jaw tightened, eyes hard again, and she hoped she wouldn't regret her words. "Those things were said in anger. Daisy knew I would never…" He seemed to lose focus, his head coming up as if he heard something. Or saw something.

Charity followed his gaze and saw a bright red sports car zip by. His daughter, Desiree.

Wade pushed off the car, stumbling back as he turned and walked away, his gait slow and awkward, the movement of a defeated man.

Charity watched him go, stunned by what she'd just seen and heard. Could she be wrong about Wade? But then how did she explain Bud Farnsworth's final moments? It was clear with his dying breath that Bud had been trying to tell Wade something.

She checked her cell phone. She'd reached Mitch's voice mail. She wondered what kind of message she'd left. Mitch wasn't going to like this any better than the newspaper article. She hoped it wouldn't change his mind about that possible marriage proposal he'd started to offer her this morning at Betty's.

Roz turned from the highway onto Maple Creek Bridge Road and followed the narrow, sheltered road until it ended in a small wide spot.

She was glad to see there were no other vehicles parked at the end of the road. But as she looked around, she wondered where her dad's truck and camper were. How odd that the pickup hadn't turned up. Was it possible someone had stolen it? Or dropped him off? Then where were the pickup and camper? More to the point, where was that person and how come he or she hadn't come forward yet?

She realized it was possible her father had hidden his truck and camper—just as he might have hidden the bones he'd found. It didn't sound like him. Liam wasn't one to hide things, to deceive. And because of that, she doubted he would realize the danger of his discovery until it was too late.

With a start, she wondered if someone had moved the truck, hidden it—after that person had pushed her father from the cliff so no one would be looking for him here?

She got out of her SUV, loaded her backpack and tied on her tent and sleeping bag. She considered leaving her camera behind, but realized if she found any proof she'd need it to verify the find. Like her father, she never went anywhere without her camera. She wondered if he'd gotten his discovery on film and where his camera was now. His backpack wasn't at the hospital. That was odd if he'd fallen or even been pushed off a cliff. He would have had it on.

She put enough energy bars and drinking water into her pack to last her a couple of days. She would stay in the mountains tonight, a place where she felt safer than at the house with all its memories and the strange new family. She wasn't taking any chances that she might end up on that widow's walk again.

And she would be a whole lot safer out in the woods than at the guesthouse with Ford Lancaster, she thought, remembering the kiss and the emotions it stirred in her. And to think she'd been afraid of lowering her defenses around him. What a joke! He hadn't needed to scale the castle walls—she'd dropped the drawbridge.

She shook her head at the memory, pretty sure she really had lost her mind. Because even knowing what a louse he was, she couldn't help remembering the kisses and the feelings and aching for both. *Fool woman.*

She clipped the can of pepper spray to her belt—not so much for a bear encounter as a human one. If anything Ford Lancaster had told her were true, she would be in danger until the bones were secure.

And she now believed her father had found bones. She could just hear Ford if she told him she started believing it when a psychic saw her father—and bones. Ford would have a field day with that.

But what were the chances that Florie would see bones in the tarot cards?

Roz glanced behind her as she swung her backpack over her shoulder, feeling as if she was being followed. But there was no one in the small clearing and it was impossible to see into the thick growth beyond it. Nor had she heard or seen another vehicle on the highway.

She'd noticed that the vacancy sign was back up at the Ho Hum Motel. The Bigfoot hunters were leaving town, giving up since there hadn't been a sighting for several weeks now. Bigfoot sightings this time of year weren't unusual in this area. The theory was that the snow in the higher elevations pushed the elusive creatures down to the rainy areas like Timber Falls.

The Bigfoot sightings had something else in common: they were all on mountain ranges in rugged isolated country. The country beyond this road was unmapped, unexplored and inaccessible except on foot, and there were hundreds of square miles of it.

On this side of the Oregon Cascades a lot of the country wasn't even accessible on foot because of the dense foliage, steep mountain cliffs and numerous waterfalls, streams, lakes and bogs. It was the perfect place for a creature to live and avoid man.

Roz looked up at the rock rims about halfway up

the mountain and shivered. That's the area where her father must have been. Whatever he'd discovered had to be fairly close around there, she would think.

She knew she would have to find the bones before Ford Lancaster—and whoever else knew about them. She had no doubt that either would try to stop her.

The moment she stepped from the small clearing where she'd left her SUV, she disappeared into the dark coniferous forest.

She wasn't surprised so few people had ever seen what they believed to be a Bigfoot-like creature. Another life-form could live just yards off the road and remain unseen especially if, as suspected, the creature was nomadic, rare in numbers and knew to avoid man whenever possible.

As she walked, she couldn't shake the feeling though that she wasn't alone. She looked behind her but saw nothing except a dense wall of trees and underbrush. As far as she could tell, there wasn't another human being for miles.

A short way up the trail, she crossed a moss-covered log spanning a gushing stream. The water roared in her ears, reminding her of Lost Creek Falls and what she'd witnessed last night. She wondered if Mitch had found anything. Or if there had been anything to find.

She walked, concentrating on the narrow game trail through the jungle. At one point, she tripped over one of the tree roots that grew across the path and almost fell. Resting her hand against a tree trunk, she tried to catch her breath. Her chest ached and she felt tears burn her eyes.

A limb snapped off to her right. She froze, listening. She couldn't see anything in the thick vegetation nor back down the trail behind her. She started walking again. A little faster. By now Ford would know she wasn't meeting him at the guesthouse.

Morning gave way to afternoon as she headed for the band of rocks, stopping only to take a drink or catch her breath.

"Where had you been, Dad?" she said out loud as she looked up through the rain and mist at the steep rock cliffs over the tops of the trees.

She wondered about his state of mind before the fall and realized she didn't have a clue as to what her father might have been thinking. He'd married Emily, hadn't he? That alone made her wonder if she still knew her father at all.

Charity was still shaken by her run-in with Wade Dennison. She parked in front of her newspaper office and sat in her VW bug for a few minutes, trying to collect herself. As much as she suspected Wade was a murderer, she hated seeing him the way he'd been on the street.

Worse, he'd made her wonder if she could be wrong about him. Sure, he would deny everything, especially now when it appeared his house of cards was coming down. But there'd been a ring of truth in his words. And Charity knew the power of love. If Wade really had loved Daisy enough to accept not only her affair but possibly the child from that affair—

The passenger side door of her car jerked open and, in a flurry of rain and wind, Sheriff Mitch Tanner slid into the seat next to her.

Charity tried to still her beating heart, this time from being startled out of her wits on the tail of her run-in with Wade. "Hey," she said with less than her usual enthusiasm.

"Are you all right?" Mitch asked, picking up on it.

She told him about her recent encounter with Wade.

"He sounds like he might be losing it," Mitch said when she'd finished. "That could make him even more dangerous."

"I felt sorry for him," she admitted.

"Just don't let your guard down around him, all right? And try not to find yourself alone with him."

She smiled at Mitch's concern. "No dark alleys?"

"Stay away from Dennison Ducks."

He was asking her to back off from her investigation. It was like asking her not to breathe and he had to know that.

"I'll be careful," she said.

He nodded, not looking happy as he opened his door and got out. No kiss. No "see you later." No "how about a late lunch or a romantic dinner?" Or about that earlier proposal that she move in with him. No nothing.

Charity sighed as he got back into his patrol car and drove away. She waited but he didn't brake or turn around and come back. She opened her door and rushed across the sidewalk through the rain to the *Timber Falls Courier*. But as she opened her office door, she stopped dead. Wade's estranged wife Daisy was sitting in Charity's office chair, obviously waiting for her. Daisy had today's paper in her hand and she was crying.

Rozalyn was too easy to find. And that's what worried him. Anyone could figure out where she'd gone.

Ford parked next to her SUV. He hadn't seen any other vehicles on the highway but it would have been easy to hide one in this dense forest, especially with dozens of old trees partially grown in the logging roads. A car could be just a few feet off the road and completely hidden.

Is that why no one had found Liam Sawyer's truck and camper? Ford wished he thought that was the case. That Liam had hid it, but Ford's intellect told him different. Liam wouldn't know to hide his rig any more than he would have known to hide himself. He wouldn't have realized how much danger he was in until it was too late.

Father like daughter, Ford thought as he got out of his pickup, slung his pack over his shoulder and started up at the mountain. The Cascade Range formed a wall of mile-high peaks from British Columbia to northern California, running the entire length of Oregon. Sixty million years ago this was seabed. The fossilized remains of ancient fish and tropical plants were entombed beneath these mountains and foothills by layers of accumulated lava and ash.

He looked toward the mountains and the band of cliffs that could be seen over the treetops. Walls of columnar basalt, granitic intrusions, ash beds, building-size chunks of andesitic magma that cooled into granite rock.

A scientist's heaven. Or hell, Ford thought as he zipped up his raincoat and pulled up the hood, the drizzle falling around him.

For months Pacific Ocean storms moved inland across the lower Coast Range mountains to the five-thousand-foot wall of the Cascade Mountains, clouds banking up and turning to rain—two hundred inches of the stuff falling each year.

It was the rain that created the long growing season and the lush, jungle-like groves of deciduous and conifer trees, six-hundred-year-old towering Douglas fir, cedar, Western hemlock, vine maple, huckleberry bushes and understories of wild rhododendron tangles, more than thirty types of ferns, four hundred varieties of wildflowers, two hundred species of mushrooms, nine hundred types of thick mosses and twelve hundred species of lichens.

It was a jungle of sorts and the last place on earth he wanted to be. But he had no choice. Rozalyn was up there somewhere and he feared she wasn't alone—and didn't know it.

He followed the narrow animal trail and her tracks through the dense forest, brushing aside the gauzelike yellow drape of Old Man's Beard that hung from tree limbs. The lichen grew up to thirty feet long and several inches thick up here.

Ahead, he caught another glimpse of the band of rock cliffs that ran along the mountainside, and knew that was where Rozalyn would be headed.

It was easy to understand what Liam had been doing up there. The majority of Bigfoot sightings were in places just like it. There were numerous accounts of huge, hairy creatures overturning massive boulders looking for food, stacking the overturned rocks into huge cairns. Another tale told of the creatures throwing the rocks down mountainsides to chase away humans.

He sincerely doubted Rozalyn had to worry about Bigfoot. But who knew what else was in the woods today?

Something else worried him. How the Bigfoot hunters had gotten Liam down. That was a long way to bring him out. True, it was the only way out. A helicopter couldn't land near there. But still, it seemed improbable that some hunters had carried the injured man out because of the liability alone. Maybe that was why they hadn't left their names.

Ford quickened his step, his anxiety growing stronger as he caught glimpses of the cliffs shrouded in cold fog and drizzle. A stream trickled over stair steps of mossy granite. In these two hundred thousand acres of heavily wooded wilderness there were more lakes, ponds, marshes and sloughs than a man could count.

He hated it all. The rain. The dark, dank rainforest of the Cascades. The memory it always brought back from his childhood. It was one of the few places he remembered his father bringing him. It had been shortly after the divorce. Before his father had completely disappeared from their lives.

The memory still made his heart pound with the fear of the nine-year-old boy he'd been. His memory of his father and the Cascades was one of fear. And a knowledge of something he hadn't wanted to know.

Mist moved across the face of the cliffs. He concentrated on finding Roz. Then he'd look for the bones. Bones decomposed quickly in a rainforest. Those that didn't became buried beneath the dense vegetation. If there was a Bigfoot, the theory was that he hid in a cave when he became sick and was about to die. It explained the lack of discovered bones. Because this country was full of caves.

Roz's tracks were easy to follow. Nor could she be far ahead of him. He lengthened his stride, anxious to catch up with her, his discovery at Lost Creek Falls this morning making him more nervous with each step.

Not long after he crossed a huge fallen cedar that spanned a roaring creek, the trail opened into a cool green glen surrounded by the vast forest.

The rain stopped as suddenly as it had begun. He pushed back his hood and stood in the glen, listening for Rozalyn. She couldn't have had that much of a head start on him and still he'd yet to catch her.

He glanced down at the muddy trail. Her footprints held only a little rain. If he kept moving he should catch her by the time she reached the nearest end of the band of rock cliffs.

His cell phone vibrated against his hip, startling him. It surprised him he could get service here. Startled him even more since he'd given the number to only one person.

He hurriedly answered it. "Hello?"

"Mr. Lancaster, I have the results of that urine sample you asked me to put a rush on," the lab tech said.

It had taken Roz longer than she'd expected to reach the bottom of the band of rocks that ran across the mountain—and the old tree where she had often camped with her father.

The rain had stopped momentarily. She took a breather under the tree, adjusted her backpack and stretched. Her body ached. In her career, she did a lot of hiking while carrying all of her camera equipment so she was in pretty good shape.

But today she was trying to hurry. She was winded and tired and discouraged. What did she hope to find up here? If her father really had been pushed, the killer wouldn't have left any evidence. And as for the bones

her father had supposedly found, they could be anywhere. Especially if he'd had time to hide them.

She glanced up at the cloud-shrouded band of granite just above her. A hawk circled overhead and close
by she could hear a blue jay's call. Up here, she understood why her father loved the Cascades so. There are
so few places man can be completely alone, he used to
say. And few places that still held mysteries.

Oregon had once been a land of giant bison, mam-
moth, mastodon, wild horses, giant bear and ground
sloth. Today the largest animals were elk. Unless, of
course, Bigfoot was an animal—and not a form of
human. There was no doubt in her mind there was
another lifeform out there—and it was a humanoid.

She had loved to sit around the campfire and listen
to her father's stories. He often talked in awe about the
day he'd photographed the creature in these woods.

"It had a horrid smell to it," he'd said. "But what got
to me was the look in her eyes. It was a female, I'm sure
of that. She looked scared, but it was the pleading I saw
there, as if she was saying, 'Please, just leave me alone.'
I wish I'd never let anyone see those photographs."

Roz thought about that now. If her father had found
Bigfoot bones, would he tell anyone? Once there was
proof that Bigfoot existed, the next step was capturing
a live one. Her father would want to prove his earlier
photos hadn't been faked. But he wouldn't have wanted
the Bigfoot hunted down and caged. Would her father
hide the bones and protect the creatures in the end?

The hair lifted on the back of her neck. She straightened slowly and turned, positive someone was watching her. In the trees, a pine bough moved. She heard

the rustle of leaves followed by the snap of a limb, then silence.

She let go of the breath she'd been holding. No one there, she told herself. Just forest sounds. But she couldn't shake the feeling that not only wasn't she alone, but someone was very close by, watching her, waiting.

But waiting for what? Her to find the bones? Or evidence that her father's fall hadn't been an accident?

Ford lost Rozalyn's tracks just before he reached the rimrocks. Earlier the rain had fallen in a steady drizzle, the low clouds offering little light. Even now that the rain had stopped, the air was damp, everything dripped and he could hear water cascading down the rocks off to his right not far from a huge old Douglas fir. The cliffs loomed ahead of him. Rozalyn would already be at the base of them. Might have already found a cave to explore.

He found himself running to catch up to her. As he topped a rise, he spotted her just yards away standing at the base of the rock cliff.

Something caught his eye higher up the cliff. A movement on a wide ledge directly above her. A dark figure clad in a raincoat, the hood up, bent over behind a large boulder. In the time it took for his heart to beat, Ford saw the boulder tumble off the edge of the cliff headed right for Rozalyn.

Chapter 12

Charity stepped into the *Timber Falls Courier* newspaper office and closed the door behind her, bracing herself for a tongue-lashing.

Daisy Dennison looked up when she heard Charity enter. She set down the newspaper, pulled a tissue from the box on Charity's desk and dried her tears as if ashamed to be caught crying.

Charity watched her, surprised how good the woman looked considering she'd been shot in the shoulder just two weeks before and had spent the past twenty-seven years a recluse in her mansion before that.

Daisy had gained some weight, had color again in her cheeks and had put some expensive highlights in her hair. She looked damned good, and Charity couldn't help but wonder if getting rid of Wade wasn't responsible for it more than anything else. Tears and all, Daisy looked happier than Charity had ever seen her.

Charity went to the small fridge next to the bathroom and opened the door. "Can I get you anything to drink?" This definitely called for a Diet Coke—if not something stronger.

Daisy suddenly seemed to realize that she was sitting in Charity's chair and quickly got up. "No, thank you. I..." She took another wipe at her tears. "I just need to talk to you."

"If you came here to defend Wade—"

"No," Daisy said almost too quickly. "It's... I'm worried. You don't know Wade like I do. You don't know what he's capable of."

But Daisy did? "If you're worried about my safety—"

"I'm worried about my own," the older woman snapped. Her eyes filled with tears again. "I'm afraid he's going to snap and...and kill me."

Charity stared at her, speechless.

"He blames me for everything," Daisy said, her voice breaking. "For the rumors about the baby..." Daisy looked away. "I think in his mind he believes that Angela would never have been kidnapped if I hadn't..."

"Had an affair?" Charity suggested.

Daisy's gaze swept back to hers, the eyes now cold and hard. "This town is good for nothing *but* rumors. The baby was Wade's. There was never any doubt."

"Are you sure about that?" The moment the words were out of her mouth, Charity regretted them.

Daisy reached for her purse, anger giving her cheeks high color as she glared at Charity. "I thought I could appeal to you as another woman and ask you not to do any more stories about this. Just let it be forgotten. Let us try to get on with our lives."

She had to be kidding. "How is that possible, Daisy,

when you still don't know what really happened to Angela? What about justice? Surely you don't think it's been done."

"Life isn't always just," Daisy said, lifting her nose into the air. Except now everyone in town knew Daisy was no aristocrat. "Isn't it enough that the man who took my daughter is burning in hell as we speak?"

"Is it enough for you?" Charity asked.

Something dark flickered in the woman's gaze before she turned and left. She didn't even bother to slam the door.

Charity stared after her, wondering what Daisy had really come to see her about. It wasn't to ask her not to run any more stories. Daisy wasn't that naive.

No, Daisy Dennison had another agenda and Charity wondered what it was.

Roz first heard the tinkle of small pebble-size rocks trickling down the cliff. Then a rumble. If she hadn't been standing under a rock face she might have thought it was thunder.

Rock slide!

She was too far from the trees to find safety there. Her only hope was a small cave back under the cliff face. Her feet were already moving as the first boulder careened down from overhead, showering her in dirt and rock chips before it thudded to the ground just inches from her. Overhead, she heard more boulders break loose and rumble downward.

As she dove for the shallow cave, she was hit hard from behind, the air knocked out of her as she was thrown to the ground just inside the mouth of the small dark cavern and rolled back under the overhang, something heavy coming to rest on her.

The earth shook as rocks pounded the ground next to her in a shower of crashing thunder that drowned out everything else except the sound of heavy breathing next to her ear and the weight on top of her.

The rocks seemed to fall forever. Then silence.

"You're crushing me," she wheezed into the chilling silence that followed the rock slide. She would know that distinct male scent anywhere, as well as the now familiar contours of his body. "You just can't stay off of me, can you?"

He rolled from her and she gasped for breath, flipping over to stare in shock at the pile of rocks in the spot where she'd been standing only moments before. She began to shake at the realization of just how close a call it had been and looked over at Ford.

He'd moved to a sitting position against the wall of the cliff. The look on his face surprised her, a combination of anger and—fear. "You *are* crazy," he spat. "What does it take to get through that thick skull of yours that this is dangerous?"

She glared at him. "The only danger I'm in is from you."

He shook his head in disgust. "*I'm* the one who keeps rescuing you."

"Really? And why is that?" she demanded.

"I was just asking myself that very question. Obviously not to impress you, that's for sure." He cautiously crawled from under the overhang, then reached back to grab her hand and pull her out behind him. He dragged her away from the cliff before he spun around to face her.

"What the hell are you doing up here by yourself? Do you realize you were almost killed? And worse, *I* was almost killed."

"It's what you get for following me," she snapped. "And don't try to tell me you saved my life again. I was jumping out of the way when you tackled me."

"I'm not going to try to tell you anything." He swore. "I should wash my hands of you. Let you get killed."

"If you're trying to scare me again—"

"Lady, if you were a cat, you'd be out of lives by now," he said, dusting himself off.

"I know the truth about you," she threw at him, remembering what she'd found at the guesthouse in the papers he'd tried to hide under his laptop, and what Charity had told her about him being in town two weeks ago.

"Yeah, I gathered that when you took off on me," he said and turned his back on her as he started toward the cliff face again.

"Why were you in town two weeks ago and failed to mention it? Where are you going? Aren't you even going to try to deny why you're really in town?" she demanded to his retreating backside.

"What would be the point?" He started to climb up a series of rocklike steps. "You coming or not?"

"What? And let you get me up there so you can push me off?"

"Don't tempt me. I thought you might be interested to know how those rocks just happened to fall."

Rock slides happened all the time in this part of the country. "Don't try to tell me that rock slide was anything but an accident."

He stopped and turned to look back at her. "And waste my breath? I'm going to show you. Unless you're afraid to climb up here."

Was that a *dare?* Did he really think she would fall for something so obvious as a dare? She glanced up at the cliff. She certainly wasn't afraid of climbing up there. But what would be the point? Just to prove the rock slide had been an accident? Just to prove him wrong?

She clambered up the cliff behind him wondering how he thought he could prove it was anything more than a rock slide when she and Ford were the only two people for twenty miles.

As she reached the wide ledge where he was waiting for her, she saw the smug look on his face. He'd known all he had to do was dare her and she'd climb up here. But she realized that wasn't the only reason for his smugness. He pointed to one clear boot print in a patch of wet earth in a flat rock at his feet. Past it there were scrape marks where a boulder had been pushed to the rim of the ledge.

Her heart caught in her throat as she spotted something else near one of the rocks along the ledge. She stepped closer and bent down. She heard Ford move to her side, heard him swear under his breath.

"Don't touch it," he ordered. He shrugged off his backpack, removed a small plastic container and carefully scooped up the two fresh cigarette butts where someone had smoked while they waited. From this point, a person would have had a clear view of the path below—the same one she'd just come up. "The lab might be able to get DNA from a saliva sample."

She nodded. She still had her camera strapped to her chest. She took it out and, stilling the trembling in her hands, turned back to get a shot of the single boot track in the mud. The tread was worn along the outside edge and she thought she might be able to match it if she ever came across the boot that had made it.

"You can't be serious," Ford said, obviously realizing what she was thinking as he watched her take the photograph of the boot print. "This person just tried to kill you—and probably put your father in the hospital. Unless you only plan to turn that photograph over to the sheriff—"

"Whoever did this doesn't know me," she said as she put her camera back into its case strapped to her chest. "If this is the same person who hurt my father, I'm going to find him or die trying."

"Exactly." He reached for her but she stepped away. His hand brushed hers. He felt her stiffen, saw the panic in her gaze. She'd felt it, too, the heat, the electricity, the heart-pounding, brain-numbing chemistry.

"You aren't going to try to stop me, are you?" She didn't bother to give him time to reply. "No, you want me to find the bones so you can make a name for yourself. Or is it the money you're after? Or both?"

"Would it do me any good to tell you you're wrong?"

"None," she said stepping over to the edge of the cliff, her back to him. She could see another storm coming, the sky dark, the rain headed this way. A light breeze came up out of the forest below them, scented with cedar.

He cursed under his breath.

"Tell me, is this still your best behavior, because I'm having trouble telling."

Roz stared down at the pile of stones, ignoring Ford as best she could. Her heart was pounding and she felt weak at just his touch. What was wrong with her? He was the enemy. The man was despicable. He would sell his soul for money and fame. And yet her body ached for his touch.

She turned, realizing the would-be killer had gotten down from here without being seen after the rock slide. So where had he gone?

She looked past Ford to a crack in the cliff and walked over to it, ignoring him. He was watching her, studying her, a frown on his face. The crack in the rock was just wide enough for a person to slip through. Beyond it she could see where the boot prints had slid down the earthy slope to a stand of trees.

What she couldn't understand was why her father would have ever come up here. Unless... She turned and looked down the ledge to where a tree grew out of the rocks. Behind it was darkness. A cave.

As she moved to it, she could see that it wasn't very large, no more than three feet across, maybe six feet deep and about her height. It was hidden behind the tree unless you were standing at the right spot to see it. She would never have noticed it had she not been trying to determine where her assailant had gone.

She peered inside with her flashlight. The cave floor was smooth, rocky, no sign of digging. Nor any sign of bones embedded in the rock. It would have been too easy to find the bones here but she still couldn't hide her disappointment.

"What is it going to take to get through to you?" Ford asked impatiently behind her as the first drops of rain began to fall, splashing down hard on the rock ledge. She stood under the shelter of the pine tree but Ford stayed out in the rain, not seeming to notice it.

She turned, surprised how close he was. "You don't give a damn about me or my dad. That stunt at the hospital, getting Jesse Tanner to guard him night and day, was just a way to get to me. For all I know you set up everything—all the times you supposedly saved my life—including this one." She sounded close to tears and hated it.

His sea-green gaze washed over her in a warm wave. "Is that *really* what you think?" he asked quietly.

"Damn right it is," she said but her words carried little conviction and they both knew it. "You're an impossible man," she whispered, all the fight gone out of her. "Totally incorrigible."

"I've been told that on more than one occasion," he said as he stepped under the tree with her to thumb away an errant tear from her cheek.

The rough brush of his thumb pad sent a tremor quaking through her. She felt her pulse jump, her heart suddenly a drum in her chest. "What makes you such an ass one minute and such a…a…"

"A prince of a guy the next?" he asked. He was so close she swore she could feel heat radiating from his body. He looked down into her eyes. "I don't know. You probably have some theories though."

She let out the breath she'd been holding as she tried to step back, tried to put some distance between them, but there was no place to go. Her back was to rock. If she moved she would be forced into the cave. He had her trapped and he knew it.

"Don't," Rozalyn whispered. Her brown eyes swam with tears as she looked up at him. She drew in a short, shuddery breath. "Don't do this."

"And hate myself the rest of my life?" He touched her hair, not surprised that it felt as silken as it looked as he cupped her chin in his hand and turned her face up to his. Her eyes pleaded with him not to kiss her as he lowered his mouth to hers.

She seemed to hold her breath as if afraid to breathe, afraid to move. Her palms came up as if to push him away, but only rested against his chest as he deepened the kiss.

She groaned softly against his mouth, leaning into the kiss, leaning into him.

He tried to warn himself. This was crazy. If he didn't stop, there would be no turning back. But even as he thought it, he knew he'd gone way past the point of no return a long time ago with Rozalyn Sawyer. This felt as if it had always been written in the stars. As if he had spent his life headed for this moment— and nothing could stop the inevitable.

He knew he should run like hell. But running was the last thing he wanted to do right now. Think of the bones, the money, the scientific recognition. The fame.

"I want to make love to you," he heard himself say even though he knew instinctively he would be giving up both the money and the fame should they find the bones. He had a lot more to lose and he was putting it all on the line for the first time in his life. He'd never been so scared or so certain.

Roz lifted her hands from his chest as if to ward him off. He caught both in his and drew her hard against him.

His Caribbean-blue gaze locked with hers as he dropped his mouth to her lips. She felt herself diving into his gaze as if it really was tropical surf. It was heavenly. She kissed him back with a passion she hadn't known she even possessed.

A moan escaped his lips. He backed her up against the cool stone, pinning her there with the hard planes of his body. His mouth explored hers as his hands cupped her bottom and rain fell in a torrent just beyond the shelter of the tree. She'd never been kissed like this. In fact, she'd never known a kiss could have this effect.

She couldn't breathe. Her pulse boomed in her ears louder than thunder. He kissed her harder, his hands moving sensually up over her hips, over her breasts, her neck, to bury his fingers in her hair. He robbed her of her breath. Stole her good sense.

She melted against him as the rain pounded the rock ledge.

He pulled back, blew out a breath, his gaze locked with hers. "Tell me this isn't what you want."

She shook her head. She wanted this and more, so much more. She wanted to be naked with him, to make love with him. Crazy or not, she wanted to sleep with the enemy.

The rain fell harder. He dragged her down and into the cave, his mouth never leaving hers as he drew her to the floor of the cave and lay down beside her.

Her hand went to his cheek, his beard rough to her touch and she looked into all that sea-green and felt herself sinking deeper and deeper. There would be no coming up for air. Her life would never be the same after this.

"Do you trust me?" he whispered against her mouth.

She didn't want him to stop kissing her. Not now. She tried to draw him closer, but he pulled back to look at her. "Do you trust me?"

She gazed into his eyes, afraid of her answer. She looked deep and realized with a start that she did. Tears stung her eyes. She trusted him. God help her.

He smiled then. How had she not thought him handsome? He was glorious when he smiled and he was smiling at her as if he'd never seen anything he wanted more.

She wrapped her arms around his neck and drew him down until his lips were on hers, amazed at the way he made her feel. Amazed even more by the words that came out of her mouth. "I want you to make love to me, Ford Lancaster."

He seemed to breathe a sigh of relief as he drew her closer and kissed her senseless, his hands roving over her body, sending shafts of heat to her center. He freed the top button of her blouse, his gaze never leaving hers. "If you change your mind, all you have to do is tell me to stop."

He slipped another button free. His fingertips brushed her skin, making her quiver inside. "Just say the word."

She swallowed hard. Her skin ached. She could feel her nipples, hard and tender against the sheer fabric of her bra. Just say the word. Any word and he would stop. She didn't utter a word, deathly afraid he *would* stop.

She closed her eyes, leaned her head back. She felt her blouse slip from her shoulders, felt his fingertips skim over the thin fabric of her bra and the hardened tips of her nipples beneath. She groaned and pressed against his mouth as it dropped to envelop one nipple, then the other.

His fingers were at the zipper of her jeans. She opened her eyes, a flash of rational thought. Say the word. Any word. Now. Or never.

She opened her mouth as his head came up from her breast but his gaze held a kind of wonder as he looked down at her and left her speechless.

Her heart drummed like the rain beating the rocks just outside the security of the cave as she made love with him.

Naked and in his arms, he released a well of passion from within her she hadn't even known existed. No man had ever touched her like that nor had she ever wanted to explore a man's body the way she did Ford's. It was as if there was nothing between them, no secrets, no boundaries. It was as if she'd found her way to a home she hadn't known existed. And when he'd pleasured her beyond her wildest dreams, she lay spent in his arms, tears of joy in her eyes. Whatever tomorrow might bring, she would never have regrets. In her heart, she knew it was meant to be.

When Roz opened her eyes, her body still alive with his touch, Ford was gone. She sat up and looked out of the cave, surprised how late it was. The rain had stopped. For a moment, she thought he'd taken off. It wouldn't have surprised her.

She pulled on her clothes and slipped out of the cave. Ford was just climbing up over the rim of the cliff about fifty yards away. She walked along the edge of the ledge to meet him.

Her body already ached for his touch. She was almost to him when she saw his grim expression. "You're sorry, aren't you?"

He seemed surprised by the question. "You mean about you and me?" His eyes seemed more blue than green in the dying light of day. He shook his head. "Never." He stepped to her and pulled her into his arms, cradling the back of her head in his large hand as he pressed her close.

Relief made her weak. She rested her cheek against his chest, listened to his beating heart. She knew he hadn't wanted to feel anything for her—just as she hadn't for him. What they felt was overwhelming and impossible to explain. And she suspected it scared him as much as it did her.

She looked out over the rainforest, then down to the rocks below, and suddenly tensed.

Ford turned her, trying to shield her from the sight. But it was too late. She'd seen her father's backpack lying in the dirt a dozen yards below them. "Oh, God, this can't be from where he fell."

"It isn't," Ford said, clasping her upper arms to keep her from stepping around him to take another look.

She struggled to free herself, but Ford's grip was strong, his will even stronger. He was determined to protect her. Damn him.

"Don't lie to me. Not now," she cried in frustration.

"Rozalyn, listen to me. Your father was never up here."

She stopped struggling and stared at him. "That's his backpack."

"Someone tried to make it look like Liam fell from up here, okay?" Ford said. "But he couldn't have. He would have landed closer to the cliff if he'd fallen. Or been pushed."

"You've been down there?"

He nodded. "There's blood down there on the rocks. Probably your father's but it was planted there. Do you understand what I'm staying? I've spent my life investigating elaborate hoaxes and exposing the offenders. I know what I'm doing."

"You were wrong about my father's photographs," she snapped.

He winced as if she'd slapped him and his eyes grew as dark as the depths of the ocean. "What is it you want me to say? That I've been an ass most of my thirty-six years? All right, you've got it. You think all my motives are self-seeking, maybe they are. Maybe I'm kidding myself that they're not anymore. Maybe a person can't change. Especially me."

Afternoon shadows lengthened under the pines below them and the air cooled perceptively. She felt confused, afraid and angry with him. For a while she'd forgotten who he was back there in the cave. Or why he was here with her now. "If you're looking for sympathy—"

He laughed. "You're a tough one. You aren't going to cut me any slack at all, are you? Okay," he said holding up a palm to hush her before she could say anything. "I'm up here just for the money and the glory. But your father still didn't fall from this cliff. Nor was he pushed. All of this," he said, waving his hand through the air, "was *staged.* Liam wasn't found up here. Whoever dropped him off at the hospital was the person who put him in the coma. This isn't about Bigfoot bones. I doubt it ever was."

"But the doctor said some Bigfoot hunters dropped him at the hospital," she said.

Ford nodded. "I know. That's why we have to get to the hospital as quickly as possible."

Chapter 13

Once off the mountain, Ford followed Rozalyn in his pickup as far as the edge of town where she left her SUV. On the way to the hospital, he told her what he'd found at Lost Creek Falls earlier that morning.

She turned the piece of painted plastic mannequin face over in her fingers for a long time without saying a word. "I'm not crazy."

"No. What I can't figure out is why someone would do this," he said. "It was obviously planned specifically for you. Whoever did it anticipated your reaction. They had to have known about your mother's suicide, had to know you would risk your life to save the person you thought was about to jump."

"Drew told me his mother resented me and he was afraid she might have been pulling some tricks on me, trying to keep me away from Timber Falls so my father would let them move somewhere and start over fresh."

"What kind of tricks?" He listened while she told him about the phonograph.

Then he said, "Before I went to the waterfall, I dropped the sample you gave me last night at the lab. The results were positive. It's a drug used by doctors to help induce hypnosis in patients and has the same symptoms as sleepwalking. The person under the drug is very susceptible to suggestion."

She hugged herself, biting down on her lower lip. "Someone talked me up into the attic and out onto the widow's walk?"

"It certainly would appear so."

"Drew?"

"I doubt Drew would have left the note if he'd been the one to drug the chocolates," Ford said.

Anyone in the house could have known about what time Rozalyn would be coming up the road. He sighed. "If Emily is behind this, she's doing more than just trying to scare you away. And what bothers me is Liam's accident. He obviously was attacked somewhere else and his assailant didn't want anyone to know where."

"Why, if not because of Bigfoot bones?" she asked.

All Liam had said was bones. But what other kind of bones were there?

Human bones.

Ford sped up the SUV.

"I just don't understand why the person who attacked my father would take him to the hospital," she said.

"To be able to tell the story about him being found under the cliff and take away any suspicion," he said. And to make sure he died, Ford thought as he turned down the street toward the hospital, tires screeching.

Roz had Liam's backpack in her lap. She'd been going through it and looked worried and scared. "The digital camera isn't in the pack. But the usual things he always takes on his day trips like his GPS and binoculars are."

"Maybe the camera was stolen from the backpack before we got there."

"But the thief would leave a GPS and a pair of expensive binoculars." She shook her head. "I don't think the digital camera was ever in here." She turned to stare out the window, looking as scared as he felt.

"Who told you that your father had gone up into the mountains?"

"Emily, when I called the house."

"Your father has money. Who gets it if something happens to him?" Ford asked.

She stared at him. "My father insisted Emily sign a prenuptial agreement with me getting the bulk of his estate."

He nodded. "And if anything happens to you?"

"Since I'm not married and have no children it would go to…my father's wife, I guess," Rozalyn said.

Ford nodded as he swung into the hospital parking lot.

When Sheriff Mitch Tanner returned to his office, the information he'd been awaiting was on his desk.

All of Wade Dennison's and Bud Farnsworth's financial records from twenty-eight years ago. He sat down in his chair, surprised the express package wasn't thicker. Then again, twenty-eight years ago, Wade was just starting out, Dennison Ducks had only begun to establish a name for itself in the decoy world and Wade and Daisy had only been married three years. Even though Daisy had spent Wade's money as if there was no tomorrow back then, there wasn't the wealth there was now—or the paperwork.

Mitch's cell phone rang. He almost didn't answer it, anxious to see what he'd find in the finances of the two men. "Hello?"

"Mitch, it's Charity."

As if he didn't know that. Just the sound of her voice warmed him in a way that could only get him into trouble. He couldn't believe he'd suggested they move in together. Actually, he'd been just short of suggesting something much more permanent. Thank God, Roz had shown up when she did.

"I need a huge favor. Would you run the name Lynette Hargrove for me," she said. "I need it ASAP."

"Of course you do," he said and thought about arguing that his computer wasn't for the use of nosy reporters but that would have taken more time than just typing in the name. He moved the financial package aside. "Spell it for me."

Lynette Hargrove. He curbed his curiosity. Even if Charity told him the real reason she wanted the name run, which was doubtful, it would be a long, involved explanation because it was Charity. He'd just wait and see what came up on the computer screen.

"It's going to take a few minutes," he said glancing toward the package. "Can I get back to you?"

"Promise?"

"Promise."

She hung up before he did. That was odd. Not like Charity at all. He sighed and reached for the package.

As he tore it open and pulled out the papers, he put Charity's call out of his mind.

"You need anything else before I call it a day?" Sissy asked from the doorway.

He didn't look up, just shook his head and after a moment, the clerk closed the door. He knew she was dying to know what was in the package from the bank. So was he.

It didn't take long to find the first large cash withdrawal made from Wade and Daisy Dennison's personal joint checking account. Ten thousand dollars.

Mitch unlocked his desk drawer, pulled out the Angela Dennison file and flipped through it until he found her birth date. May eighth. The first withdrawal was made on August thirtieth the previous year. Like clockwork, there was a withdrawal on the thirtieth of each month. The final withdrawal was made on April thirtieth—just days before the kidnapping and unlike the others, it was for twenty thousand, for a total of one hundred thousand dollars.

"Hot damn," Mitch swore as he leaned back in his chair. "One hundred thousand dollars." He thought about the shopping trips Daisy used to take. The expensive horses Wade bought her. All of that seemed to be accounted for. This hundred thousand wasn't.

He picked up Bud Farnsworth's bank records telling himself Bud wouldn't be stupid enough to put the money in the bank.

Wrong. There it was, deposited each month just a couple of days after the money left the Dennison's private account.

"Oh man, Charity was right." Wouldn't she love to know that? She'd said all along that Bud Farnsworth never would have come up with the kidnapping idea by himself. Still, it was circumstantial evidence and Mitch was sure Wade would try to explain it away. But there was little doubt that Bud Farnsworth had been paid to kidnap Angela Dennison.

The bad feeling hit him like a brick almost doubling him over. All this information had been there twenty-eight years ago. It would have been even easier for Mitch's predecessor, his mentor, the man he'd spent his life trying to emulate. One of the first things Sheriff "Hud" Hudson would have done was check the bank records.

Mitch swore, sick at even the thought that Hud could have been bought off. It wasn't possible. So why hadn't this come out all those years ago? Why not until now?

Was it possible that Wade had accounted for the money? Is that why nothing had ever come of it?

He glanced up at the computer screen, having forgotten his promise to Charity. The information on half a dozen Lynette Hargroves had come through.

Frowning, he clicked on a link to a newspaper article about a Lynette Hargrove who'd been a nurse in Timber Falls ten years ago. That caught his attention. She was wanted for questioning in the disappearance of the doctor she'd been employed by at the time—Dr. James Morrow, a doctor who specialized in hypnosis.

He clicked on another link. Lynette Hargrove had been killed, her body burned beyond recognition after her car left the highway and rolled near Portland. The article said she had been wanted for questioning in a missing person's case. He looked for newspaper articles on Dr. Morrow. As far as Mitch could tell, Dr. Morrow had never been found.

This had to be the Lynette Hargrove that Charity was interested in. He wondered what Charity's interest was. It was better than thinking about Sheriff Hudson. Could Mitch have been that wrong about the man?

Why was Lynette's name coming up now after all these years? After Ford Lancaster had asked him to check Anna Sawyer's case file? After Mitch had seen that Lynette Hargrove had been questioned by the former sheriff about Dr. Morrow's visit to Anna Sawyer just before her suicide? Lynette had said she knew nothing about the visit, that she hadn't even been in town.

His phone rang. He flipped it on without looking to see who was calling, expecting it was Charity. "I hadn't forgotten to call you." A lie.

"Sheriff, it's dispatch. I have an urgent call from Daisy Dennison."

He sat up, surprised as Daisy was connected and he heard fear in her voice.

"Wade just phoned me. He sounded as if he'd been drinking. He said he was on his way up here. He…he threatened to kill me and I'm afraid—"

"Lock your doors, I'm on my way," Mitch said, as he dumped everything into the drawer, locked it and took off for the Dennison house.

Ford threw open his car door and ran toward the emergency room entrance, Rozalyn at his heels. *Let me be wrong. Please, let this be one of those times I'm wrong.*

But he couldn't shake the bad feeling that twisted his insides.

Rain pounded the pavement. A breeze stirred the

nearby trees emitting a low moan. Chilled, Ford pushed open the door, hoping to see that nice older nurse at her station.

The nurse's station was empty. No lights had been turned on yet, making the hallway dark. An eerie quiet moved ghostlike through the place.

Ford broke into a run again. As he burst through the door to Liam's hospital room, the first thing he saw was a water glass on its side on a dinner tray at Jesse's feet—the food on the tray floated in a sea of pink as a blob of red gelatin slowly melted.

Jesse was in his chair, slumped, chin to chest, his feet at an odd angle.

Ford's gaze shot past him to Liam lying on the bed. A startled Dr. Harris turned in surprise from where he stood over his patient, the pillow he'd just lifted off Liam's face still in his hands.

Ford didn't break stride as he dove across the bed at Harris. He hit the doctor chest high, driving him into the wall. The pillow fell to the floor as Ford punched the doctor in the face with an uppercut that put the man's lights out.

As Dr. Harris slid down the wall to the floor, Ford swung around to check Liam, afraid he was too late.

Liam's eyes were open, unblinking.

Ford swore and threw back his head, wanting to howl out his pain. He'd failed Rozalyn. Failed.

At a sound behind him, he swung around expecting to find Rozalyn in the doorway. Nurse Kate Clark blinked in confusion, a box of donuts in her hands.

"Call the sheriff, hurry," Ford barked as he ripped off his belt and grabbed some tubing from the tray next to the bed and began to tie up the doctor.

Kate dropped the donuts and picked up the phone in the room, fingers trembling as she beat out 9-1-1.

Ford heard Jesse groan in the corner. Kate was on the phone with the dispatcher. The sheriff was on a call, Kate told Ford. The dispatcher would get word to him as soon as she could.

Ford looked to the hospital room doorway. Still no Rozalyn. She must have seen Dr. Harris holding the pillow over her dad's face, must have known they were too late and taken off in her grief.

And yet, even as Ford thought it, a part of him knew she wouldn't do that. He hurriedly finished tying up the doctor, anxious to find her and comfort her, upset with himself, afraid for her. Why the hell would Harris want Liam Sawyer dead? It didn't make any sense. If he hadn't seen the doctor holding the pillow over Liam's face—

And hadn't been suspect of the doctor's story that Liam had been dropped off at the hospital by some out-of-town Bigfoot hunters.

"The doctor sent you to get donuts?" Ford asked the nurse as she hung up the phone and reached to take Liam's pulse.

She nodded distractedly. "He said he should have gotten something to eat when he brought the tray for Jesse, but that he craved jelly-filled donuts and could I—"

"What the hell?" Jesse said as he looked over at the doctor on the floor, then tried to sit up and doubled over to be sick.

"Kate, did you see Rozalyn when you came in?" Ford asked as he finished securing Dr. Harris. "Did you see which way she went?"

Behind Ford, Jesse struggled to his feet and seemed to take in the situation quickly. "Son of a bitch. The bastard drugged me."

"Did you see Rozalyn, Kate?"

The nurse shook her head. Her gaze transfixed on Liam.

Ford reached across the bed to get her attention. Bony fingers closed over his wrist.

"You look like John," said a raspy voice from the bed.

Ford blinked, then focused on Liam and the hand gripping his wrist.

"Where is Roz?" Liam whispered.

Ford shook his head in disbelief, then turned, hoping again to see her standing there. "Rozalyn!" No answer. "Rozalyn!"

"I saw her on my way in," Kate said.

And Ford breathed a sigh of relief.

"Find Roz. Not Emily," Liam whispered and Kate gave him a little water, his lips dry and chapped. "Lynette."

Ford frowned down at the man. Who was Lynette? Liam wasn't making any sense.

The old man was frantic now, gripping Ford's arm. "They'll…kill her. The…bones." He fell back, exhausted, his fingers falling away from Ford's wrist.

"I knew it!" cried a thin female voice from the doorway.

Ford swung around to find an elderly woman in a bright-colored caftan, her red hair piled high on her head, turquoise eye shadow over shining blue eyes, standing in the doorway. "Do you know what he's talking about?"

"Emily. You fool. She's really Lynette Hargrove and she's a killer!" the woman said, rushing to Liam's side.

"Florie Jenkins," Jesse said by way of introduction. "She's harmless. Thinks she's psychic."

"I'm *clairvoyant*," Florie said, cradling Liam's hand in both of her jeweled ones. "The woman was only after Liam's money. Don't just stand there," she snapped at Ford. "Your destiny is with Rozalyn and I just saw her leaving."

Kate's eyes widened. "When I saw her she was talking to her stepbrother Drew in the hallway—"

Chapter 14

Charity found herself pacing. Mitch hadn't called back about Lynette Hargrove. That wasn't like him. Maybe there was nothing to find. Or maybe there was something. Something he didn't want to see in print. That was more likely.

She started to pick up the phone and call Mitch. Instead, she dialed one of the two numbers she'd gotten from the Portland directory. Neither line had answered earlier, not that she'd expected them to since Drew and Suzanne were both in Timber Falls.

The number for Drew Lane rang and rang. She started to hang up, wondering why she didn't just call Mitch when a young male voice said, "Hello?" He sounded breathless.

"Andrew Lane?" Charity asked incredulously.

"Yes?" Now he sounded suspicious.

"I'm sorry. I'm trying to find the attorney's son."

"My father is deceased."

"I'm not sure I have the right Andrew Lane. You have a sister Suzanne?"

"Yes?" More suspicion in his voice.

"Just tell me this. Has your mother Emily remarried?"

"No," he said. "What is this about?"

"I do have the wrong number. Sorry." Charity hung up with fingers shaking, as she quickly dialed Roz's cell phone. Out of the area or turned off. Charity felt cold inside and scared. What were the chances that there was another hotshot attorney named Andrew Lane with a wife named Emily and two grown children named Andrew and Suzanne? None. Nada. Nil.

Liam's new wife hadn't just passed herself off as Emily Lane, she'd brought along two offspring. Hers? Or had she just borrowed them from some actor's school?

And the big question: Why?

For Liam Sawyer's money just as Florie had suspected.

Frantically, Charity started to dial Mitch's number but then she saw his patrol car go racing by.

Charity grabbed her purse and ran out to her car in hot pursuit.

The lights of the patrol car cut through the darkness as Mitch raced up to the Dennison house. It was a huge house with white pillars, a Southern mansion in the wilds of Oregon. Wade had built it for his young wife. Off to the back were stables from when Wade had bought Daisy expensive horses. Directly behind the house was a large indoor pool and recreation room larger than any hotel.

The last time Mitch had been out here, the drapes had been drawn and he'd had to force Daisy Dennison to come to the door. She'd been a recluse for twenty-seven years. That was until a woman named Nina Monroe had come to town with a secret. Since then, Daisy seemed to have come back to life, kicking Wade out and, if local rumors were right, talking about filing for divorce, both of which had obviously set her husband off.

And that's what worried Mitch as he noticed this visit the drapes were open, all the lights on and the front door was standing ajar. The four-car carport off to the right was also open and empty except for Daisy's SUV.

On the way through town, Mitch had seen Desiree Dennison's little red sports car parked in front of the Duck Inn bar. Today was the maid's day off. She always went to Portland on her day off and was a creature of habit like none other Mitch had ever seen.

That meant Daisy had been alone.

Mitch swore as he parked beside Wade's Ford Navigator, got out and started up the wide steps to the veranda.

"Daisy? Wade? It's Sheriff Tanner." No answer.

He stepped into the foyer, broken glass grating under his shoe sole. A pane of glass from the front door lay shattered on the floor.

Mitch drew his weapon and moved deeper into the house. In the living room, he saw the remains of what appeared to have been a struggle. An overturned chair.

A lamp base crushed on the floor next to it. More glass and—

He froze, heart hammering. The wall was splattered with what at first appeared to be blood. A broken wineglass lay on the floor in a puddle of red the same color as the spots on the wall. Mitch took a temporarily relieved breath.

"Daisy? Wade?" Still no answer. He continued through the lower floor of the house and had started up the wide staircase when he spotted the bright-colored scarf on the floor in front of a set of French doors that opened on the back of the house. Past it, he saw the lights were on in the pool house, shadows moving jerkily inside.

He ran to the pool house in time to hear the report of a gunshot echoing across the water. He didn't feel the pain until he was already pitching forward.

Drew pressed the hard, cold barrel of the gun against Roz's temple. "Stop here," he ordered.

She brought the sports car to a stop and leaned over the wheel, still fighting the heart-wrenching sobs that had made driving nearly impossible when he'd told her that her father was dead.

Drew reached over, turned off the engine and pocketed the key. A smothering darkness moved in quickly around them. The only sound was Roz sobbing softly.

"Come on."

She lifted her head, wiping her tears, anger stilling her sobs temporarily. It took a moment for her eyes to adjust. He'd forced her to drive to a spot along the far side of the house, hidden from both the guesthouse and the front driveway.

He grabbed a handful of her hair. "Get out. Go slow. I'm coming with you."

She opened her door. She'd already looked into his eyes, seen the bottomless coldness she'd glimpsed in Emily's eyes. It was what had convinced her to go quietly with him in the hospital.

Drew had come up behind her as she had stopped in her father's hospital room doorway. He'd motioned for her to be quiet or he would kill her, then he dragged her back away from the door making it clear he wouldn't just kill her but Ford also if she screamed or struggled.

She'd gone with him thinking Ford would be safe. Once in the car, Drew had told her that her father was dead. That Ford hadn't gotten there in time to save Liam from Dr. Harris, a friend of Drew's mother.

"Mother wants to see you," Drew said now as he slid out of the car behind her, still gripping a handful of her hair and pressing the gun barrel against her temple.

Roz hadn't said a word since Drew had forced her from the hospital and into his car. She'd cried but done as he ordered, all the time feeling the grief turn to rage.

As her eyes adjusted to the light, she could make out the crest of the house over the top of the trees. Drew let go of her hair to pull a flashlight from his jacket pocket. He gave it three short flashes, all pointed toward the house.

An instant later, a light came on in the attic near the widow's walk and Roz saw Emily waiting for them.

As Mitch fell to the pool house floor, the thick scent of chlorine filling his lungs, he saw Daisy and Wade on the other side of the lap pool struggling for the gun.

He saw the intensity of the struggle in Daisy's face

just before he hit the tile floor hard. Pain shot up his side and he thought he would black out. "Put down the gun, Wade," he ordered weakly.

It was an idle threat as he watched his own weapon dislodge from his fingers and skitter across the tiles to come to rest under one of the lounge chairs.

Mitch tried to rise, realized it wasn't going to happen and rolled over onto his back. He clutched his side, his uniform shirt soaked with what he knew was his own blood.

Daisy was screeching now.

Another shot reverberated through the pool house. More pain. In his left leg this time. The screeching sound ended in a loud splash.

"Daisy?" His voice came out a hoarse whisper. He turned his head. He could see her in the water now, Wade standing over her on the edge of the pool on the other side, the gun in his hand.

"Wade, don't kill him!" Daisy cried as she surfaced and began to swim toward Mitch. "Kill me. That's why you came up here. Kill me!"

"Don't do it, Wade," Mitch said, gritting his teeth against the pain. Tiny dark spots danced before his eyes and he willed himself not to pass out. "You okay, Daisy?" He could hear the lap of water next to him. "Daisy?"

"She's just fine," Wade said, his voice sounding strange even to Mitch's ears. Closer than he'd expected, too. He was standing over Mitch, looking down at him. Wade's jacket bloomed with blood from a bullet hole, shoulder-high.

"Oh God, Wade, what have you done?" Daisy said weakly from the edge of the pool.

"Shut up," Wade bellowed, his voice echoing across the water as he swung the gun on her. "I *should* kill you. You shot me. You're trying to destroy me."

Daisy pushed a lock of wet hair back from her face and looked up at her husband with hatred in her eyes. "Destroy you?!" she screamed. "Destroy *you* after what you did to me?!"

"Shut up!" Wade bellowed and closed his eyes, grimacing as if in pain. "I loved you. I *loved* you."

Mitch caught movement behind Wade. His heart stopped as he saw Charity creep into the pool house unnoticed. She carefully picked up one of the oars that decorated the wall over the pool door.

"Take it easy, Wade," Mitch said, his voice raspy with pain. Neither Wade nor Daisy had seen Charity edging toward Wade with the oar. "You don't want to kill anyone."

Wade wagged his big head. "You think I shot you? That's what she wants you to think. She set me up. Told me to come to the house to talk about things and then pulled a gun on me and shot me."

"Wade, no one's going to believe that story," Daisy said, sounding tired and depressed. "Everyone in town knows your temper. I shot you to defend myself. You were trying to kill me."

He was shaking his head. "I *loved* you." His voice broke. He sounded close to tears. "I would have done anything for you. *Anything.* Even raised another man's child."

Mitch thought of his own mother and felt a chill as he looked at the venomous way Daisy glared at Wade. This is what he feared in a relationship. That love could turn to hate just like that.

Wade opened his eyes and pointed the gun at her head. She didn't even blink.

"Go ahead, Wade. Put me out of my misery. Do it. Kill me!" Daisy cried up at him. "You weak bastard. You can't even do that."

Charity swung the oar. Wade didn't know what hit him. The force of the blow dislodged the gun from his hand. It fell into the water as he went sailing out over the pool past Daisy, belly-flopping on the water and sending up a huge splash.

Mitch closed his eyes and lay back.

"Oh, Mitch." Charity was crying as she jerked off her shirt and wadded it up against the wound in his side. He could hear the sound of an ambulance and knew she had to have called when she heard the first shot. "You'd do anything to get out of marrying me."

He opened his eyes and tried to smile.

"Damn you, don't you even think about dying on me," she said tearfully. "I swear I'll track you down in heaven."

He managed to smile up at her. At least he thought he did. She looked beautiful. Especially without her shirt. Along with the sound of the ambulance, he could hear the sound of a motorcycle coming up the road, hell-bent. Jesse to the rescue. She'd called Jesse as well. What would he do without Charity? he wondered. He hoped he never had to find out.

He heard Wade come up sputtering from the deep end of the pool, all the fight gone out of him as he treaded water, his clothes billowing around him in the water.

Mitch glanced over at Daisy. She had disappeared

under the water. He tried to sit up. Couldn't. Got out only the one word. "Gun."

Charity turned just as Daisy came up with the weapon Wade had dropped. She had it in both hands and was pointing the barrel end at Wade.

"I'm never going to have to fear you again," she said and pulled the trigger.

Wade didn't even try to duck the bullet. He just stared at her with a hurt look on his face as the bullet tore through the sleeve of his shirt and the flesh of his arm.

Charity dove into the water, coming up behind Daisy and grabbed her around the neck with one arm. As they struggled for the gun, Mitch called on every ounce of strength he had to drag himself over to the lounge chair, reach under it and come up with his gun.

He fired the shot in the air. "Drop the gun, Daisy. Now!" His voice boomed across the pool.

Daisy stilled. The weapon slipped from her fingers, made a faint splash, then floated slowly to the bottom of the pool. Charity released her hold on Daisy's neck as Jesse came racing in, took one look at the situation, pulled Mitch's weapon from his fingers and began giving orders.

Mitch lay back and closed his eyes again. He could smell Charity's perfume, feel her warm breath on his cheek, her wet hand brushing his hair back from his forehead. He was overwhelmed with his love for her. "Marry me."

Silence. "What?"

He opened his eyes and looked into hers. Any doubts he had about him and Charity were gone like a puff of smoke. In some cases, maybe love could conquer all.

All he knew was that he couldn't go on living without this woman. "Marry me." Unfortunately, he blacked out before he heard her reply.

Roz looked toward the house, her legs turning to water beneath her as she saw what Drew and Emily had planned for her. She'd been afraid at the hospital. Even more frightened in the car, thinking Drew was just going to take her out and shoot her. But now she knew that her death was to be exactly like her mother's. History was to repeat itself.

A tremor rattled through her. She fought back the terror that threatened to incapacitate her. She would die trying to avenge Liam Sawyer's death—and if she could, she would take Drew and his mother with her.

As Drew pushed her toward an opening in the dense garden behind the house, shining the flashlight beam a few feet in front of her, she wondered where Suzanne was. Hiding in a bottle or had that, too, just been an act? Was Suzanne waiting for her as well?

Three against one. The odds weren't good and Drew had a gun. Roz knew she would have to be very lucky to come out of this alive. She didn't feel lucky right now.

"Was it only for my father's money?" she asked as he pushed her down the garden path that wound toward the house while he held the gun to her back.

Drew laughed. "You think Mother cared anything about your father? The man wears flannel shirts and work boots. A man with that kind of money and he dresses like a mountain man not even to mention the difference in their ages."

"So your mother planned to kill—" her voice broke.

She couldn't say "my dad" without crying "—Liam from the very first?"

"Isn't that what you've always suspected?" he sneered as he prodded her forward with the gun.

It surprised her that her feelings had been so transparent. The hate she heard in Drew's voice threatened her resolve to fight until the very end. She thought about making a run for it. She knew Drew would shoot her in the back. That seemed far better than what Emily had planned for her in the attic.

But it also seemed the coward's way out. Given a little time, maybe she could turn the tables on her new family.

Her greatest fear though was that Ford would realize she was gone and try to help her as usual. She couldn't stand the thought of Drew hurting him, let alone killing him. That's what worried her. That and a worse thought. That someone had been waiting in her father's room, waiting to take care of Ford. That meant something had happened to Jesse, as well.

She had never felt so alone. She stumbled, fighting the horrible fear that, like her father, Ford was no longer alive. She couldn't bear the thought.

Drew shoved her again and she felt a cold, clear shot of anger race through her veins. He and his mother and sister weren't going to get away with this. She would bide her time. She would wait for an opening. She would try to keep a cool head and pray for a break.

And all this because her father had money and Emily and her family wanted it.

Roz must have said those words out loud because Drew snapped, "What would you know about being poor? Having nothing? You're a little rich girl."

She wanted to argue. Her parents hadn't lived extravagantly. Her father had never flaunted the money that had been handed down to him from past generations. If anything, he lived just the opposite and had taught Roz to live just as frugally. She'd never given much thought to the money she would someday inherit. She made her own money and lived just fine.

The thought made her angry. "Do you even have a job?"

"What? You think taking care of my mother isn't a full-time job?" Drew let out a laugh that held no humor. "You know nothing about me or my life."

How true. "Is your name even Drew Lane?" The silence chilled her. Could Florie be right? "My God, her name isn't Emily. She really is Lynette Hargrove." She heard his intake of air behind her and turned to see the answer in his startled expression.

He stepped past her to open the back door and shoved her inside. "What else do you know?"

Not near enough. "I know she faked her death in a car wreck." She stumbled into the house. It was dark except for a light over the back stairs. He pushed her toward the stairs. "And she had an affair with Dr. Morrow," Roz said, clutching at straws.

"One out of two isn't bad." He prodded her up the stairs. "You don't want to know. Trust me. It would be better to die not knowing."

She began to climb as slowly as possible, afraid he might be right. "Tell me."

"Okay, you asked for it."

She had almost reached the attic. Time was almost up.

"She killed the good doctor, Morrow, after he caught her stealing drugs."

Roz held her breath, knowing instinctively there was more.

"And the kicker? I helped her bury him in your garden," Drew said. "I was nine at the time."

"Oh, Drew," Roz said, unable to imagine the childhood he must have had.

"That wasn't the worst of it," he said. "Your mother saw us."

Chapter 15

As Roz neared the attic, she heard the music coming from the phonograph and felt her blood run cold. It was her mother's favorite record. The one Roz had broken into bits just the night before.

But it was playing again now on the old phonograph.

It took all of her strength to take those last few steps up the stairs to the attic. No one had believed her about the voices she'd heard or that loud thud over her head.

If only she had gone upstairs to see what the noise had been. If only she hadn't convinced herself it was the wind. If only her mother had cried out for help.

No, she thought. Her mother wouldn't have because she knew there was only one other person in the house that day. Roz. But her mother must have argued with Emily, Lynette, whatever her name really was. That had been the voices she'd heard. And the loud thump?

She stumbled on the last stair as she remembered turning down her stereo but she hadn't been able to hear anything overhead because... Her heart lodged in her throat. Because her mother's phonograph had been playing so loudly.

Just as it was now. The same song.

Drew jabbed her in the ribs with the gun.

Roz did it without thinking, without even considering the consequences. She spun around, bringing her elbow back hard. It caught Drew in the face, blood instantly spurting from his nose as he cried out and grabbed for the stair railing. Except there wasn't any on the back stairs.

His eyes widened as he grabbed for her with the hand without the weapon. She slapped his hand away at the same moment the deafening boom of the gunshot echoed through the stairwell.

She waited for the pain in that instant as she watched Drew flail, then fall backward to tumble down the stairs as the sound of the gunshot died away. He crashed into the door at the bottom with a groan.

It took Roz a moment to realize she hadn't been shot.

Now! Get out of here! Run!

She looked down the steps. Drew was struggling to his feet, cursing and reaching for his dropped weapon. She couldn't get down there before he retrieved the gun. Nor could she get past him if she did.

The record stopped playing. There was a soft click. And then the needle dropped on the vinyl again.

Roz turned, knowing there was only one way out of here and that was the attic. A dark shadow filled the doorway.

"Rozalyn," Lynette Hargrove said, the gun in her

hand gleaming in the dim light. "So nice that you could make it but as always you've made a mess of things."

Ford drove as fast as his pickup would allow him, around the corners and up the lane to the front of the Sawyer house. Drew had Rozalyn. This was the logical place to bring her given what Ford had seen of Drew's relationship with his mother, whoever the hell she was.

The sky was black, rain drumming down in a thick dark veil. Ford figured the front door would be locked—not standing open. It was almost as if they'd been expecting him. Waiting for him.

He hoped to hell that meant Rozalyn was all right. He'd left word for the sheriff. Whatever Drew had planned for Rozalyn, it wasn't going to work. Liam was alive. The game was over. Ford just hoped once Drew knew that—

"Rozalyn!" he hollered as he raced up the porch steps and into the house. "Rozalyn!"

He heard music. Faint, but definitely coming from upstairs somewhere. It was an old song, one he couldn't quite place but he suspected it was the same song Rozalyn had told him about, her mother's favorite record.

The living room and dining room French doors were open, the rooms empty at a glance. He rushed up the stairs, taking them three at a time, as he followed the sound of the music.

He'd been so obsessed with Bigfoot bones, he hadn't thought the bones Liam had mentioned could be anything else. He'd done everything wrong, made so many mistakes. That's all he could think about as he cried out Rozalyn's name, not bothering to stop at the first or second-floor landings. His gut instinct told him where he'd find Rozalyn. In the attic.

The music played overhead as he clambered up the steps, no longer calling her name, afraid of what he would find. Or wouldn't find.

The panel at the end of the third floor was open—just as he knew it would be. He ran to it and bounded up the stairs.

As he reached the top and burst into the attic, he saw the old automatic phonograph sitting on the floor by the doorway. A single 45 spun on the turntable, the needle scratching across the record, the music coming out the tinny speakers.

In that instant, the song stopped, the phonograph moaned and groaned, then a soft click and the record began to play again.

Past the phonograph, he saw Rozalyn by the widow's walk. Only this time she wasn't alone.

"Come on in, Mr. Lancaster," Emily said. Except she wasn't Emily, right? She was some woman named Lynette Hargrove. "You're just in time."

"I've got some bad news, Lynette," Ford said as he moved into the room. He saw her react to the name. So the old broad at the hospital with the bright red hair knew what she was talking about. But that meant that Lynette was more dangerous than even he had suspected.

Lynette stood with a gun to Rozalyn's head. Next to her, Drew pressed a blood-soaked handkerchief to his nose with one hand and held a gun in the other. The barrel was pointed at the floor and he seemed distracted by his injuries, including a nasty gash on his forehead. Had Rozalyn given that to him? Drew looked as if he'd taken a bad fall. That was his girl, he thought with pride. Off to the right behind the couch, the young blond Suzanne was sprawled in a pool of her own blood, a bullet hole between her eyes, her sightless blue eyes staring up at the attic ceiling.

Ford hoped to God that Roz hadn't seen her, hadn't completely realized yet just what her stepmother was capable of.

"We already know the news," Lynette said over the sound of the phonograph playing next to him. "Liam is dead. Such a pity."

"Wrong," Ford was happy to inform her. "Liam is alive and conscious. In fact, he is talking to the sheriff at this very moment." A slight exaggeration. "And he's not the only one talking. Your boyfriend, Mark, Dr. Harris? He's talking as well."

Lynette turned the color of her bottle-blond hair. "That's a lie." The record stopped. The room was suddenly deathly quiet. Then the song began again.

"I stopped Dr. Harris from killing him." Ford's gaze went to Rozalyn. He nodded and smiled. "Your dad's fine. Conscious. He's tough. Like you." Ford looked into Rozalyn's eyes and liked what he saw. Anger in her gaze and a steeliness to her backbone that told him she was ready to kick butt if she only got the chance. He hoped to give them both the chance.

"Right now, Liam is telling the sheriff everything—including about the bones." Ford knew he really was clutching at straws now. For a moment he thought he might have made a mistake. All Liam had said was something about finding bones. But how did that tie in with this woman and her beyond dysfunctional family?

* * *

Roz had never been so happy—or so upset—to see anyone in her life. But having Ford here only made her more determined that they would get out of this alive. Ford had saved Liam. Her father was alive!

"Lynette killed and buried Dr. Morrow in our garden," she said, wondering how much Ford actually knew. From the look of gratitude she witnessed in his expression, not much. She filled Ford in about Lynette Hargrove and the stolen drugs. "My father must have found the bones."

"What was Dr. Morrow going to do? Have you arrested for stealing drugs?" Ford asked.

"Dr. Morrow had stopped by to see my mother that day. She and the doctor had become friends. He confided in her that he'd caught Lynette stealing drugs. He was a kind, caring man. He would have hated to have Lynette arrested because she was the single mother of a son. Lynette must have followed him when he left. She might have gotten away with it except my mother saw her from the attic window."

Roz saw the shocked look on Ford's face. "She didn't commit suicide." It was little consolation.

"That must be a relief to you," Lynette said. "Unfortunately, the two of you are the only people who know the truth. Everyone will think you couldn't live with your mother's suicide, Rozalyn, and took your own life. Sadly, your new boyfriend tried to save you. A terrible mistake on his part."

"Lynette, the sheriff knows. You can't get away with this," Ford said. "Killing more people isn't going to save you. And Drew, if I were you, I'd be hightailing it out of here. You don't have to take the rap for your mother anymore."

Drew looked up from the blood-soaked handkerchief in his hand for a moment, then touched the wide open gash on his forehead, grimacing, too involved in his own pain now to even seem to realize what was happening.

Lynette shook her head as if amused by Ford's tactics. "Drew is my *son*. He is all I have. He would never leave me. We will disappear again. I am very good at it and I have enough of Liam's money socked away. I will do just fine until I find another fool to charm into marriage. I really have had the worst luck with husbands dying on me."

Another fool? Is that all Liam Sawyer was to her? Roz felt her face flame in anger. Ford must have seen it. He gave her a slight nod, then he stepped to the phonograph and kicked it hard.

The needle scratched loudly across the record. The plug jerked from the wall. The phonograph skidded loudly across the hardwood floor like a missile aimed right at Lynette.

It happened in a heartbeat. Lynette jumped back to avoid the phonograph flying toward her ankles. Roz saw her chance. She turned and grabbed the woman's wrist holding the gun and jerked her toward the open window of the widow's walk at the same time Roz bent down.

Drew, seeing what was happening, reached for his mother as Lynette began to fall over Roz toward the narrow widow's walk—and the four-story drop past the railing.

But Ford had already launched himself across the

room, hitting Drew hard, chest-high. Drew's weapon clattered to the floor but his momentum drove him into his mother. It was just enough to propel Lynette into the widow's walk railing with Drew right behind her. Off balance, she hit the railing and would have gone over right then if she hadn't grabbed her son Drew's arm.

Roz got to her feet, turning in time to see both of their faces, Lynette's caught in a horrible grimace as she fought to save herself—even at the expense of her son. Drew's expression was one of realization. If his mother didn't let go, they would both go over the railing. Or with luck, his mother would be able to pull him over past her and save herself.

In that instant, Drew could either free himself of his mother—or take the brunt of the impact.

Lynette let go as Drew hit the top of the railing next to her. Roz heard the wood crack. Nothing could save him. He must have known that. His mother had regained her balance against a portion of the unbroken lower widow's walk railing. Relief washed over her expression and resignation as she watched her son start to go over the railing.

Roz watched in horror. To the end Drew had protected his mother.

At the very last minute, Drew grabbed his mother's sleeve. Roz saw the smile on his face and heard Lynette scream as the two plummeted over the side and dropped out of sight. Then Lynette's screams stopped with an abrupt silence that shook Roz to her core.

She turned to bury her face in Ford's shirt as he pulled her into his arms.

Epilogue

The days that followed were a blur. Ford had taken Roz straight to the hospital to see her father. Liam's eyes had widened, tears flooding them at the sight of her.

He'd drawn her into his arms and, although weak, he'd held her tightly. "I was so afraid they hurt you. Roz, I'm so sorry, so sorry."

"It wasn't your fault," she tried to reassure him.

"I was such a fool, such an old fool."

"You did it to get me home," she said.

He looked into her eyes. "Your mother would have so wanted us all here. I feel that in my heart. This is where your children should grow up. On this side of the Cascades, in the one place that made us all once happy."

Roz had felt Ford behind her. "I'm not sure I can do that, Dad."

"I understand," he said. "It was a foolish dream of mine. Forgive me?"

"There is nothing to forgive," she assured him.

It was later that she had learned Sheriff Mitch Tanner had been airlifted to Eugene with two gunshot wounds. Charity had been at his side.

His brother Jesse had taken over as deputy, showing up at Roz's house only moments after Drew and his mother had gone over the broken top railing of the widow's walk to their deaths in the garden below.

Roz and Ford had given him their statements a few days later. The woman she'd known as Emily Lane was in fact Lynette Hargrove. She had only one child, a son named Robert Hargrove Junior. The elderly Robert Hargrove Senior had died in his sleep with only his nurse Lynette, whom he'd recently married, in attendance. Unfortunately, his estate hadn't been as large as Lynette had hoped.

It would take months before all of Lynette's former husbands could be found because she had used so many different names.

The blonde Jesse found dead in the attic turned out to be a third-rate actress from Portland named Sunday Brooks. Her last act was as Suzanne Lane, one she no doubt would regret for eternity.

Roz spent that first night beside her father's bed along with Florie Jenkins. It wasn't until daylight that the nurse, Kate Clark, insisted the two go home and get some rest. She promised to watch over him for them.

Ford walked Roz out and offered to take her to breakfast. She'd declined. Nor had she wanted to go to the house. She'd taken a room at the Ho Hum. Ford had offered to get her things from the house. That was one offer she couldn't refuse.

Over the days that followed, she thought a lot about what her father had asked her. Could she ever go back to that house? She felt torn between the years of happiness she'd known there and the horror. And yet the house was her last link to her mother.

She had come to grips with her mother's death, now at peace with the knowledge that her mother would never have left them the way she had if she'd had a choice.

The day before her dad was to be released from the hospital, he'd patted the side of his bed for her to sit. "I need to ask you what you want to do with the house. If you still feel the same way, I'll sell it and you'll never have to come back here. I'll go to Seattle and get a place up there closer to you. Just tell me what you want, sweetheart."

"Excuse me," Ford said from the doorway.

Roz turned and gave him an impatient look. Now was not the time to interrupt.

"We need to talk," Ford said. "Now." He looked past her to Liam. "You understand?"

"I don't understand," Roz said as Ford walked her out of the hospital.

"Liam does," he said and opened his pickup door for her.

"Where are we going? I thought you just wanted to talk? Why can't we talk right here?"

"Get in, Roz." It was the first time he'd called her that.

She slid in, her heart hammering so hard she just knew he could hear it. He had been there for her over the days since the attic, but not once had he tried to kiss her, or make love to her, or even say anything about the afternoon they'd spent in a cave in the Cascades.

"I'm hungry," he said as he slid behind the wheel.

She watched in amazement as he drove to Betty's and got out. She followed him, not knowing what else to do. Was this his idea of talking?

Only a few locals were in the café. She told herself she wasn't hungry. Her stomach was in knots. She figured Ford just wanted to tell her he was leaving. Why couldn't he just do that in the hospital hallway?

The smell of freshly baked pies drifted through the air. "I'll take a piece of banana cream," she told Betty, surprising herself. But she remembered something Charity had told her about banana cream pie.

Ford lifted a brow, then ordered an omelette. "Banana cream pie for breakfast?" he inquired.

She nodded. "It works for my friend, Charity." Hand trembling, she took a bite of the pie Betty slid in front of her and closed her eyes. Nothing. Just darkness behind her eyelids.

"Rozalyn?"

She opened her eyes, disappointed.

"There is something I didn't tell you."

She held her breath.

"When I was nine, my dad, my biological dad, John Wells, took me back into the Cascades with him on one of his Bigfoot searches. He left me alone while he climbed up to check out a cave. I saw something." He glanced toward the window. She followed his gaze to the dark green of the forest just across the street and beyond, miles and miles of wilderness. "I saw a huge creature covered with hair. It was watching me from the foliage. I have never been so terrified in my life."

He shifted his gaze back to her face. "That is, until I came into that attic and saw that woman holding a gun to your head."

She stared at him, not sure which revelation shocked her the most. "So you have known all along that Bigfoot exists?"

He looked surprised, then laughed. "I'm trying to tell you something here."

"You wanted my father's photographs to prove Bigfoot existed."

He blinked. "Yeah, I guess I did and when they didn't— Listen, I'm having a hard enough time saying this—"

"You came up here hoping for Bigfoot bones. I know how disappointed you must be," she said. "But you wouldn't have sold them to the highest bidder."

He stared at her. "How do you know that?"

She smiled. "I know."

He laughed again and ran a hand over his hair to brush it back from his forehead. "I guess I'll never know but once I met you—"

"That's why you never went with your father again, isn't it?" she said suddenly, excited. "You never told him what you saw! And he never understood why—"

He pushed off the booth, standing to lean over the table and kiss her.

She gasped in surprise.

"That is the only way I've found to shut you up," he said. "I heard what your father said about your mother and the house. I have to know something. Do you think you could live there?"

She was still stunned by the kiss. "What?"

"Let me put it this way. If I told you right now that I love you and don't want to spend a day of my life without you, would you want to stay in Timber Falls?"

She stared at him. "Are you asking me—" She couldn't bring herself to finish. She grabbed her fork, took a bite of her pie and closed her eyes tightly. And there he was. Ford Lancaster dressed in jeans and a flannel shirt sitting on the front steps of the Timber Falls house holding…holding a baby!

"Roz? In my inept way I'm trying to ask you to marry me and tell you that I'd stay here with you, if you'd have me. If it's what you want."

Her eyes flew open. The look on his face made her laugh out loud. He really thought she might turn him down? Were all men fools at heart? "Ford, oh Ford, yes!"

She slid from the booth to throw herself into his arms.

"Say the words, Rozalyn."

And she said the words she thought she would never hear come out of her mouth. "Ford Lancaster, I love you."

Of course, her father was ecstatic. Florie had been coming by every day to see how he was doing, as had Charity, who also had good news. Mitch had finally asked her to marry him and he was recovering nicely from his gunshot wounds.

Jesse had arrested Wade after his wounds had healed enough to leave the hospital. Daisy was filing for divorce. Their daughter Desiree was raising hell at the Duck Inn. Nothing new there, Charity said.

The evidence Roz and Ford had collected was turned over to Jesse. The DNA on the cigarette butts were compared to Drew's along with the tread on the boots. Both were a match. Drew had been doing his mother's dirty work since he was a boy so it came as no surprise he'd started the rock slide to kill Roz. Or that he'd staged the fake suicide at Lost Creek Falls.

Once Liam was well enough, he told Roz that a neighbor's dog had been digging in the garden and turned up the bones. That dog, Liam swore, had saved his life. If he hadn't found the old bones, he was certain that Emily, as he knew her, would have poisoned him.

He'd had doubts almost immediately about his hasty marriage. But when he'd found the bones, then later discovered rat poison in a drawer in the kitchen, he'd made that call to Roz. He had planned to get a divorce. But Emily wasn't going to let him leave. He'd confronted her. Of course, she'd denied everything. He had told her he had contacted his lawyer and that if anything should happen to him, like a poisoning, she would be the first person the police would come looking for. He'd tried to leave, but of course, Drew stopped him.

As it was, she drugged him, obviously realizing she had to move fast. He pretended to be out, then got to the phone. When he couldn't reach the sheriff, he'd hit redial since he could barely see. It was John Wells's number. That's why he'd sounded like he was drunk.

Then Drew had hit him with something. It was the last thing he remembered. He wasn't surprised that Emily had come up with the story about him falling off a cliff. She would have gotten away with it, too, if it hadn't been for Roz coming to Timber Falls.

"Thank you," her dad had said, taking her hand. "I know how hard it was for you to come back here." He was saddened to hear that his old friend John Wells had died but he had known he was ill. "I'm just glad I got to meet his son," Liam said to Ford. "I owe you a huge debt for saving my daughter."

"It was my honor," Ford said. "I had a lot of practice. By the way, your truck and camper turned up. Some Bigfoot hunters found it hidden a few miles from here." He figured Emily had wanted him in the guesthouse so she and Drew could keep an eye on him. Her mistake.

The disk Ford had started writing his article on had also turned up in Drew's things. Drew had made a copy of the article and left it in the guesthouse that morning for Roz to find. As Roz watched, Ford had destroyed the disk and the article. She would never know what he had planned to do before he came to Timber Falls. All she knew was that she loved him and he loved her, and anyone who knew anything knew that love transformed a person. Charity Jenkins would attest to that. Mitch Tanner, too.

Roz and Ford went over to her house later that day. Roz stared at the place. Funny, it looked different now that it was empty. Ford had seen that everything had been cleaned out that would even remind her of her former stepfamily. The house looked a little sad to her. Like a house just crying out for a family that could love it.

Ford took her around to the back. The widow's walk was gone. He'd hired some carpenters with her father's approval to remove it. And the garden was being plowed up. The state investigation lab had been forced to dig up most of it just in case any more bodies were buried there.

Fortunately there weren't.

"I'm thinking a swimming pool," Ford said, looking at the torn-up ground.

Roz nodded. She liked that idea. She turned to look back at the house. She knew she would grieve her mother's death wherever she lived, but here, she could hold on to all those years of wonderful memories. Here she could make new memories with her own family, her own children. And Charity's, she thought with a smile. Her mother and father had always thought Roz's and Charity's children would play here just as their mothers had.

Yes, Roz could see that happening—and maybe sooner than anyone thought.

"The first thing is paint, inside and out, bright colors," she said. "And big pots of flowers for the front porch. And we should throw a party. Yes," she said warming to the idea. "This town needs a party after everything that has happened."

Ford smiled over at her. "That's my girl."

She took his hand and they walked back toward the house. She could already hear the animated voices echoing through the old place, and almost hear hers and Ford's children running through the long hallways, laughing and calling to each other. Yes, this house would again ring with laughter. She and Ford would see to it.

It was strange but as Roz entered the house, she felt a warm breeze touch her cheek. She stopped and in that instant, she felt her mother's hand on her shoulder and heard her mother whisper in her ear, "Welcome home, dear."

* * * * *

We hope you enjoyed reading
AT HOME IN STONE CREEK
by *New York Times* bestselling author
LINDA LAEL MILLER
and
DAY OF RECKONING
by *New York Times* bestselling author
B.J. DANIELS

Both were originally
Harlequin® Special Edition and
Harlequin® Intrigue series stories!

INTRIGUE

EDGE-OF-YOUR-SEAT INTRIGUE,
FEARLESS ROMANCE.

www.Harlequin.com

NYTHI0616

I N T R I G U E

Read on for a sneak preview of
AMBUSH AT DRY GULCH
the conclusion of **BIG "D" DADS: THE DALTONS**
by Joanna Wayne

*The last person widowed Carolina Lambert would
consider falling in love with is Jake Dalton. But when
danger forces her to trust the rancher to stay alive, she
realizes only a fool would walk away from a second
chance at happiness...*

Carolina Lambert shifted in the porch swing so that she could
look R.J. Dalton, her neighbor, in the eye while they talked. He
rocked back and forth in his chair, sometimes looking at her,
more often staring into space.

Her heart ached at the way his body grew weaker each day.
He had already beaten the odds by more than two years, but
the inoperable tumor in his brain was relentless. It was only a
matter of time, and yet there was a peace to his spirits that she
envied.

He sipped his black coffee, his wrinkled hands so unsteady
that it took both of them to hold his mug. "I reckon Brit told you
that you better get over here and check on the old man while
she took Kimmie in for her checkup."

"No one has to coax me. Spending time with you is always
my pleasure," Carolina said truthfully.

But he was right. Even with a precious baby girl to keep her
busy, his daughter-in-law Brit had pretty much taken over the
job of coordinating the family's schedule so that R.J. was never
alone for more than a few minutes at a time.

"I swear you dropped off St. Peter's coattail, Carolina.

You're the best danged neighbor a scoundrel like me ever had. Best-looking, too. Can't believe you're still running around single. Hugh's been dead, what? Three? Four years now?"

"Four and a half."

"That's a long time to put your life on hold."

"My life's not on hold. I'm busy all the time with my family, friends like you and countless projects."

"Not the same as having a lover."

"Now, what are you doing even thinking about lovers at your age?"

"I'm not dead yet. If I was thirty years younger and not playing hide-and-seek with the grim reaper, I'd be after you quicker than hell can scorch a feather."

"You've done more than your share of chasing women, Reuben Jackson Dalton."

"I caught a few mighty fine ones, too."

"So I've heard."

He smiled, the deep wrinkles around his eyes cutting deep into the almost translucent flesh. "Lived life on my terms, sorry as it was. By rights I ought to be drowning in regrets. If it wasn't for taking your advice about what to do with my ranch, I would be."

"I can't take credit for you turning your life around."

"You don't have to take it, by jiggers. I'm a-givin' it to you. I offered to give you the Dry Gulch Ranch free and clear. You turned me down. Didn't leave me much choice except to try your idea."

"I suggested you leave the Dry Gulch Ranch to your family. That's not a particularly inventive idea."

"Sounded like crazy talk to me. Leave this ranch and what lottery winnings I had left to a bunch of strangers who wouldn't have tipped their hats if I'd passed them on the street."

"Until they got to know you."

Find out what happens in AMBUSH AT DRY GULCH by Joanna Wayne, available July 2016 wherever Harlequin® Intrigue books and ebooks are sold.

www.Harlequin.com

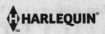

INTRIGUE

EDGE-OF-YOUR-SEAT INTRIGUE, FEARLESS ROMANCE.

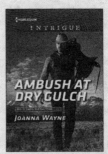

Save $1.00

on the purchase of

AMBUSH AT DRY GULCH

by Joanna Wayne, available June 21, 2016, or on any other Harlequin® Intrigue book.

Available wherever books are sold, including most bookstores, supermarkets, drugstores and discount stores.

Save $1.00

on the purchase of any Harlequin® Intrigue book.

Coupon valid until August 31, 2016. Redeemable at participating outlets in the U.S. and Canada only. Not redeemable at Barnes and Noble stores. Limit one coupon per customer.

52613728

5 65373 00076 2   (8100)0 12163

® and ™ are trademarks owned and used by the trademark owner and/or its licensee.

© 2016 Harlequin Enterprises Limited

NYTCOUP0616

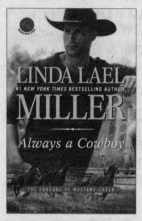